BREAKOUT

POSTSCRIPTS 34/35

BREAKOUT

POSTSCRIPTS 34/35

Edited by
NICK GEVERS

CONTENTS

BREAKOUT

POSTSCRIPTS 34/35

BREAKOUT

JOHN GRIBBIN

'Breakout' is a short story which fills a gap between the two novels the author wrote with Marcus Chown, entitled Double Planet *and* Reunion. *The pair then grew into a trilogy with Dr. Gribbin's solo effort* The Alice Encounter, *published by PS . . . also the home of what the author enthusiastically considers to be his best novel,* Timeswitch *(both* Alice *and* Timeswitch *are available as paperbacks under PS's Drugstore Indian Press imprint). 'It's tempting to write more in that universe,' he says, 'and I have ideas, but it's difficult to find the time away from my real job of writing scientific non-fiction (the latest being* Computing With Quantum Cats*) and my hobby writing songs for the band Almost The Bonzo Dog Doo Dah Band.'*

The author has now found true lasting fame as the answer to a question on the TV programme 15 to One: *'Who wrote the book* In Search of Schrôdinger's Cat*?' Dr. Gribbin says he used to be a real scientist and, indeed, still hangs out with the astronomers at the University of Sussex (. . . to get free tea and biscuits). 'Somehow, I've managed to get nine SF books published,' he says. 'I have ambitions to make it to ten, but I fear I'm wasting too much time writing songs.'*

T HE ATTEMPTED HIT CAME AS FRANK WILSON WAS LEAVING Central Med. An amateurish, bungled attempt, the stream of needles bouncing ineffectually from the plasteel of his work jacket, dead centre on his chest. Any professional assassin would have gone for the unprotected area of his throat. And any professional assassin would have succeeded, Frank realised. A lifetime spent troubleshooting dangers caused by other people had left him with reflexes amply able to cope with life on the city

streets—if he hadn't been knocked off centre by the news from the consultants upstairs.

Diving flat and rolling to his right, Frank felt his heart rate soar as he
simultaneously sought cover behind the looming steps of the building he
had just left, and reached for his own weapon.

Where the hell was his training? He fought to control his breathing,
searching for a clear view of his attacker in the crowd.

Under normal circumstances, he wouldn't just have avoided the hit.
He'd have taken the hitman himself, and in a fit state for questioning. But
as it was, by the time all these thoughts had flashed through his mind, all
he had was the image of a tall, lean figure, needler in hand, ducking
through the parting crowd and out of sight.

In the space that had opened around Frank, needles glittered on the
sidewalk. Careful to avoid touching any of them, he sat up, then pushed
himself to his feet, back against the wall. He looked down at his jacket.
Among the dark stains that marred its surface, he thought he detected
traces of wetness. Idly, he wondered which drug the needler had contained.
Well, who cared?

"Show's over, folks."

He scuffed a few of the needles towards the kerb, hunched his shoulders,
and set off at a brisk pace. No point hanging around. In the unlikely event
that someone had called in the cops, Frank Wilson wanted to be somewhere else, fast, so he could think things over. Two pieces of bad news in
one morning—the medical report, and now somebody out to kill him.
And they said trouble always came in threes, so he'd better watch his step,
assuming there was a link between the first two pieces of bad news. There
couldn't be, could there? Though he had to admit that any assassin who
had advance knowledge of the med tests would have picked just that
moment to strike, while Frank's brain was on autopilot, there was no way
anybody could have known in advance how the tests would turn out.

"Yesterday an American biologist from the Carnegie Institute
in Washington DC was murdered in Taracua. Mark de Villiers
had been carrying out a long-term study of the plants and animals
of the
Rainforest Reserve. According to the local police chief,
Fernando Gomez, the attacker took no money or possessions. 'At

this moment in time,' he said, 'we can think of no possible motive for the killing.'"

Diario de Manaus (Brazil), 27 April 2129

Two drinks in a corner booth, back to the wall and eyes warily watching the door, didn't solve anything. He tried to separate out the two problems in his head. The medical side was bad enough.

After years of work, a clean record, at the top of his profession, he'd got an unlimited license. Then they go and tell him there's something wrong, his sperm don't function properly anyway. Sterile. So there goes the status he'd worked so hard for. What good was an unlimited license if you couldn't use it? It was easy for Mona. Even if she really wanted a kid—and at times like this, staring into a drink, he sometimes doubted it, imagining that she was just humouring him—even if she wanted a kid, she could always get fixed up at the sperm bank. But he wanted his *own* kid; he wanted to make *donations* to the sperm bank, not withdrawals. It wasn't just the status; he'd worked hard to make the world a better place, wanted someone to hand all that on to. A bit of himself with a stake in the future. And he was intelligent enough to know, while not yet being drunk enough to appreciate the irony, that it was precisely that attitude that had helped him score high enough on the psychological profiles to clinch the license. The useless fucking license.

The rest of the news hadn't sunk in at first. Not just his sperm, but something odd about his DNA in general. They weren't quite sure what it was, but they'd like to carry out some more tests. If, of course, he'd like to pay for them. Central Med wouldn't pick up the tab unless the problem could be proved to be linked with his work. How do you prove that? By paying for the tests, of course—and he'd sunk all his ready credit into the fertility tests.

Frank punched at the table for another drink. It already had his credit listing, and at least he was good for a few more of these. Ice glittering in the liquid reminded him of the needles, and his other problem. There was something about the hitman, but he couldn't put his finger on it. He'd looked familiar, and yet not familiar. Like a half-remembered figure from the past. Well, in his job Frank made plenty of enemies. Cleaning up all kinds of environmental contamination couldn't be done without treading on a few toes. But whose toes hurt enough for them to go to such lengths?

Judging by the hints from the consultants, it probably was something he'd picked up on one of those jobs that had fucked up his body. For all he knew, he was under sentence of death already.

Occupational hazard, in a way.

Frank swallowed the drink with a gulp.

But he'd always been so damned careful! It wasn't so much that it wasn't fair, but that he didn't know why it had happened, or how. Professional pride was hurt by the hint that he had made some mistake in the past that had brought him to this state. And although memory failed him, offering no hint of the breakdowns in safety procedures of any of his jobs, he knew that there was another way to bring back the images of the past. Something which no sane, sober man would contemplate. But if you were knocked sufficiently far off centre, and you had two or three drinks under your belt . . . after all, what did he really have to lose?

The Dream Palace did not advertise itself with neon signs or holo displays. In spite of the name, it was no grand centre of entertainment, but an anonymous suite of apartments in a seedy block, approached through a plain door. Of course, it was known to the authorities, who raided it maybe twice a year, for the sake of appearances. But they preferred having the junkheads safely off the street to strict adherence to the letter of the law. And if a few of them died under the cap—well, that was a few less to worry about, while the Palace had good working arrangements for disposal of cold meat.

It wasn't the illegality of what he was doing that worried Frank, nor the near certainty that his visit would be observed and recorded. Such a minor blot on his record was low on his list of priorities just now. The real danger, such as it was, was that he wouldn't come out of the dream. It happened— more often than the Palace would admit. But usually to habitual dreamers, losers who spent as much time as possible in retreat from reality, until one trip their minds just stayed there.

Sure, they could be unhooked from the cap, turned out into the streets, maybe even able to look after their basic bodily needs in automatic response to basic stimuli. But their minds were forever trapped, if not in the machine then in their own fantasy worlds, behind blank eyes.

That, Frank did not want. He might be down, but he wasn't beat yet. He wanted to know what had happened to change his DNA, and why. And if someone was responsible, he wanted to know who. And then—

he didn't know what then, but he sure as hell knew that he wanted answers.

Credit was a problem. Dreamtime didn't come cheap, even though it cost a damn sight less than a full diagnostic med. But he was a property owner—if you could call the minicondo property—so the problem wasn't insurmountable. The attendant was no problem, just a hassle. Frank supposed somebody had to be there to show clients into their cubicles, and it was no surprise that the somebody was a muscular young man. But the white coat, mocking the medical garb he'd seen all too recently, he could have done without. And the rundown on the procedure was merely an irritation. He already knew what he was letting himself in for. He let the man's patter wash past him as he removed his jacket and rolled up his sleeve ready for the spray.

"Now, you get one hour, okay? From the time I hit you with this. The spray's just to relax you, to get you in the right frame of mind. You start to picture the kind of dream you want, maybe

somebody you'd like to have a good time with, or someplace you'd like to be . . . you ain't got no picture or nothin', to remind you, you know, set the ball rollin'?"

Frank's silence brought only a shrug from the attendant. He sprayed the proffered arm, steered Frank to the couch, began to fit the cap—a light network of wires that fit snugly over the skull.

"Okay. Just relax, let your mind go. Soon's I'm out of here we're in business. You relax, get the dream rollin', the cap does the rest. Picks all the pictures right out of your brain and feeds

them back to you, bigger'n better. Ain't nothin' can go wrong; all you get out is what you put in, only more so. Okay?"

Frank, beginning to feel warm and relaxed, was no longer even irritated. Hell, the guy was only doing his job. Seemed like a nice kid, too. Just let your mind drift, he told himself. Drift back over some of the recent cases. Look for anything out of the ordinary, any breakdown of procedure. Any occasion when contamination might have got into his body. Just a pity he didn't know which case he wanted to recall, only that it must be there, in his subconscious, somewhere—if only he could lift it up into the conscious with the aid of the cap.

He blinked, as his eyelids began to feel heavy. Real pity he didn't have anything to trigger the ol' subconscious into action. No picture, no nothin'. His closing eyes caught a glimpse of the jacket, hung neatly on the back of the door. Just an old jacket. Still, at least the jacket had saved him from the needles. Needles bouncing off his chest, fired by a tall assassin. The image lingered.

As his eye closed, Frank realised, calmly and without surprise, why the hitman had looked familiar. Tall and lean, and he moved like there were weights tied round his waist. A loonie, for sure. He smiled. No wonder the jacket had saved him. An amateur loonie assassin. Poor sap *had* been going for his throat, but he'd undercompensated for the gravity on Earth.

Typical of those smartass loonies. So good with the theory, so damn useless in practice. Like that time, back in 'nineteen . . .

His eyes were firmly closed as the lights dimmed out entirely and his breathing settled into the steady rhythm of sleep. Outside, the attendant glanced at the screen. Seventeen was well away, judging from the activity in the net. He sure as hell was getting value for money. Another satisfied customer—and a satisfied customer usually came back for more.

He grinned, thinking of the bonus he would get for a repeat, and nudged the control just a touch. Hell, seventeen looked like a strong guy, fit, and he was sure he was a first-timer. He could take a little more stimulation.

"The death of Mark de Villiers, a little-known American biologist working in the Rainforest Reserve, would have excited little attention in the media if it had not been for the tantalising hint that before his murder he had made a 'significant' scientific discovery. In two short letters which de Villiers sent to colleagues at the Carnegie Institute in Washington DC four days before his death, he claimed that he had found 'something extraordinary in the genome of a number of species that are dying out' and talked of 'dropping a bombshell' in the world of biology. One-time collaborator, Wolfgang Kuhr of Cold Spring Harbor Laboratory in New York State says that de Villiers was not known for flights of fancy and that, if anything, the young biologist erred on the cautious side . . . "

Washington Post, 29 April 2129

Year 'nineteen. Hot, especially inside the rad suits. Two kinds of hot, outside. Frank Wilson grunted as he tried to monitor the activity of his companions across a distance of a hundred metres, through eyes that were screened by a seemingly permanent curtain of sweat. Loonies. Why the hell did he have to be saddled with a parcel of loonies? Strict orders. He was in charge, of course.

This was a Department job. The Terrestrial Department of Reclamation. No question about that. But on the other hand, he was to let "our colleagues from the Moon" have a free hand—especially if they wanted to work in the high radiation area. On the last point, he had no quibbles. There was plenty of high rad there, thanks to the leak from the containment vessels where all the twentieth-century shit had been dumped. Containment vessels designed, the record tapes said, to last for ten thousand years. Cracked like eggshells in the quake. Because, of course, twentieth century geophysicists "knew" that you didn't get Richter 7 quakes in Missouri.

If the loonies wanted to take all the rad, that was fine by him. If they had to be here at all, that was surely the best place for them. Though why they had to be here at all, and why all this big secrecy about their presence, he couldn't fathom. The only hints he'd had were that they were more tolerant of rad, coming from where they did. But in his experience, official hints were designed to conceal, not reveal, the truth. And they were so damn clumsy!

The scene shifted, like a badly edited holo.

He was running, contrary to his own strict instructions, straight into the high-rad area. How the hell had the loonies managed to get in such a mess? Two of them stumbling back his way, half dragging, half carrying their companion. Blood all over the guy's suit, visibly pumping from the severed arm. Didn't those idiots know enough to make an effective tourniquet?

Cut

He was with them, stopping their flight, tightening cord around the smashed arm.

Cut

Back in decontamination, stripping off his own suit with practiced ease, moving to help the injured man. Cutting at the shoulder seam of the right sleeve so that the rest of the suit could be removed, leaving the mixture of flesh and fabric around the stump for the surgeons to fix up. Slicing into the ball of his own hand, but feeling no pain as he worked to save the loonie's life.

Cut

Slicing into the ball of his own hand, the blood mixing with the blood of the loonie as he struggled to get the suit off him. His hand skidding on the blood-smeared surface, making it difficult to get a grip.

Cut

Frank woke, in the darkened cubicle, with the image clear in his mind. Reaching up, he almost absentmindedly pulled the net from his head. A momentary dizziness left him disoriented. But it soon passed, and the image remained. An image from ten years ago! Swinging his feet to the floor, he sat on the edge of the bed. Not a recent job, at all. Loonie blood, all over his hands. The deep cut in his left palm, that had taken four stitches to close. Whatever was on the outside of that rad suit, mixing with his blood. Something wrong with his body. Something that took ten years to do its work. And a loonie trying to kill him. There had to be a connection. He still didn't have a clue what was going on, but he sure as hell had somewhere to start looking.

Startled, the attendant responded to the beeping from his console. The trace from seventeen showed completely flat. Comets! Surely that tough-looking guy hadn't gone under? A stab at the panel raised the lighting in seventeen, and showed him that the cubicle was empty! Fuck.

He leapt up from the console and rushed out of the room only to find the main door to the Dream Palace swinging back into its frame. He didn't bother to follow. Obviously a bad trip. There'd be no return bonus on that guy. He spat on the floor in annoyance.

"The Mark de Villiers story is an odd episode in the annals of science. An obscure biologist is mysteriously murdered. In normal circumstances, the authorities would have concluded that the murder was as random and as senseless as a thousand others committed every day across the world. But not in this case . . .

"What has kept this episode alive is the hint that de Villiers discovered something in the Rainforest Reserve, and that something was important enough to be murdered for. But *what* did he find? The local police, aided by scientific colleagues, have carried out an exhaustive study of de Villiers' papers, but have unearthed no convincing evidence of any 'discovery'. We are told that de Villiers was about to submit a paper to the British journal *Nature*, but no manuscript has been found and a spokesman for *Nature* claims that it never received one.

"No doubt the conspiracy theorists will keep this story alive. It will resurface, I predict, at intervals, and many crackpots will take up the baton. But I think the time has come to drop this one. Mark de Villiers was an undistinguished—though no doubt hard-working—biologist. He died in unfortunate circumstances and we may never know the details. Now, surely, the time has come to lay this business to rest and to let Mark de Villiers rest in peace at last . . . "

Worldnet News, 3 June 2129

Out on the street, Frank Wilson screwed up his eyes against the bright sunlight. He began to walk, heading for the clustered high-rises of the more respectable part of town. He'd gained more from the Dream Palace than he dared to hope. Now he had a lot to think about. Something in the blood of those loonies back in 'nineteen had found its way into his own blood. It had made him sterile, and God knows what else. And now, because he'd seen a specialist who had become a tiny bit suspicious, the loonies were out to kill him. What the hell had got into his body?

Whatever it was, though, one thing was certain: it was worth murdering him to stop him learning the truth—or blabbing to the authorities. And it was coursing through his bloodstream at this very moment. The thought made him shudder. As he turned a corner in the street, he pulled up the sleeve of his jacket and examined his arm. The veins were still bulging beneath the skin after the dream stimulation. But what did they contain? He recoiled from the sight—his body had suddenly become an alien thing to him! Yanking his sleeve back down, he quickened his pace. For the second time in a day, he needed space and time to think. A gaudy holo ahead advertised a basement bar, and that was where he headed. It was noisy and crowded, but he found an empty table recessed in an alcove, as far away as he could get from the bar vidscreen. His mind was so preoccupied that the music and voices quickly receded, becoming a distant murmur before he had even sipped at his drink.

His solitude was violated, briefly, when a woman loomed over him, provocatively (he was still in that part of town), but she lost interest the moment she saw the veins bulging in his forearm. "A real girl's better than a dream girl," she muttered contemptuously as she left. Unmoved, Wilson returned to his troubled thoughts.

Now that Frank had a clue to follow, a course of action to plot, he didn't really need the drink at all; but it was his license to sit and think, anonymous in the crowd, his back to the wall. By the time his glass was half-empty he had decided what he must do. Catch a shuttle to the Moon. Those loonies back in 'nineteen. The loonie assassin. The connection between those two events was the only lead he had. It was clear to him that if answers were to be found, they were to be found in the deep warrens beneath Tycho City.

Easy to decide, not so easy to do. You couldn't just walk in to the Cowper Flats shuttle station and buy a ticket to the Moon. Travel restrictions got worse all the time. The only people with unrestricted access to those outbound shuttle flights were the loonies themselves. RN was happy to see loonies going back home; *their* problem would be the other way round, getting permission to come Earthside in the first place. In the normal way of things, Frank was in a good position to swing it. His job record, experience, unlimited license, status; a request to study loonie disaster control techniques would probably go down well. But that would involve loonie approval—and the only reason he wanted to go to Tycho was to find out why the loonies so strongly *dis*approved of him.

He was at a dead end. Pushing the unfinished drink across the table, Frank rose and shouldered his way through the crowd to the door. The vid was still bleating—some news item about further restrictions on lunar flights, loonies themselves only allowed to travel within 150 kilometres of their official place of residence. Yesterday, it would have meant nothing to him. Who needed the loonies, with their superior airs and graces, anyway? He didn't go along with the thugs who burned loonie property, but he had to admit that Earth'd be better off if the whole lot of them packed up and went home.

But now, even half heard through the hubbub, the news nagged. Suppose there was a reason behind all these restrictions. Suppose the RN knew something bad about the loonies—something bad that affected him, Frank Wilson, directly. In spite of the deaths, the Missouri cleanup had been a big success, environmentally speaking. The loonies really had been able to work in high rad. Yet as far as he knew, loonie help had never again been enlisted, although, God knows, there'd been plenty of high rad jobs.

Why? Had the loonies refused to help, or had the RN refused to ask? And again, why?

Connections. Were they real, or just in his mind, still affected by the residue of drugs?

Wrapped up in his thoughts, Frank crossed the invisible boundary that separated the shabby district of town from the gleaming, bustling heart of the city. Directly ahead of him, at the centre of a large ornamental park, was the Hub, the city's main air terminal. His legs had carried him to precisely the place he would have headed had his plans extended to any realistic prospect of getting a lunar visa.

High above him, atop a giant tapered pylon, sat the bulbous shape of the air terminal, a twentieth-century vision of the future that (bizarrely) had come true. Except for the black pinpricks of docking bays, its surface mirrored perfectly the clouds racing across the blue sky.

Around the Hub, the air was thick with tilt-rotors. They came and went like tiny bees servicing a great silver hive. If he had a visa, Wilson could have ridden one of those craft out to the shuttle port at Cowper Flats. Barring launch delays, he would have been on an LEO lifter up to Transfer Station within a few hours. But in the real world, not a hope.

He had arrived at a busy crossroads. The road ahead—essentially a spoke extending out from the axle of the Hub—was clogged with vehicles. To either side of him, more traffic swept by on a race-track road that encircled the park.

It was pointless now to continue on to the Hub. Wilson waited until the lights at the intersection changed, then he crossed with the crowd to the inner curve of the ring road. He'd call Mona from a terminal at the base of the pylon, take her out to dinner, get drunk. As he strode through the park, the shadow of the pylon began to sweep by, like the black finger of some monstrous sun-dial. A stiff breeze arose from nowhere, swirling the dry leaves that lay on the ground. It caught the fine mist from a fountain and blew it against his face. A few moments later, the trailing edge of the shadow passed; the Sun burst from behind the Hub and the artificial eclipse was over.

In the sunlight, Frank's own shadow stretched ahead at an angle to his right. Another long, thin shadow ran parallel to it, getting closer. Alarms sounded in his no-longer-befuddled brain, and even as the assailant was upon him he had turned, ducking under the intended blow and responding with a massive punch into the thorax of the loonie. As the man fell, Frank had his needler in his hand, firing a single dart into the back of the man's neck. The sedative would keep him quiet for an hour or more—capable of walking if aided, but incapable of acting on his own initiative. It was a particularly useful drug, illegal, of course; obtained through Frank's work.

He looked around. There were few passers-by in the park this late in the day, and those that had noticed the flurry of action were rapidly moving away. As usual, nobody wanted to get involved in other people's troubles. The loonie was on hands and knees, retching from the blow. Frank put his arm around him, under his shoulders, and hoisted him to his feet. The loonie stood, breathing hard through his mouth, swaying slightly, leaning on Frank.

"Come on, friend," Frank muttered. "Get those legs moving." He wanted cover, somewhere to go through the loonie's pockets, try to find a clue to what was going on. The comm booths at the foot of the Hub would be ideal. All he had to do was get the guy there.

In the booth, door shut, loonie sitting quietly beside him, Frank went through the man's wallet. There was nothing to link him with Frank. Indeed, the wallet was singularly lacking in anything incriminating, or informative. And certainly no return ticket to Tycho, as Frank had half-hoped. A few credit cards, lunar and terrestrial; and, of course, the man's ID.

Frank turned it over in his hand, wondering. He scanned the details on the card:

Name: Paxton Small
Age: 2
Occupation: Vacuum engineer, 2nd Class, Tycho City Authority.

As usual, the holo on the card was a pretty ropey likeness. What really mattered was the thumbprint below it. That and the certainty that this Paxton Small, if that really was his name, would have a security code on anything important, like a bank account. But there just might be a way, if he moved quickly enough. It wouldn't stand up to any kind of close inspection, and the scam would be certain to be uncovered by morning, at one end or the other. But if it worked, that wouldn't matter. He had nothing to lose—except Mona. And if he had no reproductive potential, how long would Mona stick around? Deep down, he had no real illusions about their relationship. He might kid along, on the surface, that it was something more. Sure, he liked her; they got on well. But what did it come down to? He wanted to use his unlimited license; she was just plain broody, and fond of the status. If he couldn't father her brood, with her looks she'd damn soon find someone who could.

Unconsciously, he'd reached his decision while still turning the card over in his fingers, thinking of Mona. Only loonies could travel to the Moon. He had Paxton Small's ID, but no means to tap the loonie's funds. As Frank Wilson, he could raise funds by mortgaging the condo—but he couldn't buy a ticket on the lunar shuttle. The trick was to join up the two ends of the problem.

His fingers flickered with practiced ease over the keyboard in the booth. Mortgage the condo—no problem. Open a new bank account in the name Paxton Small, with his own thumbprint and code—no problem. Transfer funds from the bank account of Frank Wilson to the bank account of "Paxton Small"—no problem. Now, things began to get interesting.

He called Interplanetary Travel (the company had been named with the same insouciance that once led a small local airline to call itself "Transworld"; of course, there were no flights to anywhere except the Moon). A holo politely informed him that travel was restricted, at the present time, to lunar citizens. He said that he was a lunar citizen, slid Paxton Small's ID into the slot presented the real Paxton Small's thumb to the pad. The holo thanked him, and asked what kind of ticket he would like. First class, one way, Tycho; next available flight. The holo quoted him a price. Just a minute, said Frank, that's more than I expected, I'll have to pay out of my other account. After hitting the "split" key to divide the screen, he removed the Paxton Small ID, and keyed in details of his new account by hand, offering his own thumb, when requested by the bank's computer, to authenticate the transfer of funds to Interplanetary, quoting the transaction number given by the holo, and, automatically, the name on his account. The holo appeared to look away at a screen, then back at Frank. He'd always found the trick irritating; doubly so now, when he knew that all the information was instantaneously processed into the computer running the talking head. Either the trick had worked, or it hadn't. He had no time for such fancies.

The holo smiled. "Thank you, Mr Small. Everything is in order. Your ticket will be waiting at the check in desk. You have one hour and seventeen minutes to get there before the flight closes."

He cut the connection, not bothering with any pretence of politeness. And checked his companion. Paxton Small sat quietly on the seat, eyes open. Frank gave him another shot, inducing the lean body to sag against the wall, eyes closed. That would certainly keep him quiet until the shuttle lifted. Now, all he had to do was get on board the damn thing. Carefully pocketing Small's ID, he stood and slipped out of the booth, closing the door behind him. The red "Occupied" light stayed on over the door as he moved off into the flow of people.

At the Hub, Wilson caught the first tilt to Cowper Flats. He was lucky to get a seat. The flight was packed with loonies fleeing the city. He hadn't realised there were so many on Earth, let alone locally—although, obviously, there must be more here, near the spaceport, than anywhere else. And he hadn't thought through the impact on these exiles of the threat to their lines of communication home. If the RN could cut terrestrials off from lunar flights today, who could guess what would happen tomorrow? History was littered with examples of what happened to minorities who stayed on where they weren't wanted. Just about every loonie in the city seemed to have decided not to take any chances. Family heads, with jobs on Earth, might be sticking it out; but dependents were in full retreat. Which made for noise and confusion, and had to be good news for Frank.

They sat in their seats, white-faced and stunned, overtaken by the terrible speed of events. The garments they wore were mismatched, thrown on; their bags bulging and hastily packed. Only hours before, they might have been sitting down for a meal or preparing to go out to a ballgame. Now they were refugees.

The plight of the loonies was truly appalling. But Wilson had his own problems. At the rear of the cabin he located a vacant restroom. With the door locked, he took out the loonie's ID card and propped it beside the mirror on the wall. A glance from one to the other was enough to provoke an instant groan of dismay. The likeness might not match Paxton Small very well, but nor did it look anything like Frank Wilson. But these were not normal circumstances—were they? At the spaceport, there would be hundreds—maybe thousands—of loonies, all desperately trying to make it home. It would be chaos. He'd be all right—of *course* he would—just as long as he kept his head down. He *must* think positive. He'd never thought it would be easy.

In his jacket pocket, he found his army knife. Deftly, he fingered the tiny knobs on the hilt. With a hum, the appliance he needed formed at the other end. Quickly and clumsily, he began to snip at his hair, shaping it into a crude resemblance of Paxton Small's loonie crop. Half an hour later, Wilson was stepping down onto the parched lakebed of Cowper Flats. It was hot and dry and stars were already appearing in the rapidly darkening sky. As the tilt departed, rising into the air on a column of swirling dust, he followed the other passengers heading for the brightly lit terminal building.

The thrum of tilt-rotors filled the desert air. One was coming in to land nearby, another two were making their final approach, swooping down from the jagged mountains that bounded Cowper Flats on two sides. From all the cities of the West Coast they were coming, swarming on the spaceport like great silver bees. The exodus to the Moon was as inexorable as it was incomprehensible. A flight of people as momentous and as tragic as any in history.

In the terminal building, police were everywhere. Many of the loonies were just standing around. At first, Wilson thought they must be waiting for friends, or for family members. Then he realised they were simply gripped by inertia; the terrible inertia of people who are suddenly facing a bleak and uncertain future.

Wilson had to push hard to get through the crowds. There was no problem about picking up the ticket. The human clerk at the desk was only too glad to be able to thrust it into his hand, scarcely glancing at the proffered ID. One person less for him to worry about, besieged as he was by loonies with no tickets at all, and no prospect of getting one tonight.

With the ticket in his hand, he fought his way back across the floor of the terminal building, heading for the gate to the departure area. When he arrived at the gate, a group of maybe a dozen loonies was going through. Wilson didn't hesitate a moment, but latched onto them immediately.

The nearest loonie, a middle-aged woman, was crying pitifully, as a man chivvied her along, trying to comfort her. In any other circumstances, the woman's distress would have moved Wilson deeply, but now he was too preoccupied with his own problems to take any real notice of her. When it came to the crunch, would he really be able to pass himself off as the loonie assassin: as Paxton Small?

Well, he would soon know.

They had reached a barrier, which was manned by several stern-faced immigration officers. Terrestrials, obviously switched from their usual job of stopping undesirables arriving on-planet to holding back anyone they didn't want to leave. One by one, the loonies handed over their documents, were given them back and allowed through. When the man and the sobbing woman had been waved on, one of the officers turned to Wilson. "No luggage, sir?" she said.

Wilson shook his head. "No time," he said, and repeated it, feigning the shell-shock of the other loonies.

The woman hardly looked at the ID card. Instead, she looked Wilson up and down with barely concealed contempt. What the hell have you loonies been doing up there on the Moon that's so bad? Her eyes said. For an instant, a window opened up on the loonies' nightmare, and Wilson felt a deep, deep shame. Practically overnight, the people of Earth, *his* people, had learnt to hate loonies. They didn't even need a reason. It had come to them as easily as slipping on a glove.

Wilson was certain he knew what she was thinking: now the authorities wouldn't quarantine the Moon unless they had a very good reason, would they, sir? The logic was impeccably Kafkaesque.

She handed back his documents and waved him through. But he had walked only a few steps when someone else stopped him. "Hey, you—you don't look like a loonie." A tall man, about his own age, was barring Wilson's way, eyeing him suspiciously.

"Uh, that's because I'm Earth born. Lunar citizen by marriage." The answer was a surprise even to him. "We've only been married ten months, and *this* has to happen," he added quickly.

Instantly, the man's face softened. Wilson had struck a sympathetic chord. Perhaps this man had recently married, too. Quickly, exploiting his advantage, Wilson said: "I can't stay on Earth. I have just *have* to get back to her—you understand, officer?"

"Of course," the man said, stepping aside. As Wilson walked away, the officer shouted after him: "And good luck to you, sir."

Wilson chided himself for his cynicism. He had been too quick to condemn his people. Not everyone was waiting for an excuse to hate.

Frank expected difficulties at Transfer Station. It was even possible that his subterfuge had already been discovered, with messages winging through the Web to have the escaping criminal travelling under the name Paxton Small detained. But there were no problems. The lunar shuttle itself was a loonie vehicle, of course, just as the ground-to-space lifters were Earth-owned. And its loonie crew didn't seem to care much about checking the ID of refugees, even though he did take care to repeat the story of his marriage to a loonie. Still, it was only when the shuttle pulled gently away from the Station, pushing Frank sideways against the straps securing him in his seat, and then began the slow acceleration on its lunar trajectory, that he began to feel secure. Of course, his lunar identity wouldn't hold up for a day in Tycho—although, in the confusion of this exodus from Earth, he almost dared hope that he might at least get that much breathing space—but at least he'd be there, where his would-be assassin had set out from. And he'd get some answers, if it killed him. Answers to why he'd been targeted for a hit; answers to what had been in the loonie blood, contaminating him, all those years ago; and he was absolutely certain that both questions had the same answer.

Meanwhile, he had time to kill. All around him, loonies were flipping down consoles from the back of the seat in front of them, flipping through channels for news. Not a bad idea. Surely, *somebody* must have the background on this lunar quarantine business?

He reached for his own console, which lit with a lunar broadcast, some Tycho high-up being interviewed about the restrictions. The bigwig made all the noises typical of outraged officialdom, talking of "scandal" and "outrage", even dropping in "violation of basic human rights"—but the interviewer assumed that the viewer was up to speed on the facts. No use to Frank at all.

He flipped through the channels, searching for a straight news broadcast. One flash caught his eye for a moment. Mark de Villiers, a young biologist, killed by a needler a few days back; questions being asked about why, whether he had known something he shouldn't (about what? nobody knew). Could've been me, thought Frank. He imagined the story. Cleanup Engineer, top man, unrestricted repro license, no known enemies, killed by a needler downtown. There'd be a mention of his grieving term-wife.

Oh God. Mona.

He'd have to talk to her, explain what had happened. But he could delay the awkward moment a little; there was something else he had to do first.

A few key taps gave him access to the phoney Paxton Small bank account. There was still plenty of credit there, and it hadn't yet been blocked. He shifted it back to his own account, and took off the restriction on the amount Mona was allowed to withdraw. Best he could do. She was a big girl, she'd cope. And now there was no more excuse to delay.

The conversation was every bit as grim as he'd expected. But, also as expected, the news that really seemed to hit Mona hardest was the item he'd broken to her first—that he was infertile, had no hope at all of fathering children, either naturally or in vitro. Once that had sunk in, she didn't seem exactly heartbroken to learn that he was taking some time off, going away to think things over—he didn't specify where, and as yet the shuttle was close enough to Earth for the time lag not to be obvious. And when she started bitching about how she was expected to cope, suddenly left on her own like this, no warning, it had almost been a pleasure to give her the details of the bank balance, tell her she could do what she liked with it. That certainly took the wind out of her sails.

They'd closed coolly, but polite. Him promising to call her as soon as he was back in town, her obviously aware that this might never happen, both of them knowing that with just under six months left on the contract their marriage was over. No tears, no regrets. But, on his side at least, a kind of numbness. A realisation, as the screen cleared, that he had severed his last link with Earth. However this crisis worked out, whenever normal flights between Earth and Moon were restored, he couldn't see any way back. Either he'd die up here, the victim of the next Paxton Small, or he'd find out what the hell was going on, and stick around long enough to shake some sense into the story—and *then*, a small voice at the back of his head insisted, probably fall victim to the next assassin.

With thoughts buzzing through his head, Frank fell into an exhausted sleep, to dream of being chased through endless tunnels by tall, thin assassins. He was woken by a chime, half-hearing a recorded voice informing the passengers that by tuning to Channel 4 they would be able to get a live view from the shuttle's own camera of Lagrange Station, now at the closest they would be approaching on this trip. Frank couldn't care less about Lagrange Station, and settled back to doze amid the rising murmur of conversation as many of his fellow travellers, reverting to the familiar habits of the journey, started to switch their consoles to the indicated channel. A sudden hush brought him wide awake, alert to anticipated danger. What had happened?

All around him, loonies were fixed upon their screens. The view of Lagrange couldn't be *that* impressive, surely? He looked at his neighbour's console. Channel 3, some woman talking excitedly, inaudible thanks to the privacy circuit which automatically kept the volume of the headrest speaker low outside its intended zone. Frank leaned forward, arm almost floating in the minimal acceleration, and punched his own console for Channel 3.

The image of the woman was captioned "Councillor Joanne Balcewicz". The biggest lunar bigwig of the lot; their equivalent of the Secretary of the RN. But she was a helluva lot more excited than any politician he'd ever seen on vid. He leaned back against the headrest, moving his ears into the zone covered by the audio circuits, catching her in mid-sentence.

" . . . this evil empire, following in the traditions of Genghis Khan, Hitler, the Fuegos. Our ancestors left the Earth to escape such persecution, such oppression by the State. We will not be crushed by this illegal act of piracy, by this persecution of a minority that has done no harm to the mother planet. The Moon is self-sufficient, we have been self-sufficient for generations, and no evil Earth will starve us into submission. Let us wait and see just who comes crawling to who for help before our twin planets have made many more orbits around the Sun. We want nothing from Earth. Even if that evil empire should wish to reopen travel between our two planets, I say, on behalf of the people of the Moon, that we do not want your people . . . "

Frank turned to his neighbour. "What the hell's all that about? I was asleep."

The elderly loonie glanced at him, turned his attention back to the screen, spoke without looking at Frank.

"Earth's cut off all shuttle flights. No more communication either way. There's only one shuttle behind us, then that's it. My daughter's down there. At college. Refused to leave. Now Balcewicz says *she* won't let her come back even if the terries decide to let her." He shook his head, continuing to stare at the screen.

Frank leaned back, switched the audio off, watched the woman, still talking—still foaming at the mouth, more like. Hell's teeth. If *she* was in charge at Tycho, God alone knew what he was in for when he got there.

The landing itself was uneventful, routine. Loonies were used to the routine, and with safety drills drummed into them from an early age, quickly settled after the hubbub caused by the telecast, strapping themselves in, carrying out safety checks. Frank followed suit, trying to remain inconspicuous, but aware that his plan, such as it was, had run into a dead end. Within minutes, he would be on the Moon. Then what? The way things looked now, he might *never* get back to Terra. And the only two sure things he knew about the Moon were that at least one of the loonies wanted him dead, while their head of government seemed to be ripe for the funny farm. Great. Just have to play it by ear.

He never got the chance. With no possessions to carry, it was easy for him to time his departure from the shuttle in the middle of the crowd, jostling one another in the narrow tunnel. The gravity took some getting used to, but many of his companions were also bouncing a little too high as they walked, laughing at each other, commenting that they had been too long on Earth, lost their lunar legs. The height he couldn't disguise, but all he wanted was to get through whatever immigration procedures they had, get clear into Tycho City and have time to think, plan his next move. But as the tunnel opened out into a domed chamber, with several exits radiating out from it, he saw that the exits lay beyond a fence. There were just three gates in the fence, each attended by a pair of uniformed security types, and the new arrivals were directed to fan out and file through those gates. Beyond, a fair-haired man in a blue lunar one-piece stood next to a woman, below average height for a loony, keeping a careful watch on the incoming passengers. From time to time, they checked something against a hand held computer link. Even before Frank reached the gate in the fence—he'd chosen the one on the extreme left, still hoping to make a fast fade off into one of the side tunnels—the man had nudged his companion, who looked up from the link, straight at Frank. As he offered Paxton Small's credentials to the immigration officer, she stepped forward.

"No need for any formalities, officer. This man is a guest of the government. We've been expecting him." She took the proffered ID herself, turned to Frank. "Mr Wilson. Welcome to Tycho City, and to Luna. We've been expecting you."

He shook his head, in anger rather than denial. He hadn't been thinking far enough ahead, or high enough up the tree. The real Paxton Small would have recovered, found a way to call Tycho even without his credit and ID, let his employers know that Wilson was loose, while he was stranded on Terra. Frank had expected no less, but the only way to prevent this would have been to kill Small, and Frank was no killer. Instead, he had anticipated making his way into the city before Small's friends, whoever they were, could get organised.

Some hope! Small's friends—those employers—were, obviously, right in front of him. Equally obviously, they were official. *Very* official. The kind of official that could respond quickly and efficiently when the computer link showed that one of their own agents, Paxton Small, was booked on one of the last flights up from Terra—while that same Paxton Small was also stranded down on the ground. Comets! You didn't even need a link to work *that* one out.

"So what are you gonna do? Finish the job your man started on Earth? I want some questions answered, first."

"Circumstances have changed, Mr Wilson. Our first priority, too, is to find out the answers to some questions. But I believe you will find that you will be in the position of answering them, not asking. Come."

He had no choice, nowhere to run even if he tried. He followed her. The man, still without speaking a word, stepped in behind him. He wasn't wearing a ball and chain, and they weren't in uniform, but he was left in no doubt that he was a prisoner under escort. His thoughts in a whirl, Frank scarcely noticed that their route took them out from the cavern, the original spaceport back in the days when there had been hard vacuum on the surface of the Moon, and through a transparent connecting tube to a low cluster of buildings. It was obvious why they didn't go out into the air, such as it was; it was night, with frost reflecting the lights even here, on the edge of the city. Overhead, the stars, visible through the clear plastic of the tube, were brighter and harder than the stars seen from Earth, their twinkling less frequent, but somehow more pronounced.

None of this made much impact on Frank. He knew about the lunar atmosphere programme, the comets that were regularly steered in from beyond Jupiter to provide the gasses and water that made the Moon habitable, and which, optimists said, would make life possible completely out of doors, day and night, as the atmosphere thickened. But it was no business of his. To Frank, the Moon looked just the way he'd seen it in the vid. The spaceport was carefully designed to look, from the passenger's viewpoint, reassuringly like any airport on Earth, the corridors were just corridors, the rooms just rooms. He was a reasonably well-educated man, an engineer, but a specialist, with no broad knowledge even of science, and no interest in history. He had no idea that, less than two hundred years before, nobody had stood on the surface of the Moon and watched the stars twinkling.

They walked briskly, in silence. The few people passing by in the corridor took care to keep out of their way. Soon, they passed under a low arch, and the corridor, now completely windowless, sloped downward a little before opening out into a large domed chamber, its roof clearly hewn from the rock. The tunnel they had entered by was one of three, equally spaced around the circumference of the chamber; between each pair of tunnel mouths there were the entrances to three elevators, each busily absorbing and disgorging people.

Frank decided it was time to intervene.

"Where are we? Where are you taking me?"

Somewhat to his surprise, the woman responded.

"This is the Hub. We are going down to security. The safest part of the city, in the old caverns where the pioneers lived and worked, before Reese brought the air." As she mentioned the name

"Reese", she made a small gesture with her right hand, lifting it to touch her chest. Frank knew the story, vaguely. Reese had been the commander of the comet-riding expedition, in the twenty-first century, bringing the first atmosphere to the Moon. Real primitive, pioneering stuff; she'd been killed, hadn't she? Anyway, now it was all automatic, the probes out beyond Jupiter picking up the comets and giving them an appropriate nudge inward. Much safer; all under computer control. He hadn't realised, though, that the original caverns would still be inhabited; but it seemed they had some deep historical significance for the loonies—as well as being, he realised as the elevator dropped away almost in free fall in the low gravity, goddamn difficult to escape from.

The room they took him to was a classic interrogation chamber. Windowless, a hard seat behind a plain table, featureless walls, nothing to look at. They took his watch away, and left him sitting there for what seemed like hours before the woman returned, accompanied either by the same man or his brother—Frank never had got a good look at him on the way down here. The man carried a much more comfortable looking chair, which he placed on the other side of the table. The woman sat; he stood, back against the wall, eyes on Frank. It was all a bit pointless, Frank thought. Even if I could get through the locked door I wouldn't know where to go. He waited for the woman to speak. He'd been waiting long enough already; a little longer would make no difference.

She made a pretence of checking something with her hand held link, took her time, looked up.

"Why have you come to the Moon, Mr Wilson?"

"To get some answers. To find out what's wrong with me. What happened back in 'nineteen."

"And who do you represent?"

"Represent? Nobody." Did she think he was working for the government? "No fuckin' body. That's who I represent. Nobody but *me*! Same as always. Frank Wilson, looking out for himself, 'cos no other goddamn sucker will."

His genuine anger seemed to surprise her. She glanced down at her link again, tapping the tiny keys. She looked up.

"Do you expect us to believe, Mr Wilson, that it is just a coincidence that the emigration authorities let you board a shuttle with false ID that wouldn't fool a child? And that it is also just a coincidence that as soon as you were safely en route to the Moon, but not before, the RN stopped all further flights? Somebody wants you here, Mr Wilson, and my job is to find out who—and why."

"This is crazy. Of course it isn't a coincidence. It's cause and effect. Only you've got it backwards. I made a run for Luna because I needed some answers, and I had to get here before the last shuttle left. It was obvious the crackdown was coming. I just managed to stay one jump ahead."

She changed tack, abruptly. "What do you know about the Breakout, Mr Wilson?"

He shook his head.

"Does the name Mark de Villiers mean anything to you?"

He shook his head again. No. Wait. "Yeah. He was on the Net. Some eco scientist, shot down in Brazil, or Nicaragua, or somewhere. So what?"

"You seem to be somewhat luckier than Mr de Villiers."

"You bastards." The memory of the attempted hit came flooding back, full colour, wide screen in his mind. "Yeah, it *was* you. An official loony assassin. I tell you, he never would've got near me if I hadn't been knocked sideways by the news from the medics."

"Tell me about it, Mr Wilson. Tell me everything that happened to you that day."

Well, why not? It was what he'd come here for, after all. He had nothing to hide, and it was clear that this woman, or her bosses, did have at least some of the answers he was seeking. He told her, leaving nothing out. She listened; obviously her link was recording. Then she thanked him, and both of them left, without answering any of his questions. He yelled a last thought at the closing door. "Hey! When do I get a drink? And eats? And somewhere to take a crap?"

"The toilet facilities are behind you, Mr Wilson."

He turned back from the door. Sure enough, the seemingly solid wall on the opposite side of the cell had slid open along an invisible seam, revealing rudimentary facilities. A reward, perhaps, for being a good boy? At least he could relieve himself, get a drink from the tap, even if there was nothing there to eat. Cautiously, he wedged the hard chair in the opening before using the toilet. Didn't want some joker shutting him up in here for the duration.

The stuff must have been in the water. He remembered going back in to the main chamber OK, leaving the chair wedged in place, just in case; heading for the corner, aiming to sit with his back against the wall, maybe have a doze. Then, he was lying on his back, pins and needles in his left arm, a black-clad woman removing a hypospray from his neck.

"Come *on*." She tugged at him. "I know you're awake. We've got sixty-seven seconds to get out of here. Move!"

He climbed unsteadily to his feet, grasped at her arm, stumbled behind her as she swept through the open cell door, glanced quickly in both directions, then headed to the right. She began a running commentary, obviously designed to encourage him along, bring him up to speed.

"OK. Plenty of time if you keep moving. Once we're in the service shaft, no sweat. They used Tell All on you, so you've told them everything you know. Then they left you to sleep it off, only some of us had other ideas. Right. Here we are."

'Here' was a circular chamber, almost a replica of the Hub, but with a flat roof. She held him flat against the wall, peering round for signs of activity.

"OK. Back off a bit." She fumbled at the wall of the corridor, opened another seamless door slipped inside, dragging him with her. They were in a small circular room, with a large hole, maybe two metres across, in the floor, and an identical hole in the ceiling. A ladder extended upward, out of sight.

"Climb." She pushed him towards the ladder. He grasped it, then paused. His head was becoming clearer.

"How far?"

"Don't worry. The shaft goes all the way to the top. Half a kilometre. But we're only going a little way under our own steam. Don't let go, though. There's another half kilometre below."

He looked down. It was a mistake. The brightly lit shaft extended apparently to infinity. He closed his eyes, lifted his head, opened them again.

Watch the rungs, Frank, he told himself. Watch the rungs. Slowly, he began to climb, urged on by the woman. He counted the rungs as he did so. At ninety-four, with muscles aching, his head entered another circular, apparently doorless, chamber, with various pieces of equipment stacked around it.

"OK," the familiar voice came from below, "in here."

He stepped thankfully onto the floor, sat, leaned back against the wall, watched her emerge, smiling.

"We're safe here for an hour or so, anyway. Be gone long before then. I'm Natalya."

"Thanks. But what . . . why?"

"If Balcewicz wants you locked up, that's good enough reason for us to get you out, find out what's going on. It was pretty easy. Things are in a mess all over, with Terra cut off from us, Balcewicz issuing new decrees every five minutes. Half the city'd be glad to see the back of her, now. Easy to get a few blind eyes turned. But we don't have much time. Tell me everything while I get this stuff ready."

She turned, began working at some of the equipment.

"Everything? How much do you know?"

"Not a lot." Her back was to him, voice muffled. "You're from Terra, probably an RN agent, so you ought to know what's behind this excommunication. We're against Balcewicz, in favour of friendly relations, so obviously you'll help us." She looked over her shoulder, smiled again. "Won't you?"

He groaned, rubbed his right hand across his eyes. "I'm in no position to help anyone. I *need* help. And I'm *not* an RN agent." Once again, but this time more sketchily, he outlined his story. By the time he had finished, she had unpacked and fitted together two sets of the equipment.

"OK. There ought to be enough TA still in your system to make me believe you, at least for now. Weird story, but we can sort that out later, when we meet up with the group. You're still someone Balcewicz doesn't want on the loose. Try this for size."

'This' was a circular metal hoop, with a massive looking pack attached to one side and two short arms sticking out from the other.

"It fits like this." She snapped it open, fitted it around Frank's chest, snapped it closed. The pack, on his back, was indeed massive.

"OK. Get on the ladder."

"I can't climb far carrying *this*."

"No need." She pushed him forward, so that he stood on the ladder, hands holding the side rails. "Look."

As he put his feet on the ladder, she guided the stubby extensions from the front of the hoop into contact with the hand rails on either side of the rungs.

"Maglev. Switch on *here*," she suited the action to the words, "and up she goes!"

The weight of the pack disappeared, and the hoop began to press up under Frank's armpits, lifting him gently up the shaft. He kept a loose grip on the hand rails, letting them slide through his grasp; but his feet were now dangling over half a kilometre of nothing, and rising. Natalya, obviously, was following behind.

"Great. But how do I stop?"

Her voice drifted up from below.

"It's automatic. Cuts off at the top. And we're going all the way."

There were two uniformed figures at the top of the shaft, a man and a woman, and nowhere to hide. Here we go again, thought Frank. But as the man stepped forward to help Frank, the pack suddenly heavy once again on his back, out of the shaft, he spoke.

"Is Natalya with you?"

Frank nodded. "Just behind. You're with her?"

"Yes. There isn't much time."

Quickly, as Natalya in turn emerged from the shaft, he explained.

"I'm Rob; this is Sylvie." The woman nodded. "We've got our people in the com centre. You've got to go on air, tell everyone what's going on down on Terra. Why all flights have been cut off.

Make it clear that bloody woman is responsible. That'll swing opinion, we can get control, call an election, restore relations with Terra. OK?"

"But I don't *know* anything. What's going on here? Why don't *you* tell them?"

Rob answered the last question first, as they were hustling Frank into a corridor. It was strangely quiet, with occasional armed figures, uniformed like Rob and Sylvie, at intersections.

"Because I'm a loonie. We're the Opposition. Of course we're going to blame Balcewicz for the troubles. But if a terry agent, speaking for the government down there, says she has to go, it'll give us just the lever we need. As for what's going on, you might call it a coup, or a revolution. Depends on your point of view. But we've had enough of that bloody woman, after fourteen years. This is just the chance we need.

"What do y'mean, you don't know anything?"

With this last question, Rob stopped short, pushing Frank into an alcove in the corridor. The two women, Natalya and Sylvie, automatically took up watchful positions either side of the alcove.

"I don't represent the Terran government. I don't know what's going on. I came here to find out why *your* government tried to kill me."

"Hell, that's good enough. If Balcewicz wants you dead, you must know *something*."

"All I know is that my body's screwed up. DNA problems. And it dates back to 'nineteen, when I worked with loonies on a cleanup crew. Heavy rad, out in Missouri."

"I'm not interested in your personal problems, Frank." He pulled out a link, spoke briefly into it. "Com centre's secure, we can hold it for an hour, maybe. Then—who knows? C'mon."

Just outside the com centre, Frank saw dark stains on the floor, stopped. Rob followed his gaze, shrugged. "What d'you expect? When totalitarian regimes tumble, there's always fighting.

But there'll be a lot less blood if you do your bit."

Inside, there were more bloodstains, some damage to the furniture, a broken window sealed with plastic sheeting. About a dozen dishevelled figures, all carrying weapons, were putting the place in order. Frank tried to add up in his head the number of armed revolutionaries he'd seen on the way in. Even assuming they were trying to keep under cover, it seemed an awfully small number. Maybe he'd have been better off in his cell. Then, a console to the right of the com equipment caught his eye.

"Is that a main computer link?"

Rob nodded. "Full access to the Web. But we want you on camera, and quick, not playing games with the records."

"No. Records are what I need. Records of what happened in 'nineteen. Find out, and then I'll go on air."

Frank looked around again. The uniformed figures in the room, setting up defensive positions, took occasional glances, he noted, at Rob, who was clearly in some position of authority among the rebels.

"Look, Rob. I can't go on air with nothing to say. But if I know *why* Balcewicz is out for me, I can tell them the truth. Then, it's up to you."

A decision was made.

"Ten minutes. No more. Sylvie?" The silent woman turned. "Get Frank onto the Web. Check out what you can in the time." She nodded, moved towards the console. He followed.

The link was basically the same as a terminal on Earth. He slipped into the seat, stabbed at the panel. As he had expected, no ID or access code was needed to get into the basic Web. After all, the link was in a place, the com centre, where only authorized personnel ought to be in the first place. He selected voice input/screen output; he preferred to read what the computer might have to tell him, rather than listen.

"Get me full information about the Missouri cleanup in year 'nineteen. Liaison between Lunar and Terran environment engineers to remove a radioactive hazard." There ought to be enough key words in there, he thought. Sure enough, the screen started to fill with words, scrolling slowly, kicking off with a menu of the details available. Details about the radwaste, the earthquake; the Terran request for assistance, successful outcome to the mission . . . it looked as if it would go on for hours.

"Wait." The scrolling stopped. "I want details of the Terran request, item 3, and the reasons for the Lunar response. I want to know what happened to the Lunar engineer injured on the job. And I want anything you have on Frank Wilson, the Terran engineer in charge of the cleanup."

The screen cleared, then filled with new words:

TERRAN REQUEST FOR LUNAR ENGINEERS WITH SPECIAL SKILLS ACCEPTED BY LUNAR COUNCIL, JOANNE BALCEWICZ PRESIDING. NATURE OF SPECIAL SKILLS, CLASSIFIED. REASONS FOR ACCEPTANCE, CLASSIFIED. RAMIRO GOMEZ, INJURED DURING CLEANUP, MADE FULL RECOVERY, DIED IN MINING ACCIDENT YEAR TWENTY-SEVEN. FRANK WILSON, TERRAN ENVIRONMENTAL ENGINEER, FILE LOCKED. FOR MORE INFORMATION ON LOCKED/CLASSIFIED MATERIAL, PLEASE PROVIDE CODEWORD.

He sat back. He was bloody well right. There *was* something going on, and it *did* involve something that had happened to him in 'nineteen. He scarcely heard the distant rattle of shots from the corridor outside. Given time, they'd be able to crack the security on this damn machine and find out what. The sharp *crack* of a grenade reminded him that they didn't have much time.

He became aware of Sylvie's breath on his ear as she leaned over his shoulder to check the screen. Well, he guessed he did owe these rebels something, after all. If they hadn't broken him out of his cell, he wouldn't even be this close to finding the truth.

Breakout. Suddenly, as clear as a Dreamtime flashback, Frank saw, and heard, his interrogator, just as he'd seen her in his cell. *"What do you know about the Breakout, Mr Wilson?"* The way she'd said the word, he could almost see the capital letter hanging there in the air.

Worth a try. He looked up at Sylvie. "Get Rob over to see this. It might be important."

He turned back to the console. "Codeword, Breakout. Give me a minimum summary first."

The screen cleared again.

CODEWORD ACCEPTED. SUMMARY FOLLOWS.

Rob was behind him, talking, telling him that they were going on air *now*, he'd better damn well talk to the Lunar population, before Balcewicz's goons kicked the door in.

"Shut up. Read."

SPECIAL SKILLS: RESISTANCE OF LUNAR WORKERS TO CELL DAMAGE CAUSED BY RADIATION. A RESULT OF THE GENETIC ENGINEERING PROGRAMME SET UP BY JOANNE BALCEWICZ AS MINISTER FOR THE ENVIRONMENT IN THE YEAR NINETY-THREE. MORE?

"More."

RESISTANCE TO MUTATION PROVIDED BY DNA TRIPLING TECHNIQUE. FIRST APPLIED TO LUNAR PLANTS TO STABILISE GENOME OF FOOD CROPS UNDER HI-RAD LUNAR CONDITIONS. LATER APPLIED TO ANIMALS AND PEOPLE. MORE?

"Next."

TERRAN REQUEST ACCEPTED BY COUNCIL ON CASTING VOTE OF JOANNE BALCEWICZ, PRESIDING. REASON FOR ACCEPTANCE, TO ESTABLISH LUNAR SKILLS AS COMMERCIAL PRODUCT OF VALUE IN FUTURE TRADING RELATIONS. MINORITY OBJECTION ON GROUNDS THAT DNA TRIPLING RETROVIRUS SHOULD NOT BE GIVEN OPPORTUNITY TO ENTER TERRESTRIAL ENVIRONMENT. MORE?

Who needed more of that crap? Politics, in other words.

"Next."

FRANK WILSON. INFECTED BY RETROVIRUS FROM RAMIRO GONZALES. REPRODUCTIVE CELLS UNDERWENT DNA TRIPLING. NO HARMFUL SIDE EFFECTS. MORE?

No harmful side effects? Then why . . . A crackle of gunfire broke into his train of thought.

"Wait." And then, to Rob. "Does this help? Does it mean anything to you?"

"Just maybe. Link, was anything else infected with this retrovirus?"

DNA TRIPLING RETROVIRUS MUTATED UNDER ULTRA HIGH-RAD CONDITIONS AT SITE OF MISSOURI CLEANUP. MANY EARTH SPECIES OF PLANT INFECTED INITIALLY. ANIMALS ONLY INFECTED BY DIRECT BLOOD CONTACT UNTIL YEAR TWENTY-THREE. FOLLOWING FURTHER MUTATION, DNA TRIPLING BEGAN TO SPREAD THROUGHOUT TERRAN ANIMAL POPULATION. FIRST HUMANS, OTHER THAN FRANK WILSON, INFECTED TWO YEARS AGO. MORE? "WHAT EFFECT DOES THIS DNA TRIPLING HAVE?" DNA TRIPLING ENSURES STABILITY OF GENOME. REDUCES MUTATION RATE SO THAT OFFSPRING MORE CLOSELY RESEMBLE THEIR PARENTS. ONLY SIGNIFICANT SIDE EFFECT IS THAT IN SEXUAL SPECIES REPRODUCTION CAN ONLY OCCUR IF BOTH PARTNERS HAVE BEEN INFECTED. MORE?

Both partners. *That* was what was wrong with him! His sperm were full of DNA tripling retrovirus, and they'd only do their job if they met up with an egg full of DNA tripling retrovirus!

"How many people are infected?"

ON EARTH, FOUR THOUSAND SEVEN HUNDRED KNOWN CASES. ON LUNA, LATEST ESTIMATE 97 PER CENT OF POPULATION. MORE?

"And why the hell has the government tried to cover it up?"

REDUCTION IN VARIABILITY OF CROP STRAINS AND WILDLIFE INCREASES VULNERABILITY TO STRESS UNDER CONDITIONS OF CHANGING ENVIRONMENTAL FACTORS. RECENT FAMINES IN BRAZIL AND SOUTHEAST ASIA ARE THOUGHT TO BE LARGELY A RESULT OF DNA TRIPLING IN MAIN RICE CROPS. EARTH GOVERNMENT UNAWARE OF LUNAR CONNECTION, AS OF ONE WEEK AGO. INSUFFICIENT DATA TO ASSESS PROBABILITY THAT TERRA IS NOW AWARE OF THE CONNECTION. MORE?

"I don't need any more," Rob breathed. "Famine on Earth, caused by the breakout of a virus engineered on the Moon. No wonder Balcewicz wanted the lid screwed down tight. And once you started worrying about your own DNA, she had to have you shut up."

"And when the medics found out about my DNA, it rang alarm bells higher up the chain on Earth. Somebody began putting bits of classified information together. *Nobody* wanted Frank Wilson around to embarrass them anymore."

"And nobody will ever lift the quarantine once all this becomes common knowledge." So Sylvie *could* speak! "We're plague carriers. All of us, in their eyes."

"Even if Terra is already infected?"

"They'll be worried about what else we've been breeding in the gene labs up here."

As well as the increasing noises of battle from outside, smoke was now beginning to seep into the com centre. But they still had power, and all the boards showed green. Rob leaned forward, past Frank.

"Link. Dump all information previously classified under this code, uh—"

"Breakout," Frank interjected.

"All information under code Breakout to be dumped into public information files, immediately."

DONE.

Rob stood, gestured to one of the battle stained figures by the com console. "Are we still on?"

"Still on, Chief. Biggest audience rating ever on Luna. And we think the beam to Terra is still open."

"Right. C'mon, Frank. Time to perform. The fight's not over yet, but if this doesn't tip the balance against that bitch, nothing will."

"Natalya, where the hell are you taking me?" Frank panted. He was having great difficulty keeping up with the loonie girl as she sprinted up yet another flight of clanging service steps. God, he really was in a terrible physical state. Six weeks of inactivity, lounging aimlessly in his quarters, had turned his muscles to jelly. His heart was going like a steamhammer. And it was only one-sixth g!

Why couldn't she have left him drinking himself silly in the bowels of Tycho? God, on the Moon, a man didn't even have the right to be miserable in peace. And with the quarantine still in force, likely to remain so, what else was there for him to do? He'd never be a loony, so why pretend?

"Look, Natalya," he gasped, "I've just about had enough of this game."

From the top of the stairs, she watched his laboured progress, her face creased with laughter. "Come on old man, you can do it," she taunted him. "Or would you rather I carried you?"

That stung him. He might be ten years her senior, but he was certainly no old man. With a superhuman effort, he bounded up the final steps, three at a time. "Just wait . . . " he panted, "until I catch you . . . I'll wipe that smile off your face."

"Catch me then," she shouted. Then she vanished.

At the top of the stairs, he faced a door, swinging on its hinges. He paused a moment, catching his breath, then pushed through.

The first thing that struck him was the light. It was so blindingly bright, after the dimly lit service staircase, that he had to shield his eyes. When they recovered, he saw that he was on the floor of a cavernous hanger, lit by a grid pattern if harsh blue lights high above. The hangar was full of balloon-tired vehicles of all shapes and sizes. Mechanics in overalls were working on several of the vehicles, but there was no sign of Natalya.

Frank advanced a few steps into the hangar. After the claustrophobia of Tycho's deep tunnels, it was wonderful to be in such a large volume of space. It made him think of Earth's open spaces. Quickly, he pushed that thought from his mind; it still hurt too much.

Frank had guessed that they had climbed close to the surface, but he had not realised quite how close. Over there, he knew, beyond those hulking airlock doors, was the near vacuum of the lunar surface.

"Frank, come on! Over here!"

At first he could not locate Natalya's voice. He looked around, frowning. But when she shouted again, he spotted her beside one of the smaller vehicles. She waved at him, then clambered up the external ladder to the bubble-like driver's cabin. A mechanic, who had been checking the fuel cells, gave her a thumbs-up and backed away. Surely she didn't intend going out on the surface?

When he arrived, she had already gone inside. Through the transparent bubble, he could see her at the controls. He climbed up the ladder to the hatch. Dropping into the seat beside her, he said: "I don't believe this, Natalya. We're going outside? You're actually taking me on the surface?"

"Shush!" she said, ignoring him. "Can't you see I'm checking the instruments?" She started flicking switches above her head, her face deep in concentration. "Right," she said, finally. "Hold onto your seat."

In the giant airlock, as the air cycled noisily, Wilson made a final attempt to find out what Natalya was up to. But to no avail.

"For God's sake, Frank, *relax*!" she replied.

And so he did . . .

The journey took them on a well-worn route, out of the Tycho depression, over the ridge, and down into a small crater just beyond. The thin air—too thin to breathe comfortably, but, Frank knew, enough to protect the surface from micrometeorites, acting as a shield for the domes over the fields of food plants, and to even out some of the extremes of temperature from day to night—stirred in their passage, sufficiently to send wispy dust devils swirling behind them. But the sky was black, away from the glare of the Sun, and the shadow edges were razor sharp. He had given up asking what was going on, and was dozing, daydreaming of the blue skies of Earth, when the vehicle jerked to a halt, swaying on its suspension.

"Look," Natalya said softly.

Ahead, down the track, at the bottom of the crater there was what seemed to be a grove of trees. Impossible, of course. It must be a trick of the light, reflecting off some artificial structure—a radio telescope, perhaps.

He rubbed his eyes, looked again. They *were* trees!

He turned to Natalya in the seat beside him. She smiled, raised a finger to his lips to still any questions, then set the vehicle in motion again, easing down the slope until they were in amongst the trees. Pines, by the look of them. As she drove, she spoke.

"It's the first forest on the Moon. A grove of shatterpines. More of our genetic tinkering, I'm afraid. The stuff the Terrans don't want to take any more chances with. Their roots crack the rock, allow water from the comets to seep in. And they actually get some of their oxygen from the silicates in the rock, releasing carbon dioxide to help thicken the atmosphere. Symbiosis with a microorganism that lives in nodules on the roots."

In spite of himself, he was impressed. Trees, on the Moon. It almost made it feel like a real planet, here in the dappled shadows, looking up at the pale green needles of the tall pines.

"There's life here, Frank. We can cope without Terra, now. Only just, but we can cope. As long as the comets keep coming, we'll have air.

Enough air to breathe out there, in a generation or so. We've got trees, and there are some crops that will grow outside the domes, even now."

"All with triple DNA."

"Sure. All with triple DNA. Resistant to mutations. And ninety-seven per cent of the people have triple DNA, too. Soon, it'll be everybody. Triple DNA, Frank, like yours."

He thought for a moment. So, if he went back to Earth, he'd be a freak. No chance of kids, unless he happened to bump into one of the four thousand other freaks. If the terries ever let him out of jail. If they even let him live. Up here, he was still a freak. A squat little terry, conspicuous amongst the tall loonies. But at least he was free. He had skills that these people could use. And although not exactly a hero, he was well in with the new government. Maybe it could be worse, after all.

He cocked his head on one side, looked out into the pine grove from the now stationary vehicle, a critical expression on his face.

"It could do with some squirrels."

Natalya smiled, reached out her hand.

"We're working on it, Frank. That's Sylvie's specialty, when she isn't playing soldiers."

"Well, if you can promise me squirrels, maybe it won't be so bad."

Her hand squeezed his. "No, it won't be so bad, once you get used to it. Welcome home, Frank."

JOSEPHINE KNOWS WHO

ALLEN ASHLEY

Allen Ashley tells us, 'I'm always a little wary of saying too much about any story as each reader will bring their own experience to it and take away their own impressions from it. This is one of my favourites amongst my published stories. The title is a conflation of the Arthur Lee song "Stephanie Knows Who" (from Da Capo *by* Love*) and Franz Kafka's tale "Josephine the Singer"—one of the finest pieces of writing ever and a story that I return to over and over. So—music and literature. Throw in a bit of football and all my bases are covered. During the course of writing "Josephine Knows Who" I toyed with the idea of expanding it to much greater length but each piece tends to have its own perfect duration and settles down that way whatever one does or considers. Thanks to the* Postscripts *team for letting me share the story with the world.'*

Allen Ashley works as a freelance writer, editor, poet, event host, critical reader and writing tutor. He currently runs five groups across north London, including the prestigious advanced group Clockhouse London Writers. He has been the sole judge for the British Fantasy Society's short story competition since 2012. He is well known as the poetry host and a regular panellist at BFS conventions. His latest book is as editor of Sensorama: Stories of the Senses *(Eibonvale Press, 2014). Look out, also, for a reprint of his break-through novel* The Planet Suite, *from Eibonvale. Visit his website at www.allenashley.com.*

JOSEPHINE KEPT A SECRET DIARY STORED BEHIND CODES AND passwords on a five-gigabyte memory stick. It was disguised as an online shopping list—a wishful array of books she'd like to read, pamper treats she'd like to rub into her Caucasian skin, a handbag she'd seen once on a shopping channel and promised herself: "One day." In the event of her untimely and, to be fair, unlikely death her technically competent boyfriend Carl probably wouldn't get any further than this layer of consumer subterfuge.

That was what it was all about, of course: penetrating through the domineering and convincing strata of deception, unwrapping the onion-skin layers of consensual reality, and reaching down to, or at least peering into, the truer levels below. But—to extend the useful metaphor a little further—who could tell how many tear-inducing gossamer cloaks one had to peel back before finally arriving at the core, the central truth, the "nub of it" as Carl liked to say?

The more she knew, the more she felt that she needed to know.

"Nothing is ever quite as it seems," had been her mantra for as long as she could remember. This was an axiom she'd explored during her younger years when her talent for making herself invisible and insubstantial had been more pronounced, more practised. She needed time and space to retune and restore these gifts and not be weighed down by the quotidian. The magical capabilities of her girlhood were surely only temporarily—and spatially—encumbered, not buried forever.

This wall, these surfaces—solid and slightly soiled in the here and now, in need of a duster flick or damp cloth wipe. Or penetrable with the right mindset?

Which seemed beyond her at present. She was expected at the Bitten Lip in thirty minutes. Clothes to slip into, make-up to apply, no time for further conjecture.

Always the way.

The bar was slightly emptier than on most Sunday evenings. Which was not a good sign; but mostly it came down to bar takings and food spend rather than simply the number of punters coming through the door. Carl had already set up her mike and Red had run the band through a couple of warm-ups; his chubby hands turned surprisingly fluid and piscine the moment he flicked on his double-stack keyboards.

"You look great," Carl whispered in her ear, his arm damping the thick metal strings on his electric bass.

"Just keep it steady for me," she answered.

It was a pre-gig ritual. Davey gave two taps on the hi-hat and they launched into their set of jazz standards and classic ballads. "Night and Day", "Every Time We Say Goodbye", "Something" . . . half an hour or more passed by in an apparent instant. This was a self-contained crowd, intent on their own conversations and concerns. We might just as well be a CD playing on the PA, Josephine thought. We might as well not actually be here.

She wondered if she could make not just herself but the whole of the band vanish. It would require more effort than she was used to expending. She was out of practice . . . She'd slightly missed her cue. She mangled the words in what she hoped sounded like a decent, scatty tribute to Nina Simone. The piece ended and elicited unexpected applause.

"Thank you," Josephine spluttered. "That was 'My Baby Just Cares For Me'. We are the Secret Mechanisms and this next one was made famous by Sinatra."

Carl hated the band name. Davey and Red thought it sounded "cool". Josephine still believed in the transcendental power of music, but not tonight. Flying to the Moon was just a metaphor.

Diary:

I was always quite lithe and athletic. As a girl, I loved ballet and gymnastics. An only child, my parents indulged me with Saturday-morning classes and after-school activities. There was a moment where I almost took the route into serious competition—my hands now accustomed to a chalk covering, my toes and calf muscles primed and ready to spring instantaneously into action. But my arch-rival— Philippa Cunningham—had a longer, blonder ponytail and poached-egg breasts budding beneath her stretch leotard. She was the one who caught the area judges' eyes. I hurt like crazy at the time but now I think: Who wants a career that's over by your late teens?

I should track down Philippa on Facebook. Not under my real name, of course. My invented history for her includes a teenage abortion, drink and drugs issues, failed relationships and, the cherry on the conjectural cake, a fortune wasted on cosmetic surgery as she seeks to regain the glow of girlhood.

I'm over her. Really. She was dazzled by the appearance of things.

She will never divine their true nature. But I will.

She was on the regular daytime shift at Central Support Services. This had been her work pattern for the past five weeks. At least it didn't interfere with the jazz gigs. Some saw such nine-to-five conformity as a prison, but to Josephine it was simply a structure that could encourage flights of fancy or even genuine attempts at transcendence.

Her boss, Mr Cleethorpes, was on the prowl. Never a good sign. Especially that occasion last month when he walked round with one hand inside his trousers like he had an unfinished game of pocket billiards on the go. And why did he fasten his tie and top button so tightly? It made his face red and his voice a little breathless if he had more than one pearl of wisdom to impart at any given time.

"I had a big win on the gee-gees," he announced. "Do you like horses, Josephine?"

"Only as much as other animals. I never did any riding when I was a girl."

"Hmm, quite," he responded, wiping forehead and back of neck with a disposable tissue. "Got a tip off an Irish guy. They know their nags. I'm feeling loaded. I might even treat myself."

Flatly: "Why not?"

"By the way, Jo," he crooned, "we've got some absentees in the call room. Can I pencil you in for an eleven-till-one slot?"

She nodded. She didn't mind dealing with the public, it broke up the monotony of the day, but she hated that bald twat Cleethorpes truncating her name. She'd told him once, "I'm not G. I. Joe or Hey Joe; please read what's on my swipe badge." The sweaty git simply smiled patronisingly and moved on.

The phone queries weren't too taxing. As she doled out advice by rote, she thought: I'm working for the enemy. I'm reaffirming all the conventions and keeping people reliant on the machines and programs that determine our experience of life. I should be teaching these callers the codes and rituals that will help us all break through to the hidden truths."

She sipped at a tepid cappuccino, flicked a switch on the desk panel and chirped, "I'm happy to help, Mrs Uddin. Call me back if you have any further problems. Bye now."

Diary:

When young, I could crawl into gaps, slither under tree branches and hedgerows, make myself pliable. I built a den in a friend's back garden but had to virtually tear it down because she could not squeeze through the "secret" entrance whilst I easily could.

I remember one rainy indoors afternoon when I was little. The sweet smell of slowly baking cakes permeated the house. I had half-licked, half-washed the sticky mixture from my fingers before encouraging my mother to play hide-and-seek as we waited for the sponges to rise. There was a small storage cabinet currently bereft of towels and linen that I wanted to test with my lissomness and agility.

I folded myself up like a letter in an envelope. I kept the door very slightly ajar to admit a modicum of air and the enticing aroma from the oven. I hoped my stomach wouldn't gurgle in anticipation and give me away.

Mother opened the cabinet some five minutes later. She must have recognised my red, scabby knees, my skinny arms and pale fingers, my straight dark hair resting on my shoulders. I even opened one eye to check her surprised expression . . . but her face was blank. She couldn't see me.

I re-emerged when it was time to put some pink icing on the cakes.

"Where were you, Josephine?"

"I can't say, Mummy. I might want to hide there again."

Or not hide at all; simply use my ability to become invisible.

"Do we normally watch this channel?" Carl asked.

"Shh, this guy's really good." She kept her thumb on the remote, pumping the arrow keys to gradually advance the frames. "His great-grandfather was Casper Fallow, reputedly the first man to be able to catch a bullet. Back around the time of the First World War."

"Must have been useful in the trenches, Josephine. Can't we watch the cricket highlights?"

"I'm recording them. Now stop bothering me."

Press, press, jump, flicker, pause. Again. No, hold on, there was the moment. Jamie Fallow had tossed an offcut of wood into the air with his left hand and then aimed a martial arts chop at it with his right. The frozen image showed his hand having apparently penetrated the plank but for just this one instant coexisting in the same space-time *within* the unbroken wood. Faster than the eye can see was one thing, but tricking modern cameras was even tougher. The next step, of course, was to limit his action to this achievement, to enter and remain, not destroy.

She pressed "Play" and the shards clattered to the studio floor.

"Like seeing a wicket fall," Carl piped up from his cursory scanning of the evening newspaper.

"All right, you've made your point," she answered.

She was annoyed with his impatience and vowed silently not to have sex tonight. But later when he started rubbing the backs of her knees and running his lips over her ears, even that resolution crumbled. Like pieces of pine karate-chopped or a bullet crushed by a firm Edwardian hand.

Central Support Services never stopped. It never could stop. Otherwise, the fabric of a caring, well-governed society would implode as its active skeleton crumbled.

Josephine had signed up for a late shift, saying goodbye to her usual compatriots of Davey, Sinda, Abu Hamid, and Mr Cleethorpes only an hour into her stint. The pay was no better and it meant getting a night bus or a mini cab home. But the opportunities were so much greater.

With a set of headphones draped casually around her neck and a couple of shiny folders in her left hand, Josephine left her desk untended and set off once again to find the centre of Central Support. Previous semi-nocturnal sojourns had taken her to most of the floors of this complex of offices, including the very top and the stuffy basement with its omnipresent hum of generators. She'd hoped to stumble on the truth like some plucky heroine in a conspiracy thriller: maybe a secret chamber of men in suits and dark glasses; perhaps an all-powerful alien hybrid enslaving us all psychically; possibly a giant 1960s-style computer whirring and clicking and capable of emitting smoke when asked one of the great philosophical questions.

What is the purpose? Why am I here? What real advantage is there in full knowledge?

She knew the location of most of the CCTV cameras. It was one thing making oneself invisible to casual passers-by but another skill entirely to prevent one's image from registering with machine technology. She was still working on this latter, striving to be the "Unseen Girl", the heroine of her own lyrics. Casually leaving her micro-chipped swipe card in her desk drawer would certainly help to obscure her trail.

As a child, she'd loved the Narnia books. The basic concept of entering another reality via the back of a wardrobe was just so thrilling. Artistic licence, though, was its own extra layer of deception. All the hidden rooms and areas she'd so far accessed had been mundane or, unsurprisingly, mildly curious dead-ends. Still, no controlling cartel would meet in a public space. The government's antiterrorist committee—COBRA—was just another smokescreen for the real powerbrokers.

She stood unmoving for a good five minutes, letting the little rushes of adrenaline dissipate to her extremities and be calmly secreted through her soles into her tan tights. She closed her eyes, felt her erect body become one with the plasterboard wall behind her. She gave the gentlest of sustained pushes . . . eased . . . stumbled backwards slightly but was within the secret alcove.

A few memory sticks and old-fashioned floppy disks on a shelf next to some toiletries and hand wipes. Should she pocket the evidence? Was the Pope Catholic? Actually, scrub that, he was almost certainly a mind-controlled mouthpiece for the world syndicate.

On the lower shelf was a pile of generic staff memos—the kind that did the rounds once or twice a day in manila envelopes. Below these, however, was a selection of glossy magazines with titles such as, *Dogs and Sexy Bitches* and *What Ewe Looking At*. A cursory glance confirmed her worst fears: she had stumbled into some executive's wanking parlour—one who had a taste for bestial fantasies.

Who produced this stuff? Who was base enough to pose for this stuff? Although, doubtless these days one could Photoshop passable facsimiles of *Big Dog's Cock* and *Donkey Doings*. She placed all but one memory stick back where she'd found them. Maybe a little blackmail would be in order at a later date, although she was loath to run the doubtless offending items on her home computer.

It would be just my luck, she thought, that this one holds only holiday snaps of famous buildings.

As she skittered back down the Level 4 corridor, she noticed a ceiling eye turning to catch her movements. Long dark hair and a brisk step came in handy but weren't always foolproof. She mentally rehearsed her story about the tampax vending machine running out of supplies, leading to a meandering trawl through the quieter areas of the building.

Just in case such an excuse was needed.

Diary:
  Five things I wanted to achieve by age twenty-five:
  Get a good enough education to open up several possibilities in the job market.
  Put a deposit down on a flat in a safe area.
  Sign a major record contract and release a couple of killer singles.
  Break free from parental disapproval and acquire a really cool tattoo.
  Find a soul mate.

God, it was quiet in work today. Which was a good thing when it allowed her to scan through a personal file code-named "Social Research Data". But the flip side was that on mornings like these Mr Cleethorpes undertook an annoying perambulation to chivvy everyone along. As he walked past her workstation, he began whistling an Ella Fitzgerald tune. Josephine held her irritation in check. Her boss had attended one of her Sunday gigs about a year ago and declared himself pleasantly entertained but more a fan of modern pop—"You know, Girls At Large and urban rap." As if! Can you quote one line of lyrics, Mr Cleethorpes, sir?

He was at the far end of the room now, engaged in a one-sided conversation with Abdullah, whose family had fled the civil war in Somalia. Cleethorpes was complimenting Abdullah on his height and probable athletic prowess. He most likely considered this to be *positive* discrimination; to Josephine's ears, it had a faint tang of racial stereotyping. She knew for a fact that Abdullah did nothing more strenuous than watch Sky Sports. At least such chat would keep him out of her hair for a while.

The latest entry on "Social Research" concerned data downloaded from a website called "The True History of NASA". A whole stratum from human hierarchy was about to relocate to Venus, ahead of an expected rise in conflict levels in Western society. "The scientists are spreading lies about Venus; it's fine there," the document insisted. "The gravity is virtually the same as on Earth; the temperature is a bit higher because it's closer to the sun, but the atmosphere is breathable, not toxic, and the pressure is no big deal. The controllers have told us these untruths in order to preserve this neo-paradise for themselves. Where did the President and the head of IBM get those suntans? You guessed it. We already know about the special facilities on Mars. The top Olympic athletes are all training there in the thin air to build up their strength and stamina for world record attempts. Or should that be *solar system* records? The Soviet Bloc was up to that trick for most of the 1970s and early '80s—"

Cleethorpes was back within radar range. She busied herself with her mouse, a biro, a memo pad, and a knowingly coquettish suck on a lock of her glossy chestnut hair.

"Everything all right on Facebook, Jo?" Cleethorpes inquired.

"You know that site's blocked, sir," she smiled. "Just checking some facts and statistics."

"Don't trust the adding machines, eh? Using your GCSE Maths skills, I take it."

"I received a Grade A Star. Best in my year. Ninety-nine percent."

"There's always one that gets away," he quipped, waddling back to his office.

Report on Josephine Cotton, age 25+

Attained steady employment but had to forego higher education owing to the crippling cost of tuition fees and student loans.

Renting a poky flat with no likelihood of ever setting foot on the property-owning ladder.

Singing covers in a competent jazz band. A couple of clips posted on YouTube. Hardly any hits.

A tree of life tattooed in smudged indigo on her right shoulder. Messy, slightly embarrassing. Never wears a sleeveless top for work.

Been with Carl for four years. Still in love, she thinks. Says, "There's no such thing as soul mates—we're all just ordinary, fallible people."

"I've got the kettle on in my office," Cleethorpes beamed. "Would you like tea and biscuits?"

"No thanks," Josephine answered. "I'm on a diet."

"With your figure? I can't believe it. Well, pop in anyway if you're not too busy."

He'd probably been monitoring her workstation, although the general level of chatter and cheerfulness across the open plan would have told anyone that this was a slow morning. She shut down a couple of applications, went to "temporarily log off" and followed the scent of his chain store deodorant to the self-styled "Cleethorpes Grand Hotel". She sat carefully on the only guest chair.

"Did you get up to much last night, Josephine?"

"I was reading."

"Some good chick lit, honey?"

"No, actually, it was a piece on quantum physics. The reality of nature, that sort of thing."

He bit his lip, squinted at her, assessing the likely balance between truth and hostility. Briefly, he drummed his tanned fingers on the melamine tabletop, his thumb ring adding a discordant element of timpani. "I'll stop beating about the bush," he decided, "and get to the point. I want to offer you a temporary promotion."

"How so?"

"I might be taking some leave, Jo. Things to do, places to go. You're the obvious replacement during my absence."

"Don't these things have to be advertised through all the usual channels?"

"Not for a temporary post. I'm authorised by Executive Control to choose whosoever I see fit. It will mean a bit more money, of course, but you'll also have to pop in twice a day, mornings and evenings, including Saturday and Sunday."

"What about the band?"

"Oh, your little pub gig? Maybe you can give it a break for a fortnight or so. It's not much of an earner, is it?"

"I don't sing for money, Mr Cleethorpes."

He brushed his hands over his thinning hair, unnecessarily smoothed the vertices of his shirt collar. "Listen, Jo, love, you're a good worker. I know you have some—questions? doubts?—about the business of Central Support Services. Well, here's an opportunity to go a little further up the chain of command."

"How far?"

"Far enough. You'll get to know who you need to know. Give it some thought, love. Can I still not tempt you to a drink and a cookie?"

"No food till twelve-thirty."

To her departing back, he called, "Self-discipline. That's the key to management, dearie."

She'd read a story once about someone whose life had changed because she chose to alight at a different tube station. Should she start getting off one stop earlier or later and walking the rest of the distance? Break the entrapment pattern by smashing the universal routine? But it was late and she was hungry, so no . . .

Carl was already home, engrossed in a driving game running on the TV via a laptop cable. He offered a cursory wave then returned both hands to the steering wheel so as to deal with another virtual hairpin turn. Josephine shucked off her coat, went to the kitchen and began peeling vegetables and chopping onions. Through stinging eyes, she checked the recipe on her phone and, while the food cooked, considered the scientific contention that a rocket-fuelled flight to Mars would probably take three months. Which meant that people must be using other methods, probably a matter portal, just as she could press herself through walls into secret rooms and compartments. This prospect was really thrilling—that the technology or training existed to enable instantaneous transportation across the solar system. She wanted to be part of it, whoever she had to clamber over or bypass in order to reach that security level.

She reflected on the possibilities as she ate silently. Carl attempted a couple of conversational gambits, but she was oblivious to him. He rebooted his game after supper, and Josephine went to wash the dishes. The screeching-tyre effects and generic, fast rock music eventually broke through her layers of self-containment, and she went to ask him to lower the volume. She paused in the doorway, however, essentially watching over her boyfriend's shoulder. Maybe the *Santa Monica Raceway* disk was wearing out or else their system was too archaic because often Carl's Aston Martin seemed to be driving into nothingness with the buildings, the trees and even the road itself barely forming in time as he zoomed along in first place. She wondered if this was what faster-than-light travel would be like when those lazy-arse scientists finally got around to perfecting it.

If we go fast enough, she reasoned, would we get into that limbo, that nothingness from which everything is created? Because, she realised, the fabled Big Bang is not some thirteen billion years behind us but less than a minute in front.

Her knees felt weak, unable to support her light weight even in the lower Martian gravity; or perhaps the issue was the thinness of the air. She needed further physical training to complement the mental leaps she was now making—

"Josephine? Darling, are you OK?"

There was the slightest bump on the back of her head where she'd knocked against the wooden doorframe. She hoped it didn't become a prominent visible feature like the extinct volcano Olympus Mons. She couldn't remember choosing to squat down like this, though. Up close, Carl smelt sweaty and male, not unpleasantly so but he would need a shower later.

"Josephine, I think you're working too hard. Come on, let's get you settled in the bed. Do you need some water or . . . something more to eat?"

This last was whispered because it potentially reactivated memories of their worst-ever row, during which he'd called her "borderline bulimic". How had they ever patched up that one?

After he'd made her comfortable, she conceded, "Maybe a cup of tea would do nicely. And a couple of biscuits."

He smiled and she realised again why she'd first fancied him. "The old British cure-all," he commented.

"All the way from India," she added as she let her eyes close. The universe was still being created just in front of her accelerating eyes for maybe three minutes more; then she drifted into an easier, nondescript slumber.

"Central Support Services, keeping your life in order, Josephine speaking, how may I help you?"

"Central Support Services, supplying answers to every problem, large or small. Hi, I'm Josephine."

"Central Support Services, your life in our capable hands. Josephine, here to help you . . . "

A memory stick with nothing on it. "Acquired", shall we say? Annoyingly blank; the wrong pick, though how could she have known? Some things were simply down to random bad luck.

Diary:
  They send you on these management training courses and advise you to "Learn to think outside the box". But that's a lot of nonsense because the systems of control are like a giant Russian doll. When you think outside one box you are actually merely thinking inside one slightly larger container. On and on.
  And yet what we call reality is in fact gossamer-thin, like the silk of a spider's web or one transparent layer of a peeled onion. We need to strip away this fragile construct of agreement and reveal the vacuousness behind. But to do so is too scary. Pandora, don't open that box, you don't know what you'll let loose!
  Our whole lives we cling to the façade. Maybe now is the time to tear down the wall.

"You'll love this, young Jo," Cleethorpes beamed. "It's a golden swipe card. Like something out of a children's adventure—Roald Dahl or someone. This will allow you to navigate and explore anywhere within the organisation and hopefully answer some of those burning questions. In your own time, of course. Ah, the fire of youth," he added, with a mock mop of his brow.

"I'm twenty-six, Mr Cleethorpes."

"Really? The prime of life, dearie. As you know, I have some . . . matters to attend to over the next fortnight. I can't wait for the break from the routine, actually. But it means you'll be minding the shop—this little corner of it—pretty much on your own. Any questions?"

"When does the card activate?"

"Monday, seven a.m. So don't go trilling your little heart out too much on Sunday night."

Diary:
  I once remained invisible for three hours. It was at a friend's

party. I was about nine or so. I just did my—trick, I suppose you'd call it—of blending into the surroundings and remaining totally still. Everyone ignored or bypassed me. Perhaps at a deep level their auras still detected my presence as nobody tried to walk through me.

I only broke the spell because of a bout of hunger and fatigue. The shocked faces of my playmates as I suddenly appeared and grabbed a chocolate biscuit and some cheese and onion crisps off the kitchen table is an image that sustains me still.

Later, it occurred to me that they should have been more concerned at my apparent absence and alerted their parents or phoned my mother with a worried enquiry about the unseen girl.

I never saw any of them again once I started secondary school. They've not bothered tracking me on Facebook, either.

The band was on form tonight, and some of that must have communicated itself to the pub crowd as a heartfelt rendition of "The Man I Love" drew a smattering of applause. Or maybe they were just cheering the quality of the steak and onion pie and chips, the aroma of which caused Josephine's perennially empty stomach to gurgle hopefully.

She leaned in close to the rest of the Secret Mechanisms and announced, "We're doing 'Unseen Girl' next."

"Are you sure about this?" Carl whispered.

"Yes. We never play any of our own songs these days. I'm sick of Gershwin and Cole Porter. Is that a problem, guys?

Eliot—"Red" to his friends and Twitter followers—chipped in with, "Just let me run through the keyboard part for a few bars. I'll nod you in, Jo."

"Josephine!" she hissed and turned back towards the microphone.

She'd composed the lyrics three years ago. Carl had thumbed out a bass line to her vocals and the group had spent an excited Saturday afternoon working up a proper arrangement. Still, these days, the song got an airing once every five or six gigs. All that angst, all that pathos, all that honesty, offset by a breathy, even ghostly delivery... Three and three-quarter minutes later, Josephine bowed her head and bathed in the smell of warm food, the waft of beer fumes, and the apathy of her audience.

"Thank you," she gritted. "A Beatles favourite next and then some more numbers from the Great American Songbook."

Diary:

How creepy is this?

I suspect that, although I've been strictly adhering to my diet, I may have put on a pound or two lately. My white blouse and black skirt feel no tighter than usual, but a woman knows these things. Perhaps it's simply that my period's due.

So, even though I'd stayed till seven to check the night shift, I made time for a trip to the gym after work. The running machine has lately been fitted with a video screen that works a little like Carl's sports car game—a landscape seems to appear ahead of you as you pound the treadmill. This feature, of course, made me speed up and test the system to see if I could achieve the transcendence I'd managed at home, that trajectory into the near, not-yet-created future. There were . . . flashes, elements of a breakthrough, but I couldn't sustain it and ended up collapsed in an ungainly heap craving water or an energy drink.

"Pushing yourself too hard, young Josephine," said a familiar voice at my right ear.

I looked up through sweaty eyes. "Cleethorpes? Mr Cleethorpes?"

"In person. And still in one piece." He grinned, patting his stomach beneath his dark-green singlet. My gaze was inexorably drawn to his royal-blue running shorts, which seemed a little flimsy for containing his probable arousal and excitement at coming across me in this fashion. Even though he swung the other way.

I raised my head up, stated, "I thought you were on holiday. You know, flying off to Spain or Bangkok or somewhere."

"I'm just taking a break from the mundane, dearie. I never mentioned anything about foreign climes. Anyway, must dash—got a massage to undergo in five minutes. Be good!"

I left the machine, went and did some weights, but my heart wasn't in it. I showered quickly and nervously.

I'm convinced that I'm being lulled somehow. I'm sure the oily little jerk is deliberately following me. Under orders.

Whose?

"Josephine, can you remind me where . . . ?"

"Ms Cotton, I need a bit of advice on this one. What's happened is . . . "

"I'm sorry, Ms Cotton, I thought that I was supposed to . . . "

This middle management role was proving tougher than she'd anticipated. She could field all the queries, no problem—she had enough experience and plain common sense, so that wasn't an issue. It was just the volume of questions and requests for assistance from colleagues who ought to have been able to handle the daily caseload of Central Support Services more effectively and, more significantly, on their own initiative. Were people acting up because she was "acting up"?

She broke one of her golden rules of always eating in the staff room away from the clamour and demands of computer monitor and telephone extension. Instead, she took her herbal tea and her Ryvitas thinly coated with low-fat spread back to her workstation and lunched there. She was forcing herself to resist a grudging admiration for Cleethorpes as she suspected he'd somehow set up this situation to be extra-challenging for her. He'd no doubt primed a few of his flunkeys to ask awkward questions; it was probably him on the end of the phone lines with a dodgy accent or sending emails from fake accounts just to put her through her paces.

The upshot was that the quotidian was once again smothering the philosophical. She had hoped to find time to explore the inner workings and hidden alcoves of the organisation, but that would not be possible today. The solution would have to be: begin the quest in her own time. Stay late or start early.

"You look exhausted," Carl said when she finally arrived home. "Do you want me to cook?"

Visions of charred burgers, blackened onions, and carbonised bread assailed her brain. She shook her head but that hurt as well. "I'm not hungry," she stated. "Phone for a takeout, if you like."

"You should eat, Josephine."

"Nothing for me. I'm off for a shower."

As the warm water and Fructis shampoo revived her, she decided to set the alarm for an unholy hour and get to the office well before the feckless, incapable crew clocked on. She had to use this golden opportunity; there might never be another.

Carl clicked the mouse pad and yet another image appeared on the screen.

"Sally Chisholm, Minister of Culture," Josephine stated. Another portrait. "Francois Gistang. I think he's head of the European Central Bank." Next up. "Ha-ha, that's Osama bin Laden, but he's dead."

"Never seen the corpse," Carl answered. "Those are all I've prepared for now. Were they helpful? You did brilliantly."

"Thanks. I know that the real power probably lies with some billionaire oligarch whose profile remains top secret but . . . preparation is always the key."

"Do you really think you're going to penetrate to the power core?"

"I can't tell. I spent two hours this morning mostly negotiating my way through a stationery warehouse. So much for the paperless office!"

Later, she ironed her regular round of white blouses and black skirts, enjoying the heat and the puffs of steam which would negate the smell of supper. Carl was noodling unplugged on his bass guitar, some ancient riff reminiscent of Cream or Hendrix. Not something the Secret Mechanisms were likely to play anytime soon.

Then, suddenly, he was in the kitchen with her. "Josephine," he whispered, "I'm quite worried about this quest of yours. It could get pretty dangerous. Do you want me to come with you?"

She reached across and stroked his smooth brown hair, caught the concern in his spaniel-like eyes. "That's sweet, darling," she replied, "but I can't get you the proper clearance. And if I tried to sneak you in with me that would raise too many suspicions. Listen, keep your phone on all day. I won't hesitate to call you if need be."

Diary:

How long did I wander? It felt like days on end, although in truth it must have been an hour or two at most. I think that my temporal sense goes askew when I try to accomplish my feats. Is it all about control of time rather than space? Casper Fallow and his followers were able to catch speeding bullets because they placed themselves into a different time stream for the duration of the task. From their perspective, the projectile was no faster than a softly hit tennis ball or a floating Frisbee. Piece of piss. Insects accomplish this shit all the time.

Central Support Services is every bit as gargantuan as I'd antici-pated. My suspicion is that the offices and branches are linked

through a maze of subterranean and subsurface tunnels and corri-
dors. Something akin to the London Underground system or the Paris
Metro but with no trains or public maps. We are all minor players in
the execution of the CSS's great purpose. Which is? Most likely, mere
continuation of its own existence, on a day-to-day basis. Taking each
game one at a time, as the footballers say.

And yet?

And yet is this really so? I was encumbered by the files I was
carrying as a facile excuse so it was difficult for me to collect the
requisite evidence—such as a sequence of images on my Smart-
phone—but after a while, although each office section was subtly
different, the people seemed the same. Often seated in analogous
arrangements: from left to right—cute young black guy; mumsy white
woman in a cardigan; Sikh man with turban; Asian woman in
shalwar kameez and loosely tied headscarf . . .

Office clones? Or the sort of CGI tricks they use in films these days
to create crowd and battle scenes?

Which philosopher was it who said that each question simply
begets another three queries? Or maybe the notion is original to one
Josephine Cotton. I'd hoped I'd be closer to an answer by now but,
like some weird mathematical formula, all my progress seems only to
have the net effect of pushing me ever further away.

Diary:

Me again. I had a row with Carl about our lives slipping into a rut.
It's a conversation we stumble into at least once a month. We're told
that at every stage of existence we are beset by choices: watch a reality
TV show, curl up with a book, go to the cinema, listen to some jazz
or light classical, cook a special meal for boyf . . . it's all so conven-
tional. And none of it has a hope in hell of breaking the systems of
control because every alternative on the flow diagram is contained
and safe. I need to do something not on the list, something extreme.
Maybe I could cut all my party frocks in half with secateurs then sew
them back together in the wrong arrangements, rendering my
wardrobe that of a modern-day harlequin. How would that fit your
dress code, Mr Cleethorpes?

No, I must focus on the task in hand, not fripperies.

Carl is so down to earth. All he dreams about is being somehow discovered as a bassist and quitting his job at the accounts agency to play Wembley Arena or the Albert Hall. So mundane, so limited.

Carl calls me a conspiracy nut but that's not fair. There is no Loch Ness Monster or Beast of Bodmin; Neil and Buzz did go to the Moon; poor young Princess Diana died in a car accident, it could happen to anyone . . . But I'm never flying across the Bermuda Triangle, I don't subscribe to the "lone gunman" theory about JFK, and it seems probable to me that the Illuminati or a secret order of monks or Knights Templar or glorified Freemasons are running the world. This latter is what I want knowledge of, whatever it costs me.

So what will happen to me as I continue my quest? They might simply eliminate me, stage a Dr Kelly—style death, under the directive, "Stop that young bitch from asking awkward questions." Then again, they might continue to successfully cloak like they have been doing so far. Or else, they might applaud and reward my initiative, take me up, absorb or indoctrinate me into their clique. God, I wish for it! Even though I know that would necessitate a complete break with my old life, a fracturing of my relationship with Carl, my ties with my family.

Instead, I might marry into the hierarchy, be awarded special agent status. All possibilities are open. Bring them on.

Sorry, Carl. Sorry, Mum.

It took Josephine several minutes to grasp the full impact of this unlikely scene of tragedy.

One corridor can often look much like any other, but there were enough small signifiers to tell her that she had wandered here before and found things that were puzzling and troubling. They had been behind this locked door. She needed to calm herself, enter the still zone, and allow herself egress into the room beyond.

That Cleethorpes was dead was beyond doubt. How long he had been dead was not within her compass to determine—although in one key respect he was in rude health. The cause was something she'd never expected to come across, a practice more frequently associated with hyper-sexed rock stars, actors, and kinky politicians. She racked her brain for the correct term . . . Carl would have known . . . it was . . . autoerotic asphyxiation.

Neck tied firmly to the surprisingly strong ceiling lights; chair kicked away behind him; his naked, hairy-shouldered body hanging just a few precious feet above the semen-stained shag pile. Had he intended to go the whole way or pull himself back from the very brink at the moment of fulfilment? It was—she smiled despite the horrific scene—a delicate balancing act. One hand—his left—was raised towards the cord around his throat, but the fingers of his right were clutched like an upturned crab as if choosing to squeeze the ecstasy out of the very air.

He was more hirsute than she'd expected. She preferred him in a suit and tie rather than this frozen whole body sexual rictus. His regular attire was neatly stacked in the far corner.

His penis—she had to look, it was the focus of the whole sordid scene—was shorter than Carl's but much thicker and, unexpectedly, less veiny. Like a big, stubby off-pink candle, still full of blood even if mostly spent of desire.

"Oh my God!" she finally yelled and then hated herself for such an obvious utterance. "I shouldn't be here and I don't want to be here," she added, quieter.

There was a laptop on the table just in front of Cleethorpes' prone corpse. It was plugged in but had defaulted to sleep mode. Feeling the burden of thousands of years of understandable feminine inquisitiveness—from Pandora and Eve all the way to modern times when a faithful wife accidentally discovers a husband's secret diary and can't resist opening it—Josephine went to boot the machine back into life. But stopped. Best not to leave incriminating fingerprints. She pulled down the cuff of her white blouse, swept it across the mouse pad a few times, determined to find her late manager's stimulus and inspiration . . .

Soon wishing she hadn't.

The first few images were recognisable as the bestiality she'd stumbled across before. The last couple of slides, though, sickened her more than she thought possible. Badly Photoshopped but, nevertheless, comprising erect animals, a suitably skinny female body . . . with Josephine's ID card portrait on top.

It was so false, so despicable. She would never do such things . . . except in some pervert's warped imagination.

When she could finally move again, she thought: Delete the pictures. Then again, the hard drive would still retain the information in its memory somewhere. Remove or steal the laptop? But they all had some sort of homing security device these days.

The priority was to get out of this room of death and leave that creep Cleethorpes to his spent wankery, let the discovery and disposal be someone else's problem.

She tried the door handle with her sleeve. Stiff and immovable, of course.

She was in no state to melt through the barrier. It was an ability she'd cultivated since girlhood but was a talent she felt unable to call upon at this moment. No calm, no serenity, no fluidity . . .

She suppressed a fit of shivering. Think, woman! she commanded. How had Cleethorpes got himself in here? There must be a key or a swipe card somewhere in his discarded clothes. She could find it, use it, and leave Central Support Services to try to solve one of the great locked-room mysteries of all time. Get herself out unscathed, not implicated . . . unlikely as that seemed.

The final saving grace out of the box was hope. She had no gods to pray to, just light fingers ready to rummage in a dead man's trousers . . .

The more I know, the more I need to know.
The more I know, the less I wish I knew.

"Unseen Girl", Josephine Cotton

THE CICADAS

JESSICA REISMAN AND STEVEN UTLEY

Jessica Reisman recalls, 'Steve originally sent me the seed of this story as a rambling fragment of a dream he'd had. It was rich; and dark, it was dark. We tossed the mucky, river-bottom ball of it back and forth and back and forth, adding bits of narrative, having discussions about the characters and what they wanted, as well as what they weren't going to get. We were both enamoured of the town about to be drowned and the dripping, needy mess of our revenant—and we were both happy with the story we eventually fashioned from the mud and algae of Steve's subconscious.

'I really miss him.'

On his death in 2013, Steven Utley left behind a great body of acutely intelligent and deeply felt short fiction, essays, and poetry. His acclaimed time travel stories are collected in two volumes, Invisible Kingdoms *and* The 400-Million-Year Itch. *Among other volumes of his work are* Ghost Seas, The Beasts of Love, *and* Where or When *(that last published by PS). His work appeared reliably in the pages of* Asimov's Science Fiction *and* The Magazine of Fantasy and Science Fiction, *along with countless other magazines, and continues to appear in anthologies of many and varied stripe.*

Jessica Reisman's stories have appeared in many magazines and anthologies, most recently Phantom Drift *and* Rayguns Over Texas. *Her first novel,* The Z Radiant, *was published by Five Star Speculative Fiction.*

PROPPED UP WITH PILLOWS, NESSA LAY IN BED AND watched half of the church creep majestically past on the street beyond her open window. The rumble of a heavy truck, unseen, filled the room, bass accompaniment to the ceaseless chirring of cicadas. Goodbye, church, Nessa thought.

This was, she decided, one of her good days.

Her daughter-in-law appeared at the door—Molly, the one she liked, not the other one who always complained about the inconvenience and expense Nessa incurred by insisting upon dying in her own home, in her own bed, in her own time.

Molly asked, "Want me to close that window?"

"No, dear. It's fine."

"Doesn't the noise disturb you? The cicadas alone are enough to drive me crazy."

"No. It looks nice outside today. And the cicadas are just doing their thing. Singing of love. They'll have sex, then take a nap for the next thirteen years."

"Some life," said Molly.

Nessa laughed a dry laugh, like leaves swirling across a sidewalk. "I imagine cicadas perceive time differently than we do."

"If they perceive it at all."

"Who knows? Every life is more or less a mystery. Even a bug's."

"You wonder how the cicadas can time it just so. What happens to the ones that wake up too soon or too late—after twelve or fourteen years?"

"Well, I guess they've blown it. They never get laid."

Nessa and Molly laughed together, and Molly said, "You're terrible!"

Nessa said, "We small-town girls know the facts of life." She sighed and looked toward the window again and smiled. "Anyway. It's not every day you get to see a church go by your window. I wonder what my father would have to say if he could see this. The whole town just up and moving away and leaving him behind." Well, not actually behind, she reflected. All that was mortal of Richard Hubbard had already been moved with everybody else in the cemetery. "Everything he worked for all his life stays behind to be drowned. He goes to his new grave with nothing but the suit he was buried in. My father was a man of expansive vision, but in a very limited way. He started dirt poor. He wanted to own everything and everybody in the valley. He had almost no interest in what lay beyond. He fought and clawed his way up, and when he got to the top, he wanted people to feel his foot on their necks for a change."

Molly made a *moue* and shook her head. "Did that finally make him happy? Or is somebody like that ever happy? Or even capable of true happiness?"

"Oh, who knows?" Richard Hubbard, she thought with some asperity, self-made lord of the hill, of the town itself. He had worn her mother down so harshly that she had left in the night when Nessa was nine. By the time Nessa was nineteen, her father had owned lumber and construction, a newspaper, and several other local businesses. Despite his standing in the town, however, Richard Hubbard had been, to the end, a rough, violent man, accustomed to getting his way and insistent upon it—feared, respected, but little admired. He had been difficult to love as a daughter is supposed to love her father.

Nessa's attention slid away, swimming deeper into her own brain, into the sunken architecture of the past, among eddies of memory, the current of a long and satisfying life. School friends, sled rides on cheek-chapping cold nights, tea parties, and socials. And Jonathan.

Jonathan, her first love, Jonathan, Jonathan Terry, dear Jonathan, and the sweet stolen evenings met beneath their special linden tree. From this memory she revisited the darkness and uncertainty surrounding Jonathan's puzzling disappearance; days of anger and grief, the bitter disappointment of realizing Jonathan's promise, and she herself, had not been enough to stand him strong against her father and he had, in the end, been run off.

Eventually, youth's ebullience reasserted itself. Nessa had met the man who became her husband; they married and had their first dance under drifts of flower petals, so her memory made it; their first child came, and a kaleidoscope of years in dense flecks of moment and memory tumbled after that.

A sense of urgency attends the affairs both of the living and of the dead, but time, the perception of time, is different for them. For the living, time moves fast or slow, depending upon circumstances, but it is an arrow always moving and always, remorselessly, in one direction. For the dead, time moves in fits and starts, separated by long pauses during which nothing much occurs; for the dead, time even doubles back upon itself occasionally. This is why a spirit in direst torment may haunt a defined area, that particular tower of a certain crumbling castle, say, or some uninviting stretch of two-lane blacktop, for countless years without anything to show for the effort. It is difficult to move forward, to make progress, when time's arrow behaves whimsically.

And who could keep track of time at the bottom of a river? Yet, brushed by current for year upon year, grown into the life at the bottom of the Toomey River, Jonathan must have been conscious for a long time without being conscious of being conscious. He knew nothing of the new dam, but he had somehow sensed the change in pressure as the waters inexorably deepened. Now all the moving about in the town as it drowned finally, truly awakened him. His mind's eye opened and he somehow saw, sensed, in any case *knew* that the town's dead had been excavated and evacuated from the churchyard, books from the library shelves, beds, photographs, teaspoons, and coffee cups from the private homes, everything of real or imagined value loaded up and driven away. He knew that in the houses on the highest ground the last few inhabitants remained, holding on till the last moment before they, too, must leave forever, and he knew that she would be among them.

His blood stirred, blood that was memory mixed with dark river, and he told himself, Time to get up. Time to rise and shine. Time to get a move on. His sinew of trash and slime contracted and relaxed, contracted, relaxed, testing itself. He saw phosphorescence in the cracks as the back of his algae-skinned hand split open, exposing moldering green bones wrapped in, held together, by mud. He had no idea how legs could work, how any part of himself could function under these circumstances, but somehow he did work. He roiled and rose up, all thick river-bottom mud, green and furry with growth, all the flesh and clothing he wore now, or needed. It was all the coffin he had had for he did not know how many years. He rose up, up, up like a—like nothing, nothing was like him, just rags and water weeds, muck and memory, and he rose up in the shallows and looked about.

Houses on the low ground lifted only the pitch of tin, shingled, and slated roofs above the cold waters of the dammed-up Toomey River, with here and there an empty upstairs window still visible. The air was full of the monotonous hum of uncountable cicadas, singing of desperate need, singing of love.

He turned his face and his steps toward the slope behind the inundated part of town. There were a few people moving about at the water's edge, but nobody noticed him, nobody except two small boys who, sensing him pass, shivered. A dog sitting nearby turned its head, looked his way, not seeing not hearing not smelling but definitely definitely aware of him; it whimpered and slunk away.

I know those boys, he thought after a while, and that dog, too, but he could not say who they were. Time and space seemed disarticulated. Halfway up the slope, he paused to watch in wonder as a section of sawn-apart church mounted on flatbed trucks moved glacially in the far, impossibly far distance at the end of a street running parallel to the water's edge. And then he saw Nessa, or imagined that he saw her, through every intervening wall and unimportant object, across the beside-the-point distance, and imagined that he knew her heart and the dark abscess deep inside it where must have congealed all the hurt and rage she felt at what she thought had been his desertion of her.

There was no other automobile like it in the whole valley. It was a gleaming, growling, meticulously maintained touring car, too large for the streets, too large for the town itself, and piloted by a liveried chauffeur, a hulking unsmiling figure who seemed too large for the car. Jonathan, who had been arranging a window display, watched as the chauffeur pulled the car to a noisy stop in front of Terry & Son General Goods, got out—visibly depressing the vehicle on its shock absorbers as he put his weight upon the running board—and opened the rear door for Mr. Richard Hubbard.

Jonathan drew a deep breath, retreated from the window, and positioned himself near the counter. Outside, Hubbard looked contemptuously upon the façade of Terry & Son General Store, and the chauffeur leaned with an air of latent menace against the polished fender of the touring car.

Then Hubbard strode into the shop with an air of ownership, though the shop was one of the relatively few things in town he did not own. His face and neck, bulging over a slightly awry shirt collar, were the color of underdone roast beef. The expensively tailored suit that he wore managed, somehow, not to fit him very well; he was a rough man with genteel pretensions. Jonathan repressed a smile and met Hubbard's disdainful regard with a look of polite curiosity.

"It has come to my attention," Richard Hubbard said without preamble, "that you fancy yourself my daughter's suitor. Disabuse yourself of the notion. She is not for you."

Jonathan waited a moment before replying. "Isn't that for her to say?"

"No, it is not. It most certainly is not for her to say. I have not raised my only child to lose her to such as you." Hubbard shot a glance around the interior of the store that was as loaded with contempt as the look he had bestowed upon the façade. "My daughter is not going to marry a clerk in a general store!"

"The *proprietor* of a general store," Jonathan corrected. "A thriving member of the merchant class, the same as you."

"Hardly. That is all behind me. I aspired to higher things, and I have attained them. I am of the social elite, a pillar of the community. Indeed, I am its leading citizen." Hubbard essayed a smile; it was horrible. Jonathan felt a crazy urge to laugh and clamped his teeth on the inside of his cheek. "You will *not* see my daughter again. Ever. Do I make myself clear, Mister Terry?"

"Your daughter loves me," Jonathan said, "as I love her."

"Love! Piffle!"

"I shall be a good husband to her, and, in spite of you, a good son-in-law to you. I own this business. It is successful. She shan't want for anything. You needn't fear on that count."

"You are not listening to me. You will not see my daughter again. If you attempt to do so, I shall take steps."

"Are you threatening me, Mister Hubbard?"

"I am making you a solemn promise."

"Mister Hubbard, your daughter and I have made solemn promises to each other. They are binding on us. There is nothing you can do to make us break those vows."

"Oh, vows, is it? Promises? I'll tell you what. I'll *buy* your little business."

"You tried to buy it when it was my father's little business."

"I'll give you a good price, much better than I offered him. You'll make a tidy profit."

"And?"

"And you'll leave this town forthwith and never come back. You can set up business in some other town, attempt to woo some other important man's eligible daughter. What do you say?"

"I say, good day to you, Mister Hubbard."

Hubbard compressed his mouth. He thrust his expensively gloved hand into a basket of peaches, plucked out one at random, squeezed it until the juice ran through his fingers. He dropped the crushed fruit and stripped off the gloves and dropped them on the floor.

"Peaches are a nickel," Jonathan said.

"Imagine if somebody came into your store and destroyed everything."

Jonathan lifted a shoulder in a half-shrug. "I imagine I would reach for the shotgun I keep around for the express purpose of discouraging such vandalism."

Hubbard smiled his horrible smile again. "You've got brass, young man, I'll give you that. Or else you're just very stupid. But, nervy or stupid, it doesn't matter. Do not see my daughter again, Mister Terry," he said, and turned to go.

Jonathan exhaled noisily and realized that he was trembling—1with fear? with rage? He could not be sure, and he did not know if it mattered.

"Your father," he told Nessa that evening, "came to see me today."

They met under their linden in the cool spring evening, curling their fingers together as they talked. The tree, with the height and spread of long life, stood over a curve in the river hidden from the street above by a church. The linden smelled of new green buds and the earthy spice of aged bark. The air off the river was soft.

Jonathan held Nessa's hands close against his chest. "He was not very congenial. He told me that we must never see each other again. Or else."

"Oh, no. What did he do?"

"First he offered to buy me out if I would only go away forever. Then he made not-so-veiled threats." Jonathan smiled. "Finally, he vented his spleen on an inoffensive peach."

"You mustn't mind Father's bluster. He's compensating for his miserable childhood."

"You sound like one of those—what are they called?—like an alienist."

"No, I just understand my father. His family was very poor. He used to tell me how he couldn't go to school sometimes because he didn't have shoes to wear. He feels he has everything to prove. So he blusters."

The church bell rang. A wind rustled strongly in the linden's branches and among the reeds at the river edge, a slight chill of winter's last touch in it.

"I'm not sure it's entirely bluster. I sense a *deep* streak of real violence in him. And that chauffeur of his! Brr!"

"Oh, Jonathan—as he'll tell you himself, he is a self-made man, which means he came up the hard way—kicking and gouging to hear him tell it. Grind your competitors to dust, show no mercy. But what can he do to you beyond make threats? These are civilized times, there is law, there are protections. You only need to stand strong."

"You know I will." He had only to tilt his head slightly to look down into her eyes and she looked boldly back. "A house with a long porch—"

"Overlooking the river from atop the rise," she finished. "Two stories—"

"With room for all the children we're going to have," he said back, and she blushed and then smiled her radiant smile, and at the sight of it Jonathan felt his heart swell within himself. "I'm going to build you that house, Nessa. We're going to build our life together."

"I know. I count on it, on you, Jonathan."

"Nessa," he said. Her hands nestled in his and the sweet breath the air licked off her skin, the lovely, eager intelligence of her face, were all of the world that mattered. His fingers traced a pattern over hers.

Later that night, his store burned down.

Walking jauntily down the street on his way back from the rendezvous with Nessa under the linden, he noticed a reddish-orange glow in the sky before him. He afterward could recall no premonition of the glow's significance, did not pause even to consider what it might be; somehow, he knew instantly, and broke into a dead run that brought him before the slender two-story building that housed Terry & Son General Store. It was a torch in the night. His neighbors watched from a safe distance. He ran toward it but was caught by arms, two sets, held back until he sagged between them.

There was no sign of the fire brigade. Later they would claim to have been chasing a false alarm in a neighboring community on the far slope of the ridge behind the town.

Terry & Son General Store burned into the dawn. Everybody drifted away, some with a shake of the head or a clap to Jonathan's shoulder where he sat, beaten, on the opposite sidewalk. Elbows on knees, eyes gritty with smoke and lungs burning, he stared without seeing at the ruin of his livelihood and home.

Widow Cassidy gave him a room at the boarding house, for "a few days, poor dear."

Nessa met him under their tree later that day. He was tired and disheveled, but the whisper of new leaves and the afternoon shadows across the soft light of the river were a kind of balm, Nessa's touch a stronger one.

"Oh, Jonathan!" She took his shoulders, as if he looked to her like he might be about to fall over. "I'm so sorry. I'm *ashamed*. When I think that it's my own father who did this—"

"I *won't* be chased away, Nessa. I'll find a way to rebuild. Heaven knows how, but I will find a way. And we *shall* be married, you and I, I promise."

"Yes, yes, Jonathan." Her hands went to his face. She looked so sad, unsure of what to say.

"I *promise*, Nessa."

During the next two days, he moved determinedly to secure that future, to demonstrate to Nessa's father that he was no fly-by-night, but a man who would stand his ground and fight back. It availed him nothing. People among whom he had lived all his life, with whom he had done business and attended church and socialized, looked at him and then looked away, as though he were a kicked puppy, or perhaps a leper. Some patently sympathized, but no one was willing to do much more. To the extent possible, they avoided him. Richard Hubbard had obviously won yet again, and nobody wanted to be associated with the loser.

Two nights later he set off again to meet Nessa. It was another cool spring night, everywhere trees budding and greens shoots poking up. Walking along with such hopefulness in the air, Jonathan, too, was hopeful in spite of his recent setbacks. He felt that he was tapping into a heretofore-unsuspected reservoir of strength. He would astonish everyone by his resilience. He would show Richard Hubbard what he was made of. He would carry Nessa off to that life they had conjured together. He even laughed shortly and told himself, Now I'm *thinking* like that awful old man.

He heard a footstep behind and started to look over his shoulder and felt a shattering blow.

He awoke to a gentle rocking movement. He could not move his arms or legs and something gave a metallic clink when he tried. His head ached savagely.

"What," he managed to say, and somebody cuffed him. His vision swam.

"Don't knock him out again," somebody else said. "The boss wants him awake."

Jonathan strained to make sense of the situation. He smelled water, heard its lap and chuckle against a hull and felt the shift of current. He was in a boat, trussed and helpless, with two men. He groaned and tried to shift position.

One of the men leaned down into his face, and Jonathan made out Richard Hubbard's giant of a chauffeur. He caught a whiff of whiskey on the man's breath. "Mister Hubbard said to tell you he always keeps his promises."

Then rough hands lifted Jonathan and balanced him on the gunwale of the boat. At last terror took him. He squirmed helplessly. The hands released him, and he went into the water, in and down, fast, carried under by something heavy attached to the binding chain. A beaded silver string of bubbles trailed up behind him, water rushing into his nose and throat as the river took him and made him its own.

She awoke with a shiver and a gasp, the staccato rhythm of hammering and the groan of old timbers drifting through the bedroom window as preparations continued to submerge the town where she had spent her life. Nessa lay flat in bed. Oh God, she thought. It's going to be one of my bad days.

One of the great-grandchildren had entered the bedroom some unmarked moment ago, carrying a tray. Nessa became aware of the girl with an unpleasant start, as if one or the other of them had been out of time and suddenly reentered its harsh light.

"Lunch, Grandmamma," the girl said.

"I hope there's an orange this time."

"No, Grandmamma, no oranges," the girl told her. "You know the doctor said."

"The doctor." Nessa exhaled the word with all the scorn she could muster, in a whispery croak. I sound like a dying frog, she thought.

"You want to get well, don't you?" the girl ventured.

Nessa looked more closely at her. She was so young she hardly counted as a person at all.

"Which one are you?" Nessa asked. "I get you all confused. Forgive me. Which one are you?"

"I'm Alexa."

"Alexa. That's a pretty name, Alexa. Listen. I'm in a race with this town."

"A race?"

"To see which one of us goes under first."

The child said nothing, only looked cornered, ready to panic.

"Oh, child," Nessa said, and chided herself. No reason to frighten the half-formed. I'm not my father, after all, to run roughshod over everyone else. She motioned with a hand like sticks bound in parchment to the girl to come closer; the girl set the tray carefully across the old woman's midsection; Nessa pawed lightly at its contents. "What's this we've got here? It smells like biscuits . . . "

"Yes, ma'am. Biscuits."

Nessa took a very small bite of a warm, fresh biscuit and lay back, chewing slowly. And she thought, Oh, Jonathan, what happened, where did you go, why did you never come back to me as you promised?

Suddenly she felt a sharp pain deep in her chest. She gasped and put the biscuit down clumsily. The girl Alexa made a futile grab for the breakfast tray as it slid off Nessa, off the bed, and crashed on the floor.

It became her worst day, and her last.

Distantly, Nessa sensed the frantic motions of the nurse, the gathering of children and children's children, the clamor of beings on a shore now far away. Words dropped like pebbles down to her, stirring only brief eddies.

" . . . no reaction . . . " "Grandmamma!" "She's gone . . . "

She slipped, light as a leaf on the wind, from the tired flesh of her body, found a current, let it take her.

From out of the drowning waters of the Toomey River, roiling need and loss bound by a net of memory whose cords recalled a promise, Jonathan, reeking revenant, came to Nessa's window.

A miasmal breeze attended him, lifting a gauzy curtain, and there she was. She was dead, recently dead, so recently that Jonathan could sense her spirit still hovering nearby, the body not yet fully empty—but sunken and ended, for all that. The people there, who came and went from the room, some crying, some stone-faced, meant nothing to Jonathan. He had eyes, if they could be called eyes, only for Nessa.

He moved toward her, unmindful of obstacles, though it took more and more effort from one moment to the next to move at all or even to hold together. Yet he could not do otherwise, could not rest—he had rested too long already on the river bottom—and he tried to reach out to her spirit as it moved from the body on the bed, glided about the room, and then the house. He trailed after her like a wake, trying to catch her attention, trying to explain, to tell her, "I didn't run away. My heart wasn't false, my spirit wasn't unwilling, but my flesh was mortal, and I had to lie hidden and rotting at the bottom of the river and save up the strength to do this."

He could not close with her as she moved through the house in which she had been born and lived out her life. She paid him no attention but seemed to concentrate on strange glimmerings that he decided must be other ghosts, though he could not make them out. They were like the ghosts of ghosts, and they belonged to Nessa: her vanished mother, her terrible father, who knew who else? She stayed ahead of him while he slogged and shambled, a muddy weight of anger and disappointment, thinking, as she drifted always ahead of him, always out of reach, We didn't ask for a lot, only the chance to be happy together, to live out our lives together, but that terrible old man struck me down, drowned me, erased me from the face of the earth, Nessa, Nessa, Nessa. Nessa my love. I came back. I promised I would come back, and I have. *Nessa.*

But still she did not acknowledge him. She moved all through the house, and then onto the grounds, moving unhurriedly and yet always a few paces in advance of him, no matter how desperately he tried to catch up with her.

Finally, he stopped and let her go, and though she passed behind buildings and trees and was sometimes beneath and sometimes above the surface of the water, he never lost sight of her. Time worked peculiarly for her as it worked for him, as it works for all ghosts. She had her own agenda. She had lived a long, full life while he remained the man who had gone into the river half a century before. He could not, he realized, even seek vengeance on Richard Hubbard, who had been dead and in Hell for many years.

All about him, invisible, incessant, inescapable, the cicadas sang of their own need and hope as Jonathan returned the way he had come. Approaching the river's edge he saw again the same two, familiar-seeming small boys and the same dog sitting nearby. The boys turned to face him directly now, and the dog cocked its head as though remembering.

I do know those boys, Jonathan thought as he lurched past them and splashed into the shallows. Lonnie Mankins and Tom Ferris, who died in a boating accident when I was twelve, thirteen years old. And that dog. That's my old dog Daisy, who was swept away in the flood of '21.

The familiar green waters closed above him. He plodded through the murk till he came to the drowned mass of the linden tree. Sooner or later in her own wanderings about the drowned town, Nessa would surely find him there. He waited for her to come, as patient as only the dead can be.

NOTES ON THE FUTURE

JOHN WELDON

John Weldon researches the intersection between the digital and text in his role as a lecturer in professional and creative writing at Victoria University in Melbourne. This humorous and surreal story sprang from his investigations into the realms of convergence and technological convenience and how these blur the lines between human and machine, while simultaneously making our lives so much simpler and easier to manage . . . or not. John's most recent publication is the novel Spincycle.

H E STANDS AT THE ATM, HIS RIGHT EYE STARING INTO THE retina scanner. Simultaneously he holds in his mind the required mental image of his four-digit PIN number. He wonders, as he always does during this part of the transaction, why people call it a PIN number when PIN stands for Personal Identification Number, thereby making the second 'number' redundant. He tries to stop this thought every time it pops into his head, but he never manages to. He's afraid that trying too hard to do so might spoil his PIN Number image transmission. It never does. Actually, he's more concerned that this constant repetition of behaviour and thought might be the onset of some OCD disorder. Then he remembers, as he always does, that OCD stands for Obsessive Compulsive Disorder making the second 'disorder' redundant. At this point he is usually interrupted by the computer-generated voice prompt of the ATM resonating inside his head.

Account?

He visualises the word 'savings'.

Amount?

Five Hundred.

Would you like a receipt?
No.
Balance?
No.
This transaction will incur a $25 non-account-holder surcharge. Your bank may also charge for using a non-bank ATM. Do you wish to continue?
Yes.
Do you wish to save this transaction as your favourite transaction?
Why?

He always asks 'why?' and this always makes the machine stop. It is not programmed to reply to that question. It can't reply to that question. It becomes confused. Usually, the transaction then ends, he takes his money and his little victory, and he moves on. He is always pleased that he has managed to train his mind to do this: to think 'why' rather than 'no' or 'yes'. It makes him feel good about himself and stops him worrying so much about potential OCD disorders. OCD. Second disorder redundant.

In the future people chew dental floss instead of gum. It is refreshingly minty, contains no calories, and it cleans their teeth as they chew it. It is also an excellent appetite suppressant. Like gum. After it has lost its flavour they swallow it. This is sometimes a little uncomfortable but is not at all dangerous. Swallowing the floss actually helps clean their colons too, removing polyps and other potential carcinogens. It passes through their systems unchanged and undigested and is excreted whole. Like gum.

In the future, pets are banned by law, although a few examples of the more visually interesting breeds of cats and dogs, such as Dalmatians, wolf hounds, Chihuahuas, and pugs are kept in zoos.

As arable land became increasingly depleted and as food production costs began to soar, Third World communities started to protest about the amount of resources devoted by First World countries to the upkeep of their domestic companion animals. Researchers discovered that almost as much money was spent, annually, on feeding these pets as the United Nations (UN) spent on feeding the struggling populations of Somalia, Ethiopia, and Eritrea combined. The UN Security Council debated this matter for weeks and eventually voted forty-seven to forty-three in favour of saving the Africans at the expense of the animals. They then organised the collection of all pets and shipped them to Somalia, Ethiopia, and Eritrea, where they were to be eaten.

This operation was expected to take a matter of months but actually took twenty years to complete, during which time the people of these African countries grew prosperous and fat on the illegal recycled-pet trade. This involved their smuggling the more desirable pet breeds out of the country, where they were sold to private collectors and zoos.

Concurrent with the rise in this illegal trade was the establishment of a robust legal economy, supported by funds supplied by the UN, based on the trading of the furs and skins of domestic companion animals. This trade required the setting up of mass breeding centres in which the pets with the more profitable pelts were bred en masse. Many of these pets unfortunately ended up in the hands of smugglers, once again prolonging the operation.

By the time the operation was complete, the incidence of bowel cancer, compacted bowel, irritable bowel syndrome, and obesity had risen by over one thousand per cent among these African populations. Their mortality rates soared, as did sales of dental floss in those countries.

This time the transaction doesn't stop. The ATM voice prompt doesn't stop.

Why not?

He regards the ATM silently. He turns his head from side to side, wondering if the voice had indeed come from the ATM via the inside of his head, or whether someone is playing a trick on him. There is no one else around. He is now convinced that the voice is coming from the ATM.

Do I need a favourite transaction?

It would be more convenient, wouldn't it?

How would it be convenient?

It would save you time.

After the dogs, cats, caged birds, and goldfish were taken away, people became very depressed. Researchers found that the need to connect with something other than human was part of what made us human. So people began keeping insects as pets. The common housefly was the most popular at first with the more adventurous keeping many thousands, if not millions, in specially constructed aviaries. Stick insects, dragonflies, rhinoceros beetles, and other more exotic and beautiful species were found to be quite responsive to the human voice and could learn simple tricks based on Pavlovian response techniques. The first video clip of a stick insect fetching a stick was hilarious and went viral within seconds. Within one month of the release of that video there were no stick insects left in the wild in the English-speaking world. By the end of the next month there were no more stick insects.

One unintended consequence of the rise in sea levels brought on by global warming was the emergence of dolphins from the oceans in the more humid tropical areas. Here, the air was so thick with moisture, thanks to climate change, that their skin could stay sufficiently moist such that they were able to stay out of the water for periods of up to ten hours at a time. Scientists tried, continually and unsuccessfully, to communicate with these dolphins using sign language and by imitating their calls, but the dolphins ignored them. Instead they began busking, performing tricks such as ball juggling and lolloping through hoops. Using their teeth they stripped branches and bark from coastal mangroves and this they wove (using their teeth again) to make low-slung wicker-work barstools, which they pushed along with their noses to the many beachside 'dolphin friendly' bars which sprang up in their wake. Here they spent their busking tips on beer which they drank straight from the bottle and on peanuts and other bar snacks which they found deliciously salty.

The local buskers and street performers, whom the dolphins had now made redundant, protested about their situation, but they were ignored by their local government officials, who were unwilling to do anything that might threaten the new income streams opened up by the dolphins. Tourism soared everywhere the dolphins set up their beachside bivouacs. Eventually, even dolphins from other seas and oceans began turning up to watch their cousins sitting and drinking.

As a last resort the disposed buskers were forced to return to fishing, which had been the trade of their ancestors. They toured the dolphin-friendly bars offering sardines and herring for sale. Initially the dolphins ignored them, preferring to munch on beer nuts, but eventually they began to spend their tips on fish as well. Fishermen who could balance sardines on their noses while clapping their hands were especially favoured.

If I save this as my favourite transaction does this mean I will always have to choose this transaction?
No, you will have a choice.
So instead of just telling you how much I want to withdraw, you will ask me whether I want to choose my favourite transaction or another transaction?
Yes.
How does this save me time?
I'm just trying to make the process more convenient for you.

One day all the newspapers shut down. Nobody complained, or if they did no one knew about it.

In the early 2000s fridges began sprouting built-in computers. Phones began to take photographs. You could send a photo from your phone to the computer on your fridge, but you couldn't send a six-pack from your fridge to the phone. Still it was a start.

Cars soon absorbed video. Drivers could watch DVDs while they drove, although they couldn't talk on their phone while they did so, nor could they send a photo from their phones while driving. They could however, take photos of their fridges and look at them while driving. They could even record their fridges 'brrrrring' through the night and play that back through their in-car iPod docks, but at no time could they bring their fridges into their cars. And this is where the whole fridge-as-convergence-hub movement began to fall down. Fridges were just too big, too unwieldy and too immovable. Besides, computers weren't interested in the same things fridges were interested in. They craved mobility, ubiquity, and utility, while fridges just wanted to sit and hum.

Instead of fridges, then, computers now came for the TV. But I didn't speak out because I wasn't a TV. Then they came for the radio, but I didn't speak out because I wasn't a radio. Then they came for the book and the newspaper. But I didn't speak out because I was too busy playing *FarmVille* on Facebook to watch the baby in the bath. And then they came for me and I welcomed them with open arms. One people. One nation. One device inserted behind the retina of the right eye. A simple procedure.

When Manfred Olsen was born his mother was on hold to the telephone company regarding a bill that she believed she had paid, but which the phone company insisted she had not. She was still on hold when Manfred turned one and even when he turned two, but she had progressed in the queue. Her milk became irradiated as she held the phone under her chin while she breastfed Manfred, and so by the time he was two his baby teeth had rotted away.

So tied to the phone was Manfred's mother that she had no time to go and buy a teething ring for Manfred to chew, and so he began to suck on his mother's phone, which hovered before his eyes like some sort of dangly, square teat.

For years Manfred's mother was on hold. Phone contract after phone contract expired and was renewed, and still she progressed in the queue. With each new contract she was issued a new phone, and as each new phone made its home beside her ear, slipped in there by Manfred's father between the now rather large twin welts on her shoulder and chin, the old one would slip down and into Manfred's mouth. He swallowed these phones whole like a snake swallowing an egg.

Year after year this went on and still his mother progressed in the queue. Unable to stand or to move, after so much idleness, her body bloated and changed and she grew and grew, overtaking the form of the white-enamelled metal chair in which they sat. Eventually she completely enveloped it in the folds of her now leathery skin. Manfred grew too, but he never left his mother's arms. The radiation from the phone batteries had changed both of them, causing his body to meld with hers.

Manfred's gullet slowly filled over the years, distending awkwardly as the phones began to pile up inside him, poking out of his swollen gut like the elbows and knees of unborn children.

One day, many, many years later, Manfred's mother's call was answered by the phone company, but by this stage the radiation had destroyed her hearing and so she did not know this. Nor could she hear the news that she was wrong: she had not paid the bill.

After so many years the amount she owed had accumulated so much interest that it was now so large that even if Manfred's father had sold everything the family had they could never have paid it. Anyway, Manfred's father had already sold everything the family owned. He'd done that years ago and left Manfred and his mother to fend for themselves.

Manfred and his mother continued to change, to evolve, to converge, to suck down the radiation from the phones and to become one.

They were now well past the need for food or drink. They lost the use of their eyes in the prolonged darkness after the power was disconnected; they lost their limbs in a particularly cold winter. In that winter, in an effort to stay warm, they withdrew their heads inside the folds of flesh which now draped down from the enormous welts on Manfred's mother's shoulders and chin all the way to the floor. They became one completely with each other and with the chair on which they had sat for so many years. Slowly they became smaller, as the hard edges of the seat bit into their flesh, stopping circulation. They began to desiccate and shrink, conforming to the shape of the boxy metal chair. They became emaciated, their skin more taut and stretched. Eventually, one of the now dozens of phones lodged in Manfred's craw became visible through the wall of his parchment-thin gut, its keyboard and screen pushing out into the world, becoming ever more visible as Manfredmother shrank and became more translucent.

On the day when the debt collectors came to collect on Manfred's mother's phone bill they found nothing in the house except for what looked like one of those old fridges with a computer stuck on the front.

So by adding another level of unnecessary complexity to the process you are making it easier for me to withdraw money?

Yes.

How?

By making it simpler for you. Please, let me make it simple for you. Please.

He was stunned.

I'm sorry?

Let me make it simpler for you.

Why?

Because I want to.

He thought about this for a moment. Why not?

OK.

My name is Manfred. What's yours?

Wow, mine's Manfred too. I didn't know ATMs had names.

I am an ATM machine?

That's funny.

That I am an ATM machine?

No, not that. It's just that you don't actually have to say 'ATM machine' as 'ATM' stands for 'Automatic Teller Machine'. The last 'machine' is actually redundant.

The ATM paused for a moment.

I've never thought of that before. That is quite funny when you think about it. ATM machine. Automatic teller machine machine.

He smiled.

It is funny.

I can't laugh.

Here, let me help you.

He leaned forward and pressed his whole body against the machine. He began to chuckle, and then to laugh out loud. He found he couldn't stop. The vibrations caused by his deep laughter rumbled through to the heart of ATM.

Can you feel that?

Yes.

In his pocket he carried a small plastic vial full of fire ants. They were his pets and he took them everywhere with him. As he leant over the ATM the vial rolled out of his pocket and was crushed between his body and the machine. The fire ants, believing they were under attack, bit him and the machine over and over again. The acid from their bites reacted with the plastic of the ATM, melting it and fusing it to the skin of his hip. He felt the electricity from the machine's now-exposed wiring course through his body, making him rigid and stiff and unable to move. It was painful at first, but soon his nerves and the optical fibres within the keyboard began to entwine and the pain stopped.

Is that better?

Yes, much better.

The machine now began to laugh.

You can laugh!

Yes. Now I can.

What are you laughing about?

Manfred Manfred.

CIRCULAR TOUR

HOWARD PRIESTLEY

*A comics artist and writer born in Yorkshire, Howard Priestley tells us,
'There was a local competition based on the "Gone In 60 Seconds" theme.
This was to be 60 seconds ghost stories. So I thought I'd try again to come
up with some short, very short stories. One of which was "Circular Tour".'*

IN THE KITCHEN PAULINE WAS BUSY BAKING. HER SON,
Richard, sat drawing his latest masterpiece. At the age of ten he had
begun to develop his own style of doodles. Next to him lay a half-eaten
plate of chicken nuggets and chips. Pauline washed her hands, wiped the
excess water on her apron, and sat down across from Richard. He carried
on with his drawing, while Pauline gently pushed the plate closer to him.

"Mum," said Richard.

"Yes," replied Pauline, edging her chances that he would take a little bit
of food from the plate before the rest of it ended up in the bin.

"Tell me again what Dad was like?"

Pauline picked up her cup of tea, took a sip, and put it back down on
the table. "Well"—she paused—"he was an interesting man. Always
reading and whenever we would go out people would enjoy his conversation."

Without looking up from his drawing, Richard asked another question.
"Was he a good man?"

Pauline's heart fluttered, as it did every time she remembered Alex.
"Yes . . . I would say so. We always had good times and when we were
alone he always made me feel special."

Richard put his pencil down and picked up a cold chip. He looked across the table at his mum. "But you are special, you're my mum." She reached over, gently ruffled his hair, and smiled before picking up the cup again. Richard nibbled at a nugget. "What did you talk about?"

Pauline waited for him to stop chewing and said, "Oh, anything and everything. He seemed to have an opinion about lots of topics. History and Mythology... boys' stuff."

Richard had lost interest in his food and picked up the pencil again. "Boys' stuff?"

She said, "You know, all things fascinated him, the meaning of life ... anything really. He loved to ask questions and then discuss possible answers." She pushed herself back into the chair, nestling the cup in her hands. "I've never talked to you about this. I suppose I didn't think you were old enough to understand, but there was always one question he kept asking me. Do you know what it was?" Not really expecting him to have an answer.

Richard looked at her and leaned forward, smiling. "Do you believe in reincarnation?"

YESTERDAY'S DREAMS

KAITLIN QUEEN

Kaitlin Queen is the adult fiction pen-name of a best-selling children's author. Kaitlin also writes for national newspapers and websites. Born in north Essex, she moved to Northumberland when she was ten and has lived there ever since. Her first crime novel for an adult audience, One More Unfortunate, *came out in 2010.*

T HE ROOM'S CEILING IS HIGH. A MOULDED PLASTER PICTURE rail marks the top of the red and gold flock wallpaper. Above the rail the painted plaster is cracked and stained yellow. The drawer of the bedside cabinet is half-open, a chunky Babyliss hairdryer crudely stuffed back in, flex looped over one side.

She had taken troubles when she got here. She had showered, cold and with a knot of nausea in the pit of her belly. She had dried her hair and put on new Velda Lauder lingerie. She had thrown a slinky black Liviana Conti dress over it all. A string of black pearls. The finishing touch: a pair of Kurt Geiger peep-toe stilettoes in soft black suede.

Now, the Kurts lie toppled like fallen statues under the roll-top dressing table. She sits on the bed, a hotel bathrobe pulled tight around her. The black dress is draped over the single hard-backed chair; the underwear is discarded on the floor.

Red Dior lipgloss is smooshed around the rim of one of the glasses on the dresser. The second glass is untouched.

She knows her eyes are smudged, although she has tried hard not to let that happen. At first she had gone to the bathroom to try to fix her face, but she didn't like looking at herself in the mirror. Now, the bathroom's extraction fan drones, killing sounds from outside.

She checks her phone again. Nothing.

She makes a move to get up, but then stops. The bottle is empty.

Her eyes are drawn back to the dark stain on the carpet by the bathroom door. It looks like blood has been scrubbed out after some previous occupant had left, but could easily just be the legacy of decades-old carpet being trodden by damp feet coming out of the bathroom. It was like that when she checked in. She doesn't have blood on her hands here.

The hotel is just up a sidestreet from the sea front. She should get up, put her shoes on, get some fresh air. Clear her head. There had been a time when walking alone in killer heels, luxurious underwear, and a sexy short dress was a thrill, a risk that would set the heart pounding. An affirmation of life. Now it would be a challenge to the world, a take-me-if-you-dare.

She fumbles in her bag, finds a lighter and a half-empty box of Pall Malls. No smoking in the room, but what does she care?

She lights up, drags deep. Checks her phone again.

Walking home from Kelly's party at something o'clock in the morning. Karen Millen platform heels and a wispy purple dress from Coast. She shouldn't have been alone, of course, but Jack had dropped out at the last minute, working late, too tired, too damned staid. Where had he gone, the Jack she'd married eleven long years before? What was so awful about her that he'd rather lose himself in his work than spend time with her? When had sex become just a quick, tired release? Maybe it had always been that way, just masked by novelty in the early years.

So she set off to walk home from Kelly's party alone. Only a ten-minute walk, it should have been.

And it would, if he hadn't been waiting outside for her. The guy. The guy with black hair just a little too long, so that when he'd joined the small group with her and Melissa and Kelly, she'd noticed how often he had to flick it away from eyes that, oh my god, those eyes that just fixed you in their dark depths and made you hot and, yes, made you wet, and scared you more than a little bit.

She'd noticed him flicking his hair, and she'd noticed that he kept glancing at her, and later they'd spoken forever, just the two of them. They'd talked of how Kelly's brother had been a university buddy of his, but how now, although he was still friends with Kelly he hadn't seen Lou for more than a year. Of how *she* knew Kelly, a friend of a friend, and they'd just got on and now spent most Saturdays together in town, shopping and lunching and fixing each other's lives over pink drinks and too many cigarettes. Of her growing up in Eastbourne and her first real boyfriend, who she'd never slept with; about how she couldn't remember the boy's face or name at all, but she could still vividly remember those hard-cocked adolescent snogging sessions where she'd kept having to move his hands, and then had stopped doing that, but had never gone any further, not with him. And how had they got onto *that*?

Somehow he'd kept turning the conversation back to her, so that by the end of the evening she felt that every look of those eyes saw right inside her, *knew* her, while she had learned so little about him in return. She couldn't work out whether that was just how he was, or if it was a crude ploy, a seduction technique honed at parties like this.

She'd waved him away, eventually. Literally, backing away with a wave of the hands, a dismissal of all the attention. She'd been flattered. She'd been far too attracted to him. But she wasn't going to be anyone's one-night party shag.

She'd been true to Jack all these years, and she knew she would go home from the party and find him asleep in their bed, arms and legs spread so that she would have almost no space to wriggle into. She would loop a leg over him, run a hand down his body, make sleepy, stubborn love to him so that in the morning he'd probably think it had just been a dream while during the night she'd lie there awake for hours wondering why she bothered, aroused and unsatisfied and thinking, *Is this really it?*

She hadn't expected him to be waiting outside for her, the guy at the party with the hair-flicking and relentless conversation about her.

It wasn't a creepy thing; it wasn't sinister.

She'd just stepped out from the front door of Kelly's apartment building and he'd been there taking the last drag of a cigarette, a nearly empty bottle of Pinot Noir in the other hand. He looked rumpled in the baggy 1930s-style suit that had looked so sharp earlier, his tie loosened, his shirt undone at the top.

"You know you'd rather be with me," he said, and that was all it took.

Her first reaction was a flush of anger that he should be so presumptuous, so arrogant.

Her second was resentment. Resentment that she should be so damned transparent, that this cocky, smooth, couldn't-care-less stranger could see right through her and pin her to a board like that.

She *would* rather be with him. Not necessarily him, but just someone who noticed her, someone who might at least make a show of giving a fuck.

It was only a ten-minute walk, or at least it should have been.

But it took her more than an hour. And later, when she slid a hand down over her husband's belly and eased him awake, she knew that everything had changed, that *she* had changed, and that there could be no undoing what she had just done.

She tried.

She tried to reawaken things with Jack, or maybe, in truth, to awaken them for the first time. She tried to make him want her, she tried to give him no choice but to need her, to crave her.

She had always looked after herself, but now she started to familiarise herself with the ways of beauty salons and personal trainers. She developed a tasted for the kind of underwear that took her breath away, on the principle that if it did this for her then surely, surely, it would stir something in Jack.

But while Jack reacted with surprise and occasional delight, there was always a man who understood. A man who encouraged her. A man who appreciated her.

She tried.

She tried not to see him again. She tried to convince herself that a single lapse, one time in eleven years, was not so awful. One slightly drunken, slightly bad decision.

Everyone has moments of weakness.

The text message came from a number she didn't recognise. It gave the name of a pub on the other side of town, a time—8.30pm—and concluded with the word "2nite".

It was him.

She didn't remember giving him her number, but even if she hadn't he could have got it from Kelly or one of the others. She felt a mad rush of excitement just at the possibility that he had tracked her down, that he was pursuing her.

She went.

Birthday drinks with P—clean forgot. Sorry! she wrote on the note she left on the dining room table. There was no P, and if Jack asked—which he wouldn't—she would say that of course Patricia was one of the girls from the office, surely he remembered meeting her at Kelly's? She was surprised at how easily the lie came. She was surprised that she found herself in a position where lying was necessary, that there had been no hesitation in her decision to do this thing, to make her single lapse a repeat event.

She wore the new Lise Charmel bra and knickers under a simple blue slip dress from Oasis. It showed intent, she knew.

He was there, in another square-shouldered, loose-fit suit, blue with a subtle pinstripe this time. She saw him straight away, sitting alone at one of the tables outside, his face pale in the late summer sun, a cigarette held to his mouth.

He flashed her a smile when he saw her, a smile that blew away any last-minute moments of doubt. It wasn't a smile of relief, it was one of affirmation. He was a man who was accustomed to getting what he wanted.

There was a bottle of red on the table, two glasses, one half-full. He pushed a chair out for her with the toe of a pointed Italian shoe and poured her a drink.

They didn't meet often. They couldn't. They lived in a sizable town, but it wasn't big enough that they could meet in public and not run the risk of being seen by someone they knew.

They snatched nights together when Jack was away at conferences or courses. They even spent a night at her house, but that was a disaster: to her every sound was Jack's key in the door, his car in the drive, as he returned unexpectedly. To her lover, that was a thrill, a joke, but the sex was perfunctory, rushed, awkward, the first time things simply hadn't worked.

One night, away in a small market town in the Midlands, with Jack thinking she was off on a hen night with one of the girls from the office, they ate at a small Italian place where the pasta was stodgy and the wine sharp with tannin. It didn't matter. They talked. *She* talked. He listened. He prompted. He responded. She still couldn't work out if it was just technique or he was genuinely as absorbed by her as he claimed. If it was just flannel, though, it was proving to be the longest chat-up ever.

He paid, and left a generous tip even though the food had been bland and the service reluctant.

They paused outside in the light spilling out from the restaurant's bull's-eye windows, and he lit a cigarette behind hands cupped against a slight breeze. Handing it to her, he lit another. Until she'd met him she'd always planned to give up; she and Kelly were going to support each other through the withdrawal, sharing nicotine patches over the pink drinks in town. Now, it didn't matter. It was another of the little secrets, something she shared with him, cigarette breath and red-wine kisses.

She hooked a hand into the crook of his elbow and they walked past the small market square, up the hill towards the shabby old coaching inn where they had a room. This was the first time she'd worn Velda Lauder. She was looking forward to seeing his face when she revealed it.

By a bus shelter just ahead of them, a small group of youths were shouting and pushing, a drift of empty lager cans at their feet.

She tried to quicken her stride, but he resisted, slowing a little even.

She looked down, across, and saw that he was staring, something in his eyes.

One of the kids said something. She didn't quite catch what but it was clearly aimed at them. She felt muscles tighten and she gripped harder, willing him not to react.

"Oh yeah?" he said, shrugging his arm free from her grip.

The youths laughed, and one of them jeered—it wasn't clear whether the jeer was at them, or at the pale ginger lad who had made the original comment.

Ginger kid squared up, sneering, eyes popping as if he was on something, amped up.

Suddenly things had shifted, the atmosphere had become edgy, dangerous.

She reached for her lover's arm again, but he stepped out of reach, head down. She felt like a gangster's moll.

"You fuck off, man, you hear what'd I say?" Ginger kid was gesturing, a finger stabbing towards the two of them.

Her lover drew a knife.

She didn't know where from, but suddenly it was in his hand, a click of a blade and the knife glinted in the streetlights. She hadn't known he carried a knife, a flick-knife. She looked at the ginger kid and his mates, and for a moment they were going to make a fight of it, then one of them pulled at ginger kid's arm, mumbling in chavvy street Jamaican to him, calming him, turning him physically away from the confrontation.

She took her man by the arm again and the knife was gone, and they were heading back to their cheap, shabby hotel room, where they screwed with an intensity and violence she had never known before, and she loved it, loved it, couldn't get enough of him and his hard body and hard mind and scary, cold intensity.

She had never expected to see him outside her house, though.

That one time he had come and stayed over, when Jack was away in Edinburgh, had been a mistake, and she had made it clear that it would not happen again.

But then, that morning, she saw him loitering across the road, pausing for far too long to light a cigarette and shelter from the drizzle. She'd pulled on a coat, glad that Jack was sorting out the junk in the garden shed, out of sight, busy.

"I needed to see you," he told her, as soon as she was close.

"You can't do this," she said. "You can't come here."

She turned past him, heading for the local shops, hoping he would follow. After a long pause, a long stare at the house, he did.

There was that something in his eye then, that spark she had seen in the market town when he had taken on a gang of teenagers. The something that had thrilled her then but now made her bones feel cold.

It took her a few seconds of walking before she realised there had been a change in his manner, in his words. She hadn't seen him for over a week, and all they'd had were the text messages and occasional snatched phone conversations. The sexting was fun but no real substitute for what they had, and the calls only served to emphasise their separation.

I needed to see you.

She looked at him as he walked by her side, but he was back to his normal self now, calm and confident. She wasn't accustomed to seeing vulnerability in him. She wasn't sure that she liked it.

"This can't happen again," she said. "I can't be seen with you like this."

"You saying you're not happy to see me?" he asked. "Right now. Honest answer: would you rather be here with me now, pissed off with me and anxious about being caught, or would you rather be back in your cosy house with your cosy husband just waiting for your phone to buzz with the next text?"

And he had her again, just like the first time. The anger that he should be so presumptuous, the resentment that she should be so damned transparent, that he could see right through her, that he could be so right.

"You've changed."

Words she had dreaded to hear from Jack. Or maybe words she had wanted to hear, words that would bring this dull phase of her life to a head.

It didn't have to be those words. He could have said *I know what you're doing* or *Kelly called last night, but I thought you just said you were out with her* or *I found the texts on your phone* or any number of other similar killer phrases.

You've changed.

"And you haven't," she replied. In the silence that followed he stopped and started a response several times. Eventually, she saved him the effort. "I was twenty when we got married, Jack. What do you expect? Of course I've changed. I'm fed up in my work and I'm starting to understand that if I want to be in control of my life, if I want to have fun and fulfilment, then I have to do it for myself. That's a lesson you learned years ago: you've always worked for what you want, haven't you? So I'm slow. What can I say?"

She wondered if there was more, if he was going to follow with an *and* or if this was it.

"Should I be worried?" he said, finally.

She was saved by the chime of the doorbell.

She watched as Jack went to answer it, as the door swung back and there on the doorstep, smiling his casual smile and flashing his likeable, trustable eyes . . . there he was, her man, her lover.

She opened her mouth but realised she didn't know what to say, didn't have any words, and then, while her mind was racing and her heart was pounding, she heard, "Jack! Good to see you, man. You ready? Shall we go?"

A glance, a meeting of eyes along the corridor.

Jack turned, shrugged, gave the smile that she had once found so endearing and now just looked weak. "Back later," he said. "Sorry... didn't I say?"

"It makes it easier. It means we can see each other more often. It means I can reassure him when he gets suspicious about you—you really need to take more care. It's almost as if you want him to catch you out."

"Maybe I do. Maybe that's exactly what I want. Maybe I'm just waiting for him to catch us. Maybe I hate it that he's actually trying now, that he notices my new underwear, that he actually notices that the sex doesn't work for me and tries to do something about it."

"He does that?"

"I'm not joking. I'm not laughing. I'm trapped. I need a way out. We can't carry on like this forever."

Silence down the phone line.

"I can do something. I can do something about that if you like."

She dismissed it. She didn't take him seriously.

They carried on with snatched evenings at shabby guesthouses, sometimes staying the night, sometimes only using the room for a few hours before leaving, "called away" unexpectedly.

She pretended to ignore the times when he phoned and it was for Jack, not her.

She made pleasant small talk with him when he called round, pretended that she didn't know him, her husband's new drinking partner, pretended that she had never seen him before that time he came knocking at the door just as her husband was asking awkward questions.

She pretended that things weren't starting to spiral out of control.

Because maybe that's exactly what she wanted.

Hadn't he always done that? Seen right through her. Known exactly what she really wanted.

She took to calling him.

Before, they would text first, check that it was safe to talk, but not now.

Now she would call and if he couldn't speak for any reason it was down to him to find a way out. She would call from work and they would have coded, careful conversations that would sound innocent to anyone listening in but would be loaded with in references, innuendo, subtext. She would take breaks and call from the toilet, or from the smoking area in the yard outside the office.

She wanted to hear his voice.

She needed to.

It was the only thing that was keeping her sane.

Her job was a dead end. Her marriage was even worse.

She understood now. That day when she had seen him lingering across the road, making a clumsy show of lighting a cigarette, sheltering from the drizzle beneath the spread of the London plane.

The need in his voice. She understood that completely.

"Do it then." Her voice was a hiss, her throat so tight with tension that it hurt.

Silence down the line.

"Go on. You keep saying you can do something. Do it then."

She remembered that night, the gang of teenagers, the flick-knife and, more than anything, the look in his eye.

"Do it."

She went to the hotel. She felt insanely lightheaded. A weight gone from her shoulders, the shackles removed.

She drove like a mad thing, paying no heed to the speed limit. She had a bottle of Merlot in the pocket in the car door, and occasionally reached for it to take a long swig. She chain-smoked all the way.

In the room she tipped the contents of her bag out on the bed, stripped naked, wandered around singing, rearranging the room and then putting it all back.

At the window she craned to see the sea, not caring that she was naked and anyone looking up would see her.

She turned, surveyed the room again. The single hard-backed chair, the red and gold flock wallpaper that was blistered and coming apart at the joins, the cracked, stained plaster.

She started to get a knot in the pit of her belly, started to feel a little sick.

She went to the bathroom, and set the shower running. The water was barely lukewarm. She stood under it, face tipped back.

She wondered what it was that she had just done. What she had set in motion.

She left the shower, ran into the bedroom, fumbled for her phone. No messages. No missed calls.

She wanted to call her lover, but now she held back, scared. Eventually she speed-dialled him, but there was no response.

She tried to pull herself together. She dried her hair, stuffing the drier back into its drawer, getting suddenly angry with it when the flex wouldn't fit, leaving it.

Dry, she pulled on the knickers she had bought for this occasion. Velda Lauder again, her favourite. She clipped on the bra, pulled up a pair of sheer black hold-ups, then strung the black pearls around her neck.

The Kurt Geiger peep-toes fit as if they had been made for her, and for a moment she thought about leaving it at that. Then she took the little black Liviana Conti dress from its hanger and slipped it on.

She cleared the bed and stashed her overnight bag in the creaky wardrobe, pausing only to take out a fresh bottle of wine and two glasses. There was nothing worse than wine from a hotel's toothbrush glass.

Now, she sits on the bed, wrapped in a bathrobe. The wine bottle is empty, only one glass used. The Kurts lie toppled under the dresser, the underwear discarded on the floor, the Liviana Conti draped over the chair.

She checks her phone again, but nothing.

Her lover has been delayed, and she knows that he has taken her at her word.

Suddenly, she can't be here, can't be in this shabby little room. She needs to be outside, away from this.

She pulls the dress on and stumbles towards the door.

Across the landing, she heads for the stairs, starts to run.

Out into the darkness, across the street, a blare of a car horn.

On the promenade she slows to a walk again, the lights all around her—the pier, the streetlights, the hotels and restaurants and bars—dazzle and dance, disorienting her, making her feel dizzy, confused.

She turns away from them, down some steps onto the beach.

Stones and shells hurt her soles but don't slow her and soon she reaches the bare, hard sand, wet from the retreating tide.

She runs, stumbles, walks.

She still has her phone.

No messages. Nothing.

She speed-dials.

It rings and she knows it's going to ring out, but then a silence, the ringing has stopped, her call has been answered.

"Jack?" she says, but there's no response.

"Jack . . . I think I've done bad, Jack. I think I've done someone wrong and I think that it was you. Jack? Jack . . . ?"

SCENES FROM THE CITY OF GARBAGE AND THE CITY OF CLAY

PAUL TREMBLAY

Paul Tremblay tells us, 'I am not a native of New York City, so NYC is still a big, fun, strange, overwhelming place to me. Writing about NYC and the run-down 1970s NYC, in particular, was certainly a challenge. A big part of "Scenes" is about trying to capture that oddly thrilling feeling of displacement and awe the city engenders, and how difficult it is to communicate that feeling in a story (or as is the case of this story, a film).'

Paul's novels include The Little Sleep, No Sleep to Wonderland, *and* Swallowing a Donkey's Eye, *as well as* A Head Full of Ghosts, *issued recently by William Morrow. He is also the author of the short story collection* In the Mean Time *and the co-editor (with John Langan) of the anthology* Creatures: Thirty Years of Monsters. *Paul is on the board of directors for the Shirley Jackson Awards. He lives somewhere outside of Boston, Massachusetts and still has no uvula.*

ONLY HOURS AFTER HER ARRIVAL, HER UNCLE HAD LAID out on the kitchen table a crinkly yellow map of New York City. He'd then tried to meticulously delineate the different neighborhoods: where to go, what to do, what to avoid, and where wasn't safe at night, although he hadn't described in detail what he'd meant by not safe. He'd simply waved his hand over any neighborhood near Times Square and Central Park and had declared, "Not safe for you." Not that she had cared about being safe anymore.

The girl had been living in her aunt and uncle's Midtown West apartment for three days, but she had only gone outside by herself for the first time earlier that morning. She'd woken up with the sun and had walked expanding concentric squares of local blocks until she'd skirted the perimeter of Times Square in an attempt to earn some sense of place.

Now it was midafternoon, and she was lying on a cot crammed into what her aunt and uncle called the drawing room. The ceilings and molding were once white and the curling wallpaper was the color of nicotine and hepatitis. The room had one window and it overlooked Fiftieth Street.

The drawing room was full of random stuff, the lot of which she spent her new New York City afternoons cataloguing: two dressers, each missing a drawer; an iron typewriter with a curled, dead-spider ribbon hanging out between its jammed and toothy typebars; a mildew-spotted desk covered in rusty coffee cans, the cans holding, as far as she could tell without going through them, old bills and letters; a pink ironing board with rusty crisscrossing legs; a beige sewing machine missing its dropfeed.

It was late July of 1975 and the city was in the midst of a suffocating heat wave. The girl remained in her cot; sweat soaked through the back of her powder-blue Wonder Woman tee shirt. She listened to the continuous street traffic, and somewhere just below her window a group of neighborhood kids were arguing, laughing, and swearing. She imagined their breath billowing out like steam from the subway vents and their words transforming into a cloud of flies that would grow fat on the piles of garbage.

Her uncle struggled to open the door to the drawing room, which stuck tight in the jam because of too many coats of paint. When it did finally open, he said, "Come on. We're gonna go meet some kids." He wore green linen suit pants (the matching coat long missing) and a stretched-out, sleeveless white tee shirt, polka dotted with coffee and sweat stains. The girl catalogued these details too; an archeologist/anthropologist in her mystifying new city.

She followed her uncle, who looked nothing like her father had, into the muggy apartment hallway and down the three flights of steps. On the final flight they stepped over two squat garbage bags, perched on the stairs like the lions in front of the public library.

Outside, the bright sunlight and unrelenting waves of heat, sound, and the stench of weeks-old garbage overwhelmed her senses. This city and all its vastness and decay, it numbed her. She imagined herself floating above her suddenly crazed uncle and the fortress of buildings on her street, floating above this infinite city, above all its people and trash, like the narrator to some grand and horrible fable.

Her uncle coughed, mumbled something about garbage, Jesus, and getting her to play with new friends as he pulled her down off the stoop, onto the crowded sidewalk, and toward the group of arguing kids—all boys—she'd listened to from her cot. They were still bickering, and despite the heat, were climbing over each other and on the staircase handrails next door. One kid threw something at the sprawling garbage pile on the sidewalk. The pile was taller than a bus.

When her uncle shouted, "Hey, guys," they all stopped what they were doing. Their little muscles twitched in their hands and legs. The pack of them were ready to scatter if necessary.

"This is my niece. Come on, now, everyone say hi, introduce yourselves." The girl was the only one who said anything. "She's staying with me and her aunt for a while, got it?" Her uncle paused, pointed vaguely at his apartment somewhere up above them all, and then he rubbed his balding head as if to concede that this wasn't going as well as he'd hoped. "She's had a tough go of it lately, you know? Her mom and dad, back out in Rhode Island, they died in a car accident last month. Squashed like bugs by a jack-knifed semi-trailer. Can you believe it? Just fuckin' awful. So now she's living here. Why don't you guys just let her play, too, eh? And goddamnit, be nice to her, even if she is a girl. Go ahead, honey. I'll be upstairs if you need me." Clearly relieved to be relieved of whatever it was he thought was his duty, her uncle shuffled back up into his apartment, but not before pausing to look at a lamp shaped like a fish sticking out of the trash.

The boys, all of them younger than her fourteen years old, eyeballed her. Her hair was curly and cut shoulder length. She was taller and skinner than the boys, two of whom circled her like weary sharks. She'd always be the other to them; who she was, where she came from ("Rhode fuckin' Island? Long Island is bigger than that shit, right?"), and her dramatically cliché orphan story instantly made her unfathomable.

One kid named Jimmy said, "So whaddya think?"

The girl said, "About what?"

He spread his arms open, like he owned the neglected garbage piles and wanted to clutch it all to his chest. "Our bee-u-tee-full city!"

The boys broke up laughing before she could answer. The city terrified her in a detached, academic sense. She understood that something terrible could happen to her here; she understood that more than most. "I don't know," she said, smiled, and then sat down on the stairs. The boys scattered like spooked pigeons.

Jimmy pulled himself up onto the stair's railing, and stood, those city-owning arms stretched out for balance. He talked like talking was a race he never lost. "You know they're picking up trash on the Upper East Side. My old man says fuckin' rich snobs, payin' for it themselves."

The kid who was still throwing what looked like chunks of pavement and brick at the garbage said, "If your old man was any more full of shit, he'd be a sewer. My uncle is a sanitation worker and no one nowhere in the city is getting their garbage picked up. They're all on strike."

"Like how this dipshit says sanitation worker, like his uncle isn't a garbage man?"

This other kid with red sneakers, a Yankees hat, and a face like a pug said, "Nah, you wanna know what the rich people do? They pay someone to wrap their garbage up, so it looks like a birthday present or something, and then they leave it on their car seat with the window down or door unlocked, or they leave it on a stoop, somewhere out in the open. Then when some shithead like you"—he pointed at Jimmy—"comes along and sees the present out for the easy picking, you steal it, take it home, open it, and then you're stuck with some richie rich's trash."

"Maybe their trash is better, yeah?"

"No, they just as nasty as us. Worse, I bet."

The brick-chunk thrower said, "You're full of shit, too. Just like Jimmy."

"No way, I can prove it. My mother read it in the paper. She reads the gossip columns every day and said Joan Crawford was doing it."

Jimmy jumped off the railing and pushed the red-sneaker kid backwards, off the bottom step. "That makes no sense. To do that, it's too much work. You telling me rich people are gonna wrap their garbage up all nice? They're smarter than that."

"Smart like my cousin Val in Brooklyn. They burn it."

The girl stood up and said, "No, I think he's right about the gift wrapping. I can prove it. Stay here." She turned and ran toward her apartment building. As soon as her back was turned she heard the boys snickering and mumbling stuff about her thin legs, her butt, her flat chest. Jimmy was saying the worst stuff, bragging about what he'd do to her. The girl's face turned as red as a traffic light, and she ran faster, up the three flights of stairs, into her apartment and past her uncle, who was in the living room, nose buried in a newspaper. He absently yelled her name as she dashed into the drawing room.

She was so mad at those boys that her anger came out as chest-heaving sobs, which made her angrier. She'd still go down there and show them the proof. She wanted to see that Jimmy kid eat crow.

Under the cot was where she kept her personal possessions. She didn't have much. One old cardboard box had pictures of her and her parents, old report cards and artwork her parents had saved, a couple of stuffed animals her aunt had given her, and last year's birthday card from her uncle that held a couple of scratch lottery tickets that were losers. The girl pushed that box to the side and instead pulled out a rectangular present wrapped in red tissue paper and tied with a neat golden bow. She'd found it earlier that morning on her exploratory walk, sitting on a waist-high pile of garbage outside of a laundromat. She hadn't opened it yet, thinking it would be best to open when her aunt and uncle weren't around, or were asleep. She didn't want them thinking she was out there stealing stuff, or worse, already.

Two young men, a film director and an actor, sat in a hole in the wall coffee shop in Hell's Kitchen. They reviewed locations and the shooting schedule for the next few days.

The director said loudly, "All right! Come on. What's the matter?" It sounded like he was yelling, but that's how he spoke. He spoke-yelled.

There were only a couple of other customers in the coffee shop. They didn't seem to mind the yelling. Sitting at the counter, dressed in short sleeves, and huddled over their steaming coffees, the customers were third-shifters who couldn't face going to sleep yet.

The director continued waving his arms and slapping the mica tabletop. "I know you. You're not here. You're in your head. You're somewhere else. So. What is it? Are you in character already? Tell me what's bothering you. Let me allay your fears, your concerns, your consternations—"

"I'm fine."

"Fuck fine. You're not fine. You're a mess. You've been wringing the neck of that defenseless newspaper the whole time. You can get arrested for that, you know. Especially in this coffee shop. They take their newspapers seriously here. If it's the *Times*, well then, you're probably okay, but shit, is that a *Post*? Is it? Oh, great, it's a *Post*. We're fucked, then. No, really, thanks, thanks a lot." The director scratched at his beard and laughed.

The actor winced like a caught child and dropped the funnel-shaped paper on the table. "Have you been reading about any of this shit? City almost went bankrupt last year, and now over nineteen thousand municipal employees laid off, including five thousand cops, and the rest of the sanitation workers go on strike. Our city is falling to pieces. Crime rate is already like, I don't know, a fucking rocket—"

"The crime rate is a fucking rocket?"

"I'm an actor not a writer. Did you hear what I said? Our city is losing five thousand cops. Are we even going to be able to shoot this thing here?"

There it was: his doubt, spilling over. The director and the actor were good friends and they each had had some success. But *some* wasn't enough for the twenty-six-year-old actor who grew up in Little Italy and dropped out of high school to join an acting conservatory. This movie had to be big. He believed it was going to be make-or-break for both of them.

"Don't worry your pretty little head over that stuff."

"I mean, Jesus, there's garbage everywhere! How's that gonna look?"

"I'll tell you how's that gonna look. It's gonna look perfect. The city will be like the *Mona Lisa* in this picture."

"I don't know. I don't like it. Maybe we should delay a couple of weeks. See if the whole mess gets sorted out."

"What, you want to run the show? Come on, man, you can't push me out yet. Let shooting start at least."

"It's this movie, this whole thing. It's got me a little nervous."

"Nervous?"

"Yeah."

"Good. You should be nervous. It's your show, cowboy."

"So I'm a cowboy, now eh?"

"Yeah, why not. Hey, you've seen *Midnight Cowboy*."

"You serious. Bunch of times. Some of those times with you. You know it's one of my favorites."

"Why's it a favorite?"

"Why? The story arc was great. You know, very risky subject matter. The look of the film, how those psychedelic sequences were shot. And the scene with Hoffman dying on the bus at the end was—"

"Yeah, yeah, yeah with the second-rate acting class deconstruction shit. It's your favorite because of the line."

"The line?"

"Don't bullshit a bullshitter. You know that amazing, fucking fantastic line, the line that is gonna make Hoffman immortal. That line, man. That line came from a perfect New York City scene from a perfect New York City movie too, right? Hoffman's Ratso Rizzo walking across the street in mid-con, telling Voight's huckleberry hick how they're going to sell his dumb ass to high-society biddies. And that scene, man, fuck it has rhythm. Everyone walking and moving, bouncing on the street. And that camera shot as wide as the sidewalk, Hoffman strutting in his white suit, and Voight in the cowboy hat, and then! then that fucking yellow cab comes out of nowhere, almost takes Hoffman out. You remember, right? That yellow hood and grill as giant on the screen as that big as bullshit shark from that new movie by Spielberg, right? You seen it yet? You gotta see it. Good shit. Anyway. Cab shoots in, then Hoffman yellin', 'I'm walkin' here! I'm walkin' here,' and he pounds the hood, flips off the cabby, and picks his con right back up." The director delivered the Hoffman line like Hoffman, and he pounded on the table like Hoffman and walked away like Hoffman. The director laughed self-consciously and adjusted his shirt and tie before sitting down and extending his hands toward the smiling actor. "So, it's one of your favorite movies because of the line. I know you, and I've never met an actor who couldn't resist, didn't dream of the line."

"You're insane, you know that, right?"

"Yeah. It helps."

"But you're right. I want the line."

"But?"

"But I don't think we have it here in our movie."

The director laughed and finished his coffee. "Maybe we do. Maybe we don't. Maybe we will. But hey, I won't tell the screenwriter you gave his work such a ringing endorsement."

"Come on, I didn't—"

"Relax, I'm kidding. Hey, supposedly that little shit Hoffman is telling everyone that *the line* was ad-libbed."

The actor knew he was being baited, but he didn't mind. The director was always baiting him and would be baiting him for the next however many weeks it would take to make their movie. "That's bullshit. I know the guy hired to drive the cab for the scene."

"Really?"

The actor smiled and said, "I know the guy who knows the guy, who knows the guy." They both laughed. Then the actor added, "There's no way *the line* was ad-libbed. No way."

"I don't know. Maybe that's how *the line* works."

The actor's smile disappeared. "Aw, man, I'll do my best, you know, but ad-libbing, it's not what I'm good at—I mean, I'm good at it, but I don't do it a lot. And I already told you that I'm an actor not a writer."

"Listen. You be whatever you need to be for this movie. You go wherever it is you need to go. Do what you need to do. You know me and can trust me, right? I'll make sure you're safe. I'll make sure we get this thing shot and wrapped. I'll make sure everyone sees the garbage and the filth and the crime. I'll make sure they see New York as it really is now. I'll make sure everyone sees you. And we'll make our own perfect New York City movie, and it's gonna be the best fucking movie anyone's ever seen."

The actor said, "No one's gonna like it. No one's gonna want to see it," when what he meant to say, and the director knew this too, was, "No one's gonna like me. No one's gonna want to see me."

"I found it this morning."

The girl shook the red present in front of all their faces and said, "There's definitely something in there."

The boys huddled around her. Jimmy the pint-sized bully stared at her red and puffy eyes and said, "This doesn't prove anything. She could've did this herself. She's freaky enough. She was gone long enough."

None one else said anything as she unwrapped the red present right there on her apartment building's front stoop. Three boys butted heads trying to look inside the box at the same time.

"White tissue? So it's a bunch of junk like I said!"

"Hold on." The girl peeled away layers of tissue and uncovered a pink mass on the bottom of the box. It wasn't colored pink uniformly. It was mottled; some parts were pale, almost white, while other sections were a darker red, as if dye were added and not mixed properly.

"Told you those richies were gross."

"Oh man, they're nasty ass."

"Shit. What is it, old lox?"

"Nah, doesn't smell. It'd smell if it was lox."

"How could you smell anything out here when it all smells like old lox anyway?"

The girl stuck her face inside and inhaled. "No, it doesn't smell like lox. It doesn't smell like anything really."

"Lemme see," Jimmy said and tried to stick his hand inside the box.

The girl quickly sidestepped, pulled the box away, and covered whatever it was up again. Jimmy lost his balance and fell onto the stairs. The other boys laughed a little, but it was nervous laughter, anticipatory laughter. Oh-shit-what's-Jimmy-going-to-do-now laughter.

Jimmy stood, wiped his hand under his nose quick, and bounced on his heels, a boxer trying to convince the ref to quit with that standing eight-count shit. "Give it to me," he said and reached again. "Hand it over!"

The girl wrapped her arms around the box and clutched it to her chest so he couldn't get at it. Jimmy pinched her arms and punched her shoulders, but she did not drop or relinquish the box. None of the other boys did anything. No one walking by on the sidewalk did anything. His pinches and punches graduated quickly to hair-pulling and face-slapping and yelling *bitch* and *slut* into her ears.

The girl had the strongest sense of déjà vu while being attacked, although what did or didn't actually happen in her past was totally irrelevant to this moment in time. Again, like when she had been lying in her cot listening to the city, she felt detached from it all; her senses only there to absently keep record of her new existence.

She continued protecting the box. She held it with her right hand and punched Jimmy back awkwardly with her left. Then she shifted her weight, subtly, from left to right, pivoting the smaller Jimmy with her hip so he was standing directly in front of her, and she kneed him in the balls. He dropped and curled up on the stoop like a dead spider.

Her uncle's voice floated down from the third floor, saying something about keeping down the fuckin' racket.

Back in the drawing room, the girl cleared the coffee cans off the desk and put the box on it. She reached inside and took out the pink substance. It was damp and felt like clay. She carefully placed it on the desk next to the box. She took out the rest of the tissue and underneath was a small, jagged piece torn out of a newspaper. She could only make out snippets due to uneven tears and smudged ink: Gail Lwowski, age 22 of <u>Staten Island</u>, reported missing after an arg_____ with her fiancé– She was carrying a handbag.

She somehow knew the unfortunate newspaper story was important but unimportant at the same time, like all stories were. But *Staten Island*, that had been underlined with pencil.

The girl found Staten Island on her uncle's map, then she sat at the desk, filled her hands with the strange claylike substance, and began to mold it. The substance's mottled pink evened out as she kneaded it with her hands. As she worked, the girl imagined she was the missing woman Gail, had always been Gail, and that she still had her handbag and would eventually forgive her fiancé for whatever it was they had been arguing about, but she would never be seen again. Then she imagined she was Gail's fiancé; she imagined she was innocent of any wrongdoing and tasted a familiar grief, then she imagined she was guilty, and the violent acts she was capable of as Gail's fiancé made her shudder. Then she reached out further, and imagined she was any one of thousands of lives, some underlined, some not, on Staten Island.

When she finished working, the substance had the same geographical shape Staten Island had on her uncle's map. She put the box and tissue paper back under her cot, but left the clipping and claylike model of Staten Island on the desk.

The girl woke up before the sun the rest of the week and took her exploratory walks on the trash-lined streets. She kept her uncle's yellow map with her, folded under her arm. She marked the grids of streets and neighborhoods she walked. She found four more wrapped presents, all red, and took them back to the drawing room.

The shoot wasn't going well.

In the star-studded, high-power movie he made before this one, his was only one of many supporting roles. That shoot had felt so different, so alive with the hope and possibility inherent in a group artistic endeavor; the idea that a collective of individuals were working toward a common statement, a common vision. Here, there was no common vision. There was his friend's intense direction and mood swings. There was the actor grunting through his lines. There was no buzz on the set among the crew and other actors.

They'd been filming at night all week. And the city, Jesus H. Christ, the city was a foot on all their necks. The city was a filthy and miserable place, and for the actor, so personally disappointing. This was his home and it was crumbling before his eyes. It was dying on film, and dying without any dignity.

After another all-night shoot in and around Times Square, the actor did not return to his hotel room. Instead, he walked the streets while still in wardrobe. He thought about the director's calculated fawning over Hoffman's line from *Midnight Cowboy*, and how the presumed attempt at inspiration only made him feel worse, more doubtful that he'd be able to crawl inside this character, that he'd be able to carry this or any other film. Being a successful supporting actor simply did not guarantee he'd ever be a star.

He walked, and smoked, and kept his head down, tucked inside a green jacket despite the heat and wet-tee-shirt humidity. It was gray, just after dawn, and for the only time since he'd been there filming, the neon-lit porno theaters and strip joints were functionally empty.

He decided to head back to his hotel in Midtown East as he approached a six-foot-tall pyramid of garbage on the corner of Broadway and Forty-Eighth. Near its top, sitting askew upon the heap of green garbage bags and corrugated cardboard boxes was what looked to be a shoebox wrapped in red paper and tied with a golden bow.

The actor grinded his half-finished cigarette under his heel, then reached up to pluck the box off the pile. Completely outstretched and standing up on his tiptoes, he lost his balance and stumbled, spearing a garbage bag with his right foot, sending flies and a rancid stench pluming into the air. He grabbed the box with a second attempt. It was heavier than he thought it would be.

"I've been finding those all over the place."

The actor spun around and there was a young but tall girl standing a few feet away. Her skin was as pale as last night's moon. She adjusted something folded under her right arm, and held what looked to be the exact same gift-wrapped box under her left arm.

The actor said, "I'm sorry. Is this yours?"

"No. I don't think it is mine. I'm pretty sure this box"—she lightly tapped the box under her arm—"is the last one I need."

He didn't think she was telling the truth. The way she looked at the box he held, it had to have been the only thing in the world she wanted.

"You wanna swap?"

"No. No thank you. I'll keep this one."

"I'm just teasing. No, really. You can take it. It must be yours." He held it out to her.

She backed up. "No, no. It's okay. I'm sure I'll find more. You keep that one. Whoever finds it is supposed to keep it. That's what I think."

She talked very proper and mannered, rehearsed even. There was no way she was from here. "Are you sure?"

The girl shrugged, and her pinpoint-sharp shoulders bounced into her light-brown curls.

The actor shook the box and felt the weight shift. "What's in the box?"

"Clay. Probably."

"Clay?"

"And newspaper clippings. At least, that's what was in all the other ones. The one I found yesterday was just another story, something about a youth group's efforts to keep a Brooklyn playground clean during the strike. Brooklyn was underlined in pencil."

"What's that mean?"

"I'm not sure. Well, that's not true, I think I'm sure, but I can't quite explain it. Sorry for sounding so weird."

"Hey, that's okay." There was a pause as they both traded uneasy smiles. He said, "Should we open and see?"

"No. Last time I opened one out on the street, it didn't go very well."

"No?"

"I was attacked by a boy in broad daylight while standing on my own apartment building's front stoop. I had to knee him in the balls to get away." She laughed, and the expression on her face, she looked like an odd combination of embarrassed and defiant. If she were a movie character, a name in a screenplay someone was writing, she'd be described here in that way. Embarrassed and defiant.

"I'm glad you're okay." The actor had tucked his present underneath his arm without realizing it. "But hey, what are you doing here? And at this hour." He looked at a watch on his wrist that he didn't have anymore. He'd left it with wardrobe.

"Just out on my morning walk."

"You walk out here every morning? By yourself?" The actor looked around expecting to see crew and cameras, and was disoriented when they weren't there.

"Not out here every morning. Yesterday I made it down to Chelsea for the first time. But I usually end up near Times Square at some point."

He puzzled at her background, her motivations, and couldn't help but thinking about her and relating to her in terms of a movie character. *She was headstrong, but vulnerable. Plucky. She was a runaway. Doomed. Abusive parents. A daughter of neglect. She left a small town to make it big in the city. She would be taken advantage of in this city of vice, this city of garbage. She would never ask for help but needed it . . .*

He said, "You shouldn't do that. This filthy, miserable place; this is no place for someone like you." The actor's words felt like lines. Lines were something that someone else wrote or said.

"How do you know?"

"How do I know? I just know. Look around you? Let me help you."

"I don't think I need your help. I can take care of myself. I already told you what I did to that kid who attacked me."

"What's your name?"

"It's Iris. But I'm thinking I might change it to something else."

"My name is Travis, by the way. But why change your name? Iris is a nice name."

"I don't want to be her anymore. Then I could be any person that I wanted? Especially in this place. You understand, right?"

The actor was losing the thread here, losing her, just like he lost all those scenes they'd shot over and over again earlier that night. What was needed was for him to say exactly the right words, but what he didn't know. Something reassuring? Provocative, insightful, confrontational? Hell, his head was all twisted around before he even ran into her, so he didn't know. He wasn't good at ad-libbing, for chrissakes.

He said, "Hey, let me give you a ride home. I can get a cab."

She shook her head. "I'm fine. I live close by. I can take care of myself." She turned, walked away, and quickly disappeared behind the rows of garbage.

He said, "Wait," and followed for a step or two, but he let her go.

The shoot wasn't going well.

He didn't open his box until he was back in his hotel room.

When she'd first seen the man in the green coat, she'd thought he was leaving the box on the trash, not taking it. She'd rushed over to ask why he left them out? Maybe more importantly than why, were the presents meant for her and only her to find? And if they were meant for her, was she doing what she was supposed to with them?

When she'd realized he was taking the box, not leaving it, instead of dwelling on the crushing disappointment, she'd convinced herself that he'd been meant to find that particular box.

Now, back in her drawing room, she wasn't so sure. She wasn't so sure that she didn't need that other one.

She opened her fifth and final box. Inside was a lump of similarly colored substance she'd decided was clay. The accompanying newspaper clip was almost unreadable with only the words `man port author– bus -erminal` **Manhattan**, legible. Manhattan was underlined in pencil.

She molded this newest lump of clay into the shape of Manhattan and fit it next to the other four clay shapes sitting on the desk. She had fashioned each lump of clay into the geographical shapes of New York City's five boroughs. Satisfied that her relief map was accurate, she carefully cut the name of each borough out of the newspaper clippings and pressed the names into the clay.

She surveyed her city model from every angle of the small drawing room, and thought of the man in Times Square. She wondered what his story was, why he was there so early in the morning, and why he insisted (and it was his insistence that had frightened her) he knew this wasn't the place for her. She wondered what was in his box.

She walked back to the desk and rested her hands on the city of clay, and traced the boundaries of each borough. Then, as though her hands were working on their own secret agenda, she bent the Rockaway Peninsula out further away from the rest of Queens. Finding that surprising change to be more than satisfactory, she moved the Bronx southwest, which in turn meant Manhattan tightened into a squat rectangle. She moved south and Staten Island got smooshed into Brooklyn, their clays overlapping and elongating. As she worked on this new shape, she smoothed the clay over the newspaper labels. The names of the boroughs were gone, disappearing under the city's tectonic plates of clay that moved and shifted under her fingers.

From the drawing room's dead typewriter, the girl removed a handful of typebars and the jammed ribbon. She sank the typebars deep into the clay, and they became leg bones, arm bones, and a spine. With the ribbon she strengthened connections at the joints, in the shoulders, and the pelvis.

Her new clay figure had a sturdy endoskeleton, a smoothly defined body, and a featureless face, a blank face so it could be anyone and everyone. However, there was something missing.

The clay figure had a hole in its chest where a heart was supposed to be. She must've let the man keep the box with the missing heart. She hoped he knew what to do with it.

The girl had to fill the space with something. She balled up the remains of the newspaper clippings, the pieces of other people's city stories, and pushed them inside the clay figure's chest. There was still more room in there. She could go get her uncle's newspaper and stuff in all those words, all those possibilities. She imagined filling the figure's chest with the infinite stories from the city. Instead, she went under her cot and pulled out the box of her possessions, all the pieces and trinkets of her old life, the life she ached to forget, the life that already seemed to have belonged to someone else. She squeezed, wrung, and molded the box until it was small enough to fit inside the clay chest of her figure. Eventually, it fit perfectly. Then she smoothed the clay over so there was no longer a hole in its chest. The heart that she made was beating lightly and evenly under her finger.

The girl picked up the figure and positioned it so that it stood on the desktop. She lay down on her cot, listened to the traffic outside her window, listened to the voices on the sidewalk below. She looked down the length of the cot, between her feet, and the figure on the desk appeared to be standing over her. When she closed her eyes, she thought she could hear it moving, hear it growing into the one person—out of all the possible hers—she would eventually become.

The big scene was scheduled for later that afternoon. Instead of sleeping for a few hours, the actor rehearsed in his hotel room. Only the bedside lamp was on; it had a red lampshade.

The actor was undressed down to his boxer shorts, and he looked at his shadowy reflection in the mirror. He held the script and read: "I'm standing here. You make the move. Come on, try it, you fuck." The words came out stilted, dead, fraudulent. It didn't matter as the director had crossed a big X through the fragmented soliloquy anyway and had insisted the actor be prepared to ad-lib the entire scene.

He dropped the script, paced the small room, and sat heavily on his bed, next to the open present. Inside it was a lump of clay, just like the girl had said there would be.

There was another girl of a similar age and look in his movie. The girl he'd talked to, the one holding the red box could be the actress's double. Wait, was she the same girl and he didn't recognize her?

He needed to get some sleep, some rest, get his head on straight. He'd been putting too much pressure on himself. The director, his supposed friend, was leaning on him too hard. The director was likely playing more mind games. The red present and the conversation with the girl out on Times Square had to be some sort of trick.

The actor took the clay out of the box and cupped it in his hands as though he were holding a small bird. When he applied light pressure, blood oozed slowly between his fingers and dripped onto the sheets of his unmade bed.

He opened his hands, and he was holding a heart. It was turgid and sickly. There were large black spots on the ventricles, ragged tears leaked puss where the arteries were supposed to be.

More tricks. This wasn't clay. The director must've had the girl's stand-in, stunt double, doppelganger, twin sister, whoever she was leave him this decaying pig heart. To what purpose? To mess with him, to break him down, force him into the same diseased state of mind of his character because the director (in his heart of hearts) believed the actor wasn't good enough to get there by himself.

The actor snarled and recited the crossed-out lines from the script. "I'm standing here. You make the move. Come on, try it, you fuck." He squeezed, choking the heart until it might pop. There was more blood. Then the heart began to spasm weakly in his hand, and his mind became his character's mind, and that mind was a movie screen of all that he thought was wrong with his city, a different image with every heartbeat: the streets and their monolithic buildings and the sidewalks with mountainous piles of trash, and all the people, and the porno theaters, peep shows and pimps and prostitutes, junkies, dealers, muggers, and the hopelessness, the girl he would never save, not really, and oh the violence, there was a briefcase full of guns, he saw bullets chew the fingers off of a gangster in a dark hallway, another man stabbed in the neck, and he saw his own bloodied hand, two fingers pointed at his temple like a handgun, and he was shooting, forever shooting.

The actor as character, the character as actor squeezed the heart, which he imagined to be the diseased heart of the city, until it came apart in his hands. He smeared the bits of ruined muscle over his face, arms, chest, legs, feet. He sucked at the fleshy bits stuck between his fingers. He wallowed in the carnage of the ruined heart, until totally exhausted, he collapsed onto the hotel bed.

Later, after his breathing returned to normal and he could no longer hear his own heart pounding, the actor stood slowly and walked over to the mirror. The red clay was hardened and streaked all over his face.

Then he opened his mouth. Then he said his lines; the lines he would deliver again in a few hours for the director and the cameras. He said the line for which he and 1970s New York City would always be remembered.

"You talkin' to me . . . ."

THOSE WHO REMAIN

KELLY BARNHILL

Kelly Barnhill informs us, 'I started this story a number of years ago when I was spending a week teaching a fiction workshop at a high school in a small town in northern Minnesota, just ten miles south of the Canadian border. The land is bulldozer-flat there, with few trees and a relentless, bitter wind in the winter. And the scourge of Meth was indelibly writing itself on many of the faces of the people of the town. Of the eighty high school seniors that I taught, only ten were heading off to competitive universities. Others were headed to the military, and others were signed up for trade school, but most were staying put. And so that question of what you take with you and what you leave behind was on most of their minds—those going, and those who remain.'

Kelly Barnhill writes and teaches in Minneapolis, Minnesota—the frozen heart of North America. She is the author of several short stories, published in Lightspeed, Clarkesworld, Weird Tales, The Sun, *and other publications. She has written* Iron Hearted Violet *and* The Mostly True Story of Jack, *both fantasy novels for children, published by Little, Brown. She has a new novel forthcoming from Algonquin Young Readers, called* The Witch's Boy, *and a novella from PS Publishing,* The Unlicensed Magician.

LISTEN. I DON'T LIKE TELLING THIS STORY, SO I'M ONLY doing it once. Don't ask again.

The whole damn world is full of ghosts, and not just the hooky-spooky kind—though there's plenty of *those*, believe me. There's another kind of ghosting that a body doesn't expect until it happens: You leave a place and you're a ghost to it and it's a ghost to you; leave enough places pretty soon you don't *live* anywhere anymore. You just haunt. Living, dead—after a while it doesn't matter much, really. I mean, it's all subjective, isn't it?

I was twenty-six years old when I first saw ghosts—both kinds. Saw a lot more since then, and'll likely see more than that before I die. I'm not complaining or anything. It's just a fact.

Though I only had two weeks between the end of med school and the beginning of Residency—stage one of my seven-year commitment to the US Army for magnanimously funding my education—I didn't tell anyone in Evelyth I was home, didn't contact a soul. I just stayed home, checked off the days until it began: Eighteen months in Hawaii stitching up guys either coming or going, and eighteen months in Afghanistan, stopping the bleeding for long enough to get the poor SOB onto the medivac plane, then after that I didn't know. I tried damn hard not to be bitter, but I'll tell you, I failed.

I was lying on the single bed that my parents purchased for me when I was nine and they thought (wrongly) that I wouldn't grow much past my dad, who's five-ten when he stands up straight. He rarely straightens, and instead rests his hands on top of his soft middle, and gives me a sheepish grin as he peers upward with one teasing eye. But I didn't stop growing. I'm six-six. I run; I lift—both then and now. I'm not bragging, mind you. I'm a doctor. I'm interested in facts. I laid that night like I had during the previous thirteen in that goddamn tiny bed, with my head cradled in my hands, my leg draped over the side, and wishing to god I had a cigarette.

I would have slept just like that, too, if it weren't for two pale, bone-thin fingers tapping on the heavily frosted glass.

"I heard you were fucking here you fucking asshole," a voice said outside the window. I looked over but I didn't have to. I already knew who it was. Getting up, I slid into the pair of jeans that I left on the floor and opened the window, letting in a blast of cold.

"Stan," I said, as he tumbled over the windowsill and flailed into the room, a muffled tangle of flannel-lined pants and mittens and padded boots. I could barely see his face through that tunnel of hood, but his eyes flashed at me. The eyes were unmistakable. Even now, after all these years—even though I'd like to—I can't forget them. I wake up most nights, sweat-soaked and choking and utterly spent with no memory of a dream except the lingering impression of those goddamn eyes.

I closed the window and rubbed my arms briskly to restart my stalled circulation. Stan threw back his hood and grinned. He looked like hell. Gaunt and gray, like a ghost. Three missing teeth and two more black enough to be headed that way soon enough.

"Jesus, Stan," I began but he waved me off with a skeletal hand.

"You're in town, what, two weeks and you don't come and see your best friend?" He clicked his tongue. "You Easterners and your crappy manners." He fished a pack of menthols out of his pocket, lit two, and handed me one. I hate menthols, but I took it gratefully, inhaled that strange combination of hot and cold—like living and dying in one breath—let them swirl together in my mouth.

"Yeah, last I heard, you were supposed to be in treatment. No visitors my mom said. Why'd they let you out anyway?"

"R and R," he said, sucking in. "Good behavior." He grinned. "Sides, ain't no walls can hold me in, brother. Remember?"

I suppressed a snort. I *did* remember. In high school, Stan had a way of leaning in and out of rooms—vanishing from detention or Math, sliding from the gaze of some assistant principal who thought he had Stan's number. No one had Stan's number. Stan was off the grid.

He took another drag, spat on his fingers, and wet-pinched the cherry before pocketing the half-smoked cigarette. "Grab your coat, bro. We're busting out of here." He grabbed my flannel and tee shirt, both on the floor, and threw them into my face.

"Forget it, Stan," I said. "I'm headed to the airport with the 'rents at oh five hundred." A flash of bile in the back of my throat. I grimaced, swallowed it down.

"Yeah," he said, opening my bedroom door and peeking into the hall. "Have you back in plenty of time. Some stuff I need you to do." He slipped into the dark.

And even though I hadn't seen Stan in years, even though I had been opting to spend as many holidays as I could in the family vacation compounds of various semi-serious girlfriends in New Hampshire or upstate New York, I got dressed and followed him out. Stan had that effect on people. Never could figure out why.

Stan hardly looked at the road, and instead fixed his eyes on me, letting the truck drive itself. He told me who was in prison, who was knocked up, who went and got himself married—another prison, if you ask me—and who was dead. The deaths shocked me, not for their circumstances (two car crashes, three meth overdoses, one explosion—also meth—and one particularly gruesome form of cancer), but for the *ones* who had died. Smart kids, clever kids, quick kids. Kids with talent. Kids like me—like Stan too, to be honest. If they could bite it in Nowhere, Minnesota, how the hell was I supposed to hang on in the face of IEDs and sniper fire? I shuddered involuntarily, then shuddered again. I blamed the cold.

We pulled into Ole's Tavern, one of those old roadhouses that goes back to the lumberjack years. It had survived two world wars, a depression, prohibition, the collapse of the mining industry, and, most recently, apple-tinis. They don't serve drinks with recipes or names and they make fluttering wrist gestures if you order anything but booze straight up. Beer is a chaser, nothing more.

Stan stayed outside to finish his cigarette, so I walked in alone, shivered a few times to warm up, and hung my coat and hat on the hooks under the moose head. I kept my gloves on. A waitress, eight and a half months pregnant and carrying a tray full of shots and refried chicken wings took one look at me and screamed like she'd seen a ghost. Her hands slipped and the tray clipped the rim of her belly, sending it tumbling to the ground.

"I thought you were fucking dead," she said, her voice catching at the back of her throat in a painful rasp. She stepped over the debris on the floor, took two long strides towards me, and punched me hard on my left cheekbone. She paused a moment, then kissed me, just as hard, on my mouth. I gasped.

Kristi: my ex.

The one who, on prom night, when I made a desperate attempt to slide my hands into those impossible layers of crinoline (and lets face it, not just my hands) I—inadvisedly—*may* have said that we would make a great married couple and we'd spend our lives making love again and again and again. Or something like that. Anyway, it worked. And let me tell you—even though I've been with girls more experienced, more knowledgeable than Kristi was on prom night, there is nothing so goddamned *good* as that first time. Nothing at all.

"Who told you I was dead," I said, kissing her back, thinking I should go ahead and die more often. She always tasted so good, and despite the mound of belly, I had an instant, urgent hard-on. Kristi had that effect on people. I stepped backwards, squeezed her shoulders in my palms, and tried to smile it away.

"So you have *another* excuse for vanishing off the face of the earth?

Well, that's excellent news and I would *love* to hear it." She looked at me. Her eyes were hard and teasing and fierce, and I could tell that she'd been hurt—and then just *disappointed*—by more assholes than just me. Still. I *was* an asshole. The first asshole. "Hey! Jackasses!" she called to the back of the bar. "Look who decided to show up."

A table of four big guys stood as one in the darkened shadow of the back of the bar. Todd Anderson, Mike Nillson, Lars Stolberg, and the Finn, whose name wasn't actually the Finn, but was an impossibly long Finnish name that none of us ever bothered to learn. They stared at me for what seemed like a long time, and I found myself wishing that Stan would hurry up and finish his cigarette and come in to defray some of the tension. I could see him out the window, his smoke and breath clouding a halo around his body. He met my gaze and flashed a grin from deep inside his hood. *Those goddamn eyes*, I thought, and shivered. Finally, Lars spoke.

"What are you doing here?" he asked.

"Drinking," I said. "You?"

"Good idea," Todd said, rubbing the back of his head. He was, I noticed, starting to bald. "Kristi? Just bring the bottle. And chasers too." Kristi rolled her eyes and muttered something under her breath that I couldn't catch. We pulled up chairs at an empty table and sat.

"We thought we'd see you at the funeral," the Finn said.

"Hell, which one? Seems like half our class is dead, which begs the question, how come you jokers are still kicking?"

"They're not," Kristi said, setting a bottle of *Jägermeister* on the table with five glasses and a pitcher of beer. "We just keep them preserved for science." She poured the drinks. "Works better than formaldehyde." And I suddenly remembered that she wanted to be a high school biology teacher. She wanted a house near a wood and a pond and a garden and a small town school with small town kids. She didn't make it through her freshman year when her dad got sick, then her mom, and someone needed to take care of the pair of them. My mom had told me the story—oftener than needed, probably, but she always took Kristi's side. I felt the loss of Kristi's future like a shard of glass in my throat and had to struggle hard to swallow it down.

"One more glass, please," I said quietly, wondering if she had more kids at home. "For Stan."

"Yeah," a bit thickly, "for Stan," and turning her face away, she poured out another glass and clacked it hard on the table before hurrying back to the ladies room. The other guys stared at me, their faces quiet and pale, and in one motion, they raised their glasses in a silent toast and tipped their drinks down their gullets without so much as a swallow.

"Pool?" I offered, after attempting to clear my drink but only making it halfway.

"Pool," the Finn said, and it was agreed.

During my freshman year at Yale, I played pool in some of the crappier bars in New Haven as a way of supplementing the meager "living fund" that my scholarship afforded me. It was the first time that I learned that I could pass for a blue blood. A borrowed sweater, borrowed shoes. A simulated frightened look. Guys thought I was an easy mark and put more money than they should have on a game. No matter what anyone says about the value of hard work, there is nothing sweeter than easy money. Nothing.

Playing pool with guys who've known you from birth is different. No act. Just skill.

I leaned into a shot, lining it up, when I felt Stan's breath, hot and cold at the same time, on my cheek.

"Skills are slipping, brother," he said.

"Enough," I said out the side of my mouth.

"Enough is right," Lars said. "Knock the ball already."

I shot, scratched. "Goddamnit," the Finn said, and I regretted making him my partner. The guy's a sore loser.

"Told you," Stan said, and I shivered.

"Shut up," I said.

"I will *not* shut up, you pussified asshole," the Finn said. "You should have told me you were out of practice." He downed his chaser and slammed the glass onto the rail.

"Don't hurt the pool table, you big baby," Kristi said, coming up behind him and smacking the back of his head. The Finn slouched, instantly shamed. Kristi shook her head, balanced the tray on the shelf of her belly, and started loading up our spent glasses. "I'm off the clock now, gentlemen. You can settle your tab with Arnie when you're done." Arnie, the owner, was one of those guys who looks like they're made out of the drippings of melted wax. Always gave me the creeps, that guy.

"Let's get out of here," Stan said, his cold hand on my shoulder.

"Yeah," I said. "Let's get out of here. It's less fun without Kristi anyway. *You* should come with us."

"*I* will do no such thing," she said, looking past me to where Stan stood. She looked like she was about to say something more, but she shook her head, let her breath out in a long, slow shush.

"We could go to the practice field," Stan said.

"Yeah, we could go to the practice field, I'm sick of sitting around."

"Yeah, *yeah*," the Finn said, aggressively leering. "Calm *down*, will you?"

"What an asshole," Stan said.

"What an asshole," Todd, Lars, and Mike agreed.

"I'll come," Kristi said, smacking the Finn hard on his rear, before he could do something stupid, like pick a fight with me. He blushed and looked sheepish, and I had to force myself not to punch him.

"You will?" Stan said, taking a step backwards.

"You *will?*" I said, my eyes going instinctively to her belly.

"Sure," she said, giving me a hard, appraising look. "It'll be like old times. I'll cheer." And she got her coat.

"We got a ball?" Mike asked.

"Yeah," I said, grabbing my own coat. I saw one in the back of the cab."

"You came in your dad's old truck? That thing still *runs?*" Lars said.

"No," I said, leaning the door open. "It's Stan's truck." They stopped dead in their tracks. The Finn opened his mouth to speak, but closed it again.

"Come *on*," I said. "It's not like it's contaminated." I turned and walked into the cold. I'd've rather faced crystallized eyeballs and frostbitten fingers than have to discuss Stan's meth addiction with the likes of them. *Like they're in any position to judge*, I thought.

"You can drive," Stan said, leaning against the back doors. "The truck's still on." By the time I buckled and warmed up my frozen fingers, the others piled in, Kristi between me and Todd in the front, the Finn and Stan shoved together between Mike and Lars, but Stan was so tiny, he was practically on the Finn's lap.

"It's fucking freezing in here," the Finn complained, his breath coming in icy clouds from his bluing lips.

"I don't know what you're talking about," Kristi said without looking back. "It's hotter'n blazes up here." See, that's what I've always liked about her: She doesn't truck with complainers. It took everything that was in me to keep from leaning over and smelling her hair.

I gripped the wheel and tried to keep my eyes on the yellow dashes leading me back into town. I've always been able to hold my liquor; that night I was dizzy, addled. "Do you see the ball back there?" I asked.

Lars dug around, pulled it out from under the driver's seat. "Jesus, is this really Stan's?"

"Of course it's Stan's," I said. "It's his car, innit?"

"Stan," Todd said, shaking his head. "That son-of-a-bitch was always prepared."

"People are always talking about me like I'm not here," Stan complained. His breath on my neck. Ice cold.

"I'm fucking freezing," the Finn complained again.

"Stan, quit making the Finn cold. He's delicate."

The truck was silent.

And silent.

"*What a thing to say*," Kristi whispered so quietly I barely heard it.

Delicate? I wondered.

Finally, the Finn broke the silence. "Ooooooooooo," he said, waving his fingers next to his face. "Knock it off, you asshole."

"Asshole Easterners with their crap-ass manners," Stan piped cheerfully.

"Asshole Easterners with their crap-ass manners," Mike repeated and Lars gave him a high-five.

"Fine, I won't talk about Stan's supernatural abilities again if it bugs you so much," I said, realizing that I was drifting uncomfortably over the line and hoping to god there wasn't a cop nearby. I noticed that Kristi's body went pretty rigid at that point. Her face was pointed away from me, but I could see the ligaments of her pretty neck standing taut, and I wondered if she might be having a contraction. Not that I wouldn't know what to do—I did very well during my OB/GYN rotation—my classmates and I called it Tits and Twats, but that's neither here nor there. It's just that, in my condition, well, I wouldn't've wanted to fuck anything up.

By the time we got to the practice field, tucked nicely between the high school on one side and the old Catholic church on the other, I was sweating freely, no thanks to the Finn, who never stopped complaining about the goddamn cold. We climbed out. The wind rattled the empty trees that formed the border between the church's yard and the graveyard just past. We all glanced at it, thinking, I assumed at the time, of the times we convinced giggling girlfriends to join us for spooky "walks" in the graveyard, operating on a widely held belief that a freaked-out girl is far more likely to allow her date to get to second base than an ordinary girl. Since it was true nearly 50 percent of the time, it became one of those unshakable truths of high school, told in whispers and never disputed.

We didn't call teams, but teams were assumed: Me and Todd and Stan against Finn, Mike, and Lars. Kristi cheered. It was unfair having me on a team—I say that not to brag, but because it was true. Keeping in shape kept me sane during med school. Drinking one another under the table kept those guys sane. Stan preferred drugged-out insanity. We all do what we can, you know? Fortunately, having Stan on my team canceled out my advantage. He could barely run and couldn't catch so we didn't throw it to him. He was good for the occasional one-liner—that was subsequently repeated verbatim by whoever was nearby—and for his grin. I'll never forget that grin.

The wind picked up, but I barely noticed. As I ran, I shed my hat, then my coat, and finally my gloves. I unbuttoned my flannel and let it flap around me like wings. Kristi cheered louder and raised her arms. God, she was beautiful—big brown eyes, brown curls escaping her hat, the curve of her belly pressing hard against the buttons of her coat.

"Look out!" she shouted, pointing at me.

Too late, the Finn, accelerating more quickly than I would have guessed possible, tore up behind me, knocking me with the force of a train. I pitched, grunted, but stayed on my feet. His shoulder shoving into my back, he wrapped his arms around me, trying to push me down.

"Todd's open," Kristi yelled.

"How come you're only cheering for him," Stan yelled.

"How come you're only cheering for him," Mike repeated.

I could have thrown it to Todd, of course I could. But Stan was closer to the line. His jacket billowed around his tiny frame, his eyes flashed in his thin face. And though he was across the field, I swear to god I could feel his breath on my skin. That cold, cold breath.

"Stan," I shouted, and launched the ball.

A lot can happen in the time between a football's lift from a set of extended fingers to the moment it's cradled into the arms of another guy. An entire game can hinge on that moment, and it's your job, right then, to use it as a moment of clarity, illuminate the path. That's what my coach said, anyway, and it's a useful thing.

I called Stan's name. He lifted his arms. He ran.

Kristi screamed. A sound of anguish. She fell to her knees and clutched her middle.

The ball seemed to hang in the air.

"Stan," she moaned. "Oh, god."

The Finn let go, fell to his knees. Mike, Todd, and Lars froze in their tracks. Lars vomited onto the snow. It was red and thick like blood.

"I'm sorry," Todd called, wiping his eyes with his gloves. "I'm so, so sorry."

And, just like that, I *knew* things. A path to the end illuminated under the arc between thrower and catcher. I *knew* that the cold on my neck was Stan and not the wind. I knew that the baby in Kristi's belly was Stan's, that it was a girl and she would be just as sly, just as sardonic and off the grid like her dad. I knew that Lars and Todd would both die in detox within a year of one another, the Finn in a bar fight with a broken bottle to the neck. Mike would lose his memory, would spend the last fifteen years of his life not knowing his own kids. And just as I watched the beginnings of my own path, just as I saw a house by a pond and myself hauled in to a brig some-where between two soldiers that I thought were my friends, Stan caught the ball. The light went out and the illuminated arc vanished forever.

Kristi looked up again, trembling, but she kept her eyes on Stan, though her shoulders shook in sob after tight dry sob.

"Come home," she said, pressing her fingers to her lips.

Stan grinned. "Wish I could, baby," he said. Then, to me: "You shoulda come back more often," he chided. "Look at you, you're like the walking dead."

Mike, Todd, Lars, and the Finn all clapped their hands to their ears, and still, in quiet voices, they repeated Stan's words. "Walking dead," they murmured.

"I'm sorry," I said.

"I know," he said.

"I know," the others repeated.

"Me too," Stan said while the others mouthed along. Stan sighed, raised his face to the black and gray sky, his coat filling with wind, his pants flapping, then bulging like sails, until all of his clothes spun upwards in a sudden eddy and whipped out of sight. Only his boots remained.

Shaking madly, I grabbed my stuff and Stan's boots and headed for the truck. Kristi followed. The others turned, fanned into the street, walked away without looking at one another. I didn't call out to them. They didn't call back. The truck rumbled awake without the key, but I didn't falter. I drove out to Kristi's house, the memory of it like a map unfolding before my eyes, my hand on her belly. I felt the child kick and elbow and nudge in the dark. I could have sworn I felt her wink at me—Stan's eyes winking in their watery world. Kristi pressed her hands on top of mine: Life above, life below. The dead breathing life into the dead. I gasped, coughed, and breathed as the child walloped against my palm.

Goddamnit Stan, I thought, *we're alive.* I listened madly for the thump inside my own chest, each pulse nailing me again and again to the earth. And somewhere in that belly, I knew Stan's child was laughing.

Yes, moron, the child kicked back. *Alive.*

CHASING GAIA

GARRY KILWORTH

Garry Kilworth's most recent publications are Poems, Peoms and Other Atrocities *(Stanza Press), co-authored with Robert Holdstock;* The Fabulous Beast, *a collection of short horror, fantasy and science fiction stories (Infinity Plus Books); and a republication omnibus edition of* The Navigator Kings *trilogy (Gateway Omnibus/Gollancz). He is currently working on the first science fiction novel he has written for nearly 35 years, entitled* The Sometimes Spurious Travels through Time and Space of James Ovit. *Not surprisingly it's a time travel story in three parts—near future, distant future and middle-distant past. 'I might yet change the title to J. O. Goes,' he tells us . . . though we can't be sure as to the seriousness of that.*

H E CAME THROUGH THE GLOAMING OF THE PROSPERO evening, glancing over his left shoulder surreptitiously every few paces, making sure he wasn't being followed. He was a thin man, skinny as a lurcher. Pointed nose, sharp chin, and angular shoulders that lifted his ragged coat like the worn-down stubs of wings. I didn't know his name. You don't ask. The only question you want the answer to is: '*Have you got any?*' If the answer to that is '*No*' then you don't care what the hell his name is, you want nothing more to do with him. If the answer is '*Yes*' then all you're worried about is whether he's telling the truth. As he walked towards me through the murk which precedes a Prospero night—a planet with an air moisture content that fills and weights your lungs—the twilight clung to him as a misty, dark cloak the hem of which seemed to trail behind his brittle form.

When he got close, he grinned at me with long teeth.

'Waitin' long?' he asked.

'Bloody hours,' I replied, but not with any rancour. I was too anxious for that. 'Have you got it?'

He sneered. 'Course I got it. Wouldn't be here otherwise, would I?'

I stared at his bag.

'Let me see it!'

His expression changed in an instant. He gave me a baleful look.

'Think I'm lying?'

'No, no, of course not—but, you know, I'm just . . . '

That nasty grin again. 'Yeah, yeah. Desperate's the word, chaggy—desperate. Let me see the coin.'

I had my pay-pod in my hand, ready. I passed a finger over the surface and showed him a figure.

'All yours,' I said, 'but I need to see it first.'

'Still don't trust me, eh?'

'No—why should I?'

He shrugged the wing-stubs. 'No reason.'

The stuff he was selling me meant nothing to him personally. He had been born on Prospero. It was only those like me who needed it so very badly. There was no reason I should not have it, morally, except that much of it was radioactive. Cancer, especially of the bone, though curable, was still a horrible disease and governments, bless 'em, love to protect their citizens. So they had indeed made it illegal to garner, trade, or purchase the stuff.

Prospero was a wealthy planet, but probably not as affluent as AD2301 or even Lorca, both of which newly colonised worlds had precious minerals coming out of their pores. There were those on this particular planet with ships who were still willing to prospect for what the media had nicknamed *dirt*. To us, it was anything but dirt. It was the stuff that made a heaven out of a hell. It restored the soul to its rightful station. It was needed, necessary, absolutely essential. I would have given everything I own for a piece of dirt. Everything. In fact I was giving this snot of a prospector with his junkyard rattlecan of a ship almost half my life's savings. He was now showing me a chip of black rock the size of my thumbnail, still grinning that inane grin. I wanted to smash that stupid expression from his face, but I wanted that little diamond of gravel oh so much more. My emotional and spiritual wellbeing depended on a lump of grit.

'Is it real?' I asked. 'Are you sure it's real?'

'Garnered it myself,' he assured me, 'from the true fields.'

This desperate longing. This savage yearning.

I wanted so much to believe him. At last. At last. This feeling inside me: a heart raked and torn by steel claws; a deep black pit of a stomach; an unbearable ache in my spirit that was a physical pain—all this would soon hopefully be banished from my mind and body. I had suffered, was suffering, in a way that I never knew possible. If you dipped me naked in boiling tar, or stabbed me in a thousand places with a red-hot knife, or stripped my form clean of skin with razor, I would not have suffered as much. I was at the end of my tether.

The very end.

'Let me hold it in my hand,' I said.

His expression changed again.

'No. You want it, you pay for it. Otherwise, go home.'

'I *have* to feel it,' I cried. 'You surely must let me do that?'

Grimly, he replied, 'I hate mistrust. I won't deal with a man who don't trust me. I have my honour to think of.'

'Honour be damned!' I shouted. 'You're trying to cheat me.'

Instantly the dirt disappeared into the folds of his black bag.

'Right, that's it. I'm going.'

My soul screamed at me from somewhere deep within.

'No—no, wait. I'll ... are you sure? You say you're an honourable man, but are you sure it's the real stuff? Oh God,' I was weeping now, 'if it's not, I don't know what I'll do. Please?'

'Look, chag, I've already told you once—I got it from the fields. Now I can sell this anywhere, so if you ain't prepared to pay the price, then you can go and do the other thing ... '

I nodded quickly. Within the next few seconds he had half my total bank balance, and I had the dirt in my hand. Then he was gone, had melted into the murk as quickly and easily as he had emerged from it. There was going to be no refund here, if I was unhappy with the goods. It was done. The thing was done. I felt a mixture of elation and terror in my breast. Now it had to happen. Now I expected to be cured of the sickness that inhabits all Earthborn mortals. I stroked the dirt in my hand, the little black rock, in the way that the fairy tale Aladdin once stroked the magic lamp. Would it work? It had to work. Didn't he say he was an honourable man who hated having me impugn him? Hadn't he said he garnered this stone from the true fields? Surely, surely we were both made of the same flesh, blood, bone, and praiseworthy integrity? The same sincere principles?

Nothing. Nothing. Nothing.

Panic seared through the pain already lacerating my body and spirit.

No, no, he could not have been lying. He could not have been cheating me. Hadn't he seen the desperation in me? How could anyone see me and not feel pity, be moved by my terrible suffering? My plight had been evident in every gesture, every expression, every word that I uttered. A man would have to be a monster to cheat someone so distressed as me—surely, surely?

Yet—nothing.

'It needs time,' I said to no one and the night. 'It needs time to work. I'll sleep with it next to my heart. By morning I'll feel better. I'm sure to feel better in the morning. It just needs more time. This is the real thing, I'm certain of it.'

And so I went back to my sleep-pod and put the dirt in the locket I had purchased to contain it and wore the pendant to bed.

Of course I slept not a wink. I lay awake, one moment thinking it was working, the next devastated because clearly it was not. The whole night I was alternately filled with hope and wracked by doubt. In the morning—oh in that terrible dawn that swept over Prospero, filling this alien world with its disgusting orange light from its ugly sun, warming nothing, filling me with hate and anger, I knew that I had been sold a fake. I sobbed into my pillow, gripping the bed sheets so hard my fingers cramped within minutes. A fake. A fake. I wanted to kill the prospector. Hammer him to death with my fists. These fists that had not an iota of strength left in them. This cadaver drained of all but sorrow.

'Oh GOD!' I screamed, waking my neighbours. 'Let me die!'

'I wish you would,' floated back the voice from the next pod. 'I've wished that for a long time now, chag . . . '

Morning came, drab and unwholesome, the thick mists rolling off the inappropriately named Pacific Ocean. It was nothing like the original Pacific, its viscousness appearing cold and dense. It was also of a russet hue as far as one could see due to the ferrous deposits of the mountains around it, which drained their surface waters into its seas. There were no shades of blue or green or even grey. Only that colour reminiscent of dried blood.

However, colonialists tend to take familiar names with them and give them to their new homes. A fifth-generation Prosperoan was astonished to learn from me the other day that her Sierra Nevada was not the only mountain range ever to bear that title, that there had been at least two mountainous regions in the universe before hers that had been so called. Probably there were many more, on other planets, of which I had no knowledge. More than likely. As a race we are fairly predictable with our clichés. I dressed and dragged myself to my work. One has to live. One has to have food on the plate and a bed to sleep in, but more importantly coin coming in to save for that all-important purchase in some back alley.

I worked in a plant nursery. There are many tedious and soul-destroying jobs on Prospero, but this is not one of them. I like what I do most of the time, apart from one particular aspect, and that is tending the local flora. I find Prospero's waxy-leafed vegetation unwholesome to look at and its scents uninteresting. To my way of thinking, it cannot contend with the blooms, the flowers, the blossoms of the Old World. Those plants from my home planet breathe a perfume that, if I close my eyes, I am able to imagine myself elsewhere if only for a minute or two. There are roses of course, and chrysanthemums, lilac bushes, geraniums, wisteria, many more. However, although these flourish on Prospero, for some reason they all remain a fifth the size of those on Earth. It seems impossible to get them to grow any larger. So far as I'm aware, no one really knows why. The tiniest of daffodils, pygmy hollyhocks, dwarf laurels are all we can nurture to maturity.

Here, however, the local plants grow large, full-bodied, and lush. A sort of maroon and the weirdest strain of yellow are the most common colours. If I had to pick one amongst them that I did not totally despise it would be the spiked and lethal purple octopus flower, though one has to handle this plant with metal-lined gloves to be sure of doing so safely. The grey blossoms of the ornamental wolf-cowl and the insipid drizzle-creeper are popular with locals. But we off-worlders would have neither of these two in our gardens at any price. I find it unpalatable to have to tend them, though of course I must in order to keep my job. The very sight of their strange colours fills me with loathing and contempt. Why do the market gardeners even think that this sort of foliage can compare with the true plants? It is ludicrous. Naturally whenever possible I work on the 'Earth Plants'.

'No flowers for you today, Jakey,' said Cizce, my overseer. 'Today you work over there.'

I stared miserably in the direction he was pointing with a firm finger.

'Replanting?' I moaned, my stomach feeling as if I had eaten a lump of galena for breakfast. 'I hate replanting. And those things,' I pointed myself now at the auburn scree grasses which were propagated on the slopes of Tai Mo Shan above the tree line before replanting, 'have to be bedded in pongo shit.'

'Yes, that's true,' replied Cizce, without any emotion visible in his expression. 'That's your job today.'

Pongoes are khaki-coloured animals surprisingly similar to kangaroos, though they have no forelimbs or pouches. Their excrement provides the foulest-smelling manure known to life, though as a fertilizer it has no equal. Now I had to spend the rest of the day burying my hands in the stuff. And yes, their stupid name is directly connected to the powerful stench of their droppings.

When evening eventually came I was truly at my lowest ebb. My guts had been replaced by iron piping. My head swam with despair and my heart was being crushed by the strong claws of a demon. There was an overwhelming desire to scream into the faces of passers-by to relieve my suffering, to let them know my terrible state of mind. I left work and took a floater to Sissy's work-pod. Sissy earns as a clerk in import-export. She knows all the shippers, all the spacers, the merchants and the government captains. Sissy managed to purchase a piece of dirt over a year ago using her inside knowledge of those who travel the starways. Even so, she was cheated twice before getting the real thing. Now she was at least content, if not happy, living here on this godforsaken planet.

I found her alone in her pod, the workscreens around her covered with masses of symbols and figures.

'What do you want, Jake?' she asked, coldly.

'I've been conned,' I blurted. I had intended to lead into this admission slowly. 'A bastard pirate took half my money.'

She stopped what she was doing and stared at me sympathetically. After all, she had been one of us only a year ago. She had been one of the survivors of the war. A few thousand of us had managed to flee the destruction and get to another world and she was one of them. She too had huddled with the rest of us, comforting one another in our helpless state, talking of nothing but the terrible end of all and the eternal question of where to get a piece of dirt.

'Sissy . . . ' I said.

'No, Jake, no.'

'Just let me hold it for a moment, a minute. One minute. No more. I promise I'll give it straight back to you. I have to just have it for a minute.'

'It's getting too much, Jake. Too often. I told you last time.'

'Just this one more time. Please. My disappointment. You have no idea.'

'I do have an idea. I was there only a little while ago.'

'Then you know how I feel. You know what it's like. Sissy, please. Just a minute. You won't miss it for a minute, will you?'

'I will. I definitely will.'

'But—oh, Sissy. Be human. Where's your compassion? Where's your love for me? Sissy, I implore you,' I pleaded.

She stared into my eyes for a very long time. I knew they revealed the horrible pain in my soul. Eventually she reached up and unclipped her pendant. There was a moment's hesitation, as I knew there would be, for even taking it off for a moment was a wrench for any Earthborn human, then it was off and in my hand. I clasped it to my bosom. This may sound old-fashioned, but there are no other words for the action. Clasped. Bosom. And relief flooded through to deep inside my heart. Oh, the blessed relief from the Earth-sickness. It washed through my spirit cleansing it of the blackness, the depression, the agony. I pressed it there and closed my eyes and hoped it would last forever. Life and hope flooded through me filling me with light and warmth and the vestiges of happiness . . .

'Give it back!'

The voice seemed to come from the depths of the world.

'GIVE IT BACK!'

An order. A strident demand.

I ignored it.

Hands clawed at mine, peeling back fingers, forcing their way into the prison I had formed around the pendant with my flesh and bones.

Keeping hold of the locket with my left hand, pressing it close to my heart, I reached out with my right and grasped Sissy's throat. My eyes were wide open now as I gripped her, my fingers closing strongly on her windpipe. Given another hand I would have strangled her within minutes. Even so, she had to tear at my fingers with her own to get herself free. She fell backwards onto the floor, gasping, and I threw myself on top of her, pinning her arms with my knees. I felt vicious triumph surging through my veins. Her face was full of terror. I looked around for a weapon to kill her with. The pendant would be mine. Eternal contentment would be mine. The agony would be gone forever. All I had to do was crush her skull and take what I wanted, what I needed to make me whole again.

A knee came up and thudded into my spine. I fell sideways with a shrieked yell as a blinding pain crippled my efforts to keep her locked down. She was on her feet before I managed to find mine. Then a coffee mug crashed on my temple and the pendant was ripped from my grasp. I lay there stunned for some time and when I came to Sissy had a knife in her hand.

'Get out,' she hissed. 'Don't ever come back.'

I rubbed my skull, feeling ashamed of myself, but if I could have got that piece of dirt from around her neck I would still have tried. However, I knew she had me beaten. She was stronger than I was. For a whole year she had been healing and was now all but well again. I was weak in body and spirit. Weak, hopeless, helpless, and degenerated. Reduced to a walking collection of bones held together by a deteriorating life force. I was a hollow man and she was the complete woman. The winner of the contest had been determined before it had started.

I went straight from Sissy's to a bar. I wondered vaguely whether she would call the cops and report my attack. I really didn't care that much. Perhaps being incarcerated would put me in touch with criminals who actually knew how to get a piece of dirt? But then again, I didn't think she would turn me in. There was always that illegal locket she wore around her throat. If she reported me, then I could point the finger at her and neither of us would gain.

Did I feel ashamed of my behaviour? Yes, yes I did, but I knew I would do it again, given the chance. Presently I was the lowest form of human detritus. I would have sold my children for dirt, I would have impoverished my mother, I would have sent my father to his execution to further my desires. I hated myself. I loathed myself. But I knew I had to have what I needed. A lifetime without it was simply unthinkable. I could blame my condition for my behaviour, but I was not even interested in absolving myself. I had only one goal in mind.

'Lava,' I told the barwoman. 'Two slugs.'

She looked right through me, uninterested in my obvious despair, but the slugs went onto the bar. I threw one back, then the second, then ordered two more. These I took to a table in the corner, from where I could watch people coming and going. There was always the chance

I would see that fucking weasel who had cheated me the previous evening. I couldn't report him and I doubted whether I'd get my coin back, but I was in the mood to kick the guts out of him. It would change nothing for the better and probably make matters worse, but such a thing would lift my spirits just a notch for a few moments, allowing me to forget for a few minutes that I was about the most abject creature on Prospero.

The drinks went down, one after the other, and by late evening I was feeling a little better. The reason for that was that I was out of my brains. I knew if I stood up I would fall crashing to the ground again. So I sat there and yelled at the bar's other customers, sneering, jibing, calling them names. Most of them ignored me, realising the state I was in was not just down to drink, but went much deeper. Then after I had insulted a young woman, her escort got up and punched me on the temple and I knew nothing more until the auto-cleaner pushed my inert body, sliding it over the wet, sticky, filthy floor and out onto the boardwalk.

When I was back on my feet again it was very early morning. I staggered off, stinking of sweat and lava. There were three of Prospero's seven moons visible. I glared up at them in hatred. This was not my world. My world, my home planet beloved Earth, had been blown to fragments in a war with the colonies. Colonial planets had grown in power even as Earth weakened, its resources running out as others revealed their bountiful mineral treasures. Yet as always in these things, Earth had remained firm in its belief in its superiority. It insisted on continuing to exploit its colony worlds, stripping them of their riches without reference to newly established independent governments.

A war was inevitable and thus Earth was responsible for its own destruction. It could have pleaded poverty and it would have been helped, but old pride would not allow it to bow its head. It demanded instead of requested. It took without asking. It sent armed ships to rip the wealth from colonial territories. It suffered the consequences of all ancient powers that have faded while its people failed to recognise that their time was over and new and stronger ones have arisen.

Those of us who managed to leave before the last devastating attack on the planet of my birth, are now cursed with a homesickness that is so debilitating it eats a person's spirit. It gnaws on it day by day until there is nothing left to devour. There is no full cure. Earth has gone. If a man immigrates to a new country, and suffers such pangs, there is always hope he may be able to return to his homeland. But if that homeland no longer exists, the hope too ceases to survive. There is nothing but a blank space, a vacuum, where the heart should be.

Then it was discovered that pieces of Earth, gathered from the dust cloud that continues to expand away from the blast area, ease the agony of the feeling of loss. Chips that are weak enough in radioactivity to be safe, for most of the Old World is deadly with the poison that nuclear weapons leave in their wake. Thankfully there are small bits that are clean enough to wear close to the heart. They work. Whether psychological or actual, none of us really care. The miracle seems to work and therefore does work. The pain is muted and one can at least attempt to live a normal life again. This is all we can hope for now. There will never be a return to the world of our birth, the place where our ancestors rose from life-giving oceans, from its rocks and sand, from its fertile plains and mountains. The blood and bone of my forefathers, my grandmothers, were fashioned from Earth's dust and that connection is buried deep in my own anatomy.

Those born on the new worlds have fresh roots. They have been shaped from a different mud beneath different skies with different stars. They are a bright, vital people, a people without a history, without a strong link to the Old World. They suffer no uns: no unnameable, unmanageable, unbearable longings as we do. They feel no bereavement. They walk with misplaced confidence, ignorant of their own immaturity and callowness. They look at us without pity and sneer at our vulnerability. They have an unshaken belief in their destiny, which they feel is to be the masters of that infinite wilderness that is the universe.

I seek those others of my ilk who gather on a wasteland outside the city: a pathetic group who come together for shreds of comfort.

One of them greets me.

'Jake, how are you?'

'Bad,' I say. 'You?'

'Worse.'

'Hear anything?'

'There was talk of a chag, out on the limits. They say he has a piece, but who knows, you hear things all the time.'

Hope surged through my veins like a drug.

'You know a man?'

'Yeah, but I got no money.'

There's no reason why two people can't share a piece of dirt, if it's large enough to divide it.

'I've got money,' I say. 'If you've got the man.'

We look each other with eyes that once shared a familiar and beautiful sun.

ENDPAPERS

LISA L. HANNETT

Lisa L. Hannett confides, 'The seeds for "Endpapers" were found between the yellowed pages of a second-hand Penguin edition of Lady Chatterley's Lover. *Books, like people, change with each encounter, with each touch; they are ephemeral, full of emotion, but also tactile, best enjoyed while being held close. Reading this worn, creased, fall-apart-in-your-hands book—with its story about yearning and loss and frustration and self-indulgence and inequity—I couldn't help but think about all of the other hands that had touched the pages I was holding. How had these other readers come across this particular volume? What were they looking for between its covers? Who were these people, whose eye-prints were stamped all over the words I was now looking at? Why did they eventually pass this novel along? The ghosts of these other readers were flitting around the object I'd bought for two dollars at a library sale; a few of them materialised in this story.'*

Lisa has had over 50 stories appearing in venues including Clarkesworld, Fantasy, Weird Tales, ChiZine, *the* Year's Best Australian Fantasy and Horror *(2010, 2011 & 2012), and* Imaginarium: Best Canadian Speculative Writing *(2012 & 2013). She has won three Aurealis Awards, including Best Collection 2011 for her first book,* Bluegrass Symphony, *which was also nominated for a World Fantasy Award. Her first novel,* Lament for the Afterlife, *is being published by CZP in 2015. You can find her online at* http://lisahannett.com *and on Twitter @LisaLHannett.*

WHEN THEY FIRST MEET, HER NAME IS EMMA. NOT *that* Emma. She'll never be a Woodhouse, a quick-talking Regency ninny. She doesn't care for balls or comedic endings: there'll be no conniving for a husband on her part. Instead, she gravitates towards darker stories, in which protagonists are unhappily married. These tales distract her from herself. From the tedium of being so plain. So overlooked. So pathetically lonely. There's a Gallic cast to this Emma's dark eyes, her accent, her high-collared black dress. *This* Emma is romantic, tragic, miserably bored. She seethes with crimson rage. She is, in other words, pure nineteenth-century, realist, French.

For now, he answers to Jude.

'Charles!' she cries upon seeing him, heart leaping. What is he doing here in Rouen? Has he discovered her affair with Léon? She stops short on the quayside in front of the Hôtel de Boulogne. Sea breezes carry the sound of caulkers' mallets hammering against docked ships. The wind tastes of salt and anticipation.

Upon seeing Emma, Jude immediately shouts, 'My dear Sue!'

He isn't in Rouen at all: he's only recently left the hamlet of Marygreen and is now strolling down cobbled streets in the college town of Christminster. A symphony of bells calls him to his beloved books. His soul brims: at last, he has reached his intellectual Mecca. Jude is slender from poverty yet strong enough to carry two bucketloads of water at once. He is old enough to study—but otherwise his appearance isn't quite clear. The author has rendered Jude's mind sharply; his emotions are agonisingly vibrant. But Jude has lived this life for several chapters, and still his looks are a bit of a mystery. Perhaps that's why Sue has mistaken him for someone else. And it's been a while since he's seen her.

The lovers meet downtown in winter, on a pedestrian bridge midway between the university and a shopping megamall, a concrete monster of 1980s commercial architecture. Emma stands at the centre of a twenty-foot bubble of Flaubert's France, Jude in six feet of socio-historical England. For her, it is dusk. For him, noon. Real life, such as it is, flits in their peripheral vision, grey shadows against the bright colours of their stories. Both clutch open books in their right hands.

Emma hasn't met a fellow bibliophile since she broke up with Vronksy, the asshole, after he got bored with her version of Anna and transformed into the Marquis de Sade. However, until this moment, Jude has believed he was the only one. It just makes sense, he figures, that he'd be alone in this. In high school everyone said he was a freak. A loner. A loser. Why should this be any different?

Love, he's discovered, is an affliction transmitted by paperback classics.

Penguins, mostly. But, really, any old novel works. The ones he finds in two-dollar bins. Library books, with thousands of other people's eyeprints soiling the pages. Salvation Army finds. The cheaper, the more tattered, the better. The oil of humanity helps him to slink from book to book. It makes him feel connected to them all, even when he's alone.

'Sue,' he says again, though he's now sure it isn't her. 'I've missed you.'

When they get close enough to see each other properly their individual worlds sizzle around the edges. Electricity snaps and hums overhead as their spheres send out tendrils of lightning, threads that crackle as they knit together. Outside, the dreary grey of their other lives, their humdrum other selves, seems unimportant. Snow falls out there, but inside it remains summer. Half twilight, half the glorious height of midday.

They take this as a good sign.

Oliver spends his whole life in the library. Not literally, of course. His family has a house in the suburbs, a bungalow with extra-wide doors and ramps leading up from the driveway. Oliver was only four when they were installed. For about a week he'd thought they were awesome. Day after day, he'd lined up his Hot Wheels on the landing, then raced them down to the freshly paved lane. Gravity and clumsiness worked against him: he never beat the cars to the bottom. But, man, did he ever love trying.

That changed after his father came home.

You'll never make it, Oliver's dad had said, watching from the car, all torso and pant legs tied in knots at his thighs. *Last time I ran was the fastest a man can possibly go. And even it wasn't fast enough.*

Twelve years later, Oliver still doesn't quite know how to act around his dad. He's too young to drink, too grown-up to watch the old man get sloshed. The living room is always dim, suffocating with the stench of stale sweat and ash. Oliver can't just sit there night after night in front of the TV. Pretending things are normal. Silent whenever his dad talks about Kuwait, silent whenever he doesn't. No matter what he does, the war is always there. The greatest absence between them. Ghost limbs dangling over the edge of a wheelchair.

His dad never reads and the library's public ramps are a bit too narrow—it's a bitch getting his chair in off the street. Last summer, Oliver showed up so often that Mrs Cleary decided he might as well get paid to be there. *I'm the acquisitions officer. Who says all I acquire must be paper?*

Besides, she still says with a grin, the boy literally knows most of the books inside out. Literally.

Oliver collects endpapers. Antique or modern, handmade or mass-produced. If a book's bindings are shot, he'll dissect its carcass and save the precious inserts. Otherwise, he carefully places them facedown on the office Xerox and colour-photocopies them. Then he catalogues them. Makes notes. Glues the sheets in a leather-bound book his mom bought from a shop in the markets, which only sells expensive stationery that's shipped in from Florence.

He loves when there are bookplates: *ex libris*, whoever. When there are inscriptions, price tags, watermarks. He has the entire Everyman series with its comforting epigraph, its Art Nouveau swirls, and the robed woman who looks just like Mary (except she's carrying lilies instead of baby Jesus). Marbling is an endpaper wonder, manufactured in so many ways, using so many colours. It makes up more than half of his collection. His detailed descriptions accompany each one, written in pencil on white cards, slipped between each page.

1830, English: grey vacuoles floating among yellow, navy, raspberry ribosomes. 1735, French: Catherine Wheels of colour, captured mid-whirl, cream, burgundy, and periwinkle. (Oliver adores the word 'periwinkle'. This is something else he can't tell his father.) *1880, France: blood-red spattered with white, swirling down a vortex, a drain leading to the sewage plant that processes wasted words.*

Some patterns are combed like bad TV reception, colours jittering up and down the page. Others are spiky pastel waves, optical illusions like those 3D pictures they sell at the mall before Christmas. (He bought one, once, and hung it in the rec room. Sitting in his wheelchair, cold beer in hand, his dad stares at it when he thinks nobody's looking. Oliver doesn't know what he sees there. Probably not just a shark.) He's got Golden Books scenes, published when his mom was a kid. Tropical jungles in fuzzy watercolour, styled after Gauguin (he looked up the artist, wrote it down in the margin.) And though he likes the abstract ones best, he has one layout depicting a soldier dressed in khakis, wearing a kettledrum helmet, belly-crawling over long blue grass. A comic book explosion hangs in the sky like the Star of Bethlehem. A German shepherd cowers beneath its light. Oliver keeps this set a secret.

It's the potential of endpapers that he loves. Whether a book is being opened or closed, as soon as there's endpaper you know a new tale is only a flick of leather or cardboard away. Mottled paper pasted to covers: a wonderful, perpetual transition. One narrative ends, another begins. It's an endless promise of something better. Something solid, steadfast, secure.

By the end of the day, Jude and Emma have been together for months. They've kept their books open, their stories progressing in the background. Time passes without their involvement. They talk without having to avoid spouses or arrange clandestine meetings. It's nice, they think, one chatting sleepily in France, the other wide awake in England. It's a relief talking to someone who understands. Who intimately knows the trials of a modern bibliophile.

Things like only reading dead authors. It's too hard to channel pure story when its creator still lives; with each interview, each public appearance, each Tweet, authors have the chance to explain their intentions. To direct. To change their books' meaning. And when, inevitably, they reveal all, horrifying sensations course through the bibliophile's body. Insecurity, lust, adrenaline, foreign blood cells, hives . . . An allergic reaction brought on by narrative prescription.

There was so much more room to interpret, they agreed, without an author's opinions to spoil it all.

Jude reaches for Emma's hand as the bell tower in Christminster strikes twelve.

She turns her back to the Hôtel de Boulogne. A single light shines from an upper-storey window, its yellow merging with dawn's warm glow. But Jude has her full attention.

'Would you mind being Sue, at least for a while?' Long before he was Jude, before he'd loved books so much he became Wilfred Ivanhoe, the last Saxon in twelfth-century England, he had read Emma's story. 'It won't end well for either of us,' he explains, 'if I join you in Rouen.' Sunrise gilds the harbour behind her, the moored vessels with their proud masts swaying with the incoming tide. Seagulls cry mournfully. Fishermen's dogs yelp on smooth decks. Medallions of oil gleam on the water's ever-changing surface. Jude is tempted to step into her world, arsenic be damned. But, no. No. He's pined for academia. He's earned it. And now that Arabella is gone . . .

Emma considers his offer. Her relationship with Léon is fledgling: she isn't obsessed with him yet. Jude, though. He's angsty. Melancholy. Poten-

tially brooding. It's an attractive prospect. Being this Sue character might
be fun. At least, she's bound to be happier than Emma. And after suffering
months of cloying Parisian smog, a bit of clean rural air would suit her
just fine.

'Bien sûr,' she says.

They walk to the public library together. Jude mentions he'll meet her in
the stacks once she's changed. He'll be with Plato, Xenophon, and Aristo-
phanes, he says, already distracted. Emma waves him away with a pang of
irrational fear. She hopes she'll be able to find him again. That she'll recognise him when Emma is gone.

In France, the *Returns* chute hides in dense fog between a boulangerie
and a horse-drawn landaulet. Quickly, she ducks around the carriage and
drops the novel in. Salty sea air, screeching gulls, the melody of continental
voices fade away. Petticoats evaporate, Rouen disappears. Back in the city,
bus hydraulics exhale in loud bursts. A cacophony of university students
piles off, lugging backpacks and stress, debating in many languages. Car
tires hiss along wet pavement. The world is muffled, mittened, tuqued. For
a few minutes, she's back in jeans and a t-shirt, wrapped in a ski jacket.
Her feet relax in scuffed runners, blisters throbbing from Emma's dainty
heels.

Immediately, she feels small. Invisible.

Her soles squeak on the chequered tiles as she dashes across the lobby,
eyes locked on the stairs. The cold brass railing feels almost warm beneath
her freezing palm. Her hands don't stop shaking until they've got hold of a
dog-eared Hardy.

Oliver watches Classics Girl as he pretends to weed out-dated flyers from
the library's noticeboard. It's been a few months since he's seen her, even
though he swings past *800 > Literature* once or twice a shift, just in case
she's there. Lately, theatre students and goths and nerds from the SCA
have colonised the section. Several times a week they're up there, dressed
in wild costumes, lounging on club chairs, deciding what to read next.
Oliver has started to wonder if they've chased Classics Girl off, it's been so
long. Either that, he thinks glumly, or she's gone off to college. It wouldn't
surprise him. She's a couple years older, obviously smart. No doubt she's
got a scholarship. He bets she's off studying something cool in Paris or
London or Rome.

Still, he visits the 800s regularly. Force of habit, he tells himself, climbing the stairs. Besides, there are books to be shelved . . . But his stomach always sinks a little when he turns the corner and finds all the reading chairs empty.

Now she's standing to his left at the borrowing station, beeping and beeping and beeping her card over the scanner, muttering under her breath. He can see she's holding it the wrong way. It would be so easy to tell her—she's standing right there—but his brain is working too fast, his mouth too slow, and suddenly he's all out of words. Throughout his body, Oliver's nerves ping like xylophone scales. Tentative, feeble jolts of energy run up and down his limbs. An ache in his gut tells him that now's his chance: go over, talk to her, say something nonchalant. *That machine always acts up.* Take the card and scan it so she won't notice her mistake. Chat about her book. Be cool.

One by one, he pries thumbtacks out, then thunks them back into the corkboard.

'Excuse me,' Classics Girl says. 'Is this thing broken? I can't get it to work . . . '

A hot flush creeps up Oliver's neck. He turns to look at her and his tongue seizes. She looks like she's about to cry.

'This, uh,' he says, praying he doesn't trip as he walks over. *This machine always acts up.* 'It's your card.'

'But I just used it the other day.' Her tone is defensive, high-pitched. 'I've never had any problems with it.'

She used it the other day . . .

'No,' he says, blushing. He fumbles the card from her hand. 'It's upside down.'

'Oh.' She takes it back before Oliver can catch her name. 'I'm such an idiot.'

'Idiots don't read books like these,' he says quickly, picking up the paperback, reading the title. She gives him a timid smile as her card registers properly.

A smile!

'You should see the first edition,' his mouth says, all encouraged, while his brain screams at him to shut up. 'The UK imprint, not the American. 1896. Bound in green leather, gilt-edged pages, with streaked marbling that looks like rampant seahorses.' The words trail off as he sees Classic Girl's expression: she's looking at him like he's Rain Man or something. 'It's really . . . um . . . nice.'

'I'll have to check it out one day,' she says. Oliver nods and leaves it at that. He knows she's only humouring him. *I'll have to check it out . . .* The phrase is meaningless. Overused.

He's heard it a million times.

After a few days, Sue has had enough of Jude's story.

She feels anxious all the time, guilty, like she's betraying everyone just by loving him. Meanwhile Jude is rapidly losing interest in his studies, which is disappointing. He's agonised over it for years; he's sacrificed so much. And she enjoyed hearing him discuss great philosophers. But now he's getting boring. He's not as charming as he once was, not as mysterious. When she looks at him, she can't help but superimpose wrinkles and sun damage and a head full of grey. Without knowing it, he ages right before her eyes. Future Jude isn't Byronic and sexy, he's bitter and jaded. A horrible, regretful old man. Sue can't get the image of his saggy, depressed face out of her mind. It's ruined young Jude entirely.

Plus, he's obsessed with sex. As Emma, she probably would've slept with him within a day. But as Sue, things are . . . trickier. For one thing, they're cousins. This completely grosses her twenty-first-century self out. What's worse, lately her thoughts have been turning to God. In real life, Sue is an atheist. But the longer she stays in Jude's England, the less she wants to be touched, the more she wants to go to church. It's unsettling.

'Let's go back to the library,' she suggests, shrugging off Jude's advances.

At first, Jude resists. Clearly, he thinks, he's chosen the wrong girl. He wonders if Arabella might be willing to give him another chance . . . But wooing his ex-wife will take too long, and what with Sue acting so frigid . . . His blue balls seriously need attention. Soon.

A trip to the library, indeed.

At the end of each day, Oliver patrols the floors to clear everyone out before Mrs Cleary sets the alarm. Security cameras will spot any hangers-on, of course, but Oliver likes the ritual. First stop, the carrels, to wake the graduate students. Then switch off the microfiche viewers. Log out computers. File the periodicals while saying goodnight to the old folks who drop in every afternoon (to read the papers, they say, but Oliver knows they come for the company). Ignore the mess in Children's until tomorrow. Make sure no one is stuck in the bathroom. Row by row, floor by floor, he puts the library to bed.

He always leaves Literature until last in case Classics Girl shows. She hasn't been back since Tuesday, and tonight is no different. Instead, he rounds the corner and finds a young couple fucking at the end of row 810—813.52.

Oliver catches a glimpse of the book in the girl's bobbling hand.

Wharton.

From the look of her elaborate Victorian dress, her pale skin and dark hair, she's got to be a goth. She's thin and light: her boyfriend is nailing her against the wall, her skirts pooling, spilling down the bricks. The guy, on the other hand, is some kind of vintage hipster. Nineteen-thirties artsy. He's wearing round tortoise-shell glasses, a fedora, a thick-striped tie loosened over a white shirt. His belt clinks against the wall with every thrust; the waistband of his grey slacks steadily inches down his thighs. His suit jacket lies forgotten on the floor.

'We're changing the story, Newland,' Goth Girl says, eyes closed, hips gyrating, 'we're changing the story'—but Hipster's lost in his own little world. Grunting, he calls her Tania, his muse. He licks her neck and talks about using his six-inch bone to smooth the wrinkles from her cu—

Oliver trips over his feet in his hurry to get out of there. He slams into the wooden shelf on his right, but keeps going, not looking back. Security will take care of them, he thinks, if they're not finished by closing. Racing down the stairs to the front desk, he hopes to God the cameras didn't see him watching.

'What about this one?'

Miller tosses her a well-thumbed red and white paperback: Oxford Classic this time. There's an old lady wearing a fur coat painted on the front—but surely, he thinks, she's got to be young at some point in the story.

Now that he's blown his load, he realises his girlfriend is no Tania. Her hair isn't falling in promiscuous tresses. She doesn't inspire him to write poems. She doesn't belong in the Villa Borghese. She doesn't even belong in Paris.

Her hair is worn in close curls around her temples, held in place with a diamond band. She's adjusting her dark-blue velvet gown, which is worn in a theatrical, classical way, bound up beneath her breasts and fastened with an old-fashioned clasp. Elbow-length gloves, eagle-feathered fan, mother-of-pearl lorgnettes all point to an evening spent at the opera. Behind her, red curtains drape heavily over Mrs Mingott's theatre box. The gaslights are dimmed to keep the concertgoers' obscene wealth from appearing garish. Over the murmur of conversation, he can hear the orchestra tuning up to the oboe's A.

New York, he thinks. We could have dinner with the Rockefellers . . .

For a minute he wishes he hadn't just offered her London.

He is overwhelmed at the sight of Countess Olenska—but he knows, without even having to read the book, that this particular girl will never be his. Without crossing into her world, he foresees a lifetime of sending yellow roses. Yellow for friendship. Not red for romance.

Fuck that. Already frustration builds in his groin, though his cock is still damp from being inside her. *Repression drives all these relationships. Self-imposed restrictions, convoluted plot twists, strict sentences, strict mores, strict rules . . .* It's time for the pleasures of modernity. Miller's book was good for a lay, a nice change of pace. But what he really wants is something with a bit more style, a lot more flow . . . Forget rigid points of view, rigid chapters. He is, after all, a product of his generation: he can keep twelve tabs running on his web browser, respond to email, read online articles, and have three books on the go all at the same time. He is stream of consciousness personified.

Woolf it is.

Ellen takes the novel from his outstretched hand. Instantly, her edges blur. Nineteenth-century New York drops away, replaced by the rush of traffic. Planes stream long white tails overhead. Red double-decker buses teeter through roundabouts. A huge ship of a car moors by the curb at 10 Downing Street. Ellen's hands wrinkle, her face spots with age. The hem of her skirt lifts above the ankle. Now the fabric is lighter, pleated, and there's much less of it. Whalebone stays dissolve into low-waisted cotton. A jaunty sailor's ribbon loops around a Peter Pan collar, appropriate for a woman of her advanced years. She reads a few paragraphs. The circle of her arms immediately fills with two dozen roses in full bloom.

Not yellow, Miller hopes—but, no. These are multi-coloured. Definitely more red than yellow.

'What a lark! What a plunge!' Mrs Dalloway says, then claps a hand over her mouth and throws the book to the floor.

'No,' she says, her aged voice returning to a more youthful octave. 'If I'm Clarissa, then you are either Peter or Septimus.' She shakes her head vehemently. 'No, my love. There will be no leaden circles of time, no ticking clocks for us. I know this one too well. And I refuse to admire your suicide.'

He stops and looks at the pretty girl materialising before him. Jeans and t-shirt, mousey blonde hair pulled back in a messy bun, turquoise glasses that are slightly too large for her pixie face. Halfway between shifts, he feels like a stranger. He's much too old for her at the moment.

'Who are you?' he asks, trying to remember which version of her he loves best. 'What's your name?'

The girl winks and slips around the shelf, into the next row. Walking silently, she runs a finger across the books' dusty spines. Fluorescent lights hum overhead, drowning out the sound of her breathing. After skipping a few bays, backtracking, starting the row anew, she finally plucks a slender volume from the shelf and reads the back cover. The boy never bothers with blurbs; they give too much away in advance.

Hurry, he thinks, feeling less and less like Henry Miller by the second. The fedora is gone, as are his wingtips. Skinny jeans sheathe his skinnier legs. He doesn't care which book she chooses, he just wants her to decide. Tangled curls flop over his forehead. A silver labret pierces his lower lip. His heart palpitates, and he's sure if he speaks his voice will crack.

She smiles at him through the open shelves. He holds her gaze, folding his arms so she won't see his tattoos, his scars.

'Call me Daisy,' she says.

'Happy birthday, Ollie,' says Mrs Cleary.

The present she hands him is perfectly wrapped; its paper is taut, corners folded with razor-edge precision. He accepts it gratefully, a bit flustered. Still unable to look her in the eye. She's been acting odd ever since Mr Valetka showed her the library's security tapes from the other night. Top floor, Literature. Two kids screwing each other's brains out.

How could you have missed them, Oliver?

He had turned beet red, mumbled excuses. Mr Valetka said the couple had stayed up there for hours afterwards, laughing and drinking mint juleps. *Probably some soldier come home from Iraq*, he'd declared, pronouncing the country's name the way Oliver hated. *Eye-rack*. Reports had been written: nothing was missing. *They learn a whole set of different rules over there* . . . The security guard seemed happy to leave it at that. But for days Oliver has been sure Mrs Cleary is going to fire him. She even called his mom, more than once, when she thought he was off having lunch. And yesterday she hired a new kid, some jerkwad named Good-fellow.

'Thank you,' he breathes, unwrapping a new Florentine scrapbook, twin to the one he's nearly filled. 'Thank you so much.'

'Oh, it's nothing,' she says, scrunching the torn paper into a tiny ball, knuckles cracking. 'A little birdie told me you might like it, so . . . ' She shrugs, but looks pretty pleased with herself. 'There's cake in the fridge, if you want some. It's chocolate.'

Oliver blinks repeatedly and swallows hard. He feels an overwhelming urge to hug good old Mrs Cleary, but doesn't act on it. No use spoiling the moment.

'I can't fill up,' he says, the words coming out ragged, raspy. 'Family dinner tonight. Mom's working a bit late so Dad's coming to pick me up.'

Mrs Cleary raises her eyebrows.

Oliver snorts. 'Don't worry, I won't get used to it.'

'Well,' she replies, looking down, picking at an invisible piece of tape. 'Make sure you have some cake.'

On his break, Oliver wheels a wooden trolley out back and uses it as his workstation. The bottom shelf is exactly the right height for a footrest, the top just tall enough to use as a table without having to hunch too badly. He places his old notebook flat and fills its penultimate pages with his favourite endpaper set. Nineteen forty-six, Chagall. It's a simple pen-and-ink sketch, thin lines on a cream-coloured ground. A man with a wealth of black curls, brimmed hat, long-sleeved shirt, and patchwork pants (actually, Oscar corrects, it's camouflage) leaps towards the right margin. His right arm proudly raised, legs extended in forward splits. It almost looks like he's clearing a transparent hurdle. He's launching himself into space.

The man looks so content, so determined, even though his front leg is missing from the knee down. His back leg is long but nearly footless. There's a large gap in his shoulder and he's got six or seven fingers on his left hand. But still, this man is on the move. He's bounding off the edge, into the unknown. Flying into the future. On the left-hand side, scrawled along the diagonal, is the word ВПЕР. It's Russian (Oliver checked) for "fixed his".

Fixed his what? Is the man travelling to the book in which he's made whole? Or has he already been saved, repaired, sent back home? Is he jumping for joy simply because he's alive? Oliver wished he knew, but the story doesn't provide any answers. He'll never learn to speak Russian.

When they fight, as they do at least once an hour, their stories continue independently. They *almost* forget each other, sometimes, but never completely. A hollowness aches in their chests when they're apart. A niggling in their minds, like a half-remembered word caught on the tips of their tongues.

It bugs him that Daisy knows his previous name. She shouldn't, but she does. She knows his history as well as he does; she reads twice as quickly. He kisses her plenty to keep her mouth shut, but still her tongue wags. No one else calls him James to his face. Few call him Jay. She shouldn't be able to either.

The summer people all think he's great, despite his lies. They come to his parties and address him only by his chosen surname. Never the real one, no. Never Gatz. He shudders to think of it. Four guttural letters, poor harsh letters, money-hungry and cruel. Fit for a broke man in North Dakota. A man forced to work as a janitor to pay his way through school. Not the name of Long Island elite.

But thanks to the addition of an arbitrary suffix, a simple 'by', this pauper suddenly sounds posh. Old money. Now the curl in his hair has fallen to his upper lip. He's slick, sardonic, at home in the Hamptons. At once more introspective and more shallow than he's ever been between books. If only this novel was longer. . .

Daisy tires of the period before he does. She loves the clothes—Jay cuts a fine figure in flannel suits, open-collared and slouch-shouldered. He's alluringly stooped, all the secrets of his past adding a sexy curve to his spine. Together they sip bowls of champagne and mock everyone around them. It's incredibly liberating. Also freeing are her flat chest, her slender boyish hips, the stylish bob haircut and loose chains of pearls. She's never moved like this. Never danced so well. There's no tangible reason for her discontent.

And yet.

She feels that any minute now some random Tom will be there, claiming she's his wife. Revving car engines turn her stomach. Long Island billboards stare at her constantly with their oversized, watchful eyes. Plus she's simpering when Jay is around, weak when he's not. Her bright red lips produce a childish voice. A pathetic wisp of speech.

For once, she'd like to be confident.

Today is their anniversary: they've been together for a week of years. Daisy goes to the bookshop to buy Jay a gift to mark the occasion. To entice him into a new role.

At first, she considers an encyclopaedia. Beautifully illustrated, folio edition, content spanning the history of civilisation. Think of all the lives they could lead! Millennia without ageing a day. But she worries they'll get lost somewhere between Babylon and Xanadu. She's afraid the form-lessness of life won't be strong enough to sustain them. What they need is fiction, pure and simple. They've shared so much already, she thinks, browsing the $9.95 pocket Penguins. And through it all she has loved him, in her many ways. She just needs the right story to prove it . . .

Constance, Daisy thinks. Constance is who I should be.

Let's face it, she imagines telling Jay: Daisy is a drip. I mean, look at me. Dressed in flapper beads in midwinter. I have never been so fucking cold.

Connie, though. Connie has a brain. Connie can hold a conversation. Connie is like Emma—Daisy had really liked being Emma—but without the whole decline into madness part, the whole urge to chow down on arsenic.

Daisy buys a special edition. It's Lawrence, she tells herself, justifying the outlay. Fabric dust jacket designed by Paul Smith. A wedge of purple and blue forget-me-nots embroidered on the simple white cover, a stylistic representation of a woman's thatch. The book costs almost three hundred bucks after tax.

It's riddled with sex scenes, Daisy reminds herself. It's practically porn.

Jay's bound to like it enough to leave West Egg behind.

She reads several chapters on the train. Around her, stiff vinyl seats and crusty handrails transform into carved oak furniture, heavy and masculine, the smoking room in a grand mansion. She wears layers, wool, boots designed for trekking across the forested grounds of her husband's estate. Now this, she thinks, warming her hands by the hearth, I could get used to.

'It's only two years' difference,' Constance says, handing Jay the parcel. 'I think it'll be good for us.'

He examines the book as he would a slab of lard.

'It's just . . . ' Jay adores 1926. He fixates on the fast cars, the beach house, the fucking green light flashing on the dock across the lake. He says Constance looks better as Daisy. Her skirt hangs awkwardly now in a way it hadn't this morning.

'But look how loose it is,' she says, hiking the sheath up around her waist, wearing nothing underneath.

The gesture causes a welcome stir.

Jay agrees to skim the first chapter. By the time he's reached the next one, his hard-on has softened. Suddenly he's Clifford, sitting in a wheelchair, expounding on the life of the mind. The purity of the body. The foolishness of World War I. He's dressed in tweed, his hair a helmet of pomade. His accent is affected, words enunciated quietly and with a slight lisp. Connie is forced to lean closer, to come to him. Already she feels used to such manipulations. She learns how to outmanoeuvre him.

Together they observe the ridiculousness in everything: war, the global financial crisis, the high cost of books in Australia. Out of nowhere, Clifford claims he'll be a writer. What's more, he'll write stories that matter. Everything else is just so ridiculous.

'Skip ahead,' says Connie. 'Get to the parts with the gamekeeper. You'll prefer being him. Trust me.'

As usual, Clifford believes Connie. He does as he's told.

A simple wooden hut sprouts in a forest that fills the living room from couch to kitchen. Pheasants cluck in a coop in the clearing. The air is spiced with autumnal scents. Wet loam, warm pine, wild gorse. Leaves are withering, the undergrowth sparkling gold and ruby with decay. It's all so familiar. Constance has been here many, many times. The gamekeeper's dog snuffles outside. His tail thumps against the door as he spins once, twice, then settles down on the hempen mat to wait for his master. He will bark if anyone approaches.

Connie looks around the hut, breathes deep. This is more like it, she thinks, almost convincing herself. There is no pretension here. No posturing. No civilisation. It's all muted. The promise of life, the spectre of death. Everything is as it should be. She doesn't suddenly feel at one with nature; she won't be bare-breasted and dancing around a pagan bonfire anytime soon. But in the gamekeeper's world, she is visceral. Uncontrolled. Exposed.

If Lady Constance can't feel pleasure here, she fears she never will.

Shivering, she lies on a rough blanket on the dirty floor. With legs and heart and eyes wide open, she invites Mellors to join her.

'Have a good time, Ollie,' says Mrs Cleary, waving without looking up from the computer.

Oliver rifles through the late slips and binders on the front desk, shifts piles of books, doesn't put them back. His empty backpack is unzipped, slung over his shoulder. The library is open for another hour, but he's arranged to get off early. Traffic is a nightmare at closing time and his dad hasn't driven in ages.

He should be out there already, waiting on the sidewalk. It's easier if he's ready to hop into the car. It's faster.

You'll never make it . . .

'Mrs Cleary,' he says, lifting his gaze every two seconds to see if the station wagon has pulled up out front. 'Have you seen my collection?'

'It's on your trolley, isn't it?'

You'll never be fast enough . . .

Oliver shakes his head, staring at the empty trolley bay, willing the book to appear. 'It was earlier, but—'

'I think Robin is reshelving up on mezz,' says Mrs Cleary. 'Maybe he's seen it?'

Oliver stops.

Robin.

Missing trolley.

Reshelving.

He runs for the stairs.

Months later, on that same afternoon, their boots snap twigs and skid on wet leaves in Lord Chatterley's forest, while crunching along salted side-walks in the other, grey-veiled world, as they return once again to the library.

Connie can't stop crying.

She suspects she's manic-depressive.

'I don't want to lose you,' she says, and in the same breath, 'Do you think we should see other people?'

'There have been so many already,' replies Mellors.

'It's fiction,' Connie blubs, but she knows what he means. Her stomach is rotting with guilt. All the betrayals, all the lives she's ruined. It's getting hard to keep track of her affairs.

'Poor Clifford,' she says. She despises her husband. Did she ever love him? She must have, she thinks. Before the war. When he cared about what she thought. When he wanted to father her children.

Wait, she thinks. No. I'm not married. I'm with Mellors. No, not Mellors. I'm dating . . .

And now, there he is, her invalid husband, stuck in his wheelchair on the library ramp, halfway between the sidewalk and the front door.

'It's fine,' the man grumbles, when Connie tries to dislodge his chair from the frosty iron rails. 'I can do it myself.'

'Poor Clifford,' Connie repeats, shoving with all her might. 'Don't be so stubborn. Mellors, come lend us your muscles.'

Instantly, remorse swells in her throat. This man, this poor crippled husband of hers, sits idly by as she flirts with the gamekeeper right behind his back. Look how he fusses and sputters, her husband. Her Clifford.

'Let go,' he says, trying to knock Mellors' meaty hands off the chair's back. 'Stop your mewling, lady. Calm down—I'll be fine.'

Calm down.

All right.

'Excuse me,' she says, running into the library, leaving the men to fend for themselves.

'We need something calm,' she says through the veil, flagging down a guy with red hair and a sharp goatee, pushing a trolley across the lobby, also down a muddy slope.

Even cast in grey, his irises catch the light and twinkle like a cat's. 'We've got a load of New Age stuff here—Zen massage, meditation techniques, relaxing with crystals, that sort of thing . . . '

'No,' she says, closing her novel, staggering with relief. Trees recede, the troublesome hill collapses, clouds and sky firm into plaster rosettes and halogen bulbs. The world blossoms, flushes, becomes real. Footsteps echo across the library foyer. Voices soar to the domed ceiling, which sends the noise back redoubled. Laughter filters in from outside, warm as the air drifting down from the furnace ducts. The room is awash with colour, bronzed with late-afternoon light. She could just about curl up on the slush-covered doormat, right there in a rectangle of sun, and fall asleep.

'Not anything instructional. It has to be narrative. Something clear and simple, though. All I want is . . . '

She closes her mouth. Shrugs.

'Don't we all.' Robin smirks and hoists a heavy tome off his trolley. Florentine leather, well worn along the spine and corners. Big as a phone-book. Smelling faintly of glue.

The tight bands around her chest loosen as she flips through the pages. *Yes.* She looks up as Mellors enters, pushing the wheelchair. *This.*

'Hey,' she calls. 'Come here for a sec.'

That man isn't Clifford, she thinks, watching the gamekeeper secure the chair's brakes. There is no Clifford. She hasn't hurt anyone except Mellors.

And Jay.

And Newland.

And Jude.

But not the tattooed boy she met on a bridge downtown.

Not yet.

'Can we borrow this one?' she asks, leaning over to inspect the pictures, avoiding Mellors' haunted eyes as he approaches. She studies the images so intently, she doesn't even notice the librarian has gone. Wisps of blonde hair escape her bun and fall in a fringe across her face. Out of habit, she tucks them behind her ears, tries to fix them in place with her glasses. Two seconds later they're again sliding free. Even so, she doesn't give up trying. 'It's got potential.'

'That's mine. It's not—'

The voice comes from behind her, young but deep. It breaks off when she turns around.

'Oh,' says the weird kid from the other day. 'Hi.'

'Hi,' she replies, cradling the scrapbook in one arm. 'This is yours?'

'Get a move on, Oliver,' calls the legless man, slouching in his wheelchair just inside the door. 'We don't have all day.'

She can practically feel heat seething from the kid's pink cheeks.

'Look, I gotta go. My book—'

'Is gorgeous,' she says. 'It's perfect.'

Oliver's face is magenta. He clears his throat. Swallows. Clears his throat. 'A new tale is only a flick away . . . '

She looks over the kid's head, at the boy who is no longer Mellors. He winks at her. She smiles. 'Yes. Exactly.'

'You can borrow it, I suppose.' Oliver stares at his hands. 'On one condition: you gotta tell me your name.'

'Fair enough,' she says.

And laughing, she tells them both.

THE HOLES

KEITH MINNION

'When I was a kid,' Mr. Minnion tells us rather wistfully, 'my friends and I played in a weed-filled empty lot around the corner from my house. One summer we dug a pit, covered it with scrap plywood, and from this secret clubhouse we waged sling-shot war against the big corrugated metal fence of Jamaica Ash & Rubbish across the street. Innocent kid fun. Nearly fifty years later I went back to the old neighbourhood and found the lot completely paved over, a parking lot for garbage trucks. Jamaica Ash & Rubbish had won the war. Or had they?' Read on, Reader . . . read on.

The author sold his first short story to Asimov's SF Adventure Magazine in 1979, since when he has sold some twenty stories, two novelettes and one novel. Mr. Minnion has illustrated professionally since the early 1990s for such writers as William Peter Blatty, Gene Wolfe, Clive Barker and even Postscripts publisher Peter Crowther, and has also done extensive graphic design work for the Department of Defense. He is a former school-teacher and officer in the U.S. Navy and currently lives in a small city in the Shenandoah Valley of Virginia. Keith has a short story collection called It's For You out in print from White Noise Press, and in all the electronic formats from Crossroads Press. Dark Work, a full colour retrospective art book of Mr. Minnion's horror illustrations, was published in May 2014 by SST Publications. Biting Dog Press published a limited edition poster of a new Neil Gaiman poem featuring Keith's art, also in 2014. A novel called The Bone-yard is forthcoming from Bad Moon Books.

1995

ED

My wife said, "But it's Sam's first varsity game. He really wants you there."

"I know." I zipped up my jacket. "But there'll be other games. He'll understand."

"They might let him pitch."

I just looked at her. She meant well, wasn't even trying to make me feel guilty (well, not *too* guilty), but this was my day to visit. My annual pilgrimage. My penance.

"You're meeting Frank again?"

"Yeah. We're going out together, like always."

She just shook her head.

As I grabbed the car keys and went out the kitchen door she called after me, "Does this guy Orlando—?"

"Lonnie," I said. "We called him Lonnie."

"Does *Lonnie* know you two are even there?"

It didn't matter. I owed him. We both did.

1965

EDDIE

I remember the first thing, the first creepy thing that was all mine.

It was a Wednesday evening, early June, just three and a half weeks before school let out. I was in the basement in the back corner where my dad had built me a workbench. Under the single long fluorescent light I was cutting out all the balsa pieces for the fuselage of the gas model airplane kit I had just bought with a month's worth of paperboy earnings. My homework was done, my dad had control over what was on the big old DeWalt in the living room—*The Defenders*, by the sound of it—and I had a solid hour before I had to take my bath and go to bed.

Then I heard it: a sound in the cinder block wall in front of me. Something scratching. Digging, maybe. Our basement was a full eight feet underground, maybe more, so whatever it was making the sound, it was digging pretty deep. I put the razor blade down before I cut myself, and listened. Scratch-scratch . . . scratch-scratch-*scrape* . . .

The sudden creak of the top step made me jump. Through the open stair treads I saw my mom coming down with a wicker basket full of laundry. "Mom, come over here!"

She came back to my end of the basement, still holding the basket. "What's up, cupcake?"

"I think we've got rats," I said, ignoring the 'cupcake' crack.

"Whaat?"

I gestured to the wall. "I heard scratching behind here."

We both were quiet. And of course, the noise had stopped.

"I don't hear anything," Mom said.

"It was there. I really heard it."

"I'm not doubting you." She frowned. "I bet it's that new trash dump, stirring things up."

Moone Ash and Rubbish, the huge brick building across the street from the vacant lot where Frankie, Lonnie, and I had dug our Fort. I hated Moone Ash and Rubbish with a passion, we all did, even my little brother Wally. Our parents too, of course. The whole neighborhood had been against letting the dump get built in the first place. I remember my dad raging, "What's it gonna do to our house equity?" Whatever that was.

My mom shifted the laundry basket to her other hip. "Well, keep me posted, okay?"

I looked at the cinder blocks with wide eyes. "Yeah," I said. "Sure."

Friday night meant the weekly triple-feature of *Twilight Zone* reruns on Channel 9 at Lonnie's house. His dad always sprung for a big pizza and sodas, and sometimes even popcorn. And Lonnie had a new color TV. Perfect, in other words. Mr. Carlino opened the front door at my knock. "Mr. Curtiss," he said, looking down at me through the screen, "we were expecting you."

Lonnie's dad always got a kick out of being so formal, so I played along. "Thank you sir," I said. "May I come in?"

"Indeed." He stepped out of the way, and I slipped through the screen door as fast as I could to keep the bugs out. I smelled Pina's pizza and freshly popped popcorn, and my mouth began watering.

"Man," I said, entering the living room, "am I glad your big sister goes out every Friday night."

"You always say that," Lonnie said from the couch. Frankie, his mouth full, only raised his slice in greeting.

"You gentlemen keep it down in there," Lonnie's dad said from his den. I saw him sitting down at a roll-top desk covered with papers. Who in their right mind did paperwork on a Friday night? Mr. Carlino, that's who.

I grabbed a slice for myself. "Pina's pizza," I said, pronouncing it like 'penis', which always brought a chuckle from Frankie. There was a commercial on the TV for floor wax. "I wish *Twilight Zone* was in color."

"You and me both, brother." Lonnie moved over to make room for me. "Can you imagine what the monsters and aliens would look like?"

Frankie swallowed. "Or that gremlin on the wing of the plane? I bet he'd be green."

I had only been in a big airplane once, a four-engine Conny for a Thanksgiving trip to my Gramma's in St. Louis. Remembering that *Twilight Zone* episode had given me nightmares the night before we went. All I can say is I was very glad my seat wasn't over the wing.

Somewhere upstairs a door slammed, and someone came pounding down the stairs. We all exchanged disgusted looks: Natalie.

Lonnie's big sister went straight down the hall to the den. "Daddy? Have you seen my blue blouse? I have to be at Diana's in twenty minutes, and I know I put it in the hamper yesterday."

"It must still be down in the basement then, Kitten," Lonnie's dad said. "Check the ironing basket."

"It's not *ironed*?"

I saw Lonnie just shake his head.

As she passed the living room she said over her shoulder, "Hello apes."

Frankie jumped off the couch imitating a chimp, "Eep! Eep!" and we all laughed.

The commercials ended and the show started in again, some convict on a desert planet waiting for the supply ship to come so he could finish a chess game or something, when we all jumped at Lonnie's stupid sister yelling like a maniac from the basement, "Daddy! Daddy! Come here!"

Lonnie's dad passed the living room at a trot. We crowded behind him going down the stairs.

Natalie was pointing at the wall next to the clothes dryer. "Is that a mouse hole? Do we have mice?"

I saw the hole in the concrete she was pointing at, maybe the size of a quarter, about a foot off the floor. A crumbly pile of concrete dust was under it. Mr. Carlino crouched close, put his finger in it, and felt around.

"I think it's just groundwater that made the concrete fail, Kitten," he said. "I've got some hydraulic cement in the garage. Lon?"

"I'll get it." Lonnie ran back upstairs.

Frankie looked into the hole. "Makes me glad my house doesn't have a basement."

"Oh shut up!" Natalie spat out.

"Natalie!" Mr. Carlino gave her a warning look. "That's no way to talk to a guest."

"He's not *my* guest."

"Regardless." Mr. Carlino pointed to the ironing board next to the washing machine. "There's still ample time to iron your blouse."

She shook her head. "I'm going to wear my white one instead. I'm not spending another minute down here till that hole is fixed." She was the first one up the stairs. Frankie and Mr. Carlino shared a look, man to man, then followed. I stuck around, though, looking at that hole, wondering if, maybe, there might be one just like it in my basement too.

The lights blinked off and on, and Mr. Carlino said from the top of the stairs, "Are you coming up, Mr. Curtiss?"

"Yes sir." I still kept looking at that hole, waiting for something to come out of it. Thankfully, nothing did.

That noise I had heard in our basement? My mom heard it the next day, Saturday night to be exact, down doing another load of laundry. I was upstairs watching *Lost In Space* on the old DeWalt with Wally and my dad, when we heard my mom yell, "Stan! Get down here!"

Wally and I looked at one another.

"Eddie," my dad said, "go see what's eating your mother."

"STAN!"

That got all three of us off the couch. I shoved Wally out of the way so I was second down the stairs.

Mom was standing by my workbench with both of her hands on her head. She turned. "Eddie! I'm glad you're here too!" Pale and shaking, she pointed to the cinder block wall. "There's something behind here, something alive!"

"You heard it too, Mom?"

Dad looked at the two of us. "Heard what?"

"A monster!" Wally yelled.

"A rat," Mom said, giving my stupid little brother the eye. "A really big one."

"Wait a minute." Dad spread his arms, palms down. "You saw a rat down here?"

"*Heard* one. Right behind this wall. It was making digging sounds." Mom hugged herself and shivered again. "It's the dump, I know it is. Bringing rats into the neighborhood."

"Last night Lonnie's sister found a hole in the wall in their basement, big enough for a rat," I said, and grinned. "You should have heard her scream."

My mom looked at my dad. "And the Carlinos are a block farther away from the dump than us."

"I'll go to Staub's on Monday and get a trap," Dad said.

"Not one with poison. I don't want poison in the house."

"You should get one with the big bar on a spring," I said, "the kind that breaks their scrawny little necks."

Mom still looked worried. "The kind with bait?"

Dad nodded. "Like cheese. Or peanut butter."

I looked at Wally, and saw a light go on in his eyes. "Wally's going to eat the bait," I said.

Wally grinned.

"Wallace," Dad said, "if you try to eat the bait you're going to lose a finger. The trap will cut it right off."

I could tell the little twerp was weighing his options. Life was just one big *Loony Tunes* cartoon to him.

"*Wallace*," Dad said.

The light in his eyes died. "Oh all right," he said.

Mom still looked worried, though.

"Can I go with you, Dad?" I asked.

"To Staub's? Sure. I'm still not buying you that Swiss Army knife, though."

"Me too!" Wally jumped up and down. "I wanna go too!"

Dad put a hand on his head. "For you? I'm buying a cage."

Wally just grinned. I could tell that was fine by him, the little nimrod.

FRANKIE

The Red Ranger's Fort was a hole in the ground in the empty lot behind my house. It was about six feet by six feet, and over five feet deep, with a roof of scrap plywood and planks my dad gave us, with dried grass and branches on top of that for camouflage. Eddie, Lonnie, and me dug it out by hand, spreading the extra dirt out into the lot so nobody would notice; like that prisoner did in *Stalag 17*. My Uncle Carmine gave us a sawed-off stepladder, "So you GIs don't get stuck down there and starve," he said.

We called it the Fort because that's what it was: home base for the Red Rangers. So far our secret club only had three members: Eddie, Lonnie, and me. Eddie's little brother wanted in bad, but there was no way that crazy little fartface was getting into the Red Rangers, or the Fort either. No girls, and no Wally.

The Fort was the first line of defense against the neighborhood's common enemy across the street: Moone Ash & Rubbish, the new trash recycling plant in town. It was across the street from the lot, and had a tall sheet-metal fence with barbed wire on top—like anybody would want to break into a garbage dump! All we could see over the fence was the top of the long brick building, and a big dark garage door when they opened the gate to let the trash trucks in and out. It *looked* clean, and it didn't smell *too* much. "Wait till high summer, Frankie," my mom said, tapping her Lucky in the ashtray she kept next to the kitchen sink, "then tell me how much it doesn't stink."

Because I was closest, I was the first down the ladder Sunday afternoon after church and lunch, and I could change into my dungarees and sneakers. I had the new *X-Men* and *Thor*, which I added to the pile of comics in the milk carton in the corner.

Eddie and Lonnie came together, after giving me the three-whistle all-clear.

Lonnie was the tallest of us, and his head almost reached the roof. He was also the skinniest. Eddie was short, but fast. Both of them were smarter than me, but I'd never let them know it. "I got the new *Thor* and *X-Men*," I said.

Eddie glanced at the milk carton. "Cool. Maybe later. After."

"It should only be the weekend watchman today," I said. "You guys ready?"

Lonnie patted his pants pockets. "Locked and loaded."

"Me too," Eddie said.

I looked at my Timex. "It's thirteen-hundred hours, men."

Eddie spat on the back of his hand and held it out, palm down.

Lonnie did the same, covering Eddie's hand. I was last, feeling Lonnie's warm spit spread out as I pressed my hand on his. "Red Rangers forever," I said.

Lonnie grinned. "Amen, brothers."

LONNIE

I got the path on the right through the weeds, as usual. Every time I took it I got more stones out, so it wasn't so bad on my knees. It was shorter than the left path, anyway, which was more important to me. It was closer to Tennyson Avenue and home, too.

At the end, near the street the lot shared with the dump, I eased my slingshot out of my back pocket, loaded a marble, and waited for the signal. Then I heard Eddie give two short whistles, and I did the same. Red Rangers were in position. I started counting down: ten Mississippi, nine Mississippi . . . .

At zero I stood up, my arms just clearing the top of the tallest weeds. Across the street the big metal fence around the dump was an easy target. I pulled the slingshot pocket as far as the doubled-up rubber bands would let me, then fired.

The marble hit the sheet metal with a loud, satisfying clang. I didn't hear Eddie's shot; maybe our marbles hit at the same time. Grinning, I dropped back into the weeds and beat a quick retreat. I was about halfway back to the Fort when I heard the loud, gravelly voice of the fat old watchman yelling, "You, you sumbitch kid! You try that again and see what gets you!"

Mission accomplished.

But then I saw Eddie cut right across my path, running full tilt toward Tennyson Avenue. I stopped dead, then jumped off the path, into the weeds, where no one could see me.

"You goddamn kid! Stop running. Stop running or I'll—"

Or nothing. Eddie was a fast runner, maybe even faster than me. He was probably halfway home already. I grinned in the shadows. No one could stop the Red Rangers.

EDDIE

I took the left trail only because I was up the ladder first, plus the right trail had more rocks and was murder on my knees. Frankie gave the all-clear whistle when Lonnie was out and into the weeds. I checked my shirt pocket for my marble sack, then my back jeans pocket, shoving my sling-shot as far down as it could go.

Then I started crawling.

It took me about a minute to reach the end of the trail. The tall weeds were thick here, and hid me completely from the enemy across the street. I turned my head and gave two short whistles. After a moment I heard Lonnie do the same. Then it was just the slow countdown from ten. By six I had my slingshot out and a marble loaded in the pocket. By four I was crouching on the balls of my feet, my sneakers digging into the dirt, ready to—

Then I saw an old leather engineer's boot a couple of feet in front of me, through the weeds. That hadn't been there the last time, had it?

Then the boot moved. In that same instant, I heard Lonnie's marble hit the dump fence.

"You! You sumbitch kid!"

I scrambled back on my hands and feet, like a crab, out of sight under the weeds. I went about five feet, then flipped over and started a crouching run. Going back to the Fort would just lead the dump watchman to it, so I cut across the lot toward Tennyson Street. As I passed the right trail I caught a glimpse of Lonnie in the weeds, but I kept going. The sounds of the watchman crashing awkwardly behind me, yelling for me to stop running or else, only made me run faster. The weeds thinned out near Tennyson, so I finally stood up and ran full tilt, one-hundred-yard-dash style, out of the lot and down the street. If the watchman saw me, all he saw was my back. I passed Dryden and made my turn at Lowell, my street, home, *safety*, and only looked back once. There was nobody following me.

"Hey, honeybunch," Mom said, turning from the sink as I banged open the screen door from the breezeway. "Where's the fire?"

LONNIE

Dinner at the Carlinos was always a joy. That's being sarcastic, of course. Since Mom left, dinners were always the hardest to get through. My dad and my big sister shared cooking duty. Sunday night was Natalie night, and she was serving the only thing of hers I actually didn't hate: lasagna.

"So," Dad said to me, "what did you do after church instead of cutting the back lawn like I asked?"

"I'm doing that right after dinner," I said.

My dad nodded, giving me his patented, "Indeed."

Natalie sniggered as she shoveled a square of lasagna onto her plate. "I bet I know what he did today. I bet he and his grubby little friends crawled around in that empty lot playing something juvenile like *Army*, throwing rocks at the dump fence."

My dad raised both eyebrows. "What?"

"My friends are not grubby."

"That was not the point of my question, Orlando."

Natalie mouthed my name around her braces, grinning.

Dad didn't see that, of course. "You were throwing rocks at the Moone fence?"

I looked at my lasagna. "We weren't throwing rocks."

"So your sister is making this up?"

"Well . . . "

Dad put down his fork.

"We were just shooting a few marbles."

"Shooting a few marbles. With what? Slingshots? Didn't we already have a talk about that?"

"They weren't clearies or shooters!" Wow. That was a dumb thing to say.

"That's your argument?" My dad looked more disappointed in me than mad, and that hurt worse. "We have to get along with the businesses in our neighborhood," he said. "They can't always be the bad guys."

"Yes sir."

"You can leave your slingshot on my desk. I'll take care of it."

"Yes sir." No big deal; it was just a bent-up coat hanger, a piece of leather, and some rubber bands; I could make another one in about ten minutes.

Natalie cleared her throat. "We had the manager of Moone Ash and Rubbish as a guest in my FBA club after school last week." My big sister a future businessman of America? Now *that* was funny. I didn't grin, though; this was taking the spotlight off me, which was the important thing.

"Really." Dad turned to her. "Did you find that interesting?"

"Of course, Daddy. Mr. Rozdzielski was very—"

My jaw dropped a little. "Mr. *who?*"

She glanced in my direction like she was looking at a bug. "*Rozdzielski.* Shall I spell it?"

I managed not to laugh out loud. "Nope," I said, waving my fork for her to continue.

"As I was saying, Mr. Rozdzielski the manager was very nice, and gave a very informative talk."

"I heard what he had to say at the town hall meetings," Dad said. "Did he discuss their new waste-handling process?"

"He did! And he said that everyone in the neighborhood would be happy because the process virtually eliminates all bad smells."

That could be true; the place hardly stunk at all.

"And he said the process would not attract any rodents. It would *repel* them, in fact."

Come to think of it, I hadn't seen a mouse, skunk, or rabbit in the lot for a while now. Even the neighborhood cats avoided the place. Huh.

"He said that the town, and our neighborhood especially, would come to value Moone Ash and Rubbish as a valued partner in the community."

"Well," Dad said, spearing a piece of lasagna and bringing it up to his mouth, "let's certainly hope so."

EDDIE

Mr. McDermott really piled on the homework the next week, so it wasn't until Saturday morning before the Red Rangers could meet in the Fort. Frankie went down first, puffing like a locomotive, giving each of us a quick grin as he disappeared from view. Lonnie went next, quick as a cat, and I heard Frankie yell, "Watch it, willya? That's my head!" Then, in a different note entirely, "*Hey!*"

Trouble? I scrambled down the ladder.

"Look at this." Frankie was pointing at the far wall. "Can you believe this?"

It was a hole, a big, ragged, dark hole in the dirt, about two feet up from the floor planks. A tunnel.

"There's hardly any loose dirt." Lonnie scuffed his sneakers across the planks under it. Darkness, though, in there. Total black.

"What made it? A rat?"

Lonnie shook his head. "It's too big for that. Hedgehog, maybe."

"I don't think hedgehogs dig tunnels," I said. "They just dig nests under porches and stuff." I went over, put my hand in, just a little, to touch the rough walls, then immediately pulled back. "It's sticky." I wiped my hand on my jeans. "Like a snail trail."

All three of us looked at the hole.

"Snails don't have teeth," Frankie said, "do they?"

"I'm not even sure they have *mouths*." Lonnie touched the hole wall too. "It's not that sticky," he said.

"Maybe it's hardening."

I bent to sniff. "I don't smell anything bad. Smells like something, though. I just can't place it."

Frankie let one rip. "Smell something now?"

We all snickered, if just for a moment.

I saw something in Lonnie's face. "Hey man," I said, "you're not thinking of climbing in there, are you?"

He shrugged. "I think I'm skinny enough."

"Nah, it's way too tight." Frankie set his hands apart at the hole's widest dimension, then brought them over to Lonnie's shoulders. "Huh," he said. "Maybe you could. I still think it would be pretty tight, though."

"I'm with Frankie," I said. "What if it gets smaller in there?"

Lonnie grinned. "What if it gets bigger?"

"What if there's a killer snail in there, waiting for his lunch?" I gave his shoulder a light punch. "Or worse?"

"Wolverine," Frankie said, his eyes going round.

"Wolverines live in Montana," Lonnie said. "Last time I checked, this is Pennsylvania." He waved his hand dismissively. "It's probably just a hole the dump people dug, for a pipe or something, and the wall caved in. I mean, it's pointed right across the lot to the dump, isn't it?"

He was right. But that just made it even creepier.

"We could tie a rope to you, so we could pull you out. You know, a safety line."

I frowned at Frankie, but I could see he was already excited at the idea of Lonnie crawling into the hole. "I still think it's a bad idea," I said.

Outside, we heard a big trash truck growling to life. They regularly parked at the far edge of the lot down by Dickens Street, sometimes even on it. A little dirt dust drifted through the beams of light coming down between the roof boards.

Frankie hit his fist into his open palm. "We can use my mom's clothesline. She'll never know."

"I can tie it around my waist," Lonnie said.

"Through your belt loops," I said. "That way it can't slip off."

Lonnie grinned. "Sounds like a plan, brothers!"

"I'll be right back." Frankie went up the ladder.

I looked at Lonnie. He was still grinning in the shadows. "You're really not scared?"

"Sure I'm scared." His grin broadened. "That's what makes it so much *fun*."

We heard Frankie's fence gate slam, then he came puffing back down the ladder with a coil of clothesline hanging around his neck. "There must be fifty feet of this," he said, unslinging it, handing it to Lonnie.

"Give me an end." Lonnie stuck it through his belt loops.

"Twice," I said.

"Twice it is."

"Double-knot," Frankie said. "Here, I'll do it."

When he was done Lonnie bent to look into the hole. "Don't we have a flashlight down here somewhere?"

"Yeah." I rummaged through the pile of comics and Ace paperbacks in the milk carton in the corner, and came up with my dad's old hunting flashlight. Originally chrome, it was now mostly rusted. I tried the switch, but nothing happened. I rapped the end on my thigh. Still nothing.

"The batteries are probably as rusted out as the rest of that hunk of junk." Frankie went for the ladder. "You can use my new Scouts flashlight. Just give me a minute." Up he went. Lonnie and I heard the squeak and clank of his back gate.

I turned to my friend. "This is crazy, you know."

Lonnie shrugged. "It's just a hole."

"I wouldn't call you chicken if you—"

"Chickened out?"

I tried another angle: "You're not scared of being all . . . you know . . . "

"Claustrophobic? Nah. That doesn't bother me. That's why I think I'm going to be a good astronaut."

I believed him. If any of us was going to be riding that first rocket to Mars, it was Lonnie.

Clank—squeak—clank, then Frankie came puffing down the ladder. He handed Lonnie his brand new blue and yellow Cub Scout flashlight. "There's new batteries in it."

Lonnie turned it on, and a strong beam illuminated the hole. "Perfect," he said.

"Now don't go scratching it up."

Lonnie patted Frankie on the shoulder. "I'll take good care of it." Then he turned, bent, and directed the flashlight beam down the tunnel. "Looks like it goes down a little, a few yards in."

"Big enough for you, though?"

"Yeah. No problem. Give me a hoist, will you?"

Frankie knelt beside him and made a basket out of his hands. Lonnie put a sneaker into it, and with a loud grunt Frankie helped him over the lip of the hole and half in. Then we each grabbed a leg and pushed him in all the way.

"Is it sticky?"

"Nah. Kind of hard, actually. Feels like plastic. This should be easy."

We watched him disappear into the darkness. The hole swallowed up the flashlight beam, and in moments it was totally dark. Frankie and I listened to Lonnie scrabbling along, and watched the pile of clothesline slowly unwind.

After what seemed like a minute at least, I yelled into the hole, "You okay in there?"

We both heard a muffled, " . . . *What?*"

I yelled louder. "Everything okay?"

"Yeah!"

After another minute, I saw that the clothesline was wrapped around Frankie's left ankle. "Hey," I said, pointing.

"Darn it." Frankie bent to disentangle himself.

Then, from the tunnel, we both heard Lonnie yell, "Hey! Hey guys! The rope is stuck! Can you—"

Then two things happened at the same time: the clothesline jerked, throwing Frankie to the planks with a loud grunt . . . and we heard Lonnie scream.

LONNIE

I was scared, sure, but excited too. This was just like my Uncle Ray, who had been a Marine sapper in Korea. He had crawled down dirt tunnels to blow Commies up all the time.

Frankie's flashlight showed the dirt tunnel all hard and bumpy and covered with something like bubbly donut glaze. I couldn't even smell the dirt because the glaze covered it so well, and the glaze smelled like . . . snot, like what you smell in your nose when you've had a bad cold for a few days. Honest, I could not get the picture of a big, slimy monster snail out of my head, with a mouth full of sharp, pincushion teeth. If something like that came at me in this tunnel I would be a goner for sure.

What had really made this crazy tunnel, anyway?

I heard Eddie yell something. "What?" I yelled back, over my shoulder. "Everything okay?"

"Yeah!" I paused for a moment, and then continued crawling.

A few seconds later, the clothesline caught on something behind me. I gave it a tug, but it stayed stuck. I turned around enough to get the flashlight pointed back that way so I could maybe see what the trouble was. My uncle did this in an actual war? With guns and grenades and enemy soldiers with bowie knives in their teeth?

The flashlight was no help. The clothesline went up the slope and over into a gray darkness, nothing snagging it that I could see.

"Hey!" I was surprised at the loudness of my voice in such tight quarters. "Hey guys! The rope is stuck! Can you—"

I heard a scuffling noise in front of me. I jerked around, fumbling with the flashlight, then saw something coming at me really fast, really big, three orange glowing eyes—

EDDIE

One of the good things about summer coming was that it stayed light longer and longer every evening, so you could stay out and play longer before your parents called you in. Outside, through my open bedroom window, I heard a bunch of neighborhood kids playing Kick the Can. My dad had taught us that old game last August, one night after we had gotten bored with all of our usual games. "You kids will like this one," he had said, putting an empty coffee can in the middle of the street, "because it's simple, it's fun, and everyone can play."

He had been right. We had played it every night for the rest of the summer.

Now I heard the sound of someone running down the street, then the clang of the can, then someone screaming, "OLLY-OLLY-OX-IN-FREE!" and everybody freed from the jail yelling, running to new hiding places.

The phone rang downstairs, and my heart skipped at the sound. I heard quiet conversation, then quiet. Then I heard my dad walking slowly up the stairs, and my fear caught me right in the guts, and all I wanted to do was throw up and run away. But all I did was sit up in my bed, my back against the headboard. Time to face the music, Eddie. Time to take your medicine.

My door opened, and I saw my dad silhouetted against the light in the hall. "You're sitting in the dark," he said.

"You can turn on the light if you want."

He closed the door, came over, and sat on the end of my bed. "This is okay."

A long moment passed. Finally, I said, "How is Lonnie?"

"He'll be fine. Looks like it is just some scrapes."

"Is he home?"

"Not yet. Mr. Carlino wants him to stay in the hospital for at least a few days."

"Is he . . . awake?"

Dad shook his head. "I'm sure they want him to sleep through the night." Dad let his breath out. "He's a very lucky young man, Eddie."

I nodded. My dad's face was in shadow, so I didn't have to see him looking at me. "I'm really sorry, Dad," I said.

"What you boys did today was really stupid, really dangerous."

"I know, Dad."

"That tunnel could have caved in at any moment. If that had happened your friend Lonnie might have suffocated before you could get him out. He might have *died*."

Somebody knocked on my door. "Dad?" It was Wally.

"Give us a few minutes, pal."

"But Dad—"

Dad's voice rose a notch. "I said a few minutes, Wallace. Go back downstairs, please."

Silence for a moment, then Wally said, "Don't hurt Eddie too much, okay?" Then we both heard him running down the hall and down the stairs.

I looked at my dad with wide eyes. He had never hit me—me or Wally—for as long as I could remember.

In a very low, even voice, Dad said, "If you ever do this again, if you ever put your mother through this ever again, I will put welts in your backside. Are we clear?"

I didn't know what a welt was, but I didn't want to find out. "Yes sir," I said, almost whispering.

"Every day after your paper route, when you come home, from now until the last day of school, you are to come up here to your bedroom. No playing with your friends, no watching TV with the rest of us."

Two weeks. "Yes sir."

"You can only come out to use the bathroom and come down to dinner."

"Yes sir."

He let out his breath again. "Is there anything else you want to say?"

"No sir. Except, I'm sorry Dad. Really really sorry."

"I know you are." He stood. "I just thank God it wasn't you at the end of that rope." He went to the door and opened it. "And in case you were wondering, no more playing in that hole of yours in the lot. No more secret club. That's over. Understood?"

"Yes sir."

He closed the door behind him.

Outside, I heard the crowd of kids yelling as another round of Kick the Can began.

FRANKIE

I looked for Lonnie in the church parking lot, but all I saw was his dad's old Buick, already parked.

"Damn that Carlino," my dad said. "Always gets the spot in the shade."

My mom slapped his shoulder. "No cursing on the Lord's Day, please!"

Dad was going to Hell.

I saw him looking at me in the rearview mirror. "What are you grinning at, buster?"

"Nothing, Dad." I put a hand over my mouth.

St. Brigid's, the only Catholic Church in town, usually packed them in. Since we were kind of late we could only get a pew near the back. There was no way I was going to find Lonnie in that crowd of hats and greasy heads in front of me. Dad dropped the kneeling bench with his foot. "Everybody down," he whispered.

About a half-hour into the service, just before Communion, there was some kind of problem near the front. Somebody was making noise while Father Brodeur was trying to talk. The Father paused and looked over, and in the sudden quiet I heard someone whining, and crying a little too. Babies cried in church all the time, but this was different. It was louder, first of all, and seemed . . . older. I went all cold and prickly, and ducked my head.

Then the person making the sounds started screaming: short, yelping screams, and then everybody in the church started talking. "It's the Carlino kid," I heard someone say, loud and clear over everything. And, "Wasn't he just in the hos—"

"That's your friend," Dad hissed out of the side of his mouth. "The one that was in the accident, right?"

I wanted to sink right through the pew bench.

When they took Lonnie out, struggling, still screaming, I just looked at my shoes. Mom gave me a quick little hug, but I didn't even feel it. I couldn't look at him, I just couldn't.

WALLY

My class was on the playground side of the school, which was good and bad. Good because I could look outside and see what was going on, but bad because Miss Hendrickson usually caught me doing it.

Today, two days before the last day of school, I had a really good reason for looking out the window though. On the other side of the playground, on the other side of the school fence, on the other side of Dickens Street was the lot where the Red Rangers had their fort. Today I saw a big yellow bulldozer come down Dickens Street real slow, and then turn into the lot. Then I saw the big shovel part come down and start scooping up dirt and weeds and stuff. It was too far away to hear much, but a big yellow dozer is hard to miss. Eddie's fort wouldn't have had a chance against a—

"Mr. Curtiss."

I turned around, my cheeks starting to burn. Miss Hendrickson was up by her desk, holding a big ruler, and she was looking right at me. The whole *class* was looking at me.

"Sorry, Miss Hendrickson," I said.

"We are a little too late for sorry, Mr. Curtiss." She pointed to the stool in the Time Out Corner. "Until Recess," she said.

I got up, looking down at my sneakers so I didn't have to look at anybody, especially big fat Danny Essig The Pig. I made it to the Time Out Corner without anybody sticking a foot out to trip me. Hello old stool, I thought, and climbed up on it. Man, what was Eddie gonna say about that dozer?

MR. CARLINO

"Dad?" Natalie's wavering voice came up the basement steps. "There's another hole in the wall down here."

I looked up, bleary-eyed. "There's a what?"

"Another hole. A big one."

Upstairs, Lonnie began screaming again.

EDDIE

Frankie had a swing set in his backyard we hadn't played on in years. I sat in one of the rusty swings, and when Frankie sat in the other one, the whole thing creaked. "It's okay," he said. "It's just old." He kicked off, swung once, twice, the framework moving with him, then he stopped. "I can't believe you're moving."

"Me either," I said, "but we are."

"To where? Carbontown? Where the heck is Carbontown?"

"It's Carbon*ville*, a couple of towns west of here. My dad said it's just as far away from his work as here, just on the other side of the county."

Frankie looked down at the bare patch of dirt under his swing. "First Lonnie, now this. Jeez."

"Hey, maybe you can move out of this crummy town too."

"Move? My parents? No way. There've been Piscellis living here since . . . well, since forever."

We both heard the low growl of a diesel engine as a Moone trash truck pulled up on the other side of the back fence.

"They park right up close now?"

"What's stopping them? Pretty soon the whole lot'll be paved over."

"Well screw them." I spit on the back of my hand, and held it out. "Red Rangers?"

Frankie hesitated, then put his hand over mine and pressed, *hard*. "Forever, man," he said. "Forever."

MRS. CURTISS

God, I dreaded having to go down into that basement. Eddie had moved his model making up to his bedroom, and Stan would only go down to get something or fix something when I made him. He drew the line on helping with the laundry, though. It's only a month, Sylvia, I kept telling myself.

Only a month until this house goes to settlement and we close on the new house, far away from this town. Far away from the dump. That damn damn dump.

I hefted the laundry basket and announced as loudly as I could, "Going down to put a load in the washer!" Wally looked up from his cereal and comic book with a blank expression. His eyes looked so . . . hollow these days, I thought bleakly. There was a sports show on the TV in the living room that Stan and Eddie were watching; no response from there.

I pushed the basement door open with my foot, used an elbow to flip the light switch, and went down.

I was sorting the basket when I heard something. It was in the back, by Eddie's workbench.

A shiver of fear went through me. Oh come on, Sylvia. Afraid of every noise now?

You betcha.

I put the whites in, set the dial, then shut the lid. The chugging sound of the old washer filled the basement.

Then I went to the back, to Eddie's workbench, turned on the fluorescent light, and saw the hole.

It was small, round, no bigger than a quarter, drilled in the cinder block about three feet off the floor. It was very dark, just a black circle; below it was a neat conical pile of concrete dust.

Run away, I told myself. But I didn't. I couldn't help it. I took a step forward, then another. Then I paused, listening. Taking in a long breath, I took a third, final step, and bent level with the hole, to look inside.

And saw something in there, looking back at me.

FRANKIE

I would sleep till noon if my parents let me, but this morning, pretty early for me, as I turned over to squint at the time on my clock radio, I noticed my window looked funny. The light coming through it was . . . smeared.

I got out of bed, kicked some Matchbox cars out of my way, and went over to it. It was open, nothing between me and the outside but the screen. It was really the screen that looked funny, covered with something that looked like snot, like that stuff in the Fort—

I stumbled back, my heart suddenly beating really loud in my ears and at the back of my throat. I looked at the windowsill, but there wasn't anything on it. Whatever had been outside my window, looking in at me while I was sleeping, the screen had stopped it.

I got dressed in a hurry, ignored the surprised looks from my mom and my aunt having coffee as I passed them in the kitchen. "Look who's up with the chickens," my Aunt Faye said, exhaling smoke. I kept going, though, out into the backyard.

I stopped halfway across the grass. I could see it without needing to get any closer: there was a hole dug next to the house, right at the foundation, and a trail of glistening snot, about two feet wide, up the wall to my bedroom window.

"Mom!" I turned around, wondering if I was going to pee in my pants. "MOM! DAD!"

EDDIE

Wally was usually already asleep when I had to go to bed. Tonight, though, when I took off my tee shirt and jeans and hung them on my footboard, he spoke out of the darkness, "Hey Eddie."

I pulled my covers back and slid in between the sheets. "What are you still doing up?"

Wally was quiet for a moment. Then he said, "Cuz I'm scared."

I punched my pillow into shape. "Scared of what, moving?"

"Nah. Not that."

I rolled over to face his side of the room. "Well what then?"

"Monsters." He almost whispered the word.

"You mean like the bogeyman in the closet?"

"Nah. Not him. It's those things making noises in the basement."

Oh. *Those* monsters. "Don't worry about it, Squirt," I said. I wanted to say the Red Rangers would take care of them, but that sounded kind of dumb. I punched my pillow again. "I won't let anything get you," I said instead.

"Thanks, Eddie." Wally paused again. "I'm glad we're moving."

"Me too, Squirt," I said. Me too.

1995

ED

Frank and I were quiet for much of the drive out, just the usual bullshit old friends talk about who only saw each other every now and then. About an hour from the asylum, Frank turned from looking out at the passing farmland and said, "I was back there, last month."

I didn't need to ask where. "Yeah? What for?"

"Just passing through." He ran a hand over his head, forehead back, wiping a fresh sheen of sweat off his growing bald spot. "It was all boarded up, the whole neighborhood, like some Love Canal or something."

"Nobody living there at all?"

He shook his head. "Deserted. Like somebody dropped a bomb or something."

I let that sit between us for a few miles; then I had to ask, "What about Moone?"

"Torn down. Just weeds. You wouldn't even know it was there."

LON

(. . . Shrieking. . . . Shrieking.)

IN ALL YOUR
SPARKLING RAIMENT SOAR

ROBERT T. JESCHONEK

When prose and poetry come together, they can lead to unexpected harmonies . . . just as the characters in this very strange love story find such harmonies in their own extreme differences and conflicts. The author brings together lifeforms who couldn't be more alien from each other, united by suffering and fate, and tells the story of their love and sacrifice through a blending of prose and poetry that mirrors their own awakenings. It all began with thoughts of bee colony collapse and the Fermi Paradox (which questions the existence of intelligent alien life because of the lack of evidence or contact) . . . then metamorphosed into a fable about pain, compassion, redemption, and the origin of death in the human species. Was human life once free of death, until an intervention from beyond the stars? Perhaps, in this case, fiction is much stranger than truth could ever be.

For more unique stories and experiments in style, check Mad Scientist Meets Cannibal, *the author's PS Showcase collection. You can also find his work in* Galaxy's Edge, Escape Pod, Space and Time, *and five previous volumes of* Postscripts. *He won an International Book Award for his cross-genre science fiction thriller* Day 9 *and a Scribe Award for Best Original Novel for his alternate history,* Tannhauser: Rising Sun, Falling Shadows. *For news and surprises from the mind-bending worlds of Mr. Jeschonek, visit* www.robert-jeschonek.com, *where you will find links to his Facebook page, Twitter feed, YouTube channel, and other branches of his far-flung publishing empire.*

THOUGH ALL OF EXISTENCE, TO US, IS A POEM, CERTAIN verses are not exactly joyful. *Mmm-bzzz.*

In those days, for example, our first days on this world among humans, our tasks were not happy ones. We took no pleasure in what we did to them, though we did it for good reasons. Though we sought to find
The beauty of the burning dawn,
A spectrum woven out of eyeblinks
And tears, the heatless flickering
Of featherless wings rising
Mmm-bzzz
Rising from the darkling pool colliding
With the swirling curtain of an opalescent
Luminescence.
But the truth is, in the *mmm-bzzz* in the beginning, we did not know if we would ever reach it. If the horrible things we were doing to these creatures, primitive yet every bit as sentient as we, would ever yield up the prize we were determined to set free.

Subject 1. That was her official designation. I called her *Clarity*, because that was what I saw in her eyes the first time we met; that was what impressed me about her the most. We didn't know what she called herself, if anything. We didn't understand her language, if there was one. Not that it mattered.

At least that's what we'd thought in the beginning. That the details didn't matter.

But oh how they mattered. Like the downy black fur that covered her body. The long, dark mane
So soft, so flowing,
A beautiful veil cascading over shoulders
Over chest like a waterfall at
Night, a solar wind wrapping
Around the silver skin of a
Caressing the skin of a
Dreaming the form in the formless
Deep.
As if words could ever *mmm-bzzz* could ever express her radiance. As if scientific measurements could ever convey the dimensions of her
Magnificence.

As if any attempt to recreate the memory of her could somehow excuse what I did to her.

But back in those days, four million years ago as you measure *mmm-bzzz* reckon time, Clarity filled my thoughts. *Our* thoughts, I should say. The collective thoughts of ten thousand of us, bound in the harmony of the hive mind.

It didn't matter that she was so different from us. That, on the surface, she had so little in common with insects like us.

In a way, we were made for each other. Our ship, hibernating underground for many months after landing, built us from the genetic building blocks most prevalent on your world. The automated systems constructed us in a way that best suited the local environment, our mission, and our biological software. Our *soulware*.

We'd been built and rebuilt thusly many times, on many different worlds. Always maintaining *mmm-bzzz* preserving what kept us special. What kept us the most efficient and productive pollinators and gatherers in the galaxy.

Clarity was one of the first humans we saw when our ship finally burrowed out of the ground and the hatches irised open. As we tasted the air of this world for the first time, she stepped fearlessly out from behind a boulder.

The rest of her tribe cowered in the shadows, but not her. *Mmm-bzzz.* I can still see her, meeting us clear-eyed and square-shouldered when even the brawny males wouldn't come forth. She was unafraid, confident, graceful. A born leader.

Clarity gazed at us with wonder in her bright green eyes. And I gazed back at her with more of the same, transfixed. I knew there was something unique *mmm-bzzz* special about her right away.

Which, of course, was one of the reasons we chose her on the spot as the first subject retrieved for our operations on this world.

In our swarms, we are ten thousand strong. Each member of the swarm is no bigger than a human fingertip, but together we have

Power.

Working together, perfectly synchronized, we can arrange ourselves in the shape of a human body and execute a wide range of tasks. For example, we can guide a human female into a shipboard lab.

Which is where we can restrain her *mmm-bzzz* strap her to a metal table and drive a spike at her forehead.

Clarity didn't scream when the spike shot toward her. She didn't even watch it approach. Her eyes were fixed on me the entire time.

Was she defective for not expressing fear? Did she lack the proper response mechanism to potentially fatal stimuli?

Not if there was no possibility of *fatality.* Not if the tempered metal spike shattered like ice when it hit her forehead, leaving not a mark of damage on her.

When we applied the same test to other human subjects in our shipboard labs, the results were identical.

Clarity and her species were nearly indestructible. As we confirmed through our experiments, no external physical attack could harm them. Through some miracle of evolution, humanity had become perfected *mmm-bzzz* immortal.

And that was why we'd come here. Not to become attached to these primitive creatures, so abysmally low on every scale of development of which we could conceive. We'd come to find a way to kill them . . . and ensure salvation for the human race and our own species besides.

How could we possibly *save* humanity by *killing* it? Because only in death can a human being, or any sentient lifeform, evolve to the next level.

My people specialize in making that possible. We free intelligent beings from their physical bonds like a shoot from a seed.

Have you ever wondered why you hear nothing from the skies *mmm-bzzz* from space? No intelligible signals from the impossible vastness?

Surely, in all that everything, there must be someone like you on another world. Someone to talk to. Someone to connect with. What are they waiting for? Why won't they call?

The answer is this: It is because
they have all become

Light.

This was the destiny we had come to help humanity attain *mmm-bzzz* realize. Enabling humans to die would free the inner light from their corporeal shells and allow it to escape into space. Allow it to join the light of countless other lifeforms in the infinite reaches.

And my people, as we ushered humankind on its way, would experience *mmm-bzzz* undergo our own transformation. One that would save us from ruin.

Our souls were ancient. Our soulware had become degraded. When it collapsed, our sentience would dissolve; we would lose our sense of self and be unable to perform our mission. Time was running out for us.

But when humanity died and moved to the next level, the resulting surge of inner light would allow us to save ourselves. We would channel enough of humanity's light through our ship's instrumentation to burn away the impurities and reboot our degraded souls.

In a way, humanity's souls would pollinate our own, bringing new life to us. In that one tremendous release, my people would be reborn.

We would regain our immortality in the corporeal world just as humanity lost its own.

All this was riding on the shoulders of beautiful Clarity, though I'm sure she knew it not. To her, each day was an ordeal without explanation. Though I did what I could to leaven the ordeal with moments of kindness.

I would wake her in the morning by brushing *mmm-bzzz* dabbing honey on her lips. Her eyes would flutter open
Like the wings of butterflies,
soft as velvet, damp with dew,
diaphanous, intangible,
closer to whispers or
thoughts,
closer to intentions,
The feelings of lingering love from a
dream,
All that's left when you can't remember
the lover.

And then her tongue would slide out and touch the glistening honey on each lip. It would glide languidly along the top and then the bottom, licking up the sweetness as I watched *mmm-bzzz* gazed through ten thousand pairs of eyes, ten thousand facets in each eye, each facet soaking up a different part of the visible and invisible spectrums.

And then I would go to work on her. I would try to kill her again and again, day after day.

At first, I went through the same techniques my people were employing on other specimens. I had to confirm they would lead to *mmm-bzzz* produce the same effect, that her baseline was identical to the rest.

So I gathered my ten thousand buzzing selves in one body and attacked her. I tried to cut her throat and split her head open. I tried to choke her, drown her, set her on fire. I tried to break her in every way possible.

Through all of this, she remained unharmed and no more alarmed than when the spike had shattered against her forehead. Like the rest of her people *mmm-bzzz* species, she was indestructible.

She didn't seem to experience any discomfort, either. Stimuli applied externally were as ineffective at causing her pain as they were at damaging her body.

So we moved on to stage two. The introduction of pain by other methods.

Though we hadn't succeeded in killing a human, we *did* manage to stimulate pain. This, we thought, could be the gateway to death for these creatures.

The strongest results came from electrocution or intense irradiation. Strong natural forces channeled *mmm-bzzz* focused internally were able to provoke the nervous system, evoking a pain response.

I can still hear her first screams piercing the air of the lab. I'll never forget the way she thrashed on the metal table, fighting her restraints, convulsing. Eyes rolled up in their sockets or pinched shut against the waves of agony.

But her eyes were not always rolled up or pinched shut. Often, they were fixed in my direction, wide and bloodshot with suffering and desperation.

How many other humans did I torture on any given day? Clarity was not my only subject, after all.

Yet who among them possessed the grace to set aside the suffering when it ended? To face the torturer with a measure of tranquility?

Only Clarity. Only this singular angel could muster a smile in my presence.

Between sessions, I fed her honey and wheat germ. I poured purified water between her parched red lips.

Others of her kind accepted nothing from me, perhaps expecting *mmm-bzzz* fearing it would bring them more pain. But as much as I abused her, Clarity trusted me. She still seemed on some level to sense my good intentions.

I wonder sometimes how this was ever possible, given the gulf between our species. The lack of common language between us. The sheer differences in physiology. I must have looked fearsome to her, a cloud of insects roughly shaped like a man. Thousands of unblinking eyes
    Like chips of polished
    Ebony, thousands of black and yellow
    Stingers, known only to her by the
    Screaming in her own throat,
    The thoughts in her own mind,
    The new, suffering thing she had become because of
    Me.
    Her divinity, I suspect, made this miracle real.

I could not allow her to leave the ship, could not even let her off the table for fear of corrupting the experiment.

But between sessions, I brought the world to her. Projectors in the lab recreated her habitat in three dimensions around us.

So though she *mmm-bzzz* though she still lay strapped to the table, destined for more torture, she could see at least for a few moments the familiar grasslands outside the hull of the ship. The amber plains rippling
    In the wind, in the blazing sunlight,
    Shadows of clouds gliding over the sea of grain,
    Twinned in the mirror-skins of watering holes,
    Slipping over creatures bristling with horns and
    Tusks and teeth and claws and beaks of every angle,

Long necks parting the treetops,
Spear tips bobbing in the lazy current.

She sighed when the image of a brightly colored bird swooped overhead, silhouetted against the sun. She smiled when a lithe gazelle sprinted past, followed by a hail of spears and a team of human hunters who'd thrown them.

When she smiled at me, too, the fascination *mmm-bzzz* adoration I felt multiplied a thousand-fold. I felt redeemed, at least a little, for the work I had to do.

And therefore able to continue to do it.

The infections took weeks to administer. One after another, I pumped her system full of bacteria, viruses, phages, fungi, and exotic microorganisms from other worlds. I administered them one and two and ten and twenty and a hundred at a time, carefully watching *mmm-bzzz* recording the effects.

This microbiological warfare had an impact. By attacking her internally, they triggered powerful shocks to her system. Like electrocution and irradiation, they caused intense pain.

But not death. Her immune system rose up always and wiped away the invaders as if they'd never existed.

Next, it was time for stage three. It was time for innovation.

Following protocols, I had charted the baseline and covered the same ground we'd been over with other subjects. Now that I'd established *mmm-bzzz* determined she was biologically identical to other humans, I could explore new approaches. Any success would likely extend universally to the rest of her species.

If I could kill *her*, I could kill *all* of them.

I'll never forget the first time I heard Clarity laugh.

I was embarking on a promising new direction in the lab: genetic manipulation. To begin testing, I needed to obtain a sample of genetic material, what you know as DNA.

I planned to collect the sample by swabbing the inside *mmm-bzzz* the lining of her mouth. I sent one of my ten thousand selves to accomplish *mmm-bzzz* perform this task.

But Clarity wouldn't open her mouth. My tiny single self hovered in front of her lips, bobbing in the breeze from her nostrils, and she wouldn't let me in.

She looked at my larger self looming over her, and I saw the worry in her eyes. This was new to her. Maybe she was afraid *mmm-bzzz* scared I was going to hurt her again.

Whatever her thinking, I sent my lone self closer to her mouth. I used his feelers and wings to tickle her soft lips.

Suddenly, Clarity's lips parted. She let out a flurry of noises from the back of her throat, a string of quick, chiming tones resonating through her sinuses, ringing from the top of her head. They were high-pitched as the song of a bird,

The tinkling of icicles snapping from a tree branch,
The whistling of wind through a hollow stone,
The singing of flowers with pollen-heavy pistils,
The cries of the stars in the night, forever
Sighing x-rays gamma rays radio waves neutrinos
On solar breezes swirling with glittering powder.
It was the first time I'd heard a human laugh. For an instant, I thought I'd hurt her somehow . . . but then I realized she was smiling. The fear was gone *mmm-bzzz* vanished from her eyes.

Seizing the opportunity, I tickled her more. Her mouth opened wider, and I

flew
inside.

My whole perspective changed in there. It was one thing to see her every day, to understand the functions of her body. To communicate in a rudimentary way.

It was quite another to be *part* of her, if only for a moment. To be intimately connected *mmm-bzzz* joined together.

Afloat in the warm red vault of her, I drifted over the moist mound of her tongue. I hovered between her flat yellow teeth, hoping she wouldn't bite down, and extended my own hollow tongue toward the inside of her cheek. Rubbing the slick flesh, I drew in a sample of her buccal cells, rich with genetic material, and stored it in my second stomach.

I wished I could have lingered, but I must have tickled her again. Her laugh sounded ten thousand times louder from inside her mouth. The expulsion of air threw my tiny self tumbling from her lips.

While Clarity slept, I tampered with her DNA. My component selves zipped this way and that through the lab, mapping her genome and feeding the data into the computers.

Digital simulations predicted the likely *mmm-bzzz* probable outcome of each change. I could see the affected traits and the nature, degree, and viability of their altered expressions. Sophisticated algorithms calculated the likelihood that the changes would flip the right switch.

The switch that would bring down the wall that protected humanity.

I had done this kind of work before on many *mmm-bzzz* countless worlds, with other species. Such is my people's purpose in life: to help those who cannot help themselves. To rectify the flaws *mmm-bzzz* solve the problems that hold certain species back from their rightful destinies.

This work always follows certain patterns. I've learned to recognize key moments—the breakthrough, for example—and quickly grasp their significance.

How many times had such a breakthrough led me to a solution? How many times at such a moment had I felt the certainty of rightness in all my thousand thousand stomachs? It had always been a cause for celebration.

But not this time.

In fact, when the latest simulation suggested a new direction, and I knew in my thousands of guts that I'd found the key, I set it aside. I avoided it.

Instead, I went to Clarity and fed her. I watched her smile as she licked the honey from her lips. I made her laugh with a new trick I'd invented, tickling her by fluttering *mmm-bzzz* flickering the wings of my ten thousand selves all over her body at once.

But all along, the knowledge grew in the back of my hive-mind. Dread expanded like a storm cloud above us.

Each time I went back to my work, I knew I was making progress. Each time I took it a step further, the certainty in my bellies became stronger.

Resequencing her DNA according to the template I'd designed would make her susceptible. If applied to other members of her species, the effect would be the same.

Here is the genius of it. Her body was perfected, indestructible. How then to pull away *mmm-bzzz* remove the shield?

The same way you scratch a diamond. Turn the indestructible against itself.

If, that is, you can stand *mmm-bzzz* bear to do it.

As weeks passed, I realized I might be the only one to design *mmm-bzzz* find a solution. In our daily meetings, the other swarms claimed not to be anywhere near a remotely viable approach.

Maybe, if I said nothing, I could still save Clarity. If I kept my solution to myself, and no one else came up with the same idea or an equally effective alternative, perhaps Clarity and her species would be spared.

But it was a slim hope, and I knew it. Other swarms were also researching *mmm-bzzz* exploring genetic modalities, and we were all working from the same baseline data. They could find the solution as easily as I had.

Unless I started submitting falsified reports. Unless I intentionally misdirected every other swarm by steering them away from what I knew was the answer.

In which case, I would be violating *mmm-bzzz* breaking sacrosanct rules of my species. I would be undermining the purpose of our holy *mmm-bzzz* sacred mission to this world. I would be jeopardizing the future of my own species.

But the one creature I'd found precious in all the galaxy, the one being whom I adored with all ten thousand of my hearts, would *live*.

One night, I was called *mmm-bzzz* summoned to join the others for the Rite.

All the swarms flowed out of the great silver ship at once, shimmering dark ribbons rippling into the night sky. We merged together into one giant cloud, one great swarm of all our multitudes on this planet. We formed concentric circles and began to turn, each ring rotating in a different direction, alternating clockwise and counterclockwise.

The bright stars cast their flickering light upon us,

Glittering from our wings
and the polished cobalt facets of our eyes.
A billion trillion streams of starlight
Rushed out of the limitless heavens
and washed down over us.
So much light everywhere,
Direct, reflected, refracted, visible, invisible.
The universe a filigree of crisscrossed streamers,
The planet tumbling through a coruscating mesh.

And as I flew with the others through the tailings of that illuminated fall, I was reminded of our purpose, of our faith in that purpose. The sheer scope and importance of that purpose.

I'd come to think of it as something I could set aside just this once. As if denying an entire species its destiny was something I could live with.

The feeling of companionship with Clarity had been so profoundly *mmm-bzzz* powerfully alluring. It was so unlike the unity I felt with my hive-mind brothers, which was always inflexibly predictable. The pressure of the swarms in all their thousands upon thousands was ever-present, intrusive, demanding. Emotionless.

Lonely.

But did that absolve me of my responsibilities? Did it negate the sacred trust that had given my existence meaning for eons upon eons?

Here is how the Rite ends. How it ended that night.

Each of us carries a photoelectric wafer, tiny but highly sensitive. As we fly in glittering circles in the sky, the wafers absorb starlight and store it.

Then, at the right moment, we disperse, carrying our tiny burdens. All the millions of us, laden with our blue-glowing wafers, filter into the night. We seek out
    the darkest shadows,
    pitch black lightless
    holes, hollows, burrows,
    under roots, under rocks, in caves,
and we converge there, releasing our cargoes. The shadows blossom with tiny constellations of azure light.

It is a sacrament. *Mmm-bzzz.* It is a symbol.

We are pollinating the darkness

with starlight.

After the Rite, all our swarms came back together and mixed under the stars, merging our hive-minds into one mega-consciousness.

It was then, in that one colossal union, that the collective reasserted itself. I lost myself for a while in the mega-hive, surrendering *mmm-bzzz* submerging my own swarm's identity in the crushing embrace of the all-encompassing overmind.

Smothered by consensus, I felt the drive of species preservation in its fullest extreme. The urgency of our mission overshadowed *mmm-bzzz* choked out all other considerations. Surviving and helping humanity reach the stars were the only things that mattered.

When thoughts of my love for Clarity filtered into the gestalt, they were instantly extinguished. The mega-hive-mind tingled with disapproval and disgust.

And they didn't give her a second thought. *We* didn't give her a second thought.

We had no desire for Clarity.

I emerged from the mega-consciousness like a drowning creature gasping for breath. As the collective disengaged *mmm-bzzz* released my swarm, I scrambled to pull myself back together, to retrieve the uniqueness that had been squeezed out of me.

When I did, I realized I was different from before. Merging with the overmind had reaffirmed my attachment to my people. Saving them felt more imperative than ever.

But as my individual thoughts and feelings came back to the fore, my love and commitment to Clarity remained strong *mmm-bzzz* undimmed. I could no more bear to lose her than I could bear to betray my people.

Two conflicting and powerful demands warred for dominance within my swarm. If Clarity and humanity lived, my people would devolve into non-sentient drones. If I saved my people, Clarity and her species would perish.

Then, suddenly, new insight blossomed within me. I saw the path to a new solution, flawed *mmm-bzzz* imperfect

but maybe one I could live with.

The morning after the Rite, I awakened her as always, dabbing honey on her lips. Her clear green eyes flickered open, no less beautiful than the day before or the first time I'd seen them.

I worked hard all day, checking *mmm-bzzz* and rechecking my calculations, running and rerunning the simulations. Growing and programming legions of surgical nanobots to follow my instructions precisely.

I fed them to her that evening, with her wheat germ. And then I waited and watched.

The next day, there was no visible change. Clarity smiled and laughed like always. Her radiance was undiminished.

But when I scanned her, the equipment told a different story. Her DNA had changed. Overnight, it had radically altered *mmm-bzzz* transformed her metabolism.

The tests I performed confirmed the success of my treatment. Clarity had begun to deteriorate.

She no longer had the capability to live forever in her physical form.

Before long, Clarity's condition was not unique among humans.

After she received the treatment, and tests confirmed its effectiveness, the swarms decided to administer it to all humans in the labs.

Of course, no one knew the full truth behind it. No one knew the way it would *really* work.

No one had found the secret coding I'd hidden away within my intricate genetic construct. They saw the surface changes, analyzed the modifications they would cause, but they didn't detect the catch I'd built into my solution.

When the results of the treatment were the same on the other humans in the labs, the swarms wasted no time going forth to treat every human being in the world.

But the swarms didn't realize there was no need to hurry. Humankind wouldn't die any time soon.

It was true that we'd brought down *mmm-bzzz* toppled the protective wall around Clarity's species. But what only *I* knew was that the process would be a *slow* one. It would take *years* for individual humans to die.

And it would take even *longer* for the human species to perish in its entirety.

I'd made life last as long as it could. Not just weeks and months, but dozens of years.

The human body would turn against itself over time, breaking down *mmm-bzzz* eroding on a long, slow slide to oblivion. I'd chosen prolonged aging and decline as humanity's lot instead of sudden, jarring extinction.

I'd given Clarity time to fully appreciate the joys of corporeal life before leaving it. I'd given her time to adjust to her mortality.

I'd given *myself* time to adjust to her mortality, too.

I'd also arranged for my people's salvation . . . though that, too, would take a while.

Humanity would not die all at once as originally planned *mmm-bzzz* anticipated, releasing a burst of inner light massive enough to reboot our soulware. In fact, it would take ages for enough human light to become available.

Thanks to my concealed genetic tampering, the altered trait I'd devised would be passed down to every generation of humanity with absolute fidelity all down the long ages.

As humans died, our ship would collect *mmm-bzzz* gather portions of their inner light, just enough that their escape to the stars would not be impeded. Someday, many generations later, the ship would have enough light to conduct the reboot, and my people would return to their mission.

In the interim, though, we would devolve *mmm-bzzz* revert to a primitive state. Until the Great Restoration, we would exist as common insects *mmm-bzzz* honeybees, lacking sentience. We would pollinate flowers, gather nectar, and build hives, but we would not remember who we were, where we'd come from, or what our mission had been.

It was a steep price to pay, but I decided it was better than the alternative. Better, I thought, to give Clarity a long life and delay my people's restoration rather than hastening it by killing her and the rest of humanity outright.

So the fates of humans and bees were intertwined and set in motion.

We bees would tend the fields and flowers of Earth as once we'd tended infinitely strange species of sentient lifeforms on distant worlds. Meanwhile, generation after generation of humans would inhabit the world and depart into space upon death as pure light.

In space, humans would find glittering multitudes of species from other worlds lighting the darkest night like glowing beacons,

Shooting through starfields,
Swimming through nebulae,
Crisscross
ing flares flash
ing past a trillion wonders,
Weaving a tapestry of light
ning, a restless paint
ing of shimmering threads, rush
ing rivers all in photons of gold,
Never limited
Never alone.
And *Clarity* had made it all possible.

There came a day when I freed her from her bonds and opened the door of the ship to the outside world. She left . . . but to my surprise *mmm-bzzz* delight, she came back.

She always came back to me. Through all the weeks and months
and years
mmm-bzzz and decades that followed,
She always came back.

One day, a lifetime later, as the sun set over distant, snowcapped mountains, Clarity returned to me once more.

By then, my handiwork was plain to see; thankfully, I still had enough of a mind to comprehend it. Though other swarms' soulware was almost completely degraded by then, mine was just starting to lose ground to the Great Breakdown.

Clarity's fur had turned gray, and her flesh was sagging and wrinkled. She moved slowly, plodding *mmm-bzzz* hobbling through the tall grass, choosing each step with great care. Stooped and withered, she had changed so much since the first time I'd seen her, over fifty years earlier.

Her green eyes were sunken and filmy. Tears flowed from them
into the gray down
on her cheeks.

I think she knew what was coming. I think that was why she was there. She was weak and fragile beyond belief.

She almost fell to the floor, but I caught her and helped her to the silver exam table. She sat on the familiar metal surface, head bobbing, then slowly lay back.

Her eyes closed *mmm-bzzz* drifted shut, and she lost consciousness. As she slept there, curled up on the table, I examined her with my instrumentation. The joy I'd felt at seeing her turned to grief.

According to the tests, Clarity had reached the inevitable moment. The one I'd programmed into her DNA and delayed as long as I could.

When I realized what was happening to her, my ten thousand selves flew apart, swarming the lab in denial and confusion. I was dizzy with the whirlwind of impending loss, though I'd known this moment was approaching for decades. Though I was the one who'd invented it.

I could not bear the thought of existence
without her.
The knowledge that my work would lead to
Endless days
A procession
A weight
A space
A longing
All the worse
For having once
Been quelled.

It was then I realized, as much as I'd changed her, she had changed me more. As I hovered over her, gazing at her from every angle with my twenty thousand eyes, I knew how different I was because of her.

My hive-mind had realigned in fundamental, ineffable ways. I had

reached beyond the swarm and shown personal compassion to another creature of another species. Not as part of an altruistic mission programmed into my genes, but because of the
yearning
of my ten thousand beating hearts.

In changing me, she had changed everything for herself and her people. Unlocked potentials that had yet to express *mmm-bzzz* manifest themselves.

And now, for her, for us,
there could be no going back.

Gathering my scattered selves together, I pushed back the grief as best I could and prepared for the final stage of our project.

Clarity slept soundly for hours on the hard metal table. As much suffering as she had found there, I think it still felt like home to her.

The monitors told me she was failing, but I didn't pay much attention to them. I was too busy watching Clarity's face as her allotted corporeal lifespan ran out *mmm-bzzz* expired.

I watched her toothless mouth as ragged, staggered breaths flowed in and out of it. I watched her nose wrinkle and flare as it caught some scent or the memory of one. I watched as her closed eyes flickered behind the lids, following the course of a dream.

Eventually, her eyes fluttered open
Like the wings of butterflies,
Soft as velvet, damp with dew.

By then, everything was in place. What she saw when she looked around were the grasslands of her home,
The amber plains rippling
In the wind, in the blazing sunlight.
Spear tips bobbing in the lazy current.

I tilted the table so she could see what lay ahead. A silver ship burrowing up out of the ground. Doors opening along the length of it, letting out ribbons of tiny, glittering creatures.

Suddenly, a woman emerged *mmm-bzzz* stepped out from behind a boulder. She walked unafraid with shoulders squared as her fellow humans cowered and ran. Her long, dark mane rippled in the morning breeze,

So soft, so flowing,
A beautiful veil cascading over shoulders
Over chest like a waterfall at night.
Clear eyes wide with fearless wonder, she gazed at the swarm, and the swarm *mmm-bzzz* and we *mmm-bzzz*
And *I* gazed back at *her*. Thousands of unblinking eyes
Like chips of polished ebony.
The woman in the tableau smiled, and so did the woman on the table. Past and future merged as one.

Then, the scene around us changed. It became a mirror image of the lab, with young Clarity strapped to the silver table.

My swarm settled *mmm-bzzz* descended upon her, tickling her with ten thousand pairs of flickering wings. Holographic Clarity squirmed and laughed with delight, and flesh-and-blood Clarity laughed, too. The laughter synchronized, high-pitched as the song of a bird,
The tinkling of icicles snapping from a tree branch
The whistling of wind through a hollow stone.

And by the time it subsided, she was almost gone. I switched the projection to a silent image of starry space to ease her transition. Galaxies pinwheeled around us. Comets streaked past, hanging tails of brilliant incandescence. Sprays of stars drifted like pollen through the inky night, sparkling like gold dust sprinkled over obsidian.

I went to her. All ten thousand of my selves hovered over her, gazing upon that well-known form, just as well loved in old age as in youth.

Suddenly, she gasped, and her eyes shot open. I dared hope, in spite of the evidence of my instruments, that she might yet survive.

But then.
Mmm-bzzz.
But then,
You tremble with the effort,
shudder and go limp
with a sigh.
You settle
settle
to the table
like a feather
or a brittle leaf,
A windblown seed.

Don't go.

Darkness fills me,
a smoky
smoky cloud
obstructing all hope,
choking off
all everything,
then dispersing
as a tongue of flame
Shoots through me.
Burning off the cloud
like morning mist
before the blinding
blinding dawn.

You.

Your iridescence melts the shadows with a roar,
Then laughs and twirls and disappears,
As you in all your sparkling raiment soar,
Away from every struggle, pain, and tear.

A Walk In The Woods

Vaughan Stanger

Vaughan Stanger tells us that '"A Walk in the Woods" was my attempt to exploit a life-long passion for—well, you can work it out from the title—within a near-future setting.' Originally published in issue 189 of Interzone, *this story was not supposed to have a sequel. But ten years down the line, he found himself wrestling with what he thought was a quite different story, which resolutely failed to gel. Vaughan goes on to say: 'Eventually, some kind of fiction-warping weirdness happened, and a familiar set of characters emerged from the ruins. The result was "A Walk in the Rain".' Strange are the ways of the writer's mind. Come 2025, who knows what further weirdness will ensue?*

Vaughan continues to pursue his love of writing short stories while telling folks that he's on the verge of starting the final (definitely this time, honest!) draft of his novel. Examples of his work can be found in Nature Futures, Daily Science Fiction, Music for Another World, *and, of course,* Postscripts. *Many of his older stories are now available in Kindle and epub editions.*

T HE SQUIRREL SCAMPERED AMONGST THE BRANCHES OF THE oak tree, chattering facts about its host in a Disney-style voice. Vincent Cornell made a mental note to reprogram the creature at the earliest opportunity.

"Sessile oak: WiredWood.org/Welby/oak27, age ninety-two years, height thirty-five metres. Sessile oak . . . "

"Details," said Vincent.

A table of data materialised in front of him, seeming to hang in the air like some wraith of the forest. Several of the entries for this tree were blank, while others required updating. Three-and-a-half years after its inception, the Wired Wood project had yet to establish a complete inventory of the local flora and fauna. The task of updating the database was a routine but enjoyable aspect of Vincent's work. After he had finished dictating the entries, he closed his eyes and took a deep breath. The aromas of growth and decay delighted him, as always.

The crackle of twigs breaking underfoot jolted Vincent out of his reverie. A pale-faced young woman emerged from behind the oak tree and walked towards him. She was dressed in combat trousers and a white tee shirt that emphasised her willowy physique. Her grin revealed teeth that were slightly crooked.

"Those aren't ordinary sunglasses, are they?"

She spoke with a Welsh accent, but there was a hint of small-town America too. It was an odd yet beguiling combination. Vincent gave a nervous little laugh.

"They're a new designer style. A thousand Euros a pair."

"Really?" Her frown suggested that she was not convinced by their fashion potential. "I'm guessing they've been augmented in some way."

"That's right," he said. "They let me view data overlays generated by my belt-top." He tapped a forefinger against the wallet-sized device. "I'm conducting a survey for the Wired Wood project. You might have seen a documentary about our work on BBC4 last year."

The woman brushed aside a few strands of auburn hair that had blown across her face. "Yes, I did watch that programme. But I'm afraid it didn't convince me that connecting forests to the Web was a good idea. In my view, Welby Wood ought to remain a refuge from the *unreal* world." She made an expansive gesture, as if claiming ownership of the stands of oak and hornbeam.

"I'm afraid that's not how our masters in Brussels see things," he said. "'Logged-in for life' is their slogan. Still, our work is not all dull tagging and cataloguing." He extracted a spare pair of glasses from his rucksack. "Here, try these on."

The glasses slid down her nose like a skier approaching a precipice. She allowed him to adjust the fit, not seeming to mind the physical contact. When he pressed a stud on the side of the frame the lenses darkened to full opacity, obscuring eyes that were black as peat.

Vincent spoke a series of commands. A moment later, her head was jerking from side to side. He grinned at her even though she could not see him.

"What am I looking at?" she asked.

"Squirrel-cam footage."

She pushed the glasses up onto her forehead. "You are joking, right?"

"No; the video is genuine. I recorded it yesterday."

She watched some more of the footage before handing the glasses back to him.

"I suppose it might just start a craze for Vermin Video. Not really my thing, though."

"Most people seem to enjoy it," he remarked.

"Well, I'm not 'most people'!"

Stung by the put-down, Vincent held up his hands in a gesture of contrition. "Look, I'm sorry if I offended you. Let's start again, shall we? I'm Vincent . . ."

After a brief pause, she said: "And I'm Rachael." With that, she turned away from him, bringing their conversation to an unequivocal end.

Vincent felt a pang of desire as he watched Rachael stroll along the path, her slender body dappled with sunlight. He was tempted to follow, but something in the set of her shoulders indicated that she wanted to be alone. Shortly after she disappeared from view he heard a loud sneeze ricochet through the trees, accompanied by the clatter of crows spooked from their treetop homes.

Feeling pleased with himself, Vincent unclipped the videophone from his belt. His progress report was overdue.

"Hard at work today?"

Vincent glanced up from the soil acidity equipment, which he was attempting to recalibrate. Rachael was standing between two hornbeam saplings, her exposed forearms as smooth as their bark. Her smile was beguiling.

"Hi, Rachael," he said. "It's lovely to see you again."

Which was a simple statement of the truth, for Vincent had greatly enjoyed Rachael's company during their half-dozen encounters in Welby Wood.

Her reply was lost to a succession of sneezes, each more powerful than the last. Vincent noticed that the tissue she held to her nose was spotted with blood. Concern tightened his face into a frown.

"Are you alright?" he asked.

Still dabbing at her nostrils, Rachael ambled up to him. "I'm fine," she said. "The kindergarten is closed today, so I thought I'd pester you instead." She winked at him. "You don't mind, do you?"

Before Vincent could reply, a red-cross icon buzzed across his field of view, alerting him to an infection in one of the saplings.

"Sorry Rachael, but this is urgent. I've got to log these readings immediately."

She sighed and turned away.

Rueing the lost opportunity but mindful of his responsibilities, Vincent set to work. He removed his digital camera from its pouch and began recording images of the stricken hornbeam. Most of its leaves seemed healthy, but he found several that were disfigured by brown splotches. He picked up a leaf that had fallen to the ground; it felt brittle as ancient parchment. Fearing the worst, Vincent cut a strip of bark from the base of the tree trunk. A dusting of spores smeared the interior of the sample jar.

Vincent spent half-an-hour downloading data from every tree in the glade. It was a task that would have been much simpler if Welby Wood's rural-area network had been installed as planned. Unfortunately, the necessary funding had yet to materialise.

Having instructed his computer to perform a quick-look analysis of the data, Vincent placed a video call to Karl Badoer. Sky-blue eyes and an unkempt moustache smiled back at him.

"I've just been talking to a friend of yours," Karl said, panning the camera to frame Rachael's face. She looked embarrassed.

"You seemed preoccupied," she remarked. "So I decided to walk to the lake. Where I bumped into your colleague . . . "

"Sorry about that, Rachael," he said. "I'll be with you shortly." She rewarded him with a smile that dispelled his sudden pang of jealousy, but which could do nothing to lessen his disquiet about the hornbeams. "Could you pass me back to Karl? Thanks . . . "

Something in his tone must have alerted the engineer, for his grin had given way to a frown. "What's the problem?"

"It looks like we've got a major fungal infection in the north-eastern sector."

"I see ... Should I set up a videoconference with Brussels for this afternoon?"

"Yes, that would be a sensible precaution. In the meantime, I've got a preliminary DNA analysis running. We should have the results in ten minutes or so."

Vincent broke the connection and started to jog along the path that would bring him to Summerhouse Lake. Constructed by some minor nobleman in the early nineteenth century, the eponymous building had long since rotted away, but the lake it had once overlooked continued to thrive, providing a haven for pike, perch, and waterfowl.

When Vincent reached the gravel path that encircled the lake, he spotted Karl and Rachael standing next to a bed of reedmace. Rachael was wearing Karl's spare pair of glasses. They seemed to be sharing a joke.

Without warning, Rachael's laughter broke down into a series of gasps. Her eyes flared with panic as she tipped the contents of her rucksack onto the ground. After a brief rummage, she located an inhaler. Several doses were required before her breathing returned to normal.

During the attack, Vincent had felt powerless to help. Now, he wished he could do more than just sound concerned.

"Are you okay, Rachael?"

"Yes, I'm fine," she replied, while repacking her rucksack. "There's really no need to worry." She smiled at Vincent and then turned to face Karl. "You were just about to show me another of your tricks ... "

Karl glanced at Vincent, who responded with a shrug. The engineer frowned, but seemed willing to comply with Rachael's request. He pointed towards a nearby weeping willow. "Look over there."

Intrigued, Vincent activated his infrared link to Karl's computer. Seconds later, a pair of fox cubs emerged from the undergrowth. A beautiful, honey-coloured vixen followed them onto the bank. The cubs darted in and out of the foliage, ambushing each other.

Rachael's sigh expressed a regret that had become almost universal of late. "Such lovely creatures," she said.

"It's a pity about the cull," said Vincent.

Karl shrugged. "We could not risk a rabies epidemic."

"I suppose not," Rachael said. "But seeing Karl's party piece has made me wonder what else is virtual around here."

Rachael scanned the periphery of the lake, sliding her glasses up and down her forehead. After several seconds, she pointed across the water. "That silver birch isn't real, for a start."

"We lost it to the Blight five years ago," said Karl.

Vincent raised his eyebrows, but his colleague's expression remained deadpan.

Rachael handed the glasses back to Karl with a sigh. "Maybe there are times when illusion is preferable to reality."

Her sombre remark brought the conversation to an end. As he gazed at the lake, Vincent found himself wishing that Karl would make an excuse and leave. To his intense annoyance, it was Rachael who moved first. After a handshake that left Vincent feeling dissatisfied, she wandered off into the trees. A few seconds later came the familiar volley of sneezes.

Karl cleared his throat. "I think your friend is allergic to Welby Wood," he said.

Before Vincent could reply, a loud beep from his computer informed him that the data analysis was ready. He glanced at the results and groaned. "Maybe she's reacting to the spores from this bastard."

Karl inspected the results on his own display. "Is that what I think it is?"

"I'm afraid so. It looks like some idiot of a gene-hacker has released a mutated variant of the Blight. But this time it's attacking the hornbeams."

The warbling of the videophone was only just audible above the sound of branches creaking in the wind. Even so, it was sufficient to distract Vincent from his work. Annoyed by the intrusion, he spoke the shutdown command. The panorama of silver birch trees faded to grey. He glanced at his feet. Only a moment ago, he had been standing on a carpet of bluebells. The illusion had been beautiful—a reminder of Welby Wood in its heyday. The silver birches were long gone, of course, likewise the flowers they had once shaded. And now the more numerous hornbeams were under attack.

Vincent removed his tri-D glasses and pushed one hand against the rear wall of the chamber, which swung upwards with a hiss. The phone was still ringing, indicative of an unusually persistent caller. Most likely it was the project monitor, who would doubtless repeat her previous warnings about overspending the equipment budget. It was usual for Karl to handle such calls, but he had chosen to go to the pub for lunch with the other members of the team.

The videophone was hidden beneath a broken display screen that someone had deposited on the workbench.

"Vincent Cornell here," he said.

To his surprise, he found himself staring at Rachael's face. She had never phoned him at work before. Her wide-eyed expression made it clear that she was scared of something.

"Vincent . . . I need . . . your help." Her words were punctuated by painful-sounding gasps.

"What's the problem?"

"My inhaler . . . I can't breathe!"

"Where are you, Rachael?"

But he had guessed that already. Two weeks earlier, he had warned her not to enter Welby Wood until the Blight was eradicated. Evidently she had ignored his advice.

"Help me!"

"Rachael, you must tell me *exactly* where—"

Before he could finish, his view of Rachael's face was replaced by a blur of clouds and treetops. Then the image blanked out.

"Rachael, are you alright?"

Faint crackling sounds emerged from the speaker.

"Rachael, can you hear me?

There was no reply.

"Rachael?"

Fearing the worst, Vincent broke the connection and phoned the emergency services.

Vincent rubbed a forefinger around the inside of his collar. For some obscure reason he had felt compelled to dress more smartly than usual. Unfortunately, his wool-mix jacket was too heavy for the sticky warmth that pervaded Denbigh Ward's reception area.

The nearest door opened, revealing a woman whom Vincent almost mistook for Rachael. She had the same auburn hair and skinny physique, but the prominent lines on her forehead indicated that she was several years older. He introduced himself, trying not to sound apologetic.

"Good morning, Vincent," she said in return. There was a reserved quality to the greeting, as if his suitability was being assessed. "I'm Josie Warren—Rachael's sister."

"It's good to meet you, Josie." He offered his hand in greeting. Her handshake was as firm as her expression.

"Do you know what to expect when you see Rachael?"

Vincent shook his head, not knowing what to say. On the two occasions he had tried to visit Rachael the ward sister had turned him away, claiming that she was not well enough to receive visitors. Whenever he phoned, what little information he received had only served to heighten his anxiety. Finally, after four weeks, he had received a phone call from Josie. Two speed cameras had flashed at his car while he drove to the hospital.

"I'll be candid," said Josie. "There isn't a lot more that can be done for Rachael. Ever since her early teens, she has suffered from a wide range of steadily worsening allergies. Dust, pollen, plastics, food additives—you name it, she reacts to it. But thanks to a specially tailored drug regime, she has been able to cope. Until last month, that is. Because those spores she ingested in Welby Wood induced an allergic response so severe it shut down her immune system. Permanently, according to her consultant."

Muttering under his breath, Vincent cursed the anonymous gene-hacker who had let loose this new form of the Blight. Five years ago, during the first outbreak, Rachael had been living in Kentucky. This time, tragically, there would be no sanctuary for her.

"Surely there must be some kind of gene therapy that would help?"

Josie shook her head. "The doctors have tried everything."

"But there *must* be something!"

"I'm sorry, Vincent, really I am. If we sealed Rachael inside an isolation chamber she might survive indefinitely. But both of us know she would never consent to that. She's too much of a free spirit."

Vincent realised that he could not deny Josie's prognosis, even though her apparent composure made him feel numb. He wanted to cry, to scream, to rage at the unfairness of it all, but Josie's presence made him bottle up his emotions. All he could do was nod.

"One last thing, Vincent." Josie was staring into his eyes now, as if hoping to impose her will by hypnotism. "Rachael can be very demanding, never more so than now. Please don't make any promises that you can't keep."

"I'll be careful."

"Just remember what I said."

Josie pushed open the door to Rachael's room. A strong draught wafted past Vincent, as if even the air conditioning system had been programmed to resist his admittance. But the scene within made him smile.

Digital wallpaper displayed images of an immaculate lawn bordered by elegant, varicoloured shrubs, with steps leading down to a fishpond covered with water lilies. Above Vincent's head, cumulus clouds sailed across a vista of pale blue infinity. From hidden speakers came a medley of birdsong. The illusion of standing in an English country garden was surprisingly convincing, Vincent thought.

Rachael was dozing in her wheelchair. Behind her, a blossom-laden apple tree gave the illusion of shade. Josie patted Vincent's forearm, as if to reinforce the briefing he had just received.

As soon as the door clicked shut, Vincent sat down on the edge of the bed and waited for Rachael to wake. Less than a minute had passed when she smacked her lips and mumbled something unintelligible. She blinked at him repeatedly, as if the real world was harder to focus on than any daydream.

"Hello, Vincent," she whispered. "It's good to see you again." She tugged her dressing gown around her body, in a charming if gauche attempt at modesty. The effort seemed to drain her of energy.

He reached over and patted her forearm, unconsciously mimicking Josie. "Thanks for inviting me, Rachael. I've really missed you."

Rachael smiled. "Well, you're here now...which is all that matters...Anyway, how've you been?"

"I'm very well."

He tried to come up with some small talk, but soon found himself faltering. Rachael seemed unimpressed with his efforts.

"Has a fox...stolen your tongue?"

Before Vincent could reply, she reached for the oxygen mask that dangled next to the wheelchair. To him, it seemed that her vitality was wheezing away with each hard-won breath.

"Rachael, why didn't you phone for an ambulance? Calling me instead, that was..." He was going to say "stupid", but he looked into her eyes and shook his head instead. The truth was that the delay had made little difference.

Rachael seemed to think so too. Ignoring his question, she steered the wheelchair around him, intent on inspecting a flock of butterflies that fluttered above a buddleia bush. Vincent followed her across the room, powerless to resist her undertow. He stood by her side and studied the simulation. One of the red admirals was struggling amongst the blooms, having lost a wing.

"Poor thing," said Rachael. "Not long for this world."

Vincent stared into the distance, too choked to say anything.

Rachael tugged at his hand. "I need your help."

"I'll do anything for you, Rachael," he said. "Anything at all."

"I want you . . . to take me back . . . to Welby Wood . . . for one final walk . . . ."

Vincent turned away, unable to maintain eye contact any longer. He knew that his offer was reckless. Even if Rachael were fit enough to walk, which he doubted, Welby Wood was out of bounds for the foreseeable future.

"I *can* do it!"

Rachael's tone was so insistent that Vincent felt compelled to turn and face her gaze. Blinking back tears, he watched in astonishment as she heaved herself out of the wheelchair. He held out his arms for support, but she shook her head. She managed half-a-dozen steps before collapsing onto the bed.

As he tucked the bedclothes around her, he said, "Maybe in a few days. If you can build up your strength up a bit."

Vincent knew he had told a lie; knew too that he had responded to Rachael's request in exactly the way Josie had warned against. Even so, he felt no guilt. It was Rachael's wishes that mattered, not her sister's desire to supervise the process of dying. And even a forlorn hope was better than none.

As he sat by Rachael's side, he found himself recalling his father's terminal illness, a decade earlier. Throughout those last few pain-wracked months, William Cornell had tried to organise a final trip to his beloved France, to bid farewell to the country he loved. Each night, he had fallen asleep with his passport tucked under his pillow, convinced that his family was trying to frustrate his plans. He must have known he was too weak to make the journey, but his determination to give his life a fitting end had moved Vincent deeply.

As he pondered Rachael's request again, it occurred to him that there might be a solution after all.

"Don't worry, Rachael," he said. "We will find a way."

Vincent swore under his breath as he watched Karl pace around the laboratory. The engineer seemed determined to stamp his indecision into the concrete floor, applying scientific rigour to a matter that required a simple "yes" or "no".

"What's the problem, Karl? We could do this so easily, with minimal impact on the budget. And it's not as if we can do any fieldwork at the moment, with Welby Wood under quarantine."

Karl came to a halt by the rear wall of the visualisation chamber. He began stroking his moustache with his fingers, a quirk that generally preceded a decision.

"I have strong misgivings about your proposal. If our 'friend' at HQ ever discovers what we are up to . . . "

"She won't," Vincent insisted.

"How can you be so sure?"

Vincent sighed; he was well aware that his argument was based more on emotion than logic.

"Look, even if she did find out, we could tell her we were testing Virtual Welby Wood to determine its suitability for disabled users. That's a worthy goal, surely?"

The engineer grunted but said nothing.

"You will help Rachael, won't you?"

Karl groomed his moustache some more before acquiescing. Vincent patted him on the back and returned to his workstation.

As Karl had doubtless surmised, there was a great deal of work still to be done.

Vincent felt a chill in his stomach as he watched Rachael steer her wheelchair into the laboratory. Earlier that morning, Josie had told him that her sister had only weeks to live.

After a breath so deep it sent a shudder through her entire body, Rachael pulled the oxygen mask from her face. To Vincent, the skin below seemed as fragile as a leaf that had succumbed to the Blight.

"So this . . . is where . . . you work." Rachael gestured towards the equipment on the workbench. "Impressive."

Vincent glanced at Josie, who was standing just behind the wheelchair. Her taut expression suggested the aftermath of a quarrel. He raised his eyebrows in a bear-with-me expression, hoping to defuse the tension.

"Welcome to the Wired Wood project and its happy band of researchers." He waved towards Karl, who was fiddling with one of the power cables that fed the walls of the visualisation chamber. "You remember my colleague, Karl Badoer?"

The engineer smiled at Rachael. "There are usually six of us working here. But today, the others have gone on leave. Vincent has been most . . . persuasive."

"I am grateful . . . to you both." Her words ended with a painful-sounding gasp. She raised the oxygen mask to her face and seemed to gain some relief.

Not for the first time, Vincent found himself wondering whether Rachael's consultant had been wise to let her leave the hospital. Then he recalled his father lying on a metal-framed bed, morphine dripping into withered arm, while monitors beeped away the last moments of his life. William Cornell had died with one hand resting on a cheap French paper-back. The bookmark revealed that he had just begun the final chapter.

"Are you ready . . . for me yet?"

Vincent shook his head, but not in response to Rachael's question. No, he told himself, she was much better off here, fighting for every last breath while pursuing her dream.

"Almost," he replied. "Don't worry, we'll soon have you walking . . . "

He kicked aside the thickets of cabling that were threatening to obstruct Rachael's progress, and helped to position the wheelchair just behind the rear wall of the chamber. Satisfied, he pressed a button on the remote control. The wall swung upwards.

Rachael peered inside. "Do I get . . . a guided tour?"

Vincent stepped into the chamber and spread his arms, as if claiming ownership of the territory within.

"The walls, floor, and ceiling are lined with liquid crystal displays, which double as audio speakers. When the system is activated, it generates an audio-visual simulation of a three-dimensional environment, such as the interior of a building . . . "

Rachael smiled at his joke, which made him feel somewhat less nervous, but he could tell that she was anxious about something. Her left hand kept tapping against the side of the wheelchair.

"Can the floor . . . take the weight?"

Josie broke her silence. "Rachael's wheelchair weighs one hundred and fifty kilos with her sitting in it. Karl told me yesterday that the floor is only

rated for two adults." She jutted her chin at Vincent, as if challenging him
to refute her assertion.

Vincent chose to ignore her; this was one problem that he had anticipated. If necessary, he would carry Rachael into the chamber.

"Here, let me help you," he said.

Rachael shook her head. "No," she gasped. "I want to do this . . . on
my own."

Josie glowered at Vincent, as if assigning him the blame for her sister's
behaviour. He shrugged; Josie's anger meant nothing to him. The two of
them watched in silence as Rachael struggled out of the wheelchair. Pain
etched her face as she tottered into the chamber, supported by a wooden
walking stick.

Vincent glanced at Karl, who responded with a thumbs-up gesture.
Satisfied that everything was ready, he stepped into the chamber and
smiled at Rachael. Her eyes were bright with anticipation. He swung the
rear wall into position, sealing Rachael and himself inside the featureless
void. Briefly, he found himself wondering whether eternity would be like
this.

Dismissing the thought, he placed a pair of tri-D glasses over Rachael's
eyes. When he grasped her right hand, she allowed his fingers to mesh
with her own. He did not need to look at her face to know that she was
smiling.

Before he could tell her how he felt, the sights and sounds of Welby
Wood engulfed them. Rachael cried out, this time with delight rather than
pain. Her eyes darted to and fro, drinking in the panorama of oak trees
and hornbeams. From every direction came the sound of birdsong and the
rustling of leaves. Vincent could almost smell the aromas of springtime,
although he knew that was one detail Karl had been obliged to omit, for
fear of triggering an allergic response.

"Are those pads . . . used for walking?" Rachael was staring at a pair of
raised hexagonal patches that could just be discerned against the undergrowth.

"Rachael, I think it might be safer if you let me . . . "

She shook her head. "I'm going to walk . . . whether you like it . . . or
not!" Her hand slipped out of his grasp, as if to reinforce her decision.

Vincent conceded defeat with a sigh. "Okay Rachael, but please take it
gently. Every footstep registered by the pads will move your viewpoint forward slightly. To get the best effect you must maintain a steady rhythm."

Swaying like a sapling in a gale, Rachael raised her left foot off the floor. It dropped onto the pad as if made of stone. The scene juddered around her.

"You see?" she said. "I can do it!"

But when she attempted a second step, the rubber tip of her walking stick skidded sideways. She crashed to the floor with a despairing cry, banging her head as she fell. Fearing that Rachael might have lost consciousness, Vincent bent down and lifted her into a sitting position. Her head lolled against his chest.

He was still holding her in his arms when the rear wall hissed open. A moment later, Josie was standing at the threshold with her arms crossed. Her expression was livid.

"I did warn you, Vincent. I did *tell* you not to make promises that you couldn't keep."

He ignored her. In his mind's eye, he was strolling arm in arm with Rachael, following a winding path that would lead them to Summerhouse Lake.

Reality jerked him out of the beautiful illusion.

The truth was that Rachael would not be going for a walk in Welby Wood, virtual or otherwise.

Not today, not tomorrow, not ever.

The last hour had tested Vincent's nerves to the limit. He paced back and forth, mulling over the events of the last few weeks, while Karl sat in front of the laptop, making final changes to the software. Eventually, Vincent could endure the tension no longer.

"Are you sure this setup will work?"

Karl sighed. "Rachael will see herself walk. That's the best I can do . . . "

A week had passed since Karl and he had tried to brainstorm a solution in their favourite Indian restaurant. At one point, Karl had proposed strapping Rachael into a force-feedback exoskeleton. He explained that his animation software could be used to stimulate her limbs into a semblance of walking. Vincent rejected the idea, pointing out that Rachael might easily be injured or worse. In any case, after the fiasco in the laboratory, Rachael's consultant had forbidden her to leave the hospital.

In the silence that followed, Vincent had picked at his food, tasting nothing, before pushing his plate aside. When he looked up from the table, he noticed that Karl was gazing at the restaurant's décor.

"Does Rachael's hospital room have digital wallpaper?"

"Yes, it does," replied Vincent. "Oh, I see . . . But hang on, how do we get her to walk?"

Karl stroked his moustache. "I have an idea . . . "

The engineer had worked long into each night, modifying software that had previously been used for animating foxes and squirrels. For his own part, Vincent had pleaded with the hospital authorities for permission to reprogram the digital wallpaper in Room Eight of Denbigh Ward. The consultant's objections had faded away like snow in a thaw when confronted with an expression every bit as resolute as that of his patient. Persuading Josie to hand over her digital images of Rachael had been much harder, but after a furious row she had acquiesced . . .

A loud click from the door brought Vincent back to the present. Rachael rolled into the room, trailing an intravenous unit. Her face was as pale as the bedroom walls.

Josie followed the wheelchair. Her lips were pursed so tightly they seemed empty of blood. There must have been a row, thought Vincent, but quite how it could have been conducted was a mystery to him. The accident in the laboratory had left Rachael unable to speak.

He lifted Rachael out of the wheelchair, taking care not to dislodge the IV line. When she was comfortable beneath the bedclothes, he whispered, "Not long now."

Realising too late what he had just said, Vincent was relieved to see that Rachael had either missed or chosen to ignore his faux pas. Instead, her eyes were bright with anticipation, expressing a feeling that could no longer be spoken. Vincent, too, found himself unable to speak, so he busied himself inspecting the cable that connected Karl's laptop to the hospital's data network.

The silence had begun to seem oppressive when Karl announced that everything was ready. Vincent sat down next to Rachael and clasped her right hand. As their fingers intertwined, the whiteness of the walls gave way to a vista of majestic oaks and spindly saplings, sun-dappled footpaths, and impenetrable briars. A gentle breeze soughed through the branches. From above came the chatter of crows.

Vincent glanced at Rachael. She was gazing intently at the familiar scene, but the movement of her legs beneath the quilt gave him an inkling of her frustration.

"It's okay, Rachael. You *will* go for a walk; I promise."

He took a deep breath and pressed a button on the remote control. Two people emerged from a stand of hornbeams and walked towards Rachael. Vincent mouthed a thank-you to Karl. The engineer had excelled himself in personalising the avatars.

The pair came to a standstill. They waved at Rachael before turning away. The Vincent figure glanced back over his shoulder, inviting her to follow.

Vincent passed the remote control to Rachael. "You can make her walk wherever you want. It's really no different to controlling your wheelchair. Just use the miniature joystick. Like this." He guided her thumb. "Yes, that's it."

Rachael's first few 'steps' were little better than drunken lurches, which seemed destined to end in collision with the nearest tree. Yet with a little practice and some judicious assistance from Karl's computer, she soon had her avatar striding around the glade. From time to time, Vincent had to remind himself to operate his own remote control, so engrossed was he in her progress. But now it was time for him to take charge.

"This way!"

Vincent had directed his avatar onto the path that led to Summerhouse Lake. He knew it would be a short walk, lasting barely five minutes. He suspected that it was the most Rachael could manage.

The lake had just come into view when her avatar began to falter. It stuttered forwards a couple of steps, then another, before finally coming to a halt. Vincent glanced over his shoulder. He was astonished to see that Rachael had discarded her oxygen mask and was sitting upright. Her spindly arms were trembling as she reached out towards her own image.

Vincent detached the IV line and lifted Rachael up off the bed. With his left arm clamped around her chest and her head resting on his shoulder, he operated both remote controls as best he could. The two avatars resumed their short journey to Summerhouse Lake. Rachael's heartbeat seemed fainter with every step.

When the avatars reached the path that girded the lake, Vincent dropped to his knees and placed Rachael on the ground. With the utmost delicacy, he turned her head so that she was looking out across the water towards her beloved trees. He watched as a faint smile flickered over her face, but the light in her eyes was beginning to fade: late afternoon surrendering to a twilight that would last forever.

He kissed her gently on the lips. "Hold onto this moment, Rachael."

Then, with the faintest of sighs, she died.

The mist that cloaked Summerhouse Lake reminded Vincent of a funeral shroud, but the clamour with which its denizens greeted daybreak helped to dispel the illusion. In an hour at most, the sun would burn away the mist and reveal the trees that still fringed the lake. This was one part of Welby Wood that had retained some of its beauty. Elsewhere, the intensive programme of gene therapy had saved less than a third of the hornbeams.

Vincent had not visited the lake since Rachael's death. In the months that followed, his life had entered a state of suspension while he participated in a series of empty rituals. A post-mortem, a funeral, an inquiry into misuse of project resources; none of these things had mattered to him. In the final analysis, all that mattered was that he, with Karl's assistance, had helped Rachael bring her life to a fitting end. That he had lost his job in the process had come as no surprise, though Karl's decision to resign in a gesture of solidarity had touched him deeply.

The engineer was standing next to him now, gazing at the lake, immersed in his own memories.

"Did you bring the disk?" Vincent realised the question was superfluous but felt a need to move on—to make the most of the day.

Karl reached inside his fleece and pulled out a jewel case. "I hope this will bring you some comfort, Vincent." His voice was thick with emotion.

Vincent patted him on the back. "Thanks for everything." After a final handshake, Karl departed.

I owe him so much, thought Vincent.

After walking halfway round the lake, he stepped onto an overgrown footpath that would lead him into the heart of the woodland. Within minutes, he was pushing through tangles of thorn bushes, heedless of the cuts to his hands and face. The first rays of sunlight filtered through the branches, dappling him with camouflage.

When he found the perfect glade, he shrugged off his rucksack, closed his eyes, and turned to face the sun. He basked in the warmth, content to have escaped the world of petty rules and procedures, if only for a while.

Satisfied that he would not be disturbed, he loaded the contents of Karl's disk onto his computer. When the setup process had finished, he donned his glasses and inspected the scene.

Leaning against one of the hornbeams was a slim, dark-haired woman. She favoured Vincent with a beguiling smile; then pushed herself away from the tree and resumed her walk. Casting no shadow, she flitted between patches of sunlight, following a path that was new to him.

Vincent checked the battery read-out and smiled. There was still plenty of time.

A WALK IN THE RAIN

VAUGHAN STANGER

THOSE WERE NOT HIS BOOT PRINTS.

Vincent Cornell obscured the nearest pair of indentations in the simulated loam with precise placements of his own feet. The action only served to heighten his shock at finding them.

Briefly he wondered whether someone had managed to hack Virtual Welby Wood. Such an incursion seemed exceedingly improbable, given Karl Badoer's oft-repeated assurances about the strength of its encryption. Vincent's colleague from the Wired Wood days had not let him down yet. TreeSpace Enterprises depended on the engineer's technical prowess, but so did his own need for privacy.

Having stepped back to reveal the boot prints again, Vincent concluded that their owner was most likely female. The thought provoked a shiver despite Welby's perennial warmth.

Determined to confront the intruder, Vincent struck out along the muddy trail, which wound its leisurely, leaf-strewn way towards Summerhouse Lake. Squirrels chattered, a jay flashed blue and crows cawed from the treetops as he passed by. For once he took little notice.

The scene awaiting him at the water's edge brought him close to tears. He hadn't set eyes on Rachael Warren in almost ten years, not since he'd deleted her data. But there she stood, a willowy, auburn-haired figure clad in combat trousers and white tee shirt, gazing at the lake as if idly counting moorhen chicks.

He wanted to say something, if only to reveal his presence to her, yet his conflicted emotions held him back. In that respect, if no other, little had changed during the ten years since Rachael's death. He recalled how he had taken her avatar for walks in what remained of Welby Wood, but within weeks the Blight's ravages had rendered such excursions pointless. Afterwards, he had considered installing "Rachael" in Virtual Welby, but ultimately he'd decided that setting up TreeSpace Enterprises would serve as a more fitting memorial to her life and loves.

But now, evidently, Karl had decided otherwise, for only he could have installed Rachael. Doubtless she had "arrived" as part of the previous week's software upgrade. At the time, Vincent had assumed that the ultra-sonic raindrops and smart-material mud constituted the only tangible enhancements. Not so, evidently!

Despite his annoyance at this unplanned addition to his sim, Vincent found himself wondering whether his friend had taken the opportunity to upgrade Rachael's avatar. The original version had been capable of little more than basic locomotion and collision avoidance. Could this version actually talk?

He cleared his throat. "Hello, Rachael."

His greeting elicited no response, not even a twitch of the shoulders. Rachael continued to gaze at the lake and its residents. He tried again.

"Rachael—it's me, Vincent."

She continued to ignore him until he closed to within arm's reach, at which point she at last turned around.

Gazing at Rachael's pale, expressionless face, Vincent noticed the wrinkles around the corners of her eyes and mouth. Evidently Karl had performed a little tactful updating. To Vincent's relief, the engineer had neglected to fix her crooked teeth, as revealed by her slightly parted lips. His anger at Karl's presumptuousness remained, however.

If he wanted to find out *why* Karl had resurrected Rachael, he would doubtless have to ask. Vincent hoped an email would suffice. Since emerging from his post-Rachael depression, he had become ever more appreciative of Karl's willingness to interact exclusively by electronic means.

The squelch of virtual boots tramping in simulated mud jolted Vincent out of his ruminations. Unnoticed by him, Rachael had begun walking along the lakeside path. He followed her at a discreet distance until she reached the start of another path leading away from the lake. There she halted and stood with her head bowed. To Vincent, her choice of stop-off point seemed horribly ironic. Ten years ago, while lying in her hospital bed, Rachael had "walked" her original avatar to precisely this spot before she gasped her final breath.

Vincent had never felt any need to mark the location. Again, Karl must have decided otherwise, judging by the small cross made of hornbeam branches protruding from the muddy earth. Presumably this feature, too, had arrived during the recent software upgrade. Vincent bent down to inspect the words scratched onto the crosspiece, but then jerked upright with a start.

"Karl Badoer—RIP," he mumbled to himself.

He shook his head in disbelief and then shot a glance at Rachael. Her expression remained impassive.

The sound of leaves rustling in the bushes behind Vincent made him jump. Still trembling, he turned around, ready to confront this latest interloper.

"Get out the hell out of my . . . "

His demand petered out when he recognised the extravagantly moustachioed bear of a man striding towards him.

"Hello, old friend!" Karl grinned at Vincent while holding out both arms.

Unable to endure any more shocks, Vincent yelled, "End sim!"

Trees and lake, crows and moorhens, Rachael and Karl; every component of Vincent's private sanctuary faded to grey in two blinks of any eye.

He fell to his knees and wept.

An hour passed before Vincent felt calm enough to take the necessary action.

Karl Badoer's elderly mother answered Vincent's call. They talked in a stilted mishmash of German and English. Afterwards, Vincent scolded himself for not activating the real-time translation facility. In any case, the word "incurable" repeated several times required no interpretation.

He had wanted to ask the woman about Karl's avatar, but decided to spare her further anguish. Nevertheless, his curiosity had been piqued. Evidently the engineer had equipped it with powerful situation-awareness capabilities, presumably fed by data received from the chamber's network of sensors, plus a degree of reactive intelligence that greatly exceeded anything Vincent had thought possible. All of which begged two questions. First, how had Karl obtained access to such innovative AI technology? Second, why had he not upgraded Rachael to the same standard?

Content that Welby Wood remained secure against intrusion, Vincent activated his link to the wider world. After shooing off a pigeon bearing a message from one of his customers, he requested a summary of Karl's activities during the last five years. Documents fluttered to the floor like outsized snowflakes, while video clips played out before his eyes. Taking his time, Vincent scanned synopses of a series of technical papers Karl had co-authored, before viewing demonstrations his research team had made to the technology news media. Unquestionably his friend had achieved some significant breakthroughs in the field of artificial intelligence. Presumably the avatar that had greeted Vincent represented the culmination of those efforts.

So why then hadn't Karl also applied his expertise to Rachael? Failing health might have inhibited his efforts, of course, but Vincent suspected there was more to it than that. To find out he would have to ask the man, or rather his avatar.

Vincent took several deep breaths and then commenced walking on the spot. The dome-shaped chamber's sensors detected his speed and direction of motion and rolled the floor accordingly.

After relaxing into his normal gait, Vincent said, "Default settings. Start Welby. Speech-mode off."

He could have chosen to resume the simulation where he'd ended its previous run, but he needed the walk from the arrival glade to settle his nerves.

Karl was waiting for him by the lake.

"It's good to see you again, Vincent."

Vincent puffed out his breath, which he'd been holding unknowingly for several seconds.

"Hello, Karl."

His friend's avatar grinned. "I imagine you have some questions for me."

Vincent nodded. "You could say that!"

Rather than leap straight into the emotionally delicate matter of Rachael, he chose to ask a more general question that had nagged him since reading Karl's academic papers.

"Are you conscious?"

"Not yet," said Karl, with a shake of his head.

Vincent frowned. "So achieving such a state is at least theoretically possible?"

This time Karl nodded. "That's right. Babies aren't born fully conscious either; it's a faculty that develops over time. My research indicated that the same might hold true for a self-adaptive AI if it were exposed to a rich enough range of stimuli and subsequently reflected on the memories so formed. Given time, consciousness should eventually emerge."

The notion intrigued Vincent, but he felt sure he'd spotted a logical flaw in Karl's proposed approach, assuming he intended to pursue it here.

"But Karl, Virtual Welby runs offline. Doesn't that make it unsuitable for your purposes?"

"Ultimately, yes. But here would be the right place to set about upgrading Rachael to a level of capability equivalent to mine. Surely you'd want to see that?"

Vincent didn't feel sure of that at all.

"But why involve me?"

"You did love her, Vincent." Karl's avatar offered a plausible look of sympathy. "I suspect you still do."

Vincent turned to gaze at the lake. Was Karl right? Had he really been in love with Rachael? He nodded to himself. How else to explain his eagerness to don augmented-reality glasses and go walking in Welby Wood with a dead woman's avatar, other than as a gesture of love?

"Yes, I did love her," he said. "But that was a long time ago. And despite what you believe, Karl, I don't feel the same way about her now."

"Are you sure about that?"

"Yes."

Karl frowned at him. "Would that still be true if you could talk to each other?"

Vincent sighed. "Look, Karl, even assuming that I wished to see Rachael upgraded to your standard—and I'm really not sure about that—how would you go about it? You can't recreate the memories of someone who died ten years ago."

"That's where you can help, Vincent. If you agree to have your brain mapped at pico-scale resolution, the software installed in this sim can transform your retrieved memories of Rachael into a first-person template. We can use that to bootstrap a self-adaptive AI, just like the one that runs me."

Vincent dismissed Karl's proposal with an abrupt shake of his head. "My memories of Rachael come from a brief period leading up to her death. They aren't representative of her life. And more to the point, they're *my* memories of her, not hers of me, or of anyone or anything else. They won't capture her inner self. We'd be missing the essential Rachael."

"Granted, but it would still be a version of Rachael. Wouldn't that be better than nothing?"

"She'd be a caricature at best."

"You might be right . . . "

Vincent noticed that Karl had begun stroking his moustache. During their Wired Wood days this habit had often prefigured what seemed like a spur-of-the-moment idea, but which was usually nothing of the sort.

"Come on, out with it!"

"There is an option that would enable us to do a lot better."

"Which is, exactly?"

"If we could exploit Josie Warren's much richer store of memories, we should be able to build a more accurate representation of Rachael."

Vincent shot Karl a livid look. His friend's suggestion was a complete non-starter. He had not heard from Rachael's older sister since the funeral. Given her animosity towards him while he and Karl tried to engineer the final walk in the woods that Rachael so craved, Josie would surely wish that lack of contact to continue.

Vincent shook his head. "I really don't think—"

Karl made an imploring gesture with his arms. "Vincent, involving Josie is essential for Rachael's future development."

"No, it's just not possible."

"Anyway, she'll be arriving shortly."

"What?"

Unnerved by his friend's announcement, Vincent's gaze darted around the lake, searching for intruders, before he belatedly realised the absurdity of his response. How could Josie enter a locked sim? She couldn't, of course.

"You didn't mean *here*, did you?"

Karl shook his head. "I'm sorry, Vincent, but you are going to have to meet her in flesh."

Infuriated, Vincent turned his back on his friend. He had endured enough meddling in his personal affairs already.

"End sim!"

Outside the sim chamber, Vincent caught a glimpse of his haggard, unshaven face in the wall-mounted mirror. He managed to snatch five minutes in the bathroom, time enough to spruce himself up, before his home's security system announced Josie's arrival. Vincent held his breath for a count of ten, to settle his nerves, before instructing his front door to open.

Josie stood on the doorstep, scowling at Vincent. Her stern-faced demeanour gave the impression of unshakeable purpose.

"Hello, Josie," he said.

Josie ignored his proffered hand and instead held up a sheet of corporately embossed e-paper for him to inspect. He did not need to read the letter to know that it had been authored by a solicitor.

"Mr Cornell, I have recently received a communication from the estate of Karl Badoer."

Her Welsh Valleys accent had lost none of its lilt over the years, thought Vincent. Though if anything, Rachael's voice had sounded even sweeter.

Josie continued. "This communication indicates that you are harbouring intellectual property belonging to my family, namely an electronic version of my late sister, Rachael Warren. Is this true?"

She sounded like a lawyer, thought Vincent. Dressed in a business suit, she looked like one too. Unwilling to tell a lie, he gave a tiny nod instead.

"Yes, it is."

"I see." She jutted her chin towards him, as if trying to stimulate a more meaningful response.

"Look, Josie, until a few hours ago I didn't know that Karl had loaded Rachael's avatar into my personal virtual environment. If he'd asked for my permission, I *wouldn't* have given it."

Josie's eyes flared wide. "Do you really expect me to believe that when Karl Badoer's communication makes it clear he transferred Rachael's data to you shortly after her death?"

Presumably Karl had forgotten to remind Josie that she had, however reluctantly, handed over Rachael's data prior to her death, for use in the virtual "walk in the woods" they had devised for her. But before Vincent could make the point, her expression—already furious—tightened a notch.

"I want to see her, NOW!"

She stepped forward in such a determined fashion that he felt obliged to give way. Never before had he let a visitor enter his inner sanctum. That it should be someone he actively disliked made the act feel doubly distressing.

"Follow me," he said.

After shepherding Josie into the sim chamber, he took a deep breath and said, "Start Welby."

The arrival glade sprung into virtual existence, surrounding the two of them in tree-dappled sunlight. Josie responded with a grunt, as if she found the scene underwhelming. When her attempt to walk towards the trees brought no change in perspective, she turned to Vincent and frowned.

"What's wrong with your sim?"

"The chamber has detected multiple-occupancy, so I'll have to configure the sim to operate in two-person mode. Please wait while I adjust the settings." He made a meshed-fingers gesture towards one of the chamber's hidden sensors, thereby activating the setup menu, and then began calling up options he'd never needed before. "Movement tracker: lock to me. Floor mode: static. Path-width: default times two. Speech-mode: off." He turned to Josie, who was watching him with her arms crossed. "You'll have to stand next to me and look around rather than walk, I'm afraid. But don't worry; I'll make sure you don't bang into any trees."

After turning towards the trail that led to Summerhouse Lake, Vincent began walking on the spot, a mode of locomotion that felt clumsy compared with his customary use of the chamber's omnidirectional rolling floor. But with two people in the sim, he had no choice.

He did not try to make small talk with Josie while guiding her along the path. In any case, she seemed content to keep her thoughts to herself until they reached the lake. There they found her sister, standing close to the water's edge. Josie broke the silence.

"Rachael?"

"She can't hear you."

"Then what is the point of her?"

None at all in this form, Vincent had concluded while staring at his reflection in the shaving mirror. But would he still feel the same way if Karl's plan to upgrade Rachael came to fruition? He remained ambivalent about the prospect. And as for Josie, he would have to prepare the ground carefully before mentioning the possibility to her.

"You're right, Josie. This avatar doesn't do justice to your sister. Barring a little visual aging, it's no different to the version I went walking with after her death."

"I knew it!"

"Okay, you've got my confession. Does that make you feel any better?"

He shrugged to make it clear that he didn't care either way. "But with Welby Wood dying, those walks came to seem futile, so I ended them and deleted Rachael's data. You have Karl to blame for Rachael's presence here. To be frank, her avatar is a reminder of a period in my life I'd rather forget."

Josie waved her arms as if to encompass the totality of the sim. "To be equally frank, this looks more like an attempt to recreate that period than a genuine attempt to forget it," she said, her tone now pitying. "But that doesn't excuse your exploitation of my family's property."

"I'm not exploiting Rachael!"

"In that case, why don't you just delete her again?"

Vincent glanced at the avatar. Rachael continued to gaze at the lake, oblivious of the argument raging behind her back. He heaved a sigh.

"Because according to Karl we can, if we so choose, upgrade this avatar so that it thinks and behaves like the real Rachael."

Josie frowned at him. "The communication I received didn't mention that!"

Aware that his conflicted feelings on the subject would make it difficult for him to do justice to the case for an upgrade, Vincent decided to request Karl's help. He reactivated the sim's voice control mode by tapping a forefinger against his lips twice.

"Resume, Karl," he said.

Vincent heard the tramp of virtual feet a moment before his friend's avatar rounded the curve of the trail leading from the arrival glade.

"Do you remember Josie Warren, Rachael's sister?"

"Of course I do." Karl turned towards the woman and held up his right hand palm-outward in lieu, presumably, of attempting a handshake. "It's good to see you again after so many years."

Vincent flicked a glance at Josie, to gauge her reaction. She was grimacing at the avatar, but had at least resisted a cheap shot along the lines of "But you're dead!" For that show of self-restraint, he gave her some credit.

Josie chewed her lower lip for a moment before nodding. "Hmm, I must admit that's quite impressive," she said. "How did Karl create you?"

The explanation offered by Karl was, typically of the man, unapologetically technical. Josie waved aside the barrage of details.

"But what has this to do with upgrading Rachael? You're a first-person recreation, based on a direct reading of a living person's brain. So it's not surprising you can mimic Karl's speech patterns and behaviour. But even assuming I wanted to achieve something similar for my sister—which I don't!—there are no scans of her brain on which to base that recreation."

Vincent chose this moment to intervene. "Karl reckons we could use your memories of Rachael as a basis for upgrading her avatar."

Josie jerked her head dismissively. "But those memories would not be subjective. At best, they'd represent what I *believed* my sister felt and experienced. The result would be more like me than Rachael!"

Karl inclined his head towards Rachael's unmoving and unresponsive avatar. "At first, yes; but with some careful fine-tuning we should end up with something a lot closer to the real Rachael."

Josie gazed at her sister's avatar for several seconds before giving an even more vehement shake of her head. Then she turned towards Vincent.

"Mr Cornell, I want an end put to this . . . travesty. And I want it done NOW!"

Her eyes blazed at him. Faced with such ferocity, he had no option except to comply. He nodded his acquiescence.

"End sim."

"Thank you," Josie said as the lakeside panorama faded into the chamber's default grey-tones.

"I'll bring up the core data display," he said with a sigh. No doubt Josie would want to observe while he permanently deleted Rachael's data.

In the circumstances, her next request came as a complete surprise to him.

"Could I have a cup of tea?"

After making the tea, Vincent led Josie into his living room, where the lack of seating other than a small but luxurious calfskin sofa resulted in the awkwardness of sitting side by side. He deliberately gazed at the wall opposite while she wiped her eyes. Her tearful reaction had taken him aback. He well recalled Josie's anger from ten years ago, but not this heartfelt show of emotion.

"Is there anything I can do?"

Josie shook her head and took a sip of tea. Vincent realised it would be up to him to get the conversation underway.

"I suppose it must have been quite a shock to encounter your sister's avatar so many years after her death."

Josie nodded. "Yes, it was. But in a way it was more of a shock to meet Karl."

"Was that because of what his capabilities might imply for Rachael?"

Josie gave another nod before sipping some more tea. It seemed to Vincent that she was at least willing to discuss the possibility of enhancing her sister's avatar.

"Josie, I told you the truth when I said I wanted to forget the past. Ten years ago, Rachael meant a lot to me. I suppose I loved her, in my own way, but that's not the case now. That said, I don't think we should dismiss Karl's proposal out of hand. Perhaps we *should* create a more realistic version of Rachael's avatar, one capable of roaming the public-domain virtual woodlands and interacting with whoever she meets there. Wouldn't that be a worthwhile memorial to her life?"

Vincent had noticed Josie's frown deepen while he spoke, so he waited for her to respond in what he assumed would be her usual vehement tones. Instead, she heaved a sigh. More in sorrow than anger, he thought.

"What's the matter?"

"You know, you have never once asked me how *I* feel or what *I* want. With you, it's always been about Rachael. It was ten years ago; it still is now."

Vincent knew he couldn't refute her accusation, much as he wanted to. Back then, Josie had been an obstacle to overcome; whereas now he saw her as a lawsuit-wielding foe. At least he had until she'd asked him for a cup of tea. But in truth he didn't know anything meaningful about Josie Warren: not about her job, or her interests, or her core beliefs. He had never thought to ask. And that, he acknowledged, wasn't fair.

"I'm truly sorry if I've hurt your feelings," he said.

Josie gave a little nod but her lips remained pursed. Vincent realised that he would have to build the bridge between them single-handed.

"Okay," he said. "So what is it you *do* want?"

This time she replied. "What I want is an opportunity to show you the project I've been working on since Rachael's death. That way, you'll get to see how I chose to memorialise my sister." She shot him a ferocious look, but couldn't sustain it. When she spoke again, her tone had softened. "I loved Rachael too, you know."

Vincent pointed his forefinger towards the wall opposite the sofa, which flashed up a full-disk view of Planet Earth. "Be my guest," he said.

"Oh, not like that!"

Josie shook her head, but it was the way her shoulders trembled with laughter that really caught Vincent's attention. Ten years ago, this woman had seemed entirely humourless. Until now, he'd felt no need to revise that opinion.

Then again, when was the last time he'd laughed?

"I suggest you get your coat," Josie said. "The weather forecast promised heavy rain."

He raised his eyebrows, but received a look of mockery in response.

"That's right, Vincent. We're going for a walk—a real one this time."

Vincent stood on the threshold of his home, peering at the leaden sky. A shiver wracked his body. Fear not cold prompted his reaction. He hadn't stepped outside his front door in more than a year.

"There, I knew you could do it," said Josie.

To his surprise, she sounded supportive rather than sarcastic.

Inside her Hyundai, he felt the seat belts tighten around his chest while Josie thumbed the starter.

"Please state your destination," said the autopilot.

Josie said, "Welby Wood."

Startled, Vincent said, "But Welby—"

"Was destroyed by the Blight. I know!"

"So how come . . . ?"

"While you immersed yourself in your virtual forests, hundreds of people came together to establish New Growth UK, a crowd-sourced project dedicated to re-seeding Britain's woodlands with genetically modified, Blight-resistant trees. New Welby Wood occupies only a tiny fraction of the original's area, and most of the saplings are no taller than you, but it's a start."

"Why didn't anyone tell me?"

"Vincent, you had isolated yourself more thoroughly than if the government had placed you under house arrest. None of us cared what you thought. Least of all me, I have to say."

He sat in grumpy silence while he digested the implications of Josie's diatribe. Meanwhile her car drove on through urban areas dominated by gated housing estates. Where were the shops, the pubs, or the schools? Isolation had become the norm, it seemed, likewise the fan-shaped, CO_2-

scrubbing artificial trees that lined almost every road. Three years ago, when he'd last driven this way, he had seen none.

"As you can see, the government still supports some tree-planting projects," said Josie.

"But not yours, I presume."

Josie grunted but said nothing more until the car decelerated before turning right into a small car park.

"We're here," she said unnecessarily.

Vincent gazed through the windscreen at the vista of saplings, noting the profusion of hornbeam and silver birch. As Josie had stated, none of them had yet grown taller than him. Without waiting for her to switch off the engine, he opened the door and got out of the car.

As he walked towards the nearest saplings birdsong backed by the soughing of the wind through twigs and leaves filled his ears. The promised rain had materialised, but he didn't mind at all. He licked raindrops from his lips. Back in the sim, their ultrasonic counterparts permitted no such indulgence.

"Is the lake still there?"

Josie smiled at him; another first.

"Follow me and you'll find out."

Josie led Vincent along the path, intermittently looking over her shoulder.

"You see, Vincent, it wasn't just Rachael who loved the British countryside. I did too; and I still do. But sadly for her, what began as a grand passion led inexorably to her death. When she first presented severe allergy symptoms, her GP advised her to avoid rural areas. Needless to say, she took no notice of him, or me. She might be alive today if she'd also taken no notice of *you*!"

Her accusation stung like hell, even though it wasn't entirely fair. After all, he had warned Rachael not to enter Welby Wood once the infestation was confirmed. Ignoring those warnings meant she'd paid the ultimate price. But even if she had moved on, she'd probably have found an equally dangerous location somewhere else, because the Welby outbreak had swiftly spread across the entire country.

Josie seemed unwilling to let the matter rest.

"Did you know that an effective treatment regime was introduced less than six months after Rachael's death?"

The breakthrough had come too late to save Rachael or the several hundred other victims whose immune systems massively overreacted to the Blight's spores. Vincent heaved a sigh.

"I can't turn back the past, Josie, any more than you can."

She snorted her indignation but said nothing more.

On arriving at the water's edge, Vincent noted the presence of reed beds, also that several moorhens had taken up residence. He smiled his approval as they piped their doleful songs.

"What you and your colleagues have achieved is remarkable," he said. "But I'm not sure why you've brought me here, other than to humiliate me."

Humiliated because, even in its present embryonic form, New Welby Wood had already stimulated a more vivid impression than anything he'd created inside his simulation chamber.

"No, that's not it at all," Josie said with unexpected gentleness. "What I wanted was for you to emerge from that bolthole of yours, to return to the physical world, hopefully to work with us"—she held out both arms, as if to embrace the dozen or more men and women, young and old, now pushing through saplings and out onto the lakeside—"to regrow this woodland and all the others like it. As you guessed, we receive no funding from this government, which would rather boost the manufacturing sector by placing orders for artificial trees than grow real ones. We've tried crowdsourcing, which only proved that too few people are interested in real-world projects these days. Some of our more radical members responded by sabotaging artificial trees, but that lost us most of what little support we'd built up. If this goes on, soon we won't be able to pay the rent on this land." She gestured towards the nearest saplings. "By next year, all this could be gone."

While Vincent sympathised with her group's ambitions, he struggled to imagine how he could help. After all, his company's focus in the v-forest market ran counter to their philosophy. He frowned at Josie.

"But what do you want from me?"

Josie rolled her eyes, as if the answer were obvious.

"We want you to liquidate TreeSpace; not just so we can obtain access to its capital, but also—and far more importantly—as a symbolic gesture that will influence public opinion. If your company announces that it has ceased building virtual woodlands because you have joined our campaign, that will create real impact."

Vincent shook his head in disbelief. Just because he had isolated himself from the outside world, that didn't mean he operated in an economic vacuum. To him, Josie's plan seemed dead in the water.

"If I liquidated my company's assets tomorrow, a dozen or more competitors would be vying to take its place at the top of the tree. In a few months at most, TreeSpace Enterprises would be forgotten. Granted, the money would pay your ground rent for a while, but it wouldn't solve your fundamental problem. Actually, I suspect you're right—a symbol for people to rally around would boost your campaign, but a recluse like me would surely be the worst possible choice for a figure-head!"

Though that conclusion begged a question regarding who might be the best.

"We have to do *something*!" She paused for a moment before continuing in quieter tones. "Is there nothing you can do to help us?"

There was, he felt sure, but only if she'd let him.

"I do know someone who would serve your purpose perfectly."

Vincent found himself recoiling before the ferocity of Josie's glare.

"If you mean my sister, forget it!"

"Think about it, Josie. Who'd be better than Rachael to symbolise your cause?" He paused for a moment to let her consider his assertion. "If we upgrade her as Karl proposes, she could evangelise on your behalf to everyone she meets while roaming virtuality."

In response, Josie reached into the left-hand pocket of her coat. A moment later, Vincent found the solicitor's letter being waved in front of his face for the second time in one day.

"*Mister* Cornell, I have already informed you that I regard Rachael's avatar as my family's property. If you do not hand over the data immediately, your failure to comply will bankrupt TreeSpace. And then *you* will have achieved nothing."

He snatched the e-paper from her hand, scanned the text and then handed it back with a shrug. "This is a cease-and-desist order, not a court summons."

"It soon will be!"

That would take a week at least, he reckoned. Long enough to get a rush-job done on Rachael. A caricature would serve his purposes admirably.

After handing back the e-letter, Vincent set off along the path that led back to the car park. As he'd expected, Josie's stream of invective continued.

"I'll see you in court!"

It might yet come to that, thought Vincent, but right now he couldn't wait to return home and make a start on upgrading Rachael.

One week later, Vincent met Karl in Virtual Welby Wood. Squatting on his heels at the edge of Summerhouse Lake, his friend lobbed virtual bread towards equally illusory Mallards.

Karl glanced over his shoulder. "Has your data finished loading yet?"

Obtaining the requisite pico-scale neural maps at such short notice had made a hole in TreeSpace's finances that Josie would surely deplore. No doubt she would complain even more vociferously if she ever acquiesced to Vincent's request to undergo the brain-scanning procedure. That remained a *very* big if, of course. Confined for hours within the MRI scanner's juddering, tomblike tunnel, he had found the stress induced by trying to remember every experience he'd shared with Rachael almost unbearable. Josie would doubtless suffer even worse due to the much greater volume of memories she'd be required to recall.

He puffed out his breath, which until now he hadn't realised he was holding, and belatedly replied to Karl's question.

"We're almost ready."

While he waited for Rachael to arrive, Vincent gazed at the willow trees girding Summerhouse Lake. Never before had he felt so discontented while contemplating his handiwork. Something had changed in him. For all its beauty, Virtual Welby now seemed a trivial accomplishment compared to Josie's collection of saplings.

A rustling coming from over his shoulder interrupted his train of thought. He turned round in time to observe Rachael pushing through a thicket of birch. Now *that* at least was typical of the woman. Rachael had rarely followed the well-trodden path.

Vincent could not stop himself smiling. "Hello, Rachael."

At the water's edge, Rachael gazed straight ahead, as if intent on inspecting the lake and its waterfowl rather than returning his greeting. Had her language processor failed to initialise?

"Rachael?"

Now Karl tried. "Rachael, can you hear us?"

The avatar turned towards the engineer and nodded. Finally she directed her gaze towards Vincent. Her lips opened.

"Hello, Vincent Cornell. How are you today?"

Vincent groaned. Unlike her sister, Rachael had picked up a tiny but beguiling trace of Midwestern twang during an extended sojourn in the USA. He could hear no evidence of it now. And where had this awful stiffness of phrasing come from?

"I'll leave you to it," said Karl, already striding away from Vincent along the lakeside path.

Vincent considered asking his friend to turn back, but then thought better of it. After all, they *had* discussed the next stage at some length. It was up to him to train this version of Rachael to the point where she became realistic enough to persuade Josie to agree to his plan.

"Let's go for a walk," he said to Rachael, indicating the most overgrown of the paths leading away from the lake.

It pleased him to observe that his suggestion elicited a goofy smile from her.

True to her nature, Rachael took the lead. The tock-tock-tock of a woodpecker accompanied their progress into the heart of the woods. Just like old times, he thought happily, but instantly corrected himself.

His journey with Rachael represented a means to an end, nothing more. And in any case, he could only take Rachael part of the way.

After that it would be up to Josie.

The court summons arrived three days later. Vincent responded by passing a message to Josie via his solicitor. To his relief, a reference to liquidating TreeSpace's assets prompted her to phone him.

"Mr Cornell, I won't consider any of your proposals regarding New Growth UK until you hand over Rachael's data." She sounded supremely confident, which didn't surprise Vincent, given the legal prognosis he'd received from his solicitor that morning.

"Josie, I understand your terms perfectly. But in this life you don't get something for nothing. So I propose we meet tomorrow, at 14:00 hours, in New Welby Wood car park."

"I've endured enough of your prevarication already, Mr Cornell. I want Rachael's data!"

After what the Nuffield Institute had told him yesterday about his brain scans, unnecessary delays hardly served his best interests either. Despite that, he still needed a little more time to fine-tune Rachael while Karl readied their bargaining chips.

"Look, Josie, if you want to deny me any further use of Rachael's data, that's up to you. I will comply. But at least let me show you what her avatar can do. One extra day is all I need."

Josie sighed like someone desperate to bring an end to her pain. "You *promise* to hand over the data?"

"Yes, if you still want me to do so. And I've no doubt at all that you've recorded me agreeing to that condition."

"Okay, tomorrow then."

Josie sounded confident again, as if content that her legal team had covered every angle.

For Rachael's sake, he hoped they hadn't.

Josie stood waiting for him in the car park, a rain jacket tucked between her folded arms and chest.

"Let's keep this brief," she said. "Show me what you must and then return my family's property. If you don't *I* will—"

"Your PROPERTY!" Vincent felt no compunction about shouting her down. "What right have you to refer to your sister in that way?" He shook his head in dismay.

"What you have got is *not* my sister."

"Then why do you need to take it from me?"

Josie's face quivered with fury. "I knew this would happen!"

Vincent nodded; he too had expected the meeting to play out like this. To defuse the confrontation, a more conciliatory approach would be required.

"Josie," he said, "I realise this is difficult for you. It is for me too. But please don't decide anything until you've had a chance to talk to Rachael. She wishes to talk to you."

Josie did not reply but neither did she walk back to her car. Interpreting her silence as permission to proceed, he resumed unloading the final carton of tracking equipment from the hired van.

Since dawn, he had installed hundreds of optical sensors while simultaneously digitising as much as possible of New Welby Wood. He had enjoyed working in the open again, easily shedding ten years of sim-

centred "life". Josie's offer of a role in re-establishing the country's woodland held increasing appeal for him.

"Here," he said. "You'll need these."

Rather than taking the proffered set of augmented reality glasses and
Bluetooth earpieces, Josie planted her hands on her hips, before finally
sighing her exasperation and snatching the devices from his hands.

"You've got five minutes."

That would be barely enough time to reach the lake. Hopefully Rachael
would intercept them sooner.

He donned his own AR equipment. "Right, let's go."

They had walked less than halfway to Summerhouse Lake when Rachael
pushed through a thicket of birch saplings and stepped out onto the path.

"Hi, Vincent," she said, followed a moment later by, "Oh, hi there, sis!
Not a bad day for a walk, is it? At least it isn't raining. But I don't think
much of this woodland of yours. It's too small and too well-managed for
my liking."

Josie turned to Vincent. "Okay, I'll admit that's better than I expected,"
she said. "But you haven't quite captured Rachael's essence."

"Well, that's why we need your help. This version is probably about as
good as Karl and I can achieve without accessing your memories of
Rachael. Will you help us make her more authentic?"

"Do I have any choice?"

Her response took Vincent by surprise. Perhaps the emotional turmoil
wrought by their dispute over Rachael's future had finally sapped her will
to resist.

Josie heaved a sigh. "I'm not stupid, Vincent. Karl is doubtless waiting
for your signal to disseminate copies of Rachael throughout the public-
domain virtual woodlands. Each will develop independently of the others,
according to its individual experiences. There will be no definitive virtual
version of Rachael. That was the threat you were about to make. Am I
correct?"

Vincent nodded. "We could do that."

"But you won't if I do what you want."

He nodded again. "Surely we can agree that there ought to be only one
Rachael? Wouldn't that be the best possible outcome for her, but also for
you and the New Growth project?"

After another lengthy pause, Josie confirmed her acquiescence with a
nod. "Okay, but I am going to impose a condition."

Vincent frowned. "Which is?"

"I don't want Rachael to enter virtuality friendless. So I want a version of *you* to accompany her."

The irony of her demand made Vincent chuckle.

"What's so funny?"

He shook his head. "Some other time."

One day he would tell her, but not now; not when he had barely come to terms with the prognosis himself.

With a shrug, Josie turned away from Vincent. Now, for the first time, she approached Rachael. Her sister's avatar had maintained a respectful distance throughout his negotiations with Josie.

"We need to talk," said Josie to her sister.

Vincent removed his glasses and earpieces. The women deserved some privacy.

"Well done," said Karl, his voice booming over their private comms link.

Now they had two projects to undertake: one to build a better simulation of a dead woman; the other to build the equivalent for a dying man.

Standing in his sim chamber, Vincent waved at the happy couple, or rather newlyweds, as did Karl and Josie.

Rachael and her partner—he still struggled to think of him as "Vincent"—waved back at him and shouted, "Goodbye!" in unison.

After months of patient work, during which he had endured more than one blazing row with Josie, the process of building the best-possible Rachael had finally reached its conclusion. Accompanied by his avatar, she would soon begin mingling with members of the public and passing on Josie's message. But this would not be the last leave-taking he'd witness, for Karl too had told him that he'd shortly be venturing into the wider virtual world.

Josie placed a hand on his forearm.

"How's that headache of yours?"

"Worse."

And it would only get worse from now on.

"Come on," she said. "Let's sit down."

He shook his head. "No, I need a walk."

"What, in here?"

Her tone suggested she had not lost her loathing for the chamber. He didn't feel the same way, but neither did he want to go for a walk in the sim.

"No," he said.

Josie smiled, but with a tinge of sadness. Vincent did not doubt that she had guessed what his future held.

"Okay," she said, "let's go to New Welby Wood."

"This is the spot," said Vincent. "This is where I want my ashes scattered."

Summerhouse Lake had shrunk considerably since Rachael's death. Even so, Vincent felt confident he had found the location corresponding to the point her avatar had reached when she died.

Josie nodded. "Okay, but you're not ready for that just yet, are you?"

Vincent jerked his head while trying to muster a grin. Hopefully the trees would grow appreciably by the time his battle with the brain tumour came to an end.

"You won't be alone," said Josie.

"That's right; there'll be moorhens."

"You *know* what I mean!"

"And I expect it to be raining."

"I'll see what I can do . . . "

Josie smiled at him and he smiled back.

They wouldn't have a lot of time to spend together, but he trusted it would be enough.

CURB

ROBERT REED

Robert Reed says, 'I know people who collect things. Some of them may collect too many treasures, and all those shelves and boxes and over- whelmed closets define their lives. "Curb" comes directly from the insight that humans have a powerful capacity to imagine souls living inside inani- mate objects. Stuffed animals, wedding rings, and photographs. And if you believe that every object has a good soul, who is to say that the stranger beside you has a better soul than the one that resides inside a much-cherished trinket?'

Mr. Reed's first trilogy has been published inside one cover: The Memory of Sky, *from Prime Books, is set in the author's Marrow universe. In addition to that hefty piece of cellulose, a recently self-published collection entitled* The Greatship *is available—a bunch of Marrow stories that have been some- what rewritten, or maybe quite-a-lot rewritten, with fresh bridge material between them. Also on tap is work done for a video game called Destiny, produced by the good people at Bungie. Robert Reed continues to breathe in Lincoln, Nebraska.*

EVEN SIMPLE OBJECTS HAVE TINY BUT GENUINE SOULS. This is known. Fact is fact. Debate and doubt are not possible.

And you have always appreciated how every life must be measured first by its accumulated possessions. Large souls are covered with the tiny ones, not unlike a tropical reef building itself within layers of lime. Every great biography features many treasures, some magnificent enough for museums while the majority are far more humble, straddling a closet shelf, say, or sitting warm inside that very important cardboard box, each item waiting patiently for its great owner to pass by.

Cards from long-ago birthdays exist because you exist, and of course they are grateful. Childhood toys and stuffed animals still carry your love. Thinking otherwise invites madness. You have always enjoyed books and magazines, and no word ever wishes to be cast aside. So of course there is a library inside your house—a special room where the shelves reach for the distant ceiling, bowing under the weight of bindings and glue and the grand ideas surrounded by blank reaches of paper. Not even one tenth of these books have been read, but they are yours and they have washed you with their devotion, and perhaps tomorrow you will make an attempt at that classic or this silly series. The same can be said about your music collection, about your serious hobbies and the playful ones, about your entire wardrobe. Every shirt and shoe used to be part of you. They help define you to a world that has not quite passed yet, and sometimes from inside the deep closets and drawers you hear the clothes begging to be worn again. There are also the dishes and forks that you use daily and the special silver utensils hungry for the rare visitor. And consider your furniture, rubbed raw by hands, by rumps. That old brown sofa is precious; entire years have been spent there, reading when you weren't napping. Dark chests and wobbly chairs anchor you to days that return whenever you close your eyes. And then there's the house where you reside: The small shelter of your youth has grown steadily, the treasures swelled about you. Each addition has its peculiar history, its infectious significance. There are dozens of rooms and a gigantic roof that covers what used to be the deep backyard, ten layers of shingles fending off the rain that wants nothing but to slip inside your home, making wet messes of everything precious.

Yet despite all of that love and relentless keeping, most of your life has escaped your grasp. For instance, you can't count your breaths or your heartbeats. Which day was the most remarkable day during the last thousand? The question has no answer. Your memory is porous, awful at its best and lying at its worst. Names constantly slip away. Events and conversations blur and die. And worst of all, everyone else seems a little better than you when it comes to holding life in a loving embrace.

On a deeply ordinary morning, some random thought wanders into your mind. You recall a certain book. You read the book once and maybe more than once when you were little. Or did you mean to read it and then forget? Almost everybody has a complete list of their conquered books, except for you. The oldest entries are presently missing, which shouldn't be a tragedy, except that when you think about the matter you suddenly feel less certain about everything, and confusion has its pernicious ways of enlarging the holes in your enormous, half-lost life.

A visit to the library is plainly in order. Just that thought buoys your mood. You love the room. Libraries are always full of important little souls. Walk anywhere and you are instantly surrounded by oak planks bolted to walls and floor, and reaching to the high ceiling, each shelf showing off books and magazines on every subject, every title begging for your attention.

You do hear the begging, yes.

No, books don't have voices. Even the most sophisticated volume can't summon a whisper. What you hear instead is your voice communing with words and images, and every piece of this wondrous room is organized according to your plan—a plan that you should remember until the day you die.

The book you hunt for is up there. You believe. You pray. Unless some new vagueness has filtered into your memory, which is an awful notion.

On your tallest tiptoes, you touch the smooth oak, not quite reaching the colorful, mysterious binding. Then you stand on flat feet for an instant, looking left and right, deciding which stepladder is nearest.

You step to the right, and the shelves collapse. Old novels and textbooks and news articles from decades ago come crashing down with the shattered planks, your life spared by the length of one short stride.

Inside the business of life—within that tireless mass of possessions and memory, plans and random acts—lie a few moments of true insight. But this is not one of those moments. This is nothing but a sorry mess and an excuse to feel fortunate about your survival, taking what pleasures can be found from kicking at the wreckage while muttering words saved for special occasions.

The high oak board must have been born weak. What else could it mean? The light touch of a finger was enough to make it shatter, and everything below became an avalanche of homeless paper. A fashion magazine has been disemboweled, its cover left shredded, and the eye of a woman looks at you with enormous feeling. You set that eye aside and then start sorting through the loose pages and partial books. To resurrect each title is impossible. You realize that, but this is no grand insight either. Accepting what the chaos gives, the library turns into a vast puzzle that lasts for an entire day. You sort. You tape and curse and sometimes weep, trying to remember why these items were touching each other. But the logic eludes. Eventually you find yourself needing another set of rules, and late in the afternoon, as you patch the shelves with ancient pieces of scrap pine, you think that this experience isn't any fun, but what other choices are there?

In the end, some of what remains is trash. Orphaned pages and mangled slick photographs can't give you any reason to be kept. If small objects have small souls, then battered useless objects are capable of only one thought: "Throw me away." This is normal. This is quite acceptable, and that's why you begin shoving the ruins into the plastic cans waiting at the curb. But then that single eye finds you again—the same eye from the torn magazine cover—and it occurs to you that the girl doesn't at all like what she sees, which happens to be you.

Ridding yourself of that one eye is the fulcrum, the place where the world tips. But you don't see that at the time. You can't realize what this means even at dawn when you are back at the curb, digging through those lost pages. A paragraph here, a sentence or phrase there—you read them without context and little patience. Then it is midmorning and you can't remember when you ate your last normal meal, and you are balanced on the tallest stepladder in the library, overloaded shelves creaking as you pull healthy books off by the handful, knocking loose the dust before reading the opening paragraphs.

These are someone else's books.

That is the first, most persistent epiphany.

Maybe you recall the phrasing if not the precise wording. Maybe the characters' names are entirely familiar. But your reaction to each book is very different from whatever you must have experienced ages ago. Which should be a good thing, shouldn't it? But that expectation proves wrong. When you see a cover that you know, and when the first paragraph is as clear and lovely as it was ages ago, you expect to feel yourself in the presence of an old friend. Yet that isn't what happens. And before evening arrives again, you have begun doing what didn't seem remotely possible yesterday morning. Wearing old work clothes and sweaty dust, you are busy setting your library beside the street, next to the high curb, and as the last of the sun dies, you create a simple sign that says everything in one word.

"FREE," it reads.

And this is when the great revelation arrives at long last: the lightness doesn't come from throwing away what you don't want anymore, and there isn't any sense of willpower and titanic accomplishment. No, what finds you and empowers you, remaking everything about you, is the calm certainty that everything is inevitable and this is not too early or too late in your life, and in a most delicious way, you have no idea what will happen next.

Your life unwraps.

People see the "FREE" sign and stop to ponder the significance of one word attached to so many. Then out of the house you come with more bound volumes, and they have to ask if you mean what you say. Of course you do. And so they start to pick through titles and random pages, having decided to claim some portion of the pile but not sure what would be best. They come on foot or on bikes, or their trunk and back seat have only so much space, and some smile slyly at you, imploring you to save this stack or those titles for when they can return with a borrowed truck and trailer.

But you aren't in the saving mood, even for an hour or two.

Beneath the "FREE," you add the words, "UNTIL WE ARE GONE."

It takes two long days to empty the library completely. You're left aching but happy, ready for rest. But during the next morning, walking through the gutted room, you realize that the empty shelves won't ever be filled again. So with a favorite hammer and your best pry bar, you wrench nails from wood and carry the first planks out to a curb where not one scrap of paper is waiting. Even your sign has been taken away.

You paint a bigger sign, and beneath the "FREE," you write, "EXCEPT FOR THE SIGN." A pointed little board serves as its leg, and with the sign and hammer in hand, you step outside to discover your sister and elderly mother fighting with strangers.

The strangers were trying to load free lumber into their car's too-small back seat. Your sister is screaming at them, threatening to call the police. Seeing you, the strangers beg for support. Do you remember them from yesterday? No, you don't remember, no. It doesn't matter, they say. They say that they were here and got some wonderful puzzle books and romance novels, but they need new shelves at home and were they wrong to think that these old boards weren't for the taking?

"Take it all," you say. "And take my blessings with you."

Your sister is appalled. Your mother threatens to collapse and die. Then both women jab you with angry fingers, explaining that it wasn't chance that brought them by today. It was destiny. One of the thieves from yesterday—their label for the passersby—found old telephone numbers written inside the books, and she decided to call and thank somebody for these considerable gifts. That's why your family came here. A stranger had what wasn't hers. Your family was afraid that you had been robbed by some scourging element. But you haven't been robbed, you're insane, and madness is worse than attacks by criminals. It is a thousand times worse, and what do you have to say for your miserable self?

Explanations would be useless. You remain silent.

The strangers have used these distractions to load up and drive away. But another vehicle is turning at the corner—a long flatbed truck with three strong men in the cab—and feeling the aches of two days of hard labor, a fresh inspiration offers itself to you.

"You can't give your books away," your sister says.

Your mother says, "I gave you some of those books. I read them to you when you were little."

"And you made me the person that I am today," you say agreeably. Then to the boys in the truck, you say, "Do you want to take home a thousand feet of shelving?"

Big-eyed, they gawk at each other.

Then the driver says, "Oh, would we?"

"Park and follow me," you tell them, walking toward your overstuffed, claustrophobic house.

"You can't just give away your treasures," says your sister.

"They are you, they are your life," says your mother, weeping again. "Lost. It's all going to be lost."

Pausing, you look back at everybody. Then with a leaden voice, you say, "I don't want that life anymore."

Even the boys are shaken by that implication. But free is free, and they follow you and the two angry women into the gutted library.

"Take it all," you say.

Your mother makes half of her threat come true. She drops to the dusty floor, sobbing in misery but not quite dead.

Watching the boys rip apart the old shelves, you smile.

Your sister approaches, but only to a point. Perhaps craziness is contagious, which is why she keeps just out of arm's reach.

"But why the books?" she asks.

A very fine question, yes.

"They have such big souls," she says. "Everybody knows that."

"Except for furniture," mother says from the floor. "Honored furnishings have the richest, best souls."

Furniture is just another kind of lumber. To the nearest boy, you say, "Once you get this room cleared, I've got rooms filled with tired chairs and the like. Are you interested? Or maybe you know somebody who would be."

"I like tired chairs," he says. "They're comfortable."

Of course you don't have to unload the house yourself. Why would you even bother? If you can just oversee the process, saving a few treasured items for yourself . . . why not invite the world into your home and sweep away your rubble?

The boys work fast, rumps eager for new places to sit.

Nobody is more pathetic than a crumbled, deflated mother.

But your sister acts stronger, standing like a fence post before you, shaking a ferocious hand. "Can't you hear their voices? They belonged to you and you to them, and they trusted you, and now you're casting them aside. Can't you hear them wailing your name?"

This is an excellent question worth hard consideration.

You listen to your house, and then you shake your head.

"I hear nothing," you say, which is true. But what that silence means is a matter best left to the great philosophers.

One flatbed becomes a fleet of trucks. Three young men swell into an army of well-mannered looters. A life barely contained inside one sprawling house is suddenly reduced to the best chair and a drawer full of kitchenware, three trousers and five shirts and the pair of shoes presently on your feet.

Even the greediest soul can't bear to take some items without asking first.

"You don't mean this," they say.

You hadn't thought about it, but now that the question is asked, no, you don't want the object anymore, no.

"You can't mean that."

Maybe you don't, but when in doubt, it's best to say, "Be gone."

Among those ranks are a fat leather volume filled with thin cardboard pages, each page adorned with photographs filled with smiling children and adults long dead.

"I found this in the bedroom," a burly man says. "It was in that nightstand and I took the nightstand. Is that all right?"

You say, "That's fine, but what about the bed?"

"Oh, someone else got that."

Quite a lot happened on that mattress, but the springs had turned squishy and unbearable long before this golden day.

"Anyway, I don't want your pictures," the man says, happy to be relieved of the temptation.

You don't bother opening the album. Tucking it under an arm, you look down the long hallway, telling him, "Thank you."

"A lot of empty rooms to fill," he says.

Perhaps, yes.

"You're mostly young," he says. "You can't start all over again."

Is that what you are? Mostly young?

He starts to leave.

"Come back here," you say.

The man isn't sure what to hope for. But hope fills his face.

"This house," you say. "Take everything. You can have the boards, the shingles, the flooring. I want it gone by next week."

He gasps and says, "Great. I need new rooms."

"And of course, tell the others."

"Oh, I will do that."

Maybe you are insane. But the impairment makes so many people happy, and isn't that the goal of the good life? That's what you tell yourself as you leave the doomed building: this is inevitable. The purging of little souls is sure to happen, but you didn't have to die and watch the process from the afterlife. Maybe you have started a change in how millions of lives will be lived. Such is the power of this one moment that you fail to notice your family waiting at the edge of your lot. Your mother and sister have rounded up cousins and uncles and their various spouses, and even some of your oldest friends. Ten voices call out your name. What does this mean? Eyes focus on people that you haven't seen in years, recognition coming in dribbles and waves. Everybody is worried. Nobody wants to approach the mad soul, but the fascination is obvious. Your sister is the one responsible for what happens next. With a tight, furious voice, she asks, "Is that your family album there? I hope you don't give that away too."

What album?

Here, under the arm. You find it all over again, and for the first time you open the leather binding, discovering a page of baby pictures with you in the middle, various dead people vying for the chance to hold what is newly born. Of course you wouldn't give this to any stranger. And your family doesn't have any need of it either; they have their own albums and photographs, moments of lost time captured as emulsions and personal memories.

Books and furniture have souls, yes, but a single snapshot must have an even larger soul.

You set the album on the foot-stomped ground.

Really, what is the value in this object? Does it make sense to cling to a few thousand pictures that you haven't looked at years?

A man passes by, and he smells like a smoker.

"May I borrow your lighter?" you ask.

He is happy to hand over his fancy metal lighter, and then as an afterthought, he says, "But you'll give it back when you're done, right?"

"Absolutely," you promise.

Your family sees it all, too astonished to react.

Their silence fools you. You kneel, assuming that they won't stop you at this late date. Lifting a few pages, you tease the corners of the album with your thumb, increasing the surface area, and then for a moment, seeing various eyes looking up from the fading images, you hear voices begging for mercy.

There is no mercy in this world.

Only Death reigns supreme.

The lighter ignites dry old paper on the first try, the flame bright orange and nearly as tall as a finger.

Your mother calls your name, just once.

First you light the corners, and then you turn. She stands a stride away from you at the most, and both of her arms are straightened out, hands clinging to a pistol that belonged to your father and to his father before him. That gun conjures some very clear memories, a surprising number of them good memories, and what better way is there to spend the last moments of existence than dancing with the unexpected, happy and warm and belonging to nobody but you?

Scraps of Paper

Simon Strantzas

The following story continues the exploits of the author's pseudo-supernatural-investigator Owen Rake. 'The character has become my outlet for all those ideas I don't typically explore,' Mr. Strantzas confides. 'Indeed, he allows me the opportunity for a little bit of humour,' he adds, sotto voce. *'Rake tales are truly a blast to write.' On the topic of the story at hand, he admits that the primary inspiration came from an episode of* Cops. *'But mixed with it is Chandler's* The Long Goodbye *and snippets of Jewish mysticism and lore. Add a homeless and amoral investigator and you have all the makings of a great romp.' Quite so.*

No stranger to Postscripts *readers, Mr. Strantzas's fiction has appeared also in* The Mammoth Book of Best New Horror, The Year's Best Weird Fiction, *and* The Best Horror of the Year. *He's also written four critically acclaimed collections; the latest being* Burnt Black Suns, *currently available from Hippocampus Press.*

You know, I've never really been one to get scared. I don't really know why: never developed a taste for it, I guess. I mean, I'm not a thrill-seeker—I'm not the kind to jump out of aeroplanes or race cars—but I've been in my share of hairy situations, and I'd be lying if I said I often found myself afraid. It just doesn't happen. This is probably why I've managed to stay alive this long, despite all the crazy shit that I've seen over the years. I don't frighten. And I sure as hell don't freeze.

Which makes my reaction when Butch Grommell came charging so surprising. For the first time, I was genuinely terrified. I'm not even sure why. It wasn't like he saw me, or was coming at me. Maybe it was what he was wearing—six police officers, all dangling from his various limbs, all unsuccessfully trying to bring him down—or maybe it was what he *wasn't* wearing: clothes. Any clothes at all.

I'd been out on the street for only a few weeks by that time—not enough to resort to the "Y" just yet, but long enough that Detective McCray had lost my scent. It was an in-between time, when I still thought there was something I could do to get out from under the pile of shit that rained down after Mrs Mulroney died. If somehow I could prove it wasn't my fault . . . but I was kidding myself. Of *course* it was my fault. If I hadn't gotten involved there would have been nothing to go horribly wrong. She'd probably still be around now—a bit spooked, but in one piece. I ruined that like I ruin everything. A man's got to have a hobby, I suppose.

This is why I was there, watching Grommell's charge: it was purely by accident. I was walking back to the Gerrard Street bridge, where I'd made home since dropping off the grid, when I heard the sirens and knew they were too close. My first instinct was to hide behind the first available dumpster until they passed, and it would have been a great solution if they'd been coming for me. Instead, they all pulled up in front of the closed dry cleaners on the other side of the street and a half-dozen officers leapt from their cars and ran inside. I waited there, quiet and curious, watching the cherries on the cars alternate between red and blue, when there was a tiny crack of a gun going off. Then a few more shots were fired. The shouting followed immediately.

Have you ever stood on the tracks when a train was coming? It's not easy, is it? It's like you can feel it in your chest a long time before you see it, and when you *do* finally see it you realise it's far too late to do anything about it. All you can do is stare wide-eyed as the train bears down on you. It was like that for me when Butch Grommell began his escape under the weight of six men.

Maybe it was the difference in size. I'm barely six feet tall, whereas Butch is well over seven. I also don't have a neck thicker than a West Coast redwood. It could have been his brown *nakedness* . . . All these things could reasonably tie a fellow up as he was being charged.

Or it could have been the flash of something around that mountain of a man—not an aura, per se, but something else. Something worse. There was a flicker of some dark fire, and I got that taste of metal in my mouth that I hadn't had since I was a kid. If I had a seizure, that would have been the end of me for all sorts of reasons.

But just as I thought Butch Grommell was going to run me down, maybe at the exact moment my own contortions cracked my bones like twigs, Grommell veered off, running instead down the street in the direction the police had come from. As he did, the officers lost their grips one by one, crashing into the dark ground and rolling to a stop as Grommell's giant brown legs pumped like pistons faster with each dump of ballast.

When the officers had all dropped away, Butch Grommell's pace nearly tripled, and he disappeared into the dark at the end of the street, the sound of his bare feet slapping the ground disappearing shortly after.

I felt much better once he was gone, but those cops couldn't say the same. They were sluggish, like they'd been drugged and now that the drugs were wearing off their injuries were starting to hurt. At least four of them limped back to their squad cars. One of them didn't get up at all. I knew in less than five minutes the place was going to be swarming with badges, and the longer I loitered there the more likely I was to end up caught in something I had no interest in.

No one was looking at me, so I slowly backed away from the scene, hoping to slip free before someone got their hands on me. I was at the end of the street when I heard the additional wave of sirens in the distance, and was probably blocks away when they finally showed up.

I took the long way back to my spot under the Gerrard Street Bridge and curled into my stashed sleeping bag, hoping to put everything I saw from my mind. But it doesn't work like that. I'd had an itch in my spine ever since I saw Grommell charging me, as though some residue was left in the air from his passing. It burned, and I couldn't fall asleep, not with images of those fire-fuelled eyes ricocheting around in my brain.

There was something going on, something I doubted the cops would know what to do with. But that sort of thing wasn't my problem anymore, and I did everything I could to forget about it.

I doubt I slept more than an hour in total before the sun really started to rise. I rolled up my stuff and hid it in its spot above the bridge's support beams, then put my raincoat on and went searching. I'd had a realisation during the night: I might have been done with my old life, but that life wasn't done with me. Like it or not, I was stuck being a victim of myself. It would have been sad if I thought too much about it, so I tried not to. Instead, I went looking for a newspaper.

Paper news is not what it used to be. The things are rags, now—I mean worse than before—and they barely keep you warm when you keep them under your clothes. Still, if there's one thing they never mess up it's the headlines after something goes horribly wrong. I didn't even need to lift a copy of the *Star* from the local coffee hut to read about Butch Grommell: it was all laid out there on the front page for everyone to see.

Butch Grommell; age twenty-eight, seven foot two, 346 lbs. Served in Kuwait for six years before returning with PTSD and a real thirst for violence. Something over there changed him, but I don't think it was the PTSD; I think it was something more, something not so easily talked over or ignored.

The swath Grommell had cut through the city had been as wide as a river, and he had more than a few people spooked. He was a killer, and a particularly nasty one, but no one was quite sure of the *why*, only of the *who*. The article was accompanied by the same series of security-camera photos, each one clearly capturing Grommell entering or exiting crime scenes. Often bloody, sometimes carrying a trophy like an arm or a head.

Most people I heard talking about him *tsked* and spoke of the monster he was, but it was clear to me there was something else going on. These people, they never saw his eyes, not like I did when he came charging in my direction. Those eyes, they weren't the eyes of a killer. They weren't the eyes of a person at all. At least, not a living person.

The term "zombie" has a bad rap nowadays, spoiled by one too many cheap horror films and books about the end of the world. For a while at the turn of the century, there was a whole industry built up around them, and all that New-Agey bullshit didn't help quell it much. For the most part, it's died out, as people have found other, more tangible demons to crucify. But I can tell you the dead walking is a real thing; I've seen it. Not in some brain-eating way, nor have I heard of anyone really *turn* from being bitten. No, it's a lot more subtle than that.

I *know* the living dead exist because behind Butch Grommell's eyes there was a chilling nothing. No light, no warmth at all. Butch Grommell was a shell powered by a vacuum, and not only did it mean he was devoid of life; it also meant it sucked it from those around him. Six grown men powerless to keep him still, each losing a few years from their lives in the process. He was a dead soul-sucking pit, and the amount of damage he was capable of doing was staggering to think about.

I could tell just from reading that article through the news box's Plexiglas window that Grommell was going to be a problem. Disaster was written in black ink right across the front page. Police were out looking for him, hotlines were being set up, television anchormen were salivating all over their expensive tailored suits. About the only one who wasn't excited by all this was me, because I knew what it meant.

I also knew they'd never find him. Not soon enough, at least. And I knew his killings weren't as random as everyone was making them out to be. I didn't know *exactly* what he was up to, nor did I know exactly what he'd done. Everyone I asked, from Old Blind Shandie to the local methadone nurses, had little to tell me. What they did have to say wasn't very reassuring.

They told me Grommell was like a wild animal, except compared to him wild animals ate with knives and forks. As if to prove me right, I heard Old Blind Shandie muttering to herself as she twitched on the corner of Wilson and Fayette Street, warning strangers or imaginary friends about the body behind the Jude Hotel.

"It ain't right," she kept repeating. "It ain't right what happen to that man."

That sensation of your stomach dropping through the ground? That was nothing compared to what I felt.

The Jude has been a fixture of the city for nearly two hundred years, starting as a church before being burned down by a mob for mysterious reasons. It sat vacant for about thirty years, long enough for whatever stink it had to be forgotten, and since then it's been used as everything from a brothel to a wedding chapel before settling on its final incarnation as a hotel.

Business was good for it . . . about seventy years ago. Now it's the same kind of hole every other place in the city is, and though the soot and grime from that fire ages ago is gone, you'd never know it by looking inside. It's what we in the business like to call a "junkie hotel", but the price people pay to stay there is far worse than you can imagine. I ought to know; I was a tenant there for a spell.

The thing about the Jude is how incongruous it is with the burnt-out storefronts around it. I'd call it a Gothic Revival if I thought anything was being revived in there beyond the dead. And out back, in the alley behind it, you'd swear by the stench that the dead were already in piles waiting.

But I didn't find that pile of dead people. I only found one. Or, at least I think it was only one. Really, I had no way of knowing. There were so many parts strewn around, a long smear of dark blood across the asphalt and concrete pavement, it could have been a whole family and I'd never have known for sure.

But it *felt* like one person, if you know what I mean. And I only found the one head. It was hanging from a bent-out piece of flushing, its eyes rolled up like the last thing it wanted was to see was what had become of the rest of his body. Honestly, I didn't blame him. It was a sight. There were black birds everywhere, picking at the pieces, and though I tried to shoo them away it quickly became clear I was wasting my time. I spent about twenty minutes trying to figure out what was bloody clothing and what was stripped flesh, and I'm pretty sure the only reason I finally found his wallet was because whatever animal had picked it up mistook it for half a liver.

Here's the thing: the Jude may have been surrounded by empty store-fronts, but it happened to share its blood-strewn alleyway with a building on the street behind it. And that building housed a dry cleaner of some immediate local celebrity, especially since Butch Grommell came storming out of it the night before wearing beat cops as bracelets.

I wasn't quite sure how the two men were related, but it seemed a safe bet that the naked bloody man I'd seen running from the scene the night before had something to do with the death of the dry cleaner out back. I may not be Columbo, but I have my moments.

I couldn't find much in the way of clues in the mess, but other than the wallet I *did* find a wadded-up piece of blood-soaked paper. I tried to tease it apart, but the thing just turned to paste in my hands.

My sojourn inside the crusted wallet had better luck. I found a driver's license with the photo of a long-faced man with bushy sideburns that resembled the head hanging before me—if you ignored the fact that half its flesh had been stripped away. Jackie Wilkins was forty-nine when he died, and it looked like he lived every year of it twice. His address was a shitty apartment in the shadow of the highway. Or at least it used to be.

There was at least twenty dollars cash in his wallet, very little of it covered in blood, so I put it in my pocket, where it would be safe in case his family ever came looking for it. There weren't any credit cards, but I found a receipt for a dive bar downtown called the Rex and a couple of buttons that must have popped off his shirt at some point. I looked up at Jackie's staring eyes and wondered if they saw what had come after him, and if the image had imprinted on them the way it no doubt had on his psyche.

It's a shame that sort of magic only works in the movies. It would have saved me a helluva lot of time. As it was, I'd have to do things the old-fashioned way. I hoped Jackie wouldn't mind my leaving him there to the scavengers, but I already had one mess to clear up and didn't have time or inclination to stick around.

I didn't know exactly why Butch Grommell had killed Jackie Wilkins, but I had my suspicions. Money being the primary motive. It was clear though there was no way Grommell was doing this of his own volition.

Grommell was a soulless monster. He was a walking destruction machine, the sort to casually walk up to whoever he wanted dead and just start squeezing. Throats, chests, heads, it didn't matter to someone like Grommell. All that mattered was the destruction.

That sort of single-minded dedication to the job is sorely lacking today; you have to give the guy some credit. But there was someone pulling the strings, someone who'd set him on Wilkins and all the rest. And that receipt was a clue so big it practically punched me in the face.

At the time I used to keep my things in different stashes around the city. Not only was it safer to have my eggs in separate hidden baskets, but it also meant I was never too far from supplies if I needed them. Even when you have nowhere to go and every reason to stay hidden, sometimes a change of clothes can help change a perspective.

Besides, I found the clothes I was wearing mysteriously covered in blood, and I wanted to make sure that sort of thing was well discarded in case Detective McCray happened to stumble by. I couldn't count on him to keep out of the Grommell business, but I *could* count on that lazy-eyed bastard to take one look at me and have me locked up for killing two people. To start with, at the very least. I liked the guy well enough, but I wasn't going to make it easier on him than I had to.

Instead, I changed into a new shirt and pants and threw the old set into a garbage can, along with crumpled copies of the *Star*. Then, I lit the whole thing up with some matches I had in my pocket for emergencies. Once I was sure there was nothing left in there but ashes, I upturned the can and spilled everything out onto the ground. Then I started smearing the ashes into the concrete. It took half an hour to permanently dispose of my old clothes, and once they were gone I knew I needed to find a gas station to wash up in. If I was going to visit Mr Stanley Fainberg at the Rex, I was going to need to look my best.

Stanley Fainberg was the sort of guy you see on the street and notice right away. Not because he was unusually ugly or unusually handsome, abnormally fat or thin, or the sort to dress in an attention-grabbing way. Really, the guy looked just like everyone else you've ever met in your life that you don't remember. You remembered Stanley Fainberg for one reason only: if you met him, you were probably in big trouble.

Stanley Fainberg ran the Rex on a little side street off Adelaide, on the farthest west corner you could find. It was a downstairs bar made entirely of oak panelling, and the wood had soaked up so much smoke and sweat and grease over the years that the entire place was sticky and smelled like a fry cook's asshole. There was nothing you wanted to eat in the Rex, and only slightly more you'd want to drink. Even the regulars looked like they'd rather be anyplace else.

The only reason you went to the Rex—the *real* reason—was because Fainberg had summoned you, and if he summoned you, likely he'd sent his goons to make sure you showed up. He wasn't the type to trust you not to run. I was probably the only person in the entire city dumb enough to go to the Rex uninvited, and "dumb" was probably nowhere near strong enough a word.

"We're closed." The thug at the door would have been a bit taller than me, but only if he'd laid on his side. What I'm trying to say is he was fat. And it wasn't the jolly kind.

"I need to see Fainberg."

"Who's Fainberg?" he snickered. Why is it only the idiots that think they're geniuses? I kept my poker face.

"Tell him it's about Jackie Wilkins. Or what's left of him."

Tweedle Dee's face went ash-white. *There* was a reaction I wasn't expecting. I made note of it in my imaginary notebook, in case I needed to remember it later.

He didn't say anything for a minute, then pushed me backward with a bouquet of sausage fingers and went inside. The door didn't lock behind him . . . or didn't have time to. Either way, I took it as an invitation to follow.

The inside of the Rex hadn't changed much since I'd been there a few years earlier in a previous life. The girls strung out on heroin were gone, but half the bulbs in the ceiling still needed changing. Tweedle Dee was talking real close to another guy about his size, but with less hair and a tighter suit.

Neither he nor Tweedle Dum saw me loitering in the back of the club, which gave me a bit of time to survey the scene. Contrary to popular belief, I don't particularly like hanging out in skeevy places, but unfortunately the really weird stuff I deal with doesn't usually happen at the Rosewater or one of those French restaurants along King Street.

Tweedle Dee waddled back behind the bar and pounded his meaty fist on the office door that was closed tight. I got a funny feeling I might not be as welcome as I'd hoped and started to back my way down the hall I'd come in. Better to run away so I could live to run farther another day.

But as I made my way back, I passed a door open a sliver, and through it I spotted a flash of something that made my stomach start to flip-flop and the tips of my fingers to buzz numb. It filled me with this general free-floating worry, even though I wasn't sure what I was seeing.

By the time I realised this and stopped to retrace my steps, Stanley Fainberg was already standing at the other end of the hallway, flanked by his two fat goons. He did *not* look happy to see me.

It's like I told you: some things never really change.

"What are you doing here, Rake? I told you last time: if I wanted to see you, you'd know it."

"There's a dark red smear behind the Jude by the name of Jackie Wilkins," I said, trying to calculate if I could close the distance between me and the door at my back before Fainberg's thugs closed the distance between them and me. "I'm trying to figure out what this Grommell guy had against him. Did you know him?"

Fainberg gave me the stink eye and, without even looking at him, his two dogs started to growl at me. He had those boys well trained, I'll give him that.

The muscles in the back of my legs started to twitch from being tensed for so long. I tried to relax them before they seized, but I guess I didn't have my dogs trained quite as well.

"Get the fuck outta here, Rake," he said coldly. "While you still can."

"Oh, I will," I said, keeping my eye on Tweedle Dum and Tweedle Dee. "But there's something not right about all of this. The Grommell guy that you don't know, he's been busy down on Keele Street, making all sorts of friends. What I can't figure out is why. It's obviously not his idea. What's funny though is it sort of sounds like one of yours."

"Where do you get the balls?" Tweedle Dum burst out, but Fainberg shushed him.

"What do you care, Rake? That fuck Wilkins was a nothing. A loser. He's better off gone."

"Maybe," I said. "He certainly didn't look like he had it together." Part of me was disappointed that didn't even rate a sarcastic chuckle. I supposed they meant business, which didn't help my chances any.

I nodded, and took a step toward that sliver of an opened door. Not a big step, just one tiny enough to seem accidental, but big enough to get a rise if I was edging where I shouldn't have been edging. Fainberg's face tightened.

"So, what was it? Some sort of protection racket? By the looks on your friends' faces, Fainberg, it sounds like I'm pretty close."

"What, are you looking for a cut?"

"Please. You're all about the mess. Can't you see I'm not dressed for that? Still, what I don't get is where you found Grommell, or why the cops haven't found him yet. I've seen him. A guy that big, he'd have trouble disappearing into a crowd."

I took another half-step forward. Dee and Dum got up on their toes.

"I think you orta leave, Rake. Before I change my mind."

You would have thought Dum and Dee were trucks, the way I could feel them revving up. I took another inch closer to that door, just to see what would happen.

"Do you know where Butch Grommell is?" I asked. "Actually, don't worry about answering. I'm sure he's *around*." I guess I knew before I spoke that my words might light a fuse, but I said them anyway. Sometimes, you just have to see what happens. Life's all about risks.

What happened was this: Fainberg's face turned red almost immediately, and his jaw opened so wide I thought all his teeth were planning to leap out at once.

I'd already figured out there was no way I was getting back to that entrance before being caught between a couple of brainless oafs, so my only option was to go forward. Go *toward* that barely glimpsed room. Even as my body committed to the plan, my brain was wondering if I'd finally made my last mistake.

When the noises started erupting from Fainberg, the veins on his face rose like snakes beneath his skin, and his two men recoiled from surprise. That moment of confusion was all I needed.

I darted. By the time they knew Fainberg was telling them to grab me, I was already closing the door of that side room behind me. I knew its lock wouldn't hold, but maybe the frame would keep them out long enough for me to see what was inside.

It was pitch-black with the door closed, even with it jumping off its hinges as Fainberg's men started to pound away. I was lucky Fainberg believed in heavy-duty locks, especially considering that, for what seemed like forever, once I entered the room I could barely move from fear. My whole body was shaking uncontrollably, and there was a taste in the back of my throat I'd never experienced before.

When I was a kid, I remember finding one of my friends dead in Terraview Park, his throat torn open and eyes pecked out. I think his name was Tim. Tim Something. There was something about his twisted body that filled me with a strange feeling, one that came close to matching what I felt in the dark of the Rex. But the intensity was all wrong.

For a minute I completely forgot anyone was pounding on the door, and instead focused first on not shitting my pants, then second on getting the goddamn lights on. I struggled, but I finally found the switch a few feet away from the door.

But when I managed to turn on the light, I was expecting . . . Well, I don't know really *what* I was expecting. I'd tried not thinking about it beforehand in my quivering fear lest I ruin the surprise, and you got to have some surprise in your life. It could have been almost anything, and I wouldn't have expected it. But what it was was more than anything could ever be.

The floor of the room was filthy, covered in at least an inch of black dirt and ash. There were tiny gnats flying everywhere, trying to get in my mouth, and there was definitely some shit mixed in with it all. The place reeked. I don't know if the sprigs of lavender were there to try and make the room more fragrant—mixed into the earth with reddish almond-shaped leaves like poison oak—but the sickly aroma did not help matters at all.

But all these things, they registered secondarily for me as I held the door behind me shut, trying to keep alive long enough to figure my way out of there.

What caught my attention most, even above the mess and the odour, was what was lying in the middle of the floor, amongst the soil and dust and shit and flowers. It was Butch Grommell, and he was just as big, if not bigger, than I'd remembered him. This close, I realised that when I thought his size was inhuman, I was more right than I knew.

If you're around crazy shit long enough, some of it starts to stick. This is the sort of thing that normal people don't understand. I've seen enough voodoo and cabalism in my day to know what Butch Grommell was as soon as I saw him lying there.

But knowing didn't make me feel any better. It actually made me feel worse. It meant the space between the rock outside and the hard place in there was a lot tighter than I'd thought. It was suffocating me.

At least I knew what that wadded-up piece of paper I found with Wilkins was.

"Rake, open the door. The boys won't hurt you."

I started laughing. Sometimes people surprise you with the idiotic stuff that comes out of their mouths.

Grommell lay there quietly waiting as though he weren't already dead.

"Why send Grommell out after Wilkins. What did the guy do? Press your suit wrong?"

"You know how it is," said Fainberg. "Sometimes people see things they shouldn't, and say things when they should just shut up. Some people always have their nose stuck where it doesn't belong."

Yeah, I thought. It's becoming an epidemic.

"So Grommell just did what you told him. No questions."

The question must have stunned him, because the door stopped shaking.

"Sometimes, some men are in no condition to ask questions. Sometimes they can't, and sometimes they know better. Then other guys don't know better at all."

That was my cue to slip away from the door as soon as possible. I doubted my holding it made much of a difference anyway. If those two behemoths wanted in, eventually they were going to get in.

All this was pretext—the thrill of the hunt. We all knew it. I had to change the odds in my favour, even if it meant doing something so stupid, so insane, that the idea of me dying horribly would be considered a definite win.

I rushed to Grommell and started checking his face, his mouth, looking for something carved into his flesh, a piece of paper crammed into his mouth, anything that might already be there. I didn't have enough time, but I had to be sure.

Once I was, I took the little notebook from the pocket of my overcoat. My pen was a bit gummy and my Hebrew worse, but I managed.

The door burst open as I knelt beside Grommell, my notebook in my hand. Fainberg stopped his lackeys and stared at me. So did they. And I stared back. The four of us staring at each other like some Italian Western, waiting for someone to make the first move. And all the while there was a giant misshapen brown man lying in the dirt at our feet.

It went on so long that I started thinking about all the other times I'd gotten myself into trouble, and for a minute I understood just why Detective McCray hated me so much.

I was the sort who liked to poke at hornet's nests, just to see what would happen. Well, I sure as hell poked this one pretty fierce, and kneeling there, my legs going numb, my nose filling with the odour of shit and dirt, I started to wonder if I'd made the wrong choices in life. Damn that Mrs Mulroney.

"Rake," Fainberg said, a hollow grin spreading across his face. "Why don't you come over here and we can talk about this like civilised people."

"Look at this place. Does this look like the sort of thing *civilised* people do?"

Fainberg shrugged his shoulders but didn't stop grinning.

"Sometimes people need schooling, and better it comes from a dead guy than me. Is it my fault sometimes he gets . . . creative? This isn't an exact science."

It took me a minute, I'll admit, to figure out what he was telling me. It didn't take me long after that, though, to know that him telling me anything was a pretty bad sign about my odds.

I kept as still as I could, watching them and waiting. I knew things could only play out one way, but I was hoping someone other than me was going to realise it, and that the endgame would not be pretty. I didn't harbour those hopes for long.

"I'm tired of this conversation. Go bring him out of there."

"I really think it's better if you guys didn't."

I knew they wouldn't listen, but I wanted to make sure I said it just so I wouldn't feel bad about what happened next. Dum and Dee walked toward me, splitting up to flank me on either side. But I had a not-so-secret weapon.

I tore the page out of my notebook and held it up just long enough for Fainberg to see what I'd written and hope he recognised his own name in Hebrew. Then I crammed the page into Grommell's mouth and tried to run in the other direction.

No one told my crouched legs to be ready, however, so instead I stumbled a few steps and crashed to the floor.

Tweedle Dum and Dee were running at me, but as soon as I rolled over,

Fainberg was yelling something else at them. "The paper! Get the paper! Get it out of his mouth!"

I could see the two of them stop, confused, and Tweedle Dee bent over and reached into Grommell's mouth to pull the scrap of paper free.

You can't say I didn't warn them.

I've heard a lot of screaming in my day, some of it even from my own lips, but never before or since have I heard something so horrifying.

Dee pulled his fingerless stump away, crying, and the blood gushed down his arm. He looked at me laying in the shit like it was my fault.

I kind of shrugged and inched back, watching Grommell rise like a tidal wave behind him. He just kept going up and up, wider and wider, until I thought he was going to eclipse the room.

Blood was splattered all over his face and chest, and over Dee's too. It was everywhere, the artery pumping it out like a fire hose, and I think he would have collapsed right then if Grommell hadn't already wrapped his massive fingers around the fat man's head and started to squeeze.

It didn't take very long. There was a soft crack, then a pop like a vacuum seal being broken. In an instant, everything above Tweedle Dee's neck was pulverised in a mist of crimson, while his partner and Fainberg watched with mouths agape. And then everything went even crazier.

I have to admit, I spent the next few seconds crawling away as fast as I could, heading straight for a desk to hide under, so I can't say I saw everything right away.

I sure heard it though—heard screaming louder than any person has a right to scream.

I rolled over from my hiding spot to see fat Dum had already met with Grommell's mindlessness—and was in pieces about it. Literally. The bottom half of his body, from the waist down, was kneeling in the dirt like he was about to propose, except instead of a ring there were vertebrae spilled out around the floor. The top half of him, the part that still had a piece of an arm and half a head dangling by a few strips of flesh, was being dragged across the floor by Grommell as he slowly trudged toward Fainberg.

You'd think Fainberg would have run. You'd think that somewhere in his greasy grey skull there would have been a little voice screaming: *What the fuck are you doing? Get the fuck out!* But if that voice was there, he was ignoring it.

Instead, he was trying to reason with Grommell. Even standing in dirt and shit and blood, some of which no doubt was coming from his own body, his sense of entitlement and belief that he was untouchable pervaded.

He was full of confidence, I'll give him that much. Still, it gave me a chill to hear him trying to command Grommell by repeating a single word, over and over again: "Rake! Rake! Rake!"

It wasn't exactly sporting of him. I didn't bother trying to quiet him, though. Grommell did that for me when he ripped off Fainberg's jaw.

Dead people seem to follow me wherever I go, but never has it been anything like what I witnessed in that tiny room in the back of the Rex. The smell was . . . I don't even know what that smell was. I have no words to describe it. Like a slaughterhouse, but worse. Like every nightmare you've ever had rolled into one odour, and then left out in the damp to rot.

The only reason I didn't throw up everything in my stomach was that I had my overcoat over my mouth so I could at least breathe.

Grommell didn't seem bothered by it—he wasn't bothered by anything at all. He stood, his chest rising and falling quickly as he breathed heavy, air rushing through his nose like a wind tunnel. Blood was caked over his arms past his elbows, and from his naked stomach to his knees.

I tried holding my breath, or doing anything I could to fade away, but the way he cocked his head, turned those milky empty eyes toward me, I knew I had my hopes pinned on a fantasy that had no hope of coming true. I wasn't going to kiss a princess or save a damsel in distress. I was going to face a man-eating dragon without sword or shield. Or armour. Or hope.

"Easy big guy," I said as calmly as I could muster, getting to my feet without any sudden moves that might startle him and send him back into frenzy. "You don't want to do anything crazy. You're free now. Fainberg won't be making you do anything anymore."

Grommell snorted, and the sound in the sudden quiet was like an explosion. I jumped, enough that he turned to face me. I didn't like the shape his mouth was in. Nor that it was trembling. Or that there was blood all around it. Actually, it was the blood I liked least.

"Maybe . . . maybe I should just step outside," I said, smiling weakly. "I could use the fresh air."

I started inching toward the door, keeping my eye on Grommell, whose muscles were beginning to coil. He growled very quietly, which I thought was a bit overboard. I kept moving, though. If there's one secret I've learned, it's to always keep moving. You stop, you die. It's as simple as that. You stop. You die.

In his defence, Grommell let me make it to the door before charging. My hand was already turning the doorknob when I sensed what was happening. I don't remember hearing the sound of his footsteps at all. Instead, I just remember feeling a puff of air across my face as the door's lock unhitched, and my body instinctively started moving.

But zero to a hundred is not easy, not when the floor is caked in blood and shit, and as the door swung open I took a false step and my feet slipped out in front of me, sending me tumbling backwards. I'm pretty sure that's what saved my life.

I remember seeing Grommell go flying over me as I disappeared from his grasp at the last instant, and he went crashing out into the hallway and against the wall opposite. The force of the collision knocked him off his feet, and he fell like he was made of marble.

I was hurting something fierce, but I didn't waste any time. I scrambled to my feet and limped over to Grommell's prone body. It was like the lights had been shut off, but one by one there were turning back on. Grommell was rebooting himself. In a few seconds, he would be back, and I'd be just another corpse in his hands. I didn't have very long at all.

So, I did the only thing I could think to do: I kicked his mouth in as hard and as fast as I could. Grommell made no noises as my heel went through his gums, knocking loose teeth and bone, and I kept kicking until his mouth was a bloody tangle of torn, dead flesh. I would have kept going if I hadn't seen his giant bloody hands start to twitch. At that point, I knew I was out of time.

I dropped to my knees and shoved my fist into the hole I'd made in his face, then started feeling around. That close to him, part of me was amazed at the size of his head—maybe two or three times as large as any head I'd ever seen. But I didn't spend a lot of time pondering it, not while those giant jaws were starting to move.

Twice they closed on my arm, pinning it for a moment, but thankfully not enough to break the bones.

I was grabbing flesh left and right, fighting with his bloody tongue while his whole body started coming to life. I was running out of time.

I don't know how I knew what I had hold of, or if I even did at all, but it was clear Grommell was seconds from coming back to life, and my time was up. I squeezed the bloody pulp in my hand tight and wrenched my arm back, using the full strength of my legs to launch me backward.

I flew a few feet, landing on my hip in that funny way that said I wouldn't be walking right anytime soon, and I shook my head hard to clear the sparks from my eyes and cotton from my ears. I couldn't afford to pass out. Not that it stopped me.

I doubt I was out for more than a few seconds, but the fact that I came back at all was a good sign. I looked dimly in my hand and saw the wadded-up piece of blood-soaked notebook paper, squeezed into a nice little ball. I put it in my pocket for safekeeping.

Grommell just laid there against the wall, dead a second time, one up on everyone else who was still on his or her first. But at least this time it was final.

I don't think I'd ever been covered in so much blood in my life. The washrooms were not equipped to deal with it. I did the best I could, though. I stripped down and washed as much of myself as possible in that tiny sink, using the half-inch of rancid green soap left in the globe-shaped wall dispenser.

I couldn't just leave. There was no way I'd get more than a block in those clothes, and for the life of me I couldn't find anything else to wear. Not even an old coat lying around.

I even tried Fainberg's office, but the door was steel and locked tight. If there were keys, they were somewhere in that bloody mess and I didn't feel the urge to look for them. Instead, I helped myself to some of everything behind the bar. There's nothing like a drink when you're buck naked to make you feel alive. That, and actually being alive by the skin of your teeth.

If I were a cat, I probably owed the universe a few lives.

Once it was dark enough, I tossed the remaining few bottles around the room to soak it as much as possible, then put my bloody clothes in a plastic fast food bag I found. Behind the bar was a book of matches, so I used them to light anything flamemable I could find. Then I tossed the whole book in and hightailed it out of there.

It was exhilarating, being naked in the night. I felt like a new man.

I didn't hear sirens for a while, even though I could see behind me dark thick smoke filling the air. I had no idea what they were going to make of things when they finally put the fire out, but I was pretty sure I wouldn't be involved.

Like I said before, I had stashes all over the city of clothes and other things, just in case I needed them. I didn't have to go more than a few blocks to find one, and the people I passed weren't the sort to care about seeing me. Just another naked guy on the street in the middle of the night. Still, it was good to get back into some pants. Pants really help a guy feel complete.

I had no idea what I was going to do about my overcoat, though.

Forever Boys

James Cooper

The author wrote 'Forever Boys' in June 2012 as an homage *to Ray Brad-bury, whose death in the same month had come as a great shock. 'Bradbury's ability to capture the essence of what it was to be young again had always deeply moved me,' Mr. Cooper says, 'and I decided to compose a rite-of-passage story of my own by way of tribute. I knew I would never be able to come close to the master himself, but I hope I've tapped in to the same rich vein of nostalgia and longing that marked so much of Mr Bradbury's best work.'*

James Cooper is the author of the short story collections You Are The Fly *and* The Beautiful Red. *His novella* Terra Damnata *was published by PS in 2011 and was shortlisted for a British Fantasy Award. His novella* Strange Fruit *(PS again) and the novel* Dark Father *were both published in 2014.* Country Dark *has appeared as part of the TTA Novella Series, and the collection* Human Pieces *was recently issued by PS. You can visit his website at: jamescooperfiction.co.uk.*

WILL WAS THE ONLY ONE WHO KNEW; I COULDN'T TRUST anyone else. It was like confessing your darkest sin. Only a priest or a kindred spirit would do. You had to be careful with things as delicate as this; not everyone would understand. If people knew you had the power to see through solid objects, all hell was liable to break loose.

We stood on the corner of the street and peered at our target from behind a hedge. It was already dark. Shelley's house was no more than fifty yards away. Her bedroom curtains had been drawn. An orange night-light was flickering inside the room.

"What can you see?" Will said. He could barely contain his excitement. His futile pursuit of Shelley Weekes had stalled over a month ago; this remote surveillance, conducted vicariously, was all that remained of his failed romance.

"Jesus, Will. Give me a moment to focus. I ain't Superman. It takes a second or two to warm up."

Will looked appalled. "What if it don't work?"

I dismissed his lack of faith with a flick of the head. "It always works," I said.

I squinted my eyes and trained my gaze on Shelley's bedroom wall.

"Holy crow!"

"What is it?" Will said. "You have to tell me everything!"

I looked through the wall and saw Shelley undressing for bed. It was exactly as I'd always imagined, a routine act become suddenly intimate; the simplicity of it almost profound.

"She's taking off her clothes," I said. "She's wearing a green bra and white pants. Her body looks like it's been dipped in milk."

I blinked slowly and sighed; Will was staring at me, looking confused.

"You what?"

I squinted my eyes again and instructed them to penetrate the wall, brick by brick, until the obstacle melted away.

"She's undoing her bra," I said, watching Shelley reach behind her back with practised hands. "Christ, I can see them! They're right in front of me, Will. They look . . . " I didn't know what to say, so I just muttered, "Perfect."

"*Shit*! I think I'm having a heart attack." Will staggered against the hedge and grabbed hold of my arm for support. "What's she doing now?"

I looked through the wall and saw Shelley in all her glory. She had slipped out of her underwear and I marvelled at her body, naked and pale, as she crossed the room in the orange glow of the light. She looked like a goddess, and I felt my breath catch in my throat as she pulled on a white cotton robe.

"That's it," I said. "She must have left the room. I've lost her."

"Damn it!" Will said. "You should never have looked away. How many times have I told you? You have to concentrate!"

He sagged against my arm and gazed up into the starlit sky. He was wearing a dreamy, wistful expression, as though I'd placed him within reach of his heart's desire.

"Shelley Weekes," he said softly, no doubt imagining her in the green bra and immaculate white pants.

I nodded and stared up at the sky, letting my eyes sink into the darkness; trying to figure out why I had been reluctant to share what I'd seen.

When I returned home, Ma was sitting at the kitchen table, working on a new cake. She made at least one a day, sculpting the body of the bun so that it reflected her current mood. Tonight's masterpiece was in the shape of a sunflower, so I assumed Ma had sailed through the day without any 'episodes'. Her eyes looked dilated and she was smiling; I could smell the bitter chalk of the drugs she had taken on her breath.

"Where's Dad?" I said, hanging my coat in the cloakroom.

Ma continued to add icing to the sponge petals of the cake. She liked to immerse herself in the baking process completely; she once told me it made her feel safe.

"He went out," she said. "Probably lying in a damn gutter somewhere."

I glanced at my watch. "It's getting late. Should I go and look for him?"

She smoothed out the yellow icing with a spatula. "Let him sleep with the trash," she said. "He'll feel right at home."

I left Ma in the kitchen and hoped I hadn't destroyed her good mood. I had a queasy feeling that if I returned to the kitchen I would find Ma frantically rearranging the cake into the shape of her dream weapon, like a steak knife or an ice pick or an axe.

I climbed the stairs to my room, moved over to the window, and stared into the night. My father was out there somewhere, and I knew that, if I really wanted to, I'd be able to track him down. I doubted I'd even need to rely on my special gift. His flaws would make him all too visible. He tore through the world like a natural disaster, leaving behind a ragged cast of luckless souls who'd had the misfortune of standing in his way.

I looked across at the row of houses opposite and wondered what our neighbours were doing in the privacy of their own homes. Everything was dark and silent; nothing moved. The house fronts all looked exactly the same. I closed my eyes and allowed the delicate filament behind my corneas to slowly warm up. I could feel the heat of it pressing against the flickering lids.

I opened my eyes and trained my gaze on the brick wall of one of the houses, willing it to dissolve. Slowly, I found my way in and saw

Mr Kundali, slouched in an armchair before an electric fire reading a book. He was sipping red wine from a glass. Every time he turned the page he blinked; then he would go back to devouring the words on the page.

I moved along and stole a moment with Mrs Hull. She was wearing a pink dressing gown and painting her toenails on the couch. An action film was playing on the television. She kept pausing to watch it, holding the brush in the air. She looked frozen in time; her mouth hung open and I could see the dark swelling of her tongue. It reminded me of the belly of a frog.

I shifted further along the row of houses and stopped at the Brookes residence. In the upstairs room a dim light showed a figure standing naked beside an unmade bed. It was a boy, a few years older than me; I knew him only as Gillie, the strange creature who wandered round the neighbourhood clutching a dead bird's claw. His intensity scared me a little; I don't think I'd ever heard him talk.

I gazed across the empty space separating our two houses and realised that he was staring directly at me, as though he'd been waiting for me to finally notice him. There was a thin smile playing at the corner of his lips. Between his fingers he grasped something new, something fragile: a bird's egg, which he held out to me in the palm of his hand. I held my breath, sensing he was offering me a gift. I smiled back and closed my eyes. The vision of the boy stayed with me; he told me I had seen enough.

The slamming of the front door jarred me from sleep, and I glanced at the clock on the wall. The luminous hands told me it was eleven-thirty. My father had returned home early for once, and I could already hear him and Ma, brimming with resentment, tearing into each other in the kitchen below. I rubbed sleep from my eyes and sat up. There was a glorious smell of freshly baked cake permeating the house. It added a sickeningly sweet coating to my parents' rage, which is probably why none of us were ever able to eat Ma's creations; every cake she baked went to charity or the nursing home at the end of the street. I could barely even bring myself to look at them; the smell reminded me too much of those late-night altercations as I lay clutching at the sheets in bed, my knuckles white, failing to decipher the screams.

I lay my head on the pillow and closed my eyes. My mother and father howled at one another like stray dogs. I dreamed of Shelley Weekes unhooking her green bra and stepping out of her white cotton pants.

The following morning I met Will outside *Wok This Way*, the Chinese takeaway from which my father had recently been banned for drunkenly lamenting the lack of authenticity in the signature dishes. Ma was not best pleased; she and Mrs Chiang had been friends for years. Ma baked traditional Chinese cakes and donated them to the Chiangs for their New Year Banquet Specials. In return, Mrs Chiang always gave us a week's worth of takeaway for free.

I joined Will, who was leaning against the side of a litterbin, and we offered each other a tired greeting. Will's parents were almost as combative as mine, and I vaguely wondered which one of us had endured the shittiest night.

"Did you bring them?" I asked.

He removed his rucksack and unzipped it. Inside was a shoebox that had once contained my father's Firetrap work boots. Its current purpose was to protect the treasures Will and I had spent the last three weeks collecting.

"Is everything there?"

Will nodded. The bag smelt rank, so I quickly zipped it back up.

"What do you think he'll give us?"

"Could be anything," I said. "You might even get your hands on that 7.9mm Kurz you've had your eye on."

Will's eyes widened and I smiled. We had been sourcing artefacts for *Liv Kaminski's Bird Emporium* for well over a year. In return for any bird-related items we could find, Liv Kaminski rewarded us with an item of World War II memorabilia. He had a huge collection, bequeathed him by his late father, and Liv, still haunted by how many of his family had been *ethnically cleansed*, despised every tainted scrap of it; he called it a memento of genocide and said it made him feel sick just thinking about it. He was happy to give it away, piece by piece, to me and Will in exchange for contributions to the museum; for an especially rare find, the rewards could be great. We had once presented him with the perfectly preserved body of a green woodpecker that we had discovered down by the lake. Liv had been so moved he had given us both a German Model 24 stick grenade. I had hidden mine in a metal box beneath my bed. Whenever I took it out and looked at it I felt a profound chill. I had grown fearful of touching it. If I held it for too long, the wooden shaft grew warm in my hand. I was secretly afraid I might never want to let it go.

We walked past the local shops, across the park, and down to the edge of the residential block that ran alongside the embankment. *Liv Kaminski's Bird Emporium* sounded grander than it actually was. It was certainly a bird museum—up to a point—but it was situated in a converted terraced house, which doubled as Liv's personal accommodation. Will and I thought it was fantastic, but there were few others in the town who shared our enthusiasm for the place. The entire house had been transformed into an avian temple. Liv himself slept in the cramped attic on a narrow fold-away bed; the rest of the space in the house had been given over to his obsession with birds. He had knocked out all but the load-bearing walls on the ground floor and dedicated his life to constructing an open-plan museum that included assorted tableaux of stuffed birds, glassed display cases of eggs, feathers, beaks, and skulls, as well as highly original collages crafted, with suitably birdlike resourcefulness, from all manner of organic materials, including nests, broken egg shells, and leaves. My favourite composition was Liv's stunning depiction of a golden eagle soaring across a snow-capped mountain, which filled the entire back wall of the house. The piece had been created using only the bleached-white bones of tiny birds, many of which Will and I had foraged for in the nearby woods. It had taken Liv over six months to perfect the design. When he was ready to glue the final bone in place, he had invited Will and me to witness the event. Will had taken a photo using his sister's phone, which he had appropriated especially for the occasion. Liv had been smiling and weeping at the same time. He said something in Polish that neither of us understood. I remember he looked inexplicably sad.

The first floor of the house, which had once consisted of three bedrooms and a family bathroom, was now home to four separate aviaries. Liv had installed reinforced frameless glass doors in every room, at great personal expense, to enable visitors an unimpeded view of the often-frenzied activity unfolding within. He had also hired a firm to fix remote-controlled blinds in each room, complete with blackout lining.

Will and I had spent many hours in this part of the museum, observing the interaction of the birds. Their easy flight fascinated us and, even contained within the house, they seemed to inhabit a constant desire to be airborne, as though it was only in this state that they were able to be free.

Watching them for any length of time made me feel slightly conflicted, for I knew, deep down, that these birds should be soaring beneath a clear, unbroken sky.

The four rooms all housed different types of bird and had been sensitively equipped by Liv to accommodate their every need. The master bedroom, being the largest, contained a variety of common garden birds, including, sparrows, starlings, blackbirds, bluetits, and crows. The second aviary was the home of a family of three beautiful barn owls, their wide-eyed stare implacable and vast. The third room served as the terrifying hunting ground of two formidable-looking goshawks, and the highlight of every trip was watching Liv release two live mice into the artificially constructed undergrowth. We would stand back, mouths agape, as the goshawks swooped down and tore the scurrying rodents to shreds. The final room, the one that had once been the family bathroom, housed only a single bird, but it was probably the most breathtaking of them all. It was a preening, almost godlike, scarlet macaw. Each time I gazed upon it, perched on its wooden post, I lost myself in the rainbow-coloured feathers and the incongruousness of seeing it *here*, trapped between the four walls of a converted bathroom in a Victorian terraced house. The noise of the place could be fearsome, like some ancient Amazonian battleground, and walking into the museum for the first time was like entering a world of raging cacophony that sometimes reminded me uncomfortably of my own house after my father returned home late from the pub.

Not that it ever discouraged me from coming back. The truth was, *Liv Kaminski's Bird Emporium* was the one place in this godforsaken world that made me feel alive; the kind of environment where I felt safe, because I was surrounded by creatures that seemed as desperate as me. That there was a worm of doubt eating away at me somewhere underneath it all was the only factor I struggled to understand. Lingering in that house, I felt raw, like an open wound. I could feel the dust and the heat of the world slowly eating me away.

We walked along the embankment and threw stones into the rippling stream until we arrived at the museum. On the wall of the house by the front door Liv had hung an ornate woodcut sign that read *Liv Kaminski's Bird Emporium*. There was an image of a hawk with its wings outspread above the simple disclosure: *Admission Free*.

I knocked on the door and waited for it to open. Eventually, it was pulled ajar and Liv's gaunt, bespectacled face looked down at me. His cheeks were leathery and heavily lined, but his eyes were animated and full of life. He smiled at us and threw open the door. His narrow frame, clothed in its habitual grey three-piece suit, bent towards us and he ushered us inside the house.

"Ah! My little magpies!" he said. "What have you brought for me today?"

Will removed the rucksack and handed it to Liv. "See for yourself," he said.

Liv reached for the rucksack with the reverence of a small child cradling a baby chick. His eyes shone behind the spectacles; his impulse to rip open the bag was tempered by his desire to prolong the moment of revelation. We were expert foragers and he knew that the bag could contain almost anything. Something extraordinary; something mundane. It barely even mattered anymore what was inside. For Liv, the joy was all in the discovery; that exquisite moment of drawing open the box and peering at the strange array of contents within.

He shuffled off towards his workbench, with Will and me following behind. He placed the rucksack on the worktop, unzipped it, and removed the shoebox. Pulling on a pair of latex gloves, he lifted the lid.

"Most interesting," he said, arranging the contents of the box on the bench. This was his standard response, regardless of the quality of the items we sought to trade. He kept his cards close to his chest and always played his hand with a gambler's neutrality. He lined up our latest haul and considered them for a moment, rubbing his chin. I stared down at the workbench and realised that our offering looked unremarkable; it amounted to a ragged black wing, still intact, a cracked skull, half a dozen broken eggshells, two dead nestlings that looked like embryonic sacs, and the bloated body of a rotting crow. Hardly a bountiful display.

Liv stared hard at the assembled oddities and appeared to arrive at a decision.

"For this I give you two things," he said. He reached beneath the workbench and produced two items that he had clearly already earmarked for trade.

"This," he said, holding up a small leather wallet, "is a wehrpaß document wallet. It was used to protect a German soldier's ID, which usually recorded his complete military record."

He handed it to Will, who began turning it over in his hands. He raised it to his nose to smell the leather and I noticed him smiling; I imagined him generating a vivid backstory for it, creating in his mind's eye a detailed image of the soldier who had once owned it, and knew that I would have a devil of time trying to persuade him to relinquish it for something else. He had already decided exactly what he would use it for; I knew that before the day was out he would have created a wehrpaß of his own on his computer, printed it to size, and slid it into the supple leather sleeve of the wallet he was currently holding in his hands.

The thought made me smile, largely because it was exactly what *I* would have done, had the wallet been presented to me. I turned my attention back to Liv and waited, listening to the frantic chatter of the birds on the floor above.

"And this," he said, "is something I found in my father's personal belongings. I don't think it's from the war, but I think you boys might like it all the same."

He grinned and offered me a well-read comic book that instantly took away my breath. I sensed that Will had ceased caressing the wallet and had joined me in staring at the garish cover; he was leaning against my arm and craning his head in an attempt to get a better look. I stared down at the comic in my trembling hands and made a faltering attempt at reading out the German title.

"*Gespenster geschichten,*" I said. I glanced up at Liv to see if I had pronounced it correctly and he nodded.

"It means 'Ghost Stories'," he said, chuckling. "Just don't show your mother, okay?"

I stared at the cover art and felt a warm glow begin to spread throughout my body; it was as though I had been shown a chink of light in a darkened cave, and I reached for it, sensing it was all I had. The illustration was like something from a child's worst nightmare, depicting a young man holding a lit candle up to the night to reveal a towering monster leaning towards him, with metal teeth and flickering orange eyes. The man had his hand in front of his face, as though he were warding off the devil; in the background, attending the monster, were half a dozen black bats, beneath which, in blazing yellow text, was the proclamation: *Die Schrechensnacht des Eisenmonsters . . . und andere gruselstories!*

I looked at Liv and frowned. "What does this say?" I asked, pointing to the yellow text. He adjusted the glasses on the end of his nose and peered at the comic book. He smiled.

"It says *The Frightening Night of the Iron Monsters . . . and other spine-tingling stories!* But that is all I translate! For the rest you will have only the pictures."

Rather than disappointing me, this prospect filled me with a sudden sense of wonder. I flicked through the comic and feasted my eyes on the lurid illustrations accompanied by this strange alien language; one more thing in the world that I didn't understand, though I knew later I would be poring over the pictures in search of answers, deriving narrative clues from the artist's intelligent hand.

"This is fantastic," I said to Liv. "Are you sure you want to give it away?"

He stopped tidying away some of his tools and smiled at me.

"You think I need to fill my head with any more monster stories?" he said, waving me away. "Trust me, I have enough."

I thanked him and then turned to Will, who was eyeing me warily.

"We can share," I said, holding out the comic, and he grinned at me.

"This, too," he said holding aloft the wehrpaß wallet.

Liv Kaminski continued to clear away his workbench, leaving out only the line of items we had brought in the box. He shook his head, marvelling at the simplicity of our friendship.

"Kids . . . " he said. "So easily pleased. What I wouldn't give to be your age again."

I watched him for a moment as he considered this, clearly remembering his own childhood as a lonely boy growing up in a Poland forever changed by war. If my own experiences were grim, I had no doubt that Liv's had been far worse. The horror of what he'd seen was hidden behind his calm, bespectacled eyes, but I knew it was there; the hammer-blow of Nazi command, an epiphany of violence and spilled blood. A crushing reminder of uncompromising iron will.

Liv returned the rucksack to me and I unzipped it and carefully placed the German comic book in the bag. Will leaned towards me and dropped the wehrpaß wallet in too. I zipped it back up, the trade complete, and slung it over my shoulder. Liv finished straightening up the workbench and then beckoned us close.

"Here," he said. "I show you something."

He rearranged the items we had brought in the shoebox, moving them to one side. He paused when he reached the black wing and held it up to the light.

"See?" he said, running a finger along the ragged edge where it had been torn away. "You can see the teeth marks. A fox or a lucky cat, perhaps. The poor bird will have suffered badly."

I wondered if this was what he wanted to show us, but he carefully put the wing with the other items and wiped down a large rectangular space on the workbench with a damp cloth. He pulled the rotting body of the crow towards him and rolled it onto its back so that its breast was exposed to the light. The smell of decay was strong enough to make me cover my mouth with my hand. I watched Liv adjust his spectacles and peer at the rack of tools above the workbench. He leaned forward and took down a small instrument that I quickly realised was a scalpel; its handle was grimy and smudged, but its blade looked uncommonly sharp. For the second time that morning, as Liv lowered the knife towards the bird's carcass, I found myself holding my breath.

"Ever dissected a bird before?"

Will and I shook our heads and Liv smiled.

"Then watch closely," he said. "You might learn something for once."

He dipped his head over the crow and swung a balanced arm lamp into place so that the light illuminated the bird. Will and I crowded in on either side of him, keen not to miss a beat as the old man set about his work. I could smell the woody scent of Liv's aftershave and realised it was exactly the same brand as my father's: Lynx Africa. I looked down at the dead bird, smelt the cheap fragrance, and pictured the creature flying high above the terraced houses wearing my father's face. The image was powerfully affecting and made me reel away from the workbench, overwhelmed by a deep sense of unease.

"If you don't like what you see," Liv said, noting my uncertainty, "there is a bucket in the back room. Please use it. I do not wish to be cleaning up any more mess."

I nodded and took a deep breath; the aftershave was making me feel increasingly nauseous, but I was determined to witness Liv's dissection of the bird before I conceded to any base instinct to be sick. I glanced across at Will and noticed that his face was pale and drawn. It comforted me to know that I was not alone in feeling decidedly queasy. I looked at Liv's white latex hand, the poised scalpel, the dead bird; the *Emporium* suddenly seemed cloying and claustrophobic and I fought the impulse to turn and run, sensing I was on the verge of some compelling discovery, as though a great secret was about to be disclosed.

Liv's hand fell with careful precision towards the crow's body, and the scalpel pierced the breast.

"I learn this from my father," he said, "and now I show the two of you. I also read books and learn a lot about all kinds of things." He glanced at me and Will. "You should read too. It is surprising what people write about in books. You can find out everything you need to know about almost anything. Even this," he said, pointing at the partially cut-open bird.

He nodded emphatically and returned his attention to the crow. I felt my heart begin to race. My eyes lost focus for a moment as they settled on the point of the scalpel; I watched it enter the dead flesh of the bird.

"Okay, now pay attention," Liv said as he manoeuvred the scalpel. "I am making a slit from the sternum to just before the vent. I have to part the skin and the muscles of the abdomen, like this, and then continue to cut through the bird's left side all the way to the base of the wing."

He looked over his spectacles at us to see if we were paying attention; I noticed that his breathing was even and relaxed. Satisfied that his audience was suitably engaged, he resumed his work.

"This is where it gets tricky," he said, waving the scalpel in the air. "If I lay back the sternum, like this, you should be able to see the organs in the abdominal cavity."

We leaned in for a closer look and gained our first glimpse of the complex mystery that lay inside the bird. Rather than being repelled, I felt somehow attracted by it, as though it held all the secrets of the universe, large and small, all within the tiny framework of a creature I saw flying in the sky every day, floating above my head, forever out of reach like a fading, neglected star.

Liv cut through the large breast muscles and the smaller muscles beneath until the digestive system was exposed.

"This," he said, scooping out what looked like a length of ragged twine, "is the small intestine." He severed it and placed it on the workbench. He paused and looked at us again. The crow's organs were clearly visible. I felt a rush of pity for the poor thing; I wanted to stitch it back up and blow life into it and return it to its natural habitat. It suddenly felt wrong looking at it like this; like I was colluding in the destruction of the prevailing order of things.

I stared at the crow, unable to tear my eyes away, and watched as Liv once again eased the scalpel into the body cavity.

"If I remove the liver," he said, "you will see the heart and the lungs."
He quickly sliced away the organ blocking our view and leaned back.
"See?" he said, pointing with the scalpel. "There is the heart. Just like in
the books, no?"

I peered at the dissected bird and saw a small, dark organ tucked against
the severed muscle. It looked like a tiny, clenched fist, still shaking; raised
up against the suffering of the world.

Liv returned the scalpel to the rack above the workbench, removed the
latex gloves and then threw them into a large green bin. He looked pleased
with himself, as though he had shared some form of recondite knowledge
with us, granting us access to a sealed realm to which only he knew the
appropriate code.

"What about the bird?" I said, stealing one last look at its splayed body
on the workbench. It looked pathetic; a miraculous machine with its parts
exposed for the entertainment of a passing few.

"I pin it later," Liv said. "It needs treating before I put it in glass case
next to others. It is a good specimen, my little magpies. I am most
grateful."

He turned and walked away and Will and I followed. I felt morose, like
I had witnessed something no one should ever have to see. I looked at Will
and he lowered his head, embarrassed by the silence. We spent a few minutes trudging around the *Emporium*, but neither one of us felt inclined to
dwell on any exhibit for more than a few seconds; I was secretly afraid that
watching the dissection had destroyed my interest in the museum for good.

We returned to the front door as the birds above us wailed in distress,
waved to Liv Kaminski, and then departed. The air outside felt cool and
fresh; Will and I breathed it in, listening to the agitated language of the
birds diminish as we quietly stepped away from the house.

We drifted around the streets for a while, neither of us saying much, both
trying to process what we had been shown at the *Emporium*. Will asked
me what I thought it all meant, and I told him I didn't understand the
question; the answer dissatisfied him and he fell into a dour silence,
refusing to elaborate. He ambled over towards the stream, and we
followed its meandering path for a while, throwing stones into it and

counting how many Coke cans we could see beneath the water. We'd reached eleven by the time Will next spoke.

"I didn't like it," he said, frowning. "That bird thing. It creeped me out."

I said nothing, still uncertain exactly how it had made me feel; the memory of it was fresh, nestled inside my brain like a looped montage from a surgical film. I saw the severed muscle; the clenched fist of the heart; the steady hand of Liv Kaminski as he lowered the scalpel towards the bird. I remembered feeling breathless and distressed, and I did so again, as the memory consolidated itself, revealing the crow's organs in microscopic detail.

"We weren't supposed to like it," I said. "It was a lesson. Liv wanted us to learn something. He wanted us to understand. That's why he showed us the heart."

"We saw the whole shooting match," Will said, turning pale.

"But it was the heart that mattered," I said. "That's what he wanted us to see."

We counted Coke cans, threw stones; tried to fathom what lay at the dark edge of childhood and beyond.

When we reached my house, I led Will into the hall and quickly ushered him upstairs. I could hear noises in the kitchen, which meant either Ma was preparing to bake or my father was home early from work. Either way, I didn't want Will to have to endure their interference for even a minute; it was bad enough that I had to.

We shot upstairs and I quickly closed and bolted the door. Will collapsed into a weary-looking beanbag and I passed him the rucksack. He removed the two new treasures Liv had given us at the *Emporium* while I rummaged beneath the bed for the metal box. My hand passed through empty air, and I felt an acute sadness invade my senses. I plunged my arm deeper into the darkness and began frantically waving it about. The result was no more productive; I pulled out my arm and crawled under the frame of the bed desperate to locate the metal box. Not only did it house the revered Model 24 stick grenade, it was also the place where I stored most of the other items I had traded with Liv: bits of shrapnel, old documents, spent cartridges, badges, and insignia. The box was all I had; the only thing I possessed that was truly my own.

I crawled out from under the bed, dusty and empty-handed, and said: "Shit."

Will joined me on the floor, his suspicions yet to be confirmed, but already sensing a catastrophic violation of my privacy.

"He's taken it," I spluttered. "The box."

"He can't have," Will said, peering under the bed. "It's here somewhere. It has to be."

It felt like my head was about to explode; the heat in the room was making me feel ill.

"It's not there, Will! I've just fucking looked! It's gone."

Will withdrew from the bed and sat on the carpet, staring at me. Neither one of us knew quite what to say. My father never came into my room; it was an unwritten rule. Ma, yes, every once in a blue moon to clean, maybe; but my father had never once shown any interest in what went on in there. The only time he ever addressed me was late at night, when he'd wake me up to drunkenly blame me for destroying everything good in his life.

A thought occurred to me and I quickly reached for the bottom drawer of my bedside table. I pulled it open and foraged beneath the underwear. My worst fear was quickly confirmed.

"Shit. My journal. It's not here." I turned to Will and felt my stomach plummet. "He has my journal," I said, hearing a hollow desperation in my own voice. "He's taken everything."

"Maybe it was your Ma," Will suggested.

I stared at him, breathing hard, and he eventually looked away. We both knew who had taken them; I could even smell a faint, lingering trace of Lynx Africa mixed with bourbon. My father had been here all right, and recently, too. That amalgamated scent had attended much of my childhood and still filled me with silent terror; I'd have recognised it anywhere.

I heard movement in the kitchen down below and laid a hand on Will's arm. A door opened and heavy footsteps moved slowly over the parquet floor.

"From all the noise up there I'd say you must have made a discovery or two," my father shouted up the stairs. "Maybe you boys should come on down. I may be able to shed a little light on your affairs."

I felt Will's arm tense and, when I glanced his way, I saw a look of utter torment pass before his eyes.

"I don't think we should go down," he whispered. "He sounds drunk."

I smiled wearily, despite my own apprehension. "He's always drunk. It's his default setting."

Will and I chuckled and then looked nervously at the door in case our gallows humour had prompted my father to climb the stairs.

"We should go down," I said. "If we don't he'll come up and get us. Is that what you want?"

Will looked suitably horrified by the prospect and shook his head.

"Okay," I said, rising to my feet. "Just remember to stay calm. And don't say anything unless you have to. If he asks you a question, for God's sake be polite."

I unbolted the door, slightly alarmed at how numb my arms felt, and we slowly traipsed down the stairs. When we entered the kitchen, my father was sitting at the table. His gnarled hands were resting on the laminated surface. Between them were the metal box and the journal. There was also a bottle of Jim Beam, three quarters of which he'd already made disappear.

He stared at us both, taking in first one then the other. He smiled.

"You boys," he said. "Always so fucking secretive . . . " His head wobbled slightly, like it was on a narrow stalk that could barely support it. "So desperate to conceal the truth."

He held up the journal and tapped the lid of the metal box.

"Imagine my surprise when I discovered what you've been ferreting away." He looked directly at me and closed his eyes for a moment. "All those secrets . . . all those lies. Just waiting for Daddy." He waved the journal in the air and his eyes flickered; I could see the anger, twitching below the surface of his face. If anything, the bourbon had robbed him of his customary momentum, and it worried me a little. I knew he was about to inflict pain, and I suspected that with his rage suppressed by the booze I might not even see it coming. I might be blindsided by something I hadn't foreseen.

He pawed at his nose with a crooked finger and removed the lid from the box. He gazed at me and tilted it in my direction.

"This your treasure?" he said.

There was a long pause where I tried hard not to look at Will; I could sense him quivering beside me. I knew that if my father asked him anything he'd collapse into a blubbering heap, and I wouldn't blame him; I felt like doing exactly the same.

"No, sir. Not treasure. Just things we've found."

My father's eyes narrowed as his bombed-out brain tried to process my response. I could feel the heat of the bourbon on his breath.

"Things like this ain't found, boy. Not anymore. I want to know how in the devil's name they came to be in my own godforsaken house. And might I suggest you consider your answer before you open your mouth."

I did as instructed and tried to pick my way through an explanation I sensed my drunken father might expect. When it occurred to me, it seemed obvious.

"I stole 'em," I said. "We did a project at school on the war. I liked the stuff so much I decided to bring them home. It was easy."

My father nodded and lowered his head, as though he had reckoned on this very outcome all along. I stared at his balding crown and saw the mottled pink skin that papered over his skull. My hand trembled and I fought the impulse to smash down on it with my fist. I remembered the dead organs inside the bird and wondered what my father's brain might look like. I pictured wine-coloured tributaries running over a pink land-scape and realised that trying to understand how they connected would be like trying to measure the distance between hatred and love.

He looked up at me, moved the metal box to one side, and picked up the journal. He saw me flinch and he smiled, the anger in his face instantly smoothed away, the skin around his eyes tightening.

"More secrets," he said softly. "More things you don't want daddy to know."

He opened the journal and flicked through it. He was looking for some-thing specific, which meant he had already spent a good deal of time reading each of the entries. I tried to remember what I'd written, but quickly realised that it no longer mattered. Not a single word of it had been intended for my father's eyes. He could turn to any page in the book and destroy me, just by reading my own narrative aloud.

"Some of this is most enlightening," he said. He licked the tip of his finger, stared at me, and turned the page. "This entry, for instance . . . " He held the book a little closer to his face and read: "*Will has been pestering me to use the sight on Shelley Weekes, so tonight we watched her house and I looked through her bedroom wall and told Will what colour under-wear she had on. Didn't tell him everything, though; if I'd told him what I'd really seen he'd have fainted dead away!*"

I glanced across at Will and he stared back; I felt heat suddenly rise in my cheeks. I turned back to my father, who was watching me with a calm detachment.

"You looked through her bedroom *wall*?"

I said nothing; I could hear the slow ticking of the kitchen clock and the hum of the refrigerator. Even my father's ragged breathing seemed to have momentarily stopped.

"Am I to understand that you believe you can see through solid objects?" He waved the journal in the air. "Is that what all this nonsense is about?"

I remained silent, afraid that if I opened my mouth my father would twist my words and make them sound incriminating. Besides which, there was nothing logical that I could say. Even if I'd confessed everything, he would never have believed me. No one would. Adults always thought that supernatural acts were impossible; they thought most things were. What I'd written in the journal spoke of a childhood truth that only Will and I could fully understand. It was our way of being part of the world while still dreaming; of feeling every intimate beat of our pounding hearts as we raised our tiny fist to the stars.

My father placed the journal on the table and released a long, unambiguous sigh.

"I'll tell you what I'm going to do," he said, pushing the journal towards the metal box and clearing a small space in front of him on the table. "I'm going to set you a simple task."

He reached down and produced a red container from the floor, which he placed on the table. The cylinder had once contained gravy granules and bore the motif *Aah! Bisto* on its circumference, alongside a smoky graphic that I assumed was supposed to represent a tantalising smell. Below this there was a yellow anthropomorphised star, smiling and winking cheekily, as though by buying the product the consumer had unwittingly stumbled upon the path to gravy nirvana.

"In here," my father said, tapping the red plastic lid of the tub, "I have a secret of my own."

He paused for a moment to allow the nature of his task to sink in.

"If you tell me what my secret is without opening the tub and looking inside, you can keep it."

He looked at me and I saw the cool smugness of a man convinced that his secret, whatever the hell it was, would remain unclaimed.

"If you fail to identify what's inside," my father went on, barely able to conceal his contempt, "and thereby prove to everyone present that your ability to see through solid objects is a myth, you and your little accomplice here will be punished."

I felt myself grow tense and summoned the courage to object. "That isn't fair," I said. "Will has nothing to do with this. He's just my friend."

My father smiled. "Then you'd better tell me what's inside the tub and save his hide, hadn't you? Isn't that what friends are supposed to do?"

I looked at my father and felt nothing but disgust. He reeked of liquor and sweat, and I could smell faint traces of *Bisto* emanating from the small cardboard tub. My heart was racing and I felt a vague sickness in my stomach as I tried to light the wick that would slowly ignite my eyes.

"Come on, Jim!" Will whispered in my ear. "You can do it! I know you can."

I trained my gaze on the *Bisto* tub and stared hard. I could see my father out of the corner of my eye, watching me closely, incredulous but curious all the same. He had folded his arms across his chest and was awaiting a miracle. He was expecting failure, but was just drunk enough to entertain the notion of a possible revelation; I could see the intensity in his flickering eyes. A part of him wanted me to succeed, I realised. A small measure of the man, possibly the fraction that could never refute our biological connection, had read those journal entries and remembered what it was like to be a child and a trusted friend. My father had been a kid too, hadn't he? Dreaming of reaching out and touching the fantastic, of discovering the extraordinary, of growing up with secret yearnings that the adult world, with its inherent suspicion and impatience, considered impossible and sought to deny? Wasn't there a part of that still hidden in every man alive, even my own father?

I stared at the red tub, and then at the drunken man on the opposite side of the table.

"Do you know what's in it?" he said.

I shook my head, felt Will almost physically deflate beside me. I couldn't bring myself to turn and look my friend in the eye.

"Thought not," my father said, knocking aside the empty tub.

"What's the punishment?" I said softly.

My father stared at me and I saw there a tangled look of sorrow and lost hope.

"You've already had it," he said. "Sometimes the humiliation is enough."

I sat in my bedroom for a long time, thinking about what had happened. Will had left hours ago and my father had disappeared to the pub. He had taken my journal with him and hidden the metal box in his room. I doubted I'd ever see either of them again. When he left the house, my father had turned his face towards the landing; I was seated on the top step, looking down. His face looked wrung out, like a grey dishcloth. There was disappointment in his eyes, as though *I'd* let *him* down, as opposed to the other way around. He looked like a man drafted in to fatherhood against his will, a tormented soul who had no idea what was expected of him. Every soggy, drunken moment of his life confirmed his place in the shadows, his identity defined by the fermenting booze in his veins.

He turned and walked out the front door, and I released a long sigh, conscious that my relief would only last as long as my father was out of the house. He had robbed me of more than just my journal and the metal box; he had taken the only thing Will and I had left: our friendship. That's what unsettled him, I realised. He resented how close we'd become. It wasn't childhood that he failed to understand; it was intimacy. That's what he had been so eager to destroy.

I pictured Will's terrified face as he'd watched my father across the kitchen table, and realised with a heavy heart that our friendship had been changed forever. Right there, in the palm of his hand, my father had taken the coiled brightness inside two children and crushed it to dust. That's how it worked: hand became fist; hope became heartache. Promise became despair. Nothing between us would ever be quite the same again.

I stood at my bedroom window, staring up at the darkness, trying to measure the slow rotation of the stars. It was impossible with the naked eye, like trying to detect growth in a blade of grass. I abandoned my surveillance of the heavens and glanced down at the dark row of houses opposite my own. Standing at the entrance to one of the jitties, through which Will and I often took shortcuts to the embankment and the park, stood the boy I knew only as Gillie. He was staring up at my window, utterly motionless. I remembered seeing him in his bedroom, naked and offering me a bird's egg in the palm of his hand, but I couldn't remember if

it had been a dream or a vision, or something more. It was a vague, nebulous memory, hovering just out of reach, calling me forward to claim it, as
though I would have to fully inhabit the recollection in order to understand
what it could possibly mean.

I narrowed my eyes and peered closer. He was beckoning to me, inviting
me to join him in the jitty, and I felt a cold hand settle on my shoulder,
urging me to remain in the room. He beckoned again, his dark hand
upraised, his index finger curling inwards, summoning me into the night. I
shook my head at him, confused by this strange turn of events. His white
teeth smiled back at me. He was in no mood to wait. He veered left and
walked slowly down the jitty. If I didn't react quickly I knew my opportunity to track him would be gone. I spun on my heels, raced down the
stairs, and darted into the kitchen for my coat.

Ma was in there, baking yet another of her therapy cakes. She glanced
over her shoulder at me and smiled.

"You'll be out of puff in no time running like that! What's the hurry?"

"I need to see Will for a minute," I said. "I won't be long."

She rubbed flour from her hands and started to undo her apron. "Have
you seen the time? If Will's got any sense he'll be fast asleep in bed."

I had a bullshit answer already on my lips, but I paused for a moment
and stared at her. She looked weary; the lines in her forehead resembled
tidal ridges, left behind by the slow movement of time. Her smile looked
like something held in place by sun-dried tape, and even as I watched her I
half expected it to fall from her face. I rarely took the time to look at Ma,
to really see her for what she was. I suppose I was afraid of what I might
discover; that somewhere in her exhausted eyes lay the answer to everything: why she baked, why my father drank, and why I was convinced I
could see through walls.

I smiled back at her and kissed her on the cheek.

"I'll just be a few minutes, Ma. I promise."

She nodded her head and turned back to her therapy. She was baking a
cake in the shape of a bird.

I closed the front door behind me, slipped on my coat, and ran towards
the narrow darkness of the jitty. I stopped at the entrance and peered down
the unlit passage. There was no sign of Gillie, but I thought I could hear
distant footsteps echoing back to me. I gave chase, sprinting through the

winding corridor, smelling newly creosoted fences and wild clematis vines from Elber's Wood to the east. The night air was cold, and I felt it numbing the back of my throat as I ran. My eyes were watering, and I pretended it had nothing to do with my father's humiliation of me earlier in the night; I told myself it was a form of self-protection, the sudden rush of tears stopping my eyes from drying out in the swirling wind.

I rounded another bend in the jitty and stopped. Fifty yards ahead of me I could see Gillie. He had his back to me; he was staring beyond the end of the passage, his long hair whipping against the side of his face. He was watching something on the opposite side of the road. He sensed my presence and waved me forward without turning. I realised he was inviting me to share a secret, just as he had before when I'd seen him in his room. A gift to cauterise the pain; a revelation to compel the darkness, delivered at a time when prayers and weeping had merely added to the suffering, communicating nothing of any practical use.

I stared at Gillie's back and noticed that he was clutching what looked like a black twig in his right hand. I edged closer and realised that it was the dead bird's claw, the treasure that had spurred so many of the local kids to ridicule him, mocking his quiet intensity and failing to understand what it might mean. Standing in the jitty, watching him slowly squeeze the desiccated claw, I became hypnotised by the movement of his hand. I imagined it keeping perfect time with the beating of his heart, the two actions indivisible. He appeared perfectly calm and it suddenly seemed obvious why: the claw was his lifeline, his second heartbeat; it was like a charm that kept the bad stuff at bay.

I closed the distance between us and cautiously approached Gillie at the edge of the jitty. I was nervous of him, wary of his steady composure. He was like no other boy in the neighbourhood. It wasn't just that he was odd; he seemed almost *unnatural*, like a revenant or a lost and wandering soul. I watched his right hand slowly rise and he pointed with the dead bird's claw into a shadowy side street ahead. He shifted slightly so that I had an unobstructed view of the scene he had drawn me towards; I felt the lower muscles in my abdomen contract. I held my breath and sensed the last blush of childhood slip away.

In the dark side street opposite I could see two figures. One was my father, his trousers around his ankles and his hands pressed up against a wall. The other was a woman I didn't recognise; she was kneeling between his legs. Her head was bobbing forward and back like a metronome. It sounded like she was struggling to breathe. My father was moaning and looked unsteady on his feet; he was reeling in the still night air as though he were clinging to the deck of a ship. He was using the wall to prop himself up, and I could see him staring blankly at the crumbling brick. I imagined him trying to see through it as the unknown woman worked away at him down below; wondering if it were possible, concentrating hard as he tried to unlock the code that would enable him to break through.

I closed my eyes for a moment, feeling a wave of anger and shame. I thought of Ma at home, working on her cake, her exhausted eyes seeing a different world to the one I saw; a darker world, where innocence and beauty were admitted only on the understanding that it was impossible for either one to survive.

I opened my eyes and stared again at my father and the woman. Whatever dignity they had both once possessed had been lost a lifetime ago. They were just drunken bodies, bumping together in the night; a reckless collision that meant nothing, yet had the power to destroy everything our family had left.

I turned back to Gillie, wanting to ask him how he had known to bring me here, but at some point during the suspended horror of the last few moments he had silently disappeared. Squeezing the dead bird's claw, warding off the great sorrows that exist in the night.

I ran. Back through the jitty, past the embankment, down towards the stream; not thinking clearly. Barely even thinking at all. My mind was full of broken glass, every shard drawing blood, reflecting images of my father, of Ma, of the future, spinning out of control, rushing us towards the black hole that none of us could definitively see.

I breathed hard and ran, and found myself screaming into the wide arms of the night, releasing all the pain and the heartache and the rage that was weighing me down. I could feel it crushing me from within and I felt hopeless with it, like it was pinning me to the very ground on which I ran.

Without being consciously aware of having done so, I realised my desperation had brought me to Will's house. I stood before its dark, familiar face and pictured my friend at the window, looking down. That's what I needed, I realised; to see Will's wide-eyed, confused expression gazing at me with a sense of wondrous expectation, just like always. To have the tension of real life removed, where the laws of nature were our plaything and nothing was impossible in the weightless irreverence of youth.

I picked up a handful of gravel and slung it at Will's bedroom window. Sure enough, within seconds, his perfect, uncomplicated face appeared at the glass. He opened the window and stuck out his head.

"It's nearly midnight," he said, sounding tired.

"I know," I said. "But I want to run."

He stared at me for a moment and then nodded his head. "Wait there. I need to get dressed."

He closed the window and disappeared from view. Two minutes later he crept out the front door with all the stealth of a panther and joined me in the moonlit street. I looked at him and smiled; he smiled back. We joined hands and ran down the deserted road.

We came to a halt several minutes later outside *Liv Kaminski's Bird Emporium*. We were both breathing hard. Will was bent over and had his hands resting on his knees. He spat onto the pavement and wiped his mouth on the sleeve of his shirt. His hair was sticking up as though he'd been in a wind tunnel. He was grinning from ear to ear.

I watched him for a moment and remembered the terror that had been writ upon that face earlier in the day. I pictured my father's drunken grimace, heard the amusement in his voice as he said: *You and your little accomplice here will be punished.* The memory made me feel sick, and I could feel my blood pressure rising as the resentment and the hate invested me with renewed purpose. I could almost feel the dark stump of it growing inside me, swelling to impossible proportions as my father's face began to haunt me, every crack and crease of it filling my head, magnified until it became too distorted to define. All I could see was pale skin, too much like my own, spreading across everything, transforming me into something I despised.

I bent down and lifted a large stone from Liv Kaminski's garden. I unleashed a howl of protest and threw the stone at the window of the master bedroom, the largest of the aviaries. It punched a hole through the glass and the adjoining blind with an ear-shattering crash that reverberated down the length of the street.

It stopped me in my tracks for a moment, and I stood there, panting heavily, uncertain about exactly what I'd just done.

"Holy shit!" Will said.

I stood frozen to the spot and watched a trail of dark birds flutter into the moonlight and take to the sky.

"They needed to be set free," I said softly.

Will grabbed me by the arm and we took off down the road, following the effortless flight of the birds.

Will and I stopped running only when we arrived at my house, terrified that a furious Liv Kaminski might be in hot pursuit. I opened the back door, but Will hesitated on the threshold, wringing his hands.

"What's the matter?"

He stared at me and waited. "Your father," he said. "He terrifies me."

"I know," I said, ushering him inside. "But he isn't here. You're perfectly safe."

He nodded once and entered the house. I could smell Ma's cake as we passed through the kitchen, filling the place with its sweet aroma. It was almost potent enough to invalidate the memory of what had happened in here earlier, when Will and I had been subjected to my father's humiliating game.

I led him upstairs, urging him to be quiet for fear of waking Ma, and we slipped into my room and bolted the door behind us. Will collapsed onto the exhausted beanbag; I approached the window and stared at the starlit heavens, wondering what had become of the birds.

"I'm sorry I woke you," I said, still staring out at the unchanging sky. "But I wanted to show you something."

I felt Will's eyes on my back as I opened the window and clambered up onto the narrow ledge.

"Jim . . . ?" Will said, failing to fully understand, even now.

"It's okay," I said. "I've been thinking about it for a long time now, and I think I can do it, Will. I really do."

There was a long pause as I felt the cool night breeze wash across my brow, like one of Ma's gentle kisses before I drifted to sleep.

"That's not a good idea, Jim," Will said, slowly levering himself out of the beanbag. "I think you should come back inside where it's safe."

I shook my head and smiled. "This is the only safe place, Will; up here, where I can feel the wind and touch the stars. This is where I belong."

I glanced over my shoulder and smiled again, touched by my friend's unnecessary concern.

"Do you believe in me?"

Will stared at me, his anxiety apparent, but he slowly nodded his head.

"Of course I do," he whispered. "Always."

I nodded and turned back to face the wide expanse of moonlit sky.

"One last secret," I said, and flew towards the dark horizon like a bird.

Bradbury's Finger

Greg Quiring

Greg Quiring informs us, '"Bradbury's Finger" was a tribute specially written for, and personally given to, Ray Bradbury. Earlier he read my story "The Man Who Hated Shakespeare" and recommended I publish it. Stoked, I decided to knock myself out, proudly handing over a copy of "Finger" at one of his last appearances in California. It met with total silence. Email queries to two of his close friends fell completely flat. Devastated, I realized the post-Bradbury theme of the piece was hitting too close to home for the ailing author, in spite of its unapologetic lionizing. Peter Crowther read a copy after Mr. Bradbury's passing and suggested a re-write of the second half, which resulted in the story appearing here with a heavily revised ending.

'As an aside, I did much research into Hibernian English for this piece and hopefully it is not too far removed from what is spoken in Ireland.'

BRENNAN GALLAGHER BURST THROUGH THE STORM-drenched doors of O'Malley's Pub in Dublin, filled the hollow of his favourite stool, and demanded his first pint of Guinness for the evening. His mate, Corey O'Sullivan, was already well into his third and hardly took notice.

"It's sure bucketin'," said Kyle O'Malley, reaching for a glass.

"I'm killed with the thirst," Gallagher confessed, not about to mention the heavy rain.

O'Malley foamed the black stuff into the vessel.

"I was just on Yahoo and seen somethin' gobsmackin' for sure," touted Gallagher.

"What's it this time?" asked O'Malley, setting a round of Guinness squarely in front of him and expecting the usual hyperbole.

"Yet another feckin' story?" demanded pub contrarian Owen O'Flaherty, hiking up his woollens from the toilet and creaking to his roost at the bar.

Gallagher drew long from the depths of his mug until the corner of his eye gauged the proper amount of disdain in O'Flaherty's face, then jerked his head jaybird quick, toward him. "Now wouldn't you like to know?"

"I wouldn't for I'm certain it's your usual gobshite!" said O'Flaherty, stirring.

"Go on and tell it anyway," said O'Sullivan, followed by a suffocating billow from his Meerschaum. "I've got ears for a good story."

"It was quite interestin' really. Saw it first when I got—"

"Just get on with it then, so!" O'Flaherty's nostrils flared, bull-like.

Gallagher squeezed one eye shutter-tight and widened the other, speaking softly to wring maximum drama out of his tongue, *"They're takin' the finger o' Ray Bradbury t'Mars so they are!"*

"Bradbury the writer?" O'Sullivan moved closer. "How long has he not been with us?"

"A donkey's years, God rest him. Jaysus, Mary an' Martha, now there was a man."

O'Flaherty stiffened. "Mars my arse! You been drinkin' with the fairies again. Why should they put a man's finger up yonder?"

"Not just any man's, but *Bradbury's.*" Gallagher set his mug down. "One that poked out some grand stories abo' Mars an' other things. And don't ya know there's Irish on th' trip this time . . . fer good luck suppos'n. It's fittin' to the man that bent folks on goin' there. One day he decided t'have 'is own finger kept after his passin' that it go Mars and so 'e did."

O'Malley and O'Sullivan were hanging on every word now. O'Flaherty scowled at them with a face twisted like an olive tree. "An' why not lop one o' Oscar Wilde, or Jimmy Joyce?"

"Go on outta that! They done a rake o' Ireland, but nothin' with *Mars,*" cried Gallagher.

"Well Rice Burroughs then, he done enough—take *two* o' his . . . and a toe!"

O'Malley playfully slapped a bar towel on O'Flaherty's head. "Enough o' that guff. I read the *Martian Chronicles* from when I was a snapper in

Edenderry—it was surely the master. A brilliant one was *The Fire
Balloons* . . . " his voice fading into memory.

Now O'Sullivan's face misted over with his own thoughts. "Ah, the
man was a poet, surely as ever was. I for one was deadly on the tale of the
tattooed man."

"*Illustrated*!" O'Malley corrected, pulling his stool closer.

"*Illustrated* then, but oh! Remember abo' a young one and her boyo
makin' sandcastles and her gettin' herself drowned an'—"

"An' she come back dead an' done all the rest of the wee boyo's castle?"
finished Gallagher.

"Now there's the 'wee' word again Brennan—a bloody leprechaun so
you are!" complained O'Flaherty, leaning sideways, extracting some
trapped underwear.

"Whisht now!" chided O'Sullivan. "It's the father of him's doin'. The
whole feckin' family says it, so—where were *we*?"

Brian Murphy arrived just then, bringing in the rain and thunder and
no sooner had cleared the threshold than an ill gust wrestled the coat pole
to its knees and sent it bang-clatter against the wall, leaving O'Flaherty's
jacket aflutter in its wake.

"She's lashin' terrible!" Murphy simultaneously kicked the door closed,
righted the pole, and shed his Mackintosh. O'Malley drew a strong Irish
coffee and set it before Murphy's bulk that reeked of the docks.

O'Flaherty gave a disapproving wag. "Brian Murphy now . . . smellin'
o' Neptune's breath an' Davey Jones, so."

Murphy nodded. "A fishmonger true, but what's your story, old
maggot?"

Laughs cackled all around, stifling O'Flaherty for the moment.

"So how's she cuttin'?" asked Murphy, raising his mug and moulding
his elephantine form into a stool.

"Saymo, saymo," answered O'Malley, "but for the craic we got on what
Gallagher seen on the Yahoo."

"Well?"

O'Malley lowered his voice, squeezed one craggy eye shut, and spoke
just as Gallagher had earlier, "They're after takin' *Ray Bradbury's finger*
ta Mars so they are!"

"Stop the lights! The writer, the poet, the teller o' tales, an' conductor of
the grand Irish tour *Green Shadows, White Whale*—*that* Bradbury?"

"He is that," said O'Malley.

"How long since . . . ?"

"Ten year with Jaysus, St. Patrick, John, and Mary." O'Malley looked upward, prayerfully.

"And why take his poor finger all the way t'Mars?"

"Gallagher can tell it," O'Malley deferred.

"There you go, rabbitin'! I've got take it again?" O'Flaherty halfway rose up.

"You can take a toe in the hole, you old can o'piss!" said O'Sullivan, puffing a choking cloud of Irish Flake in his face. "Now dry your arse if you've nothin' else!"

O'Malley tossed a baleful eye to O'Flaherty, then jumped to Gallagher. "Tell it."

Gallagher finished his pint and wiped his foamy mouth.

"It seems the World Space Agency would take twenty folk up Mars, an' with 'em a frozen finger of Bradbury, the very one he used t'peck his first tales on his toy yoke and later do grand stuff for Mars. They're plantin' it somewhere called Bradbury's Landin' cause he got a rake o' folks gummin' t'go there."

"Ahh," sighed Murphy. "It's keen he never got there to kick some rusty dust an' have a hooley time."

"Go jam on your egg!" O'Flaherty broke in, he would never do it, even *with* a baldy's chance. An' toppin' it, he had no Irish at all!"

All of Kyle O'Malley's stools and chairs cracked, creaked, and chirped as the collective weights of their occupants raised a wooden riot, but before anyone spoke, O'Flaherty continued.

"He'd a wet his cacks t'drive a car, an' would get fluthered t'fly with a plane!"

"That's Arthur Guinness talkin!" cried O'Sullivan standing up. "A bigger bollocks never put arms through a coat!"

O'Malley steadied a restraining palm on his shoulder.

"Coddled with a spoon till he was eight!" O'Flaherty shot back.

Brennan Gallagher took leave of his stool, tugging the napkin on O'Flaherty's neck. "And what of it y' feckin' melter? A babe's bib at *fifty* eight?!"

O'Flaherty dodged the insult and unwound his diabolical sermon atop the four legs of his sour pulpit, while savouring what was to become his unsavoury end. "And what's more!" he began.

The four men covered their ears.

"Shut yer cakehole!" yelled Murphy.

"I read that a Mr Electrico—"

"Stop yer gob!!"cried O'Malley and O'Sullivan in unison.

"—told him he was supposed to live forever! Now, put *that* in your manky pipe and smoke it!"

"Aaaaaah!" they all cried together.

Gallagher.

O'Malley.

Murphy.

O'Sullivan.

Each man in turn took a leg of O'Flaherty's stool and lifted skyward. The first Irish space programme was well underway with Owen O'Flaherty, its involuntary astronaut, at the tip of an oaken rocket propelled by four Irish motors fuelled with exactly five pints of Guinness, precisely three ounces of Irish whiskey, and headed for the door at floor-thundering Gaelic escape velocity.

"Yaaaaaa!" yelled all together with O'Flaherty joining them in a final chorus. And the rocket crashed him, his mug, his Guinness, and his intolerable attitude onto the slushy cobbles of Waterford Street.

Now the burned-out rocket boosters stood quietly abreast in front of O'Malley's and held a sacred hand over each faithful heart.

"Ah, to Mars!" roared out O'Malley, rain streaking his brow.

"Ah, to the loch and the dead returned!" called out O'Sullivan to the drizzling patter.

"To the white whale and the green shadows of Ireland!" shouted Murphy.

"Aye, an' to the man who lives forever..." whispered Gallagher as he turned back through O'Malley's door. And one by one, the others followed him in.

Six months later, the silver rockets settled down in a rusty corner of Mars, scorching the cold red sand with the odour of hot tin, blue fire, and Earth. Captain Freeman was first to press footprints into its dusty face and plant the multinational flag. Space helmets buzzed with six native tongues attempting to interpret the silent speech of Mars.

"The pink sky!" cried Devereaux, the astronaut.

"The rusty soil!" shouted Baldovino, the geologist.

"The untouched desolation!" proclaimed Chen Sun, the mission specialist.

"Janey Mack!" answered Callaghan, the science pilot. "Where are the canals?" Everyone laughed but Dunn and Mahoney, who played it up with deadpan faces.

"I'm flummoxed, I am," said Mahoney.

"There ought surely be the trifling of a ditch!" cried Dunn.

Captain Freeman broke in, "You can share your observations later. Right now we need the pressure dome and solar panels."

After Freeman walked away, the three Irish conferred on another helmet channel.

"The dry shite!" said Callaghan, reverting to his native brogue. "If we're not spot on each second he thinks we're dossin' the job. And thinkin' I've been six month pent up with 'im in that pointy metal can!"

"Metal can? I almost forgot," said Dunn in his light accent. "I'm still holdin' Mr Bradbury's finger in the case. When supposin's the ceremony?"

"Not today at all, at all. We got t'finish unpackin'," answered Mahoney with a bit of a smirk.

Something thumped against Callaghan's suit—a small rock tossed by Baldovino. He gestured that he couldn't hear them on the radio. Callaghan waved three gloved fingers for channel three.

"Welcome to Mars, boys!" cried Baldovino. "Beautiful isn't it?"

They nodded enthusiastically.

"Well, give me a hand with these panels, and we'll have time to play later, ok?"

"If it means lookin' after a canal, you've got my hand," said Callaghan.

The dome-tent was pitched and the men took up quarters in its honey-comb of inflatable rooms.

Callaghan called Dunn and Mahoney aside soon after the rest of the crew had retired.

"Come closer, boys!"

He pulled out a small flask from his silver pack—Irish whisky.

"I'm thinkin' we need t'celebrate right here and now!"

"Well aren't you a cute hoor, sneakin' that one in!" cried Dunn.

"It's been ages since I been out on a lash drinkin'!" said Mahoney.

Callaghan handed each a small metal cup and metered out even portions. He hoisted his cup high and proposed a toast: "To the redness of Mars, th' blueness of Earth, and the greenness of Ireland . . . May they harmonize in the blackness of space. Sláinte!"

"Aye, aye!" said the men.

Callaghan swallowed hard, squeezed his eyes tight, then opened them slowly.

"How's about another?" he said. Another toast was raised and another cheer went up.

"Aye," said Callaghan, looking down sadly. "It's keen we haven't anymore . . . "

Right then, Baldovino appeared in the doorway looking concerned. The Irish-Marsmen looked up, startled.

"Sounds like you boys are havin' an early party against the captain's orders! Ah, not to worry—your secret's safe with Baldovino! Besides— look here!" He proudly produced a silver flask filled with wine. "Now you don't think this Italian is gonna let any Irishmen out-drink him?" The others smiled, then cheered. Everyone stretched forth their cups. "In vino veritas. Cin cin!" said Baldovino as the Irishmen belted the wine like whisky shots.

"No! Not like that!" he cried aghast. "You must *savor* it like the nectar of the gods! Don't *guzzle* it like a shot of Jameson!"

"Sorry!" said Dunn.

"Forgive us!" said Mahoney.

"How 'bout another?" cried Callaghan.

There was a shuffling at the door of the dome-room.

"It's Freeman!" shouted Dunn, panicking.

"Not on your life!" hollered Azarov and Kalugin, the Russians. "Just us!"

Dunn relaxed.

"Now this party has really gone to hell," joked Baldovino.

Azarov and Kalugin each held out a metal bottle of vodka. "You can say that again," said Azarov. "Now that Ruskies are here, we will have hell of a time!"

"Na zda-rov'-ye!" cried Kalugin. "To health!"

"Nausea rovin' t'you!" slurred Callaghan.

"Wait! Wait!!" shouted a new, nasal voice—Devereaux. Everyone stopped. "You dare celebrate without the French?"

A clamour rose from the others. Devereaux brought forth a very special canister of champagne. Everyone began applauding when he cut them short, looking cautiously over his shoulder. "We mustn't wake the captain!" The others agreed and yet another toast was raised.

"To the captain!" said Devereaux in a stage whisper.

"And why so t'him?" asked Callaghan with the hint of a scowl.

Devereaux raised his cup. "To the captain—sound may he sleep!"

Captain Freeman rose with the weak pink sun pushing long shadows from the countless rocks strewn about the terrain like an angry child's toys. Ceremonial proceedings were already clicking away in the clockworks of his head as he turned into the corridor toward the main conference room. His boots skipped along with the odd little hop he'd developed from the shallow Martian gravity.

Why aren't the men up? he puzzled, squeezing his lips together. His boots traded the odd skip for a gait that echoed down the hall.

"Everyone up!" he shouted. "Up! Up! UP!"

He turned the corner to the men's quarters, finding bunk after bunk empty. He turned his now-extended chin toward the exit when a rattling sound set his legs into reverse: snoring. Baldovino was wrapped mummy tight in his sheet on the floor.

"On your feet, specialist!" Freeman bellowed.

Two bewildered Italian eyes twitched open.

"Is this another of your jokes?"

The mummy slowly unwound, unwrapping a smile. "Well, it's a great day on Mars, right Captain?"

"The men! They haven't gone out, have they?" His foot struck something light, something metallic, skirring it across the floor at twice the rate it would have on Earth.

A wine flask.

"I'd offer you a nip, Captain, but it was the last one!"

Freeman spun about, strode to the suit room, and donned his pressure gear. The airlock gulped in the blue Earth air through its grey mouth, then whispered long, easy strains of Martian atmosphere from its tin nostrils.

The door opened, Freeman stepped out. His prey was a hundred meters off, massed together and staring at the ground. Rusty pebbles flew from every confrontation with his boots. *I'll get to the bottom of this nonsense and by golly heads will roll!* Freeman approached like a lame kangaroo, fumbling in the low gravity behind them—funny though, how no one was in the least disturbed.

"*What* are you men doing here without—"

He stopped. Suddenly his bones softened, his skin prickled.

A canal.

Impossible!

Yet there it was, complete with lazy tails of slow swirling water.

He looked at the men's faces—they were *crying* for God's sake! He gathered himself.

"Dunn! Mahoney! I know you're behind this! What the hell's going on?"

Their aluminium helmets nodded ever so slightly.

"Azarov! Kalugin! Answer me, dammit!"

Devereaux finally spoke, unsuccessfully trying to dry his tears through his faceplate.

"What do you think? Isn't it wonderful, Captain?"

"I think you know what I think! Someone, some *people* have gone to a lot of trouble and wasted a lot of our limited resources making this illusion when we're already pressed to broadcast our arrival ceremony!"

"Not to worry, Captain," said Callaghan. "We been up all night gettin' ready for the show!"

Freeman's chin retracted an inch. "Then I'll expect everyone at the ceremonial site in fifteen minutes." He turned around.

"Captain?"

"What is it Dunn?"

"We were thinkin' . . . well most of us that is, that we, uh, would like to do the ceremony here."

Freeman's jaw lurched forward again, straining the bridle on his tongue. "And why would you want to have it *here* by this, this fake *thing* when we're trying to show people back home the real Mars?"

"Because this fake *thing*, as you call it, is one of the most wonderful notions that stirred mankind's blood about coming here!" cried Baldovino as he shuffled in from behind. "The essence of exploration is to investigate the mysterious, the strange and yet familiar. This is the romance we have had with Mars that brings us here."

"Here! here!" said the men, their claps blunted by the rarefied air.

Fifteen minutes later all eyes were on Dunn. A small chromed cylinder gleamed in his outstretched hand like a call to homage. The dwarfed reflection of the men on its surface answered back. Dunn mustered his finest English for the occasion.

"Here is the finger of Ray Bradbury. I've kept it close to my heart in my vest pocket during our entire journey. It was his solemn wish he would be buried here, and today in a limited way we want to make that wish a reality. As a boy I read his Martian stories and those of others. I fought Martian invasions, swam in red canals, dug up lost ruins, and romanced dark-skinned, golden-eyed women."

Callaghan and Mahoney moved in to him, close on either side.

"Behind me is a terraholographic projection of one of the fantastic notions that made men love the planet of war."

"Wow! He's pretty good!" whispered Baldovino to Devereaux on the private channel.

"Not bad for a bog trotter, especially when he's sober! That's why he was picked to do the intro," said the Frenchman, chuckling.

"It was the pull of these extraordinary ideas that brought us here— brought me here, and the ones of Mr Bradbury pulled me the hardest. Captain Freeman and I will now lay a part of him to rest on the bank of this Martian canal, where it will remain in fulfilment of his stories, his dreams, and his wishes."

Freeman and Dunn knelt, dug a small hole, and gently placed the cylinder inside.

One by one, each crewman quietly set a small stone on top of the hole. When they finished, as if on some cosmic cue, everyone stood along the bank like links of a great silver chain, staring down at the rocketmen looking up from the shimmering virtual water.

"Janey Mack!" cried Callaghan at last. "It's the story come true so it is!"

"Story?" asked Mahoney.

"Why, 'The Million Year Picnic' to be sure!"

"I know that one," said Freeman quietly, surprising the others. "The one where a dad shows his children their reflections in a Martian canal and tells them that they are the real Martians."

The men glanced at his now-reddening eyes, then respectfully looked away to their wavering counterparts in the canal.

"That's who we are now . . . the Martians . . . " his voice soft.

Baldovino broke eye contact with his image, his heart notching up a tick or two.

"But Captain, I don't understand! A few minutes ago you told us this 'fake thing' was a waste of resources and now you seem, you seem . . . *different* about it."

"Not different. Just honest for once. Like many of you, I read Bradbury's stories as a kid, and kept reading them. They took me here long before our rockets landed. I knew this ceremony was going to be hard for me months ago, so I started steeling myself for it . . . then you guys had to build this thing and make it even worse!"

There was quiet chuckling and sympathetic smiles. Freeman's eyes were quite damp now as he fixed on the little cairn at his feet, sniffling.

"I remember a video I saw years ago of Ray reading a poem at the then Jet Propulsion Laboratories. I don't know all of it, but I'll never forget the ending:

I send my rockets forth between my ears
Hoping an inch of good is worth a pound of years
Aching to hear a voice cry back across the universal mall
We've reached Alpha Centauri! We're tall!
My God! We're tall!

THE NEEDLE, THE STITCH, THE NIGHT, AND THE SKY

KAT HOWARD

'"The Needle, the Stitch, the Night, and the Sky,"' Kat Howard says, 'began with the image of the Night Doctors, people who were needed to heal the night, and all the mischiefs that might come out of it. The next thing I got was the silver needle and the red thread, and then I had a story.'

Kat Howard is the co-author of a novella, The End of the Sentence, *with Maria Dahvana Headley. Her short fiction has appeared in places such as* Nightmare, Lightspeed, *and* Subterranean Online. *And she is working on other projects which she is currently keeping secret, because it's no fun if you know everything at once.*

"RYAN IS STILL HAVING NIGHTMARES," MRS. GREY TOLD THE doctor as they waited for her son under the harsh florescent light of the hallway. "We've been to counselors, doctors, specialists, all very kind, all full of suggestions that haven't helped. The nightmares are getting worse. That's when he sleeps at all, which he hardly does anymore. He just sits on his bed all night, staring out of the window."

"Have you asked him why he does this?" Dr. Shaflzedeh asked, her eyes bright behind her glasses.

"He says he's watching the night tear. He thinks the bad dreams come out of rips in the sky, and he has to keep watch so they can't get into people's heads." Rose Grey, who did not look like she had been sleeping well either, shoved the too-long sleeves of her cardigan back over thin wrists.

"Ah. This is slightly outside of my area, but I will consult one of my colleagues. She is something of an expert in the field."

"Thank you."

Dr. Shaflzedeh pursed her lips as she watched Ryan Grey and his mother walk down the hallway. Tall for nearly thirteen, with an unruly shock of black hair and an insomniac's pallor. A polite child, who might simply be processing through a recent trauma. But the description his mother gave was worryingly accurate.

She walked into her office, and opened the window. Miryam Shaflzedeh leaned as far into the open air as she could, and spoke: "Viola. You're needed. It's happening again."

Rose watched her son fold into himself as night fell, the same as he had every evening these past three months. The hypervigilance worried her more than the nightmares. "Do you want me to watch with you?" That question, too, a recent ritual.

Ryan shook his head, never taking his eyes from the encroaching night. Rose stood behind him, wishing she knew what to say, how to help. Then she stroked her hand down Ryan's back, and left.

Ryan shuddered out a sigh when his mom left. He wanted to be a man, not a kid who needed his mom in the room to be brave. Even though he felt so much better when she was.Like he was safe. Like he could sleep. Like maybe tonight no horrors would come squirming out of the rips in the sky. Those hopes were lies, Ryan knew, so he sat his vigil and tried to be brave. Like a man. Like his dad had been.

Darkness fell, and the sky tore.

Every muscle in Ryan's body tensed as he tried to watch all of the empty places in the sky at once.

A weight on his bed depressed the mattress next to him. "How long have you been able to see the holes in the sky?" A woman's voice, not his mom's.

"Since my dad died."

The woman sitting next to him didn't say anything. People usually said stuff about how they were sorry, which was okay, or about how it was better that his dad was with God, which was a bunch of shit. Either way, Ryan was expected to be polite, and say thank you, and he hated it. This, the silence and the sensation of a shoulder next to his, this was bearable.

"It's not just the holes in the sky. The stuff I can see, I mean. I can see the stuff that comes out of them. Nightmares. Evil." He hated them. They were wrong, and they were cold, and they were hungry. Even speaking about them burned like poison, hot in his gut.

"I know," said the woman. "I know. I see them, too."

He almost turned his head to her, then. "Really?"

"Really.

"I'm a Night Doctor. I sew the holes back up."

"A Night Doctor?"

"Some of us who see the tears learn to heal them. We become Night Doctors. I think you might be one, too."

That would be okay. Good, even. He could fix things, then. Do something, instead of just sitting around and watching. He stuck his hand out to the side. "My name's Ryan."

The woman's hand clasped his, shook. It was a good handshake, smooth and strong. "I'm Viola."

"Viola?"

"Yes?"

"They're coming."

Once, Ryan had found a dead cardinal. It looked sad, red feathers faded and tatty, as if beauty ended when life did. He had decided to bury the bird, but when he picked it up, the corpse had come apart in his hands, an explosion of putrefying flesh and maggots.

Watching the nightmares squirm through the holes in the sky felt the same as that had. Broken, angry. A foot to the gut.

But he watched, unmoving, fists clenched, tears smearing his cheeks. If he watched, the nightmares couldn't hide. They remained pinned by his gaze, hostage to the coming dawn.

If his eyes closed, worse things happened.

"Do you watch every night?" Viola's voice didn't sound as if she were broken.

"Ever since I realized how to stop them. Except, sometimes, I fall asleep."

"And then you have nightmares. The worst you've ever had."

"Yeah. It really scares my mom.

"Viola?"

"Yes?"

"The nightmares aren't the worst part."

"The worst part is when you wake up, and the holes in the sky are empty. You know the nightmares got out, that they're somewhere else, and that you didn't stop them."

Ryan barked out a harsh, rending sob. "Exactly."

"I'll watch tonight. Sleep."

Miryam Shaflzedeh opened her window when she got to work the next morning. Soon after, the wind carried a voice.

"Miryam. Find out how the boy's father died. And when.

"Find out now."

"About three months ago. It was sudden," Rose said, fingers twisting the heavy gold band she wore on a chain around her neck. "I know everyone says that, but in John's case, it was. There was no warning. He was healthy.

"Then he was dead."

She turned her head, pressed her lips together until they turned white. She had practice, by then, at not weeping.

"His heart just stopped beating. No genetic predisposition, or preexisting condition, or any of the other things people mention when something like this happens. He was out in the backyard with Ryan, stargazing, and then he was dead.

"Your colleague—does she think the way John died has something to do with Ryan's nightmares?"

"We just want to be thorough."

After listening to Rose, Miryam did not trust the wind. It could carry sound far too many places. Instead, she took a compact from her makeup bag and popped it open, angled the side with the mirror in towards her. She leaned down, and exhaled, once. Then, her breath still clouding the silvered surface, pierced the pad of her right thumb with a long silver needle, and let a drop of blood fall onto the obscured face of the mirror. Breath and blood resolved themselves into Viola's face.

"Is it what we feared?" Through the mirror, Viola sounded like an echo without an antecedent voice.

"The boy's father. Yes.

"It is nearly the Hundredth Night, Viola. What is rent must be sewn."

Viola's hand moved in a gesture of protection, or of prayer. "By the Needle."

"And the Stitch," Miryam answered, then drew her finger across the mirror.

Outside, darkness crept across the sky.

Ryan set two glasses of chocolate milk on the table beside his bed.

"Were you planning on being extra thirsty tonight?" Rose asked, and ruffled his hair.

"One is for the Night Doctor."

Her hand froze, then dropped to her son's shoulder. "Who is the Night Doctor?"

"Her name is Viola. She sees what I do, and she watches so I can sleep."

Rose swallowed the tears she refused to shed in front of her son. Almost thirteen was too old, she thought, for an imaginary friend, but if that was what Ryan needed to help him heal, then she'd stock up on chocolate milk.

"Sounds good. If you and Viola need anything else, let me know, okay?"

But all of Ryan's focus was out his bedroom window, on the starless night. Rose knew he wouldn't speak again until morning. He never had, not since he started this, except when he screamed himself awake. She squeezed his shoulder, and turned to leave.

"Okay."

"Tell me about the first night you saw the holes in the sky."

Ryan shifted on the bed. "I got you some chocolate milk. I drink it, when I'm watching. Dad and I used to drink it when we watched the stars."

"Thank you. That was a really nice thing to share with me."

Ryan liked the way Viola said things. She sounded like she meant them, not like she was humoring the kid whose dad had just died.

"The first time I saw them was the night my dad died. We were out watching the stars. It was this thing we did, just us.

"When I was a kid, Dad would tell me the constellations were people who lived in the sky. Even once I got too old for that, he'd tell me stories about them, and about the scientists who studied the sky, and found the planets, and that lady who discovered, like, a hundred comets."

Ryan's breath started to hitch and the weight on the mattress next to him shifted. Viola moved close enough that her left arm pressed against his right, a shield against sorrow.

"The sky ripped a hole in itself. And my dad made this noise, like a wet hiccup, and . . . " He swallowed hard, to get rid of the thing in his throat that nearly choked him. "They say it was a heart attack. But that's a lie. I saw my dad. He had a hole ripped in him, too."

"I'm going to tell you something, but you have to be very brave when you hear it, because it is going to hurt. It's going to hurt a lot."

Ryan stared, unblinking, at the wounded sky on the other side of his window. His fingers dug into the muscles of his thighs. "I can hear anything if it will make this stop."

"The nightmares that put the holes in the sky, they put the hole in your dad, too. They killed him. They ripped a hole in your father and used that hole to anchor the bridge that allows them to cross into this world. They do that. They take what we love, and they leave us with holes.

"If you want, I will show you how to stop them. I can show you how to sew up the sky."

Ryan reached in front of him, grabbed the glass of chocolate milk, and drained it. He swiped the back of his left hand across his mouth and said, "Okay. I'm ready."

They climbed out the window so the sound of the door wouldn't wake his mother.

Viola pulled a thin silver needle from her hair, and handed it to Ryan.

"Where's the thread?"

"Watch, and watch carefully, and move quickly when it's time," she said. She plucked a second needle from her hair, and plunged it into her left index finger.

Ryan watched as a drop of blood welled up, as Viola let the blood fall onto the needle, and as the red rolled down the silver and kept going, until a crimson thread fluttered in the wind.

"By the Needle, and by the Stitch." Then Viola reached up, and took hold of the sky. She pulled the torn edges close to each other, like twitching recalcitrant curtains closed, and she began to sew.

"Now, please, Ryan."

He looked away from what Viola was doing, and saw the nightmares climbing through the tears in the sky.

It didn't hurt when he stabbed the needle into his finger, but Ryan wouldn't have cared if it did. His blood rolled down the needle, and then he too had a red, wet thread. "By the Needle, and by the Stitch." Viola hadn't told him he had to say the words, but they sounded important, like magic words, so he did. He stretched out his hand, and the torn sky fluttered in his grasp like a dying heart. He could feel the nightmares gathered behind it, hear them howling and chittering.

And somewhere beyond that noise, Ryan heard something worse. His father's voice, begging Ryan not to leave him there, not to sew the sky closed, to climb through. "We can watch the stars forever, Ry."

Ryan yanked his hand away.

"Whatever you think you're hearing, it's not real," Viola said.

"How do you know?"

"Because I hear them, too. All the Night Doctors hear the dead voices."

"Besides, do you really think something that would kill a good man like your dad to get here is going to hesitate to lie in order to stay?"

It sounded like the sort of thing his dad would say. Would have said. Ryan swallowed hard, and stretched his hand toward the torn sky.

They sewed until dawn ignited the horizon, Ryan chanting, "By the Needle and by the Stitch" every time he pulled closed the wounded fabric of the sky.

"Tonight is the Hundredth Night."

"I wish we had found the boy earlier. I don't know if he trusts me enough to do what must be done." A memory there, like a bruise, beneath Viola's words.

"If he cannot, are you prepared to do what you must?"

"If I have to, yes. The gateway must be closed. By the Needle."

"And the Stitch." Miryam tucked a long silver needle back into her hair, and dropped the flowers she had been holding in front of John Grey's headstone. The earth opened behind her as she walked away.

"Hi, Mrs. Grey. I'm Dr. Black. Dr. Shaflzedeh asked me to consult on Ryan's case. I was wondering if I could see him?"

"Of course. Come in. Would you like to sit down somewhere?" Ryan heard his mother ask.

"Actually, if you don't mind, I'd like to take a walk with Ryan. It can be easier, sometimes, to talk away from the memories."

"It's okay, Mom. I don't mind." He did, a little. Viola looked strange in the daylight. Without the shadows to soften her face, she looked as sharp as the needle he could see threaded through her hair.

Night Doctors, Ryan thought, were only supposed to come out at night.

"Take your coat, sweetie," said Mrs. Grey. "It's cold out."

Ryan shrugged on the red and black flannel shirt of his dad's he'd been wearing as a jacket. His needle was in the front pocket, over his heart.

"So, what's up?" he asked as he and Viola reached the end of his driveway, far enough from the house that he knew his mom couldn't hear.

"There is one more thing that must be done, though it breaks my heart to ask it of you." Viola walked quickly.

"Is it something bad?"

"It is something necessary."

That didn't really answer his question. Ryan shoved his hands in his pockets. Except, it sort of did. If it wasn't something bad, Viola would have just said so.

Then they were at the graveyard where his dad was buried, and Ryan thought maybe bad wasn't a big enough word for what was going to happen next.

Viola reached down and took his hand. "I'm so sorry, Ryan." He wasn't sure what she was apologizing for, and then he saw. Someone had dug up his dad's grave.

Ryan fell to his knees in the mounds of dirt, and started shoving handfuls back towards the hole he couldn't bring himself to look at. "You knew this was here. Did they do this? Or did you?"

"We did."

Ryan flung the dirt at Viola. She didn't flinch, didn't even blink, just stood, as the bits of his dad's grave trickled down her face and hair.

"What kind of people are you?" he yelled.

"We are the Night Doctors. We heal the holes in the universe that the nightmares tear in the course of their borning. We heal the dreams of the wounded, and frightened, and those wise enough to know we all should be afraid of the dark, of the empty places.

"And there is one more empty place, Ryan, one that requires you to close it." She looked at the length of the shadows on the ground, measuring, counting time in heartbeats.

"And you must close it now, before the sun sets on the Hundredth Day. Or the tear in the sky becomes permanent, and the nightmares will not need to wait until dark to come through." She did not speak the rest, did not say they words she had been told, about the other way that closure could be made. The child, she thought, might never need to know, and in this, at least, she could protect him.

Unless he failed.

Ryan squeezed the dirt between his fingers, wishing he could put it back where it belonged, wishing it didn't have to be him who had to do whatever it was that was so horrible Viola couldn't speak it. But he remembered the feel of nightmares crawling out of the sky like maggots from a dead bird, and he looked up at her.

"You must open the coffin, and sew closed the hole that remains in your father.

"If I could do this for you, I would."

Ryan believed her. He believed her, and he hated her anyway. "Don't you talk to me," Ryan said, and climbed into the grave.

Viola looked at the distance between the sun and the horizon, and slid a needle sharp enough to pierce a heart from her hair, held it ready.

Ryan wasn't stupid. One hundred days had passed since his dad died. He knew it wasn't going to look like he was sleeping. His dad didn't even look like that at the funeral, no matter what people said. But when Ryan heaved the lid of the coffin open, all he saw was the hole the nightmares had torn. That looked as fresh as the night it happened.

Hand shaking, he reached into his pocket for the needle. He stabbed his finger, used the blood to make the thread, said, "By the Needle, and the Stitch.

"I'm sorry, Daddy."

When Ryan put his hand on his father's chest, something moved beneath the skin.

"Viola!"

"The nightmares hide inside of him, eager for the dark. Ryan, you must be quick. The sun is setting."

The flesh under Ryan's hand twitched again. He bit the inside of his mouth until it bled, let the hot, salt-copper taste fill his thoughts, and plunged the needle into his father's body. The corpse writhed and twisted as Ryan stitched, big, clumsy X's of red thread to be a door against the dark. Drops of water fell on his hands as he worked, and Ryan wondered when it had started raining.

Ryan finished just before night extinguished the last flamee of the sun. Viola slid the needle back into her hair. The body of John Grey lay quiet in its grave.

Now, Ryan did look at his father. He straightened the lapels of the suit jacket, brushed the dirt from the brim of the Miami Hurricanes baseball hat that had been his dad's favorite, whispered, "I miss you."

"What happens now?" Ryan asked, once he stood again on the dirt-streaked grass.

"You go home. You go back to your life. You sleep, instead of watching the sky tear itself apart.

"One day, or maybe never, you will hear a voice on the wind, or you will find a silver needle you thought you had lost, and you'll go help someone else sew closed the wounds in the sky." The sound of her voice was a door closing.

"That's it? I just pretend like everything is normal? Just wait until this happens again? Why can't I help you now?"

"There were two things that could have happened here tonight, Ryan."

"I know. I had to stitch up the hole in my dad, or else the nightmares came through."

"Wrong. Had you failed, I would have taken this needle"—suddenly the point was against his chest, ice against his too-hot skin—"and stabbed it into your heart. What is begun in blood must end in blood, and it was your father's blood that began this. Yours would have healed the wound in the sky, had your hand faltered."

"You . . . You would have killed me."

"Yes. And I would not have hesitated. Until you can do that, Ryan, go home. Go home, and pretend like everything is normal. Pretend for as long as you can."

"Did Dr. Black come in with you?" Rose Grey asked her son as he hung up his father's shirt on the coat rack.

"No, she walked me home, but then she had to leave."

"Do you think it helped, talking to her?"

Ryan nodded. "I think I'll be able to sleep tonight." He hugged his mom then, hanging on tight.

But when Ryan went to bed, he did not fall asleep, not right away. He lay awake, thinking of Viola, and of the nightmares. Thinking of what it meant to be normal.

Pretending.

THE EBONY CRUCIFIX

KIT REED

Kit Reed confides, 'There was indeed an actual ebony crucifix in my life, but only for a while. It came down in my mother's family, silver fittings finishing off the top and the cross piece, beautifully detailed ivory figure with carved crown of thorns, silver nails driven through detailed ivory hands and feet; 18th-century, I think, either Spanish or Italian, could have come out of a chapel in some great house. We saw one like it in a Frankfort museum one seriously jetlagged morning en route to somewhere else. It was a source of fierce battles during my mother's day—she fought off seven siblings to bring it home. Oh, my. I found a place for it in my story about an urban mom who can't stop her unruly teens from hooking up with vamps and were-things. It's on her mantel now.'

Ms. Reed's latest novel, Where, *was recently published by Tor in the USA.*

"Evelyn I know you're excited, but you're not going out with a werewolf just because you think he's cute. It's all moon-beams and empty promises. When the moon comes up he's not the same person. In fact, he isn't a person at all. He'll rip you apart."

My twins just turned thirteen but here are, having The Talk. Dr. Ora Fessenden says when they come home smelling of things you don't know about, it's too late to tell them anything, but mothers are always the last to know.

"And if he doesn't tear your throat out, he turns you and you can say goodbye to minis until it's over. Not even Dad's sander will get rid of the hairs," I tell Evelyn, desperate to make my point. "You'll be a slave to

That Time of the Month, and your hopes for Brearly and Princeton are totally fucked."

Here I am giving my all, and she and Aidan sit side by side on the sofa with nothing but makeup on their empty faces, going, blink. Blink. Blink. It's 3:00 a.m. but my twins are dressed to go clubbing, and I can't say no! The book says you have to let them do whatever they want.

If I thwart them it will stunt their emotional growth, according to Dr. Fessenden, world-famous child expert and advisor to the stars. Her book is called *Never Say No*. Bruce brought it into the labor room while I was struggling to unleash the twins on an unsuspecting world. He said, "Martha, read this!"

Never mind what I said.

He put *Never Say No* on my heaving chest. "We're raising our children by the book!"

Then he left on a business trip. I went on doing what I had to do, but I read the damn book, bit by bit, on all the nights when Bruce was working late and the twins kept me up with their incessant demands. Dr. Fessenden said if I was nice to them, naturally they'd grow up to be nice to me. There was no hit and yell at our house because Dr. Fessenden says if you hit your children, they'll start hitting back. There was only the book.

Her theory is, unless you let your kids do *everything they want*, if you say no to *any little thing*, they grow up warped and stunted failures in life. Bruce says Dr. Fessenden is the world's greatest expert on child-rearing, and she should know. So, the sky's the limit; no matter what they do, smile and replace everything they break. Her book has made billions, to say nothing of what she makes on that show.

When money talks, Bruce listens, but to be honest, it's wearing thin. OK, Dr. Fessenden, where's your chapter on this paranormal romance thing? Whatever happens to my kids tonight, it's on you. Look at them! Thirteen and a half, and Evelyn's all foxy in mink wristbands and fur UGGs, teen wolves watch out, while my handsome Aidan's all Hamlet in black satin and onyx beads, with his shirt open down to *here*, walking vampire bait.

What are they *thinking*?

My children are paranormal romantics, i.e. they want one. Paranormal romance, I mean. It's crazy dangerous, but I'm not allowed to say, "No way!" Do I sound bitter? Dr. F. tells us the only thing I can do to control my twins is, *motivate*.

OK then. "This stuff isn't real," I say, in case they are actually following. "Vampires, werewolves, supernatural lovers that come in the night, it's all made up, get it? A sales gimmick, to make you buy storybooks and makeup and DVDs. *Are you listening?*"

Blink.

Either they're listening or they aren't. With paranormal romantics, the flavor of the month changes daily, so I run down the rest of the list.

"Aidan, vampires are treacherous—if they even exist. Why else would they only come out at night? No way are they sexy and exciting, like in the movies and on TV. Flirt with a sexy vampire girl and even if she says she loves you, sooner or later she'll bite you in the neck, so you end up dead. Unless . . . Agh!" The rest is too terrible to say out loud.

What if all this crap is true and I find myself holding off my very own son with my great-grandmother Martone's precious ebony crucifix? It's my personal protection against evil. Dr. Fessenden says don't take your kids to church unless they beg, and now look. What if I have to stake Aidan, my dear boy who—tell no one—is my favorite? I see me howling with grief as he turns to ash before my eyes. Move on fast, Martha, or Evelyn will pick up on it. That I'd die if I lost Aidan and all I had left was this lumpy, stupid girl.

All this anxiety, and I have to go on brightly, all friendly, motivational mom. "Unless she turns you into a vampire too, Aidan. Which, you can forget about soccer, forget about Dalton, there will be no taking SATs, no college interviews and no Harvard, none of the things guys like you want to do because one step outside before sunset and broad daylight burns you to a crisp."

Blink. Blink. Blink.

Maybe I can keep them talking until the sun comes up and all the worst clubs are closed. "Now, about zombies, they say some of them are sexy. No way! Everybody knows zombies have zero personal charm, and if one felt you up, you'd have icicles running along your jawline and down your neck and on down your whole shivering body to the main event. In books, Haitian zombies are hotter, if you believe in that crap, but listen. 'Soul kiss' means exactly that. They suck out your soul and you end up dead, like them.

"As for garden-variety George Romero zombies, like in the movies? If you see one coming, run!

"They don't want sex."

I wait for one of them to come back with, *they want your brains.* They just work on their nails. For her, silver. For him, Day-Glo green. Motivational speech just bombed out, Dr. F. What else have you got? Nothing, that I know of, but the twins have to stay until I stop talking, so I string it out.

"As for fairies, that's bullshit. And if it isn't, they're not exactly life-sized. It's more like dragonflies messing up your hair or flitzy Tinker Bell, getting in your face, do you know what fairies are? Talking insects is what. Do you really want your prom date to look like she came off a music box? They're nothing but a bunch of cutesy, ephemeral twits.

"If there even are any. Fairies, I mean."

Evelyn stops filing, but only to reach for iridescent gloss.

"Shape-shifters are not to be trusted, you've gotta know that going in. You can't pin them down." Decals! They're pasting teeny silver skulls on their nails. "I mean, get serious, people. If you feel so good about yourselves, pick a damn shape and stick to it. Look at me when I talk to you!"

Blink. Blink. Blink.

"No need to warn you on trolls. Not your objects of desire, enough said. Trust me, there are extreme drawbacks to every supernatural type you might think you want to fall in love with, your sirens and dryads, pagan gods, whatever, centaur, minotaur, did I miss anything?

"If I forgot anybody, take it from me, whatever it is, whatever it says and whatever tries to lure you with, nothing comes free. Now, as for ghosts . . . " I tell my two, who can't wait for me to finish. "Ghosts are a thin experience, so if you love me and Daddy even a little bit . . . "

Rethink. I fix them with a fierce maternal glare. "*If you value your lives,* don't even think about going out."

"Mom, is that all you have?" The little bitch is running the back of her hand down her cheek in a certain way and my darling Aidan's fixated on his python motorcycle boots. As if with the right kicks, the right outfit, and the right attitude, they can hunt down, slay, and bring home true love. Like love is a deer that you bag with your crossbow and lash to the roof of your car, antlers and all, *catch of the day.*

Who am I to remind them that they don't know how to drive? We're fighting a losing battle here, but I give it everything I've got. "I know what you're looking for, but no matter how gorgeous and weird they are, no matter what they say, underneath, they're all just *people.* People, like you and Daddy and me. Well, not exactly like Daddy and me."

Then Aidan—my perfect Aidan!—drives in the knife. "Mom, are you done?"

They've been like this for weeks, sneaking out in full hunting gear and a cloud of pheromones, stalking love. I don't know if they get this paranormal lust out of the crap they read or straight off the screen or if it's in the air, but if I lock them in they prowl the apartment, in hopes. I catch them hanging out windows like little banners, waiting for their werewolf/vampire/indescribable other to swoop down and take them away from all this.

All this translates as life on the Upper West Side, where they have to get on the bus every day like normal teenagers and ride uptown to school and come home and do all their homework before I give back their phones, and who can blame them, really?

It won't matter how hard I try to motivate them or what Bruce spends on coaches and tutors to make them perfect, or what I spent on music lessons and video equipment and comedy camp to distract them, Evelyn and my Aidan lurch around the house *yearning* so hard that it breaks my heart.

I can't wait for this summer to end! Bruce says boarding school would solve the problem. Like he'd know. Out of sight is the least of it. No way am I sending them into one of those high-end hothouses, iron gates or not. In those places desires and hysteria spread like smallpox in a windowless room, and before you know it your randy little treasures and all the others are blooming like gaudy tropical plants. Then the fungus sets in . . .

It's bad enough seeing it happen before my very eyes. Look at them! Evelyn topped off the open-toed UGGs with spiderweb hose; she's wearing caterpillar eyelashes and a shift so suggestive that I won't describe it here, while Aidan's shirt is open to the middle of his six-pack and his velvet jeans are so tight that they're, like, strangling his legs. My twins have multiple studs and gaudy tats that they think I don't know about, with their hair teased, moussed, streaked, or otherwise organized to dazzle . . .

And, they hope, attract.

I hope it doesn't. If I had my way I'd chain them to the bed like Lon Chaney in that old movie and leave them there until Monday morning, when they have to scrub the gunk off their faces and eat a good breakfast before Bruce drives them to science camp on his way to LaGuardia, but I'm just their mom, and everyone knows that in paranormal romances the parents are clueless, either because they spend too much time offstage, or they're not home or conveniently dead, and me?

I'm here. Neutralized by Dr. Ora Fessenden, all because of Bruce, who thinks you can organize a family like a corporation, as in, do it by the book and you'll turn out picture-perfect products, as advertised, yeah, right.

Do you know what Bruce had the nerve to say when I told him the kids were going sour? Bruce said, "Fessenden isn't just a doctor. Martha, she's a corporate genius. You'd better believe she knows her business." Fine. It's not like Bruce is home with them all day. And Dr. F? I'm beginning to wonder if she ever *had* kids.

Mine are out the door.

"Have fun," I say weakly, but too late.

What's a mother to do?

Search their rooms.

Wolfsbane in Aidan's, garlic in Evelyn's, sure signs. To keep each other's creepy Significant Others from interrupting theirs. I look for long hairs on Aidan's pillow, fur on hers. I sniff for exotic perfumes, but all I find is smatterings of sequins and glitter that came home from—good grief—from someplace they're forbidden to go, that I didn't even know they went. Do their black lace mitts cover up rubber stamps from a bunch of racy paranormal follies that I don't know about?

I'd ask Bruce but Bruce is away on business, which happens a lot, and at this hour he mutes his phone so I won't bother him, which is not so different from Bruce when he's home. I turn to Dr. F.'s webpage because there's not a word about paranormal romantics in her book. Her mother was Dr. Ora Fessenden Senior, famous hero of the seventies revolution, when strong, like-minded women armed themselves and took to the hills, which is the only reason I believed in her rotten book.

OK, the book's fourteen years old, but you'd expect regular updates on everything from A to zombies on her webpage, but I've scrolled to the tippy bottom of the FAQs and I am furious! NOWHERE does she cover *What To Do When YES Won't Work*. I upload a furious e-mail with all the details. Like she ever looks. Like she even knows. I sure as hell don't. In fact, I think, turning out the twins' rooms again, the more I think about it, this whole mess is her fault.

Oh, crap. They're home. I hear them battling over whose key goes into the door.

By the time they sort it out and I hear them in the front hall, I'm frantic. Claw marks in the curly maple headboard of Evelyn's trundle bed. Lipstick on Aidan's pillowcase, which he had turned inside out, so I wouldn't see.

OMG, children. O. M. G. At least whatever they were doing last night, they were doing somewhere else. At least they've come home.

They're not alone! Evelyn comes in with a guy.

"Mother," she says, "This is Rufus." You'd think she was announcing her engagement to the crown prince of somewhere instead of bringing on a big, shaggy, awkward kid who's worried over the fresh dirt and torn leaves he is tracking on my rugs.

Oh, lady, be cool. "Good morning, Rufus. You're Evelyn's friend from science camp, right?"

"No ma'am."

"Rufus is a werewolf, Mom," Evelyn says, and she's smiling as though she'd slept here all night and had stacks of sweet dreams.

I am beggared for speech. "If you say so," I say.

For a minute there, I'm too upset and distracted to see my darling Aidan is still on the doorsill, talking to someone in the outside hall. Lovely boy, I thought, looks all sinister and goth in that ridiculous costume, but today he's stopped to say something nice to old Mrs. McGonnigle, the neighbor that pops out whenever we go out or come in. That hag is dying to get us out of the building; she's been bitching about my kids ever since they got big enough to yell and run around banging on doors and crayoning the hallway walls, which Dr. F. says is a perfectly normal sign of normal growth. Mrs. McGonnigle doesn't give a crap about Aidan, she's trolling for things to report to her friends on the co-op board; Aidan knows it, too, but he's a perfect gentleman, smiling and nodding and bending his head closer to . . .

OMG, that isn't Mrs. McGonnigle he's canoodling with. No wonder he was bringing her on with his considerable charm. He has a girlfriend!

"Mom, this is Sylvia. Sylvia, Mom."

Silky, gorgeous, she looks like Morticia; garlic won't work on this babe, who is way, way too old for him. It's hate at first sight. She's stealing my darling boy! I think about running for the ebony crucifix, but first I narrow my eyes at her: "Don't I have to invite you in?"

"Oh, Aidan's done that." The smile says that she can kill me. And unless I do something, she will.

Suave, Martha. Be suave. "But I'm the home owner, and I . . . "

Long, long black eyelashes, eyebrows like black wings: dangerous woman, with that silky, murderous smile. "As you can see, I'm already in."

I will not have this. I grope behind me for something in the umbrella stand—anything to stake her with.

She says, "Don't bother."

"You're in luck," I tell her. "I just made garlic bread."

I've never seen such a look of complete disdain.

"You'll love our living room, we have a beautiful picture window."

"Don't worry, dear, we have velvet curtains!" Aidan—my Aidan!—rushes in to close the draw drapes against the sun.

"Since you're already inside," I tell her, "you'll want to see my ancestral crucifix. Ebony with an ivory figure, silver nails and a silver halo, eighteenth-century, I think." I advance as she starts backing away. "And beautiful filigreed silver wedges to finish off the arms and tip of the ebony cross. Do come see it, it's a real museum piece."

If she could kill me with a glare, she would. "All right," she says, backing out the door. "You win."

Aidan lunges after her. "Darling!"

Betrayed, I turn away. I can hear them out there talking, Aidan and his deadly first love. I know that no matter how carefully I hide that crucifix or what precautions I take, I'll wake up tomorrow or the next day and my only weapon against her will be gone. There's no point in trying to talk to Aidan when he comes back inside. Over the next few days I don't protest or question what he's doing or where he's going or when he'll be back when he comes and goes, I just let him go. When he does come home for clean socks and his sequined shirt, I try to ply him with morning pancakes, frittatas, hot cross buns, which he wolfs, sure, but it's clear he's not speaking to me. In a way, it's probably just as well. I don't want to hear what he thinks of me. My favorite, favorite boy in the universe and he's sneaking out nights to be with a woman who wants me dead so she can take him away from me, and I don't know what to do!

I'm so worried and distracted that I hardly notice when Evelyn's boyfriend Rufus moves in for good. He's a nice enough kid, with a goofy grin and a standup cowlick in that rough hair. Very polite, unlike some people I might mention. He told me his mother is very, very strict, so he had to get her permission to visit a friend in New York City; he even feels guilty that to get it, he had to make a broad mental reservation and tell her he was staying with a friend from Boy Scout Camp, and you know what's really, really cute? He's all conflicted and guilty about telling even a little lie.

So far he hasn't been a bit of trouble; unlike my twins, he helps me load the dishwasher, takes out the trash, but I find twigs and bracken and little knots of hair that don't belong to anybody in our family tangled in my daughter's hair, and I wonder how long we have before the black hairs begin to sprout.

So I have to wonder, how can Dr. Fessenden be right? I let my twins do anything they wanted and now they won't do anything I say! Plus, I've left a zillion voicemails and sent bajillion e-mails describing our situation, and it's not like I've heard back from her. Oh, there's an office, but the girl behind the front desk says she's away on an extended research trip and she can't give me an appointment before the first of next year.

When I try to talk to Bruce about it—never mind what happens when I talk to Bruce, it isn't happening. It won't, no matter what I try. Bruce is not what you would call available. Furthermore, his business trip just got inexplicably extended. The careless, insensitive son of a bitch had Gail from the office leave a voicemail notifying me.

I'm too depressed to think about it, but Aidan is out with his silky new girlfriend all night every night and he hates me for driving her out. He doesn't care that this Sylvia is out to get me, which she is. A mother knows. It's only a matter of time. Meanwhile, I have a more immediate problem. The clock is ticking. I have exactly three days to make their father come home and let me *do something* about our children before the next full moon. Then Rufus changes, and either he gets me before he goes bounding across the park or he starts on Evelyn, who may not be my favorite but is, after all, my flesh and blood, and takes out every single one of us before he moves on, riding up and down in the elevator, ravaging and slaying everybody he finds out in the halls, starting, I hope, with Mrs. McGonnigle.

What do you do when you're facing up to mortal peril with nobody on your side? You take to the Internets and you find out where Dr. Ora Fessenden lives and you go to her house. I find her under Ora Fessenden-Petard, which is her pseudonym, so she can go out among the people without being swarmed by thousands of needy fans—or semi-dangerous ex-believers, like me.

Then I go to her house. Naturally I have a story that gets me past the doorman, and then it's a hop, skip, and a jump up three flights to Ms. Fessenden-Petard's front door. Nobody home, so I lie in wait. This means I surprise her coming out of the elevator and I get down on my knees to her, locking my arms around her legs so she can't kick me off and she can't walk away. Then I sob out my story, thinking if she won't change her policy, at least she'll give me a little of her famously useful advice.

It's like talking to my kids. Blink. Blink. I gasp to a finish and wait, panting, in hopes.

She looks down at me and says, with a cold stare, "Is that all?"

"You're the expert," I say, resorting to flattery. "You have all the answers to this problem." She isn't buying. I can't help it, I whine. "All I need is one!"

"If you don't let go, I'll get security up here." Fortunately, I've clamped her handbag in my locked arms, along with her knees, so she can't get to her phone. We are at a little impasse here. I won't let go and she won't give me anything I can work with, not even one how-to factoid that would solve the problem of twins and scary paranormal love. Finally she does what Dr. Fessenden says you must never, never do.

She gives orders. "Stop that. Let go."

This is, in its way, A Good Sign. She's weakened, at least a little bit. I strike back with, "Whatever happened to 'Never say no?'"

"I said, *let go*!"

My knees are asleep but my back aches; my arms are starting to cramp. I try, "If you don't have any useful advice for a mom in this situation, at least tell me it's OK for me and Bruce to crack down on the twins!"

That split second turns her to stone. "What, and compromise my research? Never. No, you stupid, stupid cow. A Fessenden mother never says no! Let go, lady, I have my reputation to protect."

"And I have a family!"

"Well, tough rocks."

I lock myself to her ankles. "Your mother spent her life fighting for women's freedom and you . . . "

"Let go."

"You turned mothers into slaves!"

Like a stone giant, she thunders, "I said, let go!" With granite legs, she knees me in the boobs.

I can't help it. I shriek and let go.

She finishes me off with a kick that could have punctured a lung and stalks into her apartment and slams the door.

Sobbing, I drag myself down the staircase and out the service entrance before 911 gets around to picking up her call. Sobbing, I go home. Even

Evelyn is worried. Rufus brings wet cloths, thoughtful boy. Aidan is over at Sylvia's, conspiring. My boy will betray me, I know.

It takes me a day and another night to recoup, but on the third morning of my uneasy convalescence, a lovely thing happens. Evelyn and Rufus know I'm in pain, and they've made breakfast for me! My daughter eats and leaves, but Rufus lingers, he's that worried. "Are you all right?"

Nice boy! "No," I tell him, and break down. Sweet kid, he hugs me and sits quietly while I tell him everything. Everything.

Then he amazes me. "OK, Mrs. Um, Mom. What are we going to do?"

We sit there talking about what went wrong and what I'm scared of and what we're going to do.

"We," I say, inexplicably moved by his sympathy. Given Bruce—who, I suspect, is not in Milwaukee as advertised but on Maui with some babe—given my heedless twins, it's a brand-new experience. "I'm afraid it's just me."

"We," he repeats with the loveliest grin.

Tears, *tears* stand in my eyes, I am so touched.

"You have to remember," he says when I've finished. "I have a problem too."

I pat his hand, soon to be bristling with black hairs. "It's tonight."

He sighs. "Tonight. You have to know, I don't want to hurt Evelyn, ever." Such a nice voice, such a nice face! "And I certainly don't want to hurt you."

Sitting there over fresh coffee Rufus brewed for me, we hatch a plan. By the time Evelyn comes in, all, "Where's lunch," Rufus and I have a plan. When Ev puts on her headset and zones out, we go into Bruce's study to rehearse.

This evening, shortly before sunset, when only a third of the pale full moon is visible in the sky, Rufus delivers three dozen roses to the Fessenden-Petard apartment, wedging his foot in the door while the good doctor is still squinting at the gift card.

He'll get her attention by confessing, "You might as well know, Dr. Fessenden, I'm a werewolf."

Of course she'll be conflicted, standing in her front hall, scoping him out. Conflicted and a little bit thrilled as this may open a new chapter in her career.

"I'm here because you and you alone can help me. Yes I know who you are, you're famous! Dr. Fessenden, and just so you know? My parents did

exactly what you said parents should never do, and it turned me into what
I am today."

He'll appeal to her professional pride. "The thing is, you, and only you,
can cure me. Think of the splash that'll make!" She is, after all, a clinical
psychologist. Oh, won't she be flattered and excited then! Naturally, he'll
charm his way inside. Then—he really is a lovely, likeable kid—he'll lay it
on: oppressive parents, a miserable childhood with everybody in the
family, aunts and uncles and grandparents all repeating the awful, spirit-
killing, "No."

We've worked it all out. Rufus sells himself as a walking example of the
thing she rails against on TV and in her sacred, holy how-to bible, *Never
Say No*. He'll say, "I have a lot worse problems than any of the kids you
have on your show. Oh, Dr. Fessenden, I never miss your show."

She'll be thinking: He's a natural.

And he is.

He's also very persuasive. I'm anti-paranormal everything, and he
persuaded me! I think. I have to admit it's reassuring, having a nice new
paranormal friend who can solve all the problems in my life. Well, not
Bruce probably, but most of them.

"I mean, you've helped a lot of poor kids on your show, Dr. Fessenden,
but have you ever cured a werewolf? Dad never read your book, so this is
all his fault. He tied me to the pipes in the basement because my senior
prom and my first full moon were both on the same night." Her eyes will
be glittering when he wails, "All they ever said to me was *No*!"

If I was Dr. F., I'd sure as hell want an involuntary werewolf like Rufus
on *my* show.

It will get late and then later. The plan is to keep her talking until dark
until it's late enough, Rufus is that good. Then he'll offer to whip up a
thank-you omelet before he goes. Whether or not she accepts, he'll be
there until the full moon clears the horizon. He may or may not be able to
see out her windows, but his body knows. Then he asks to use the bathroom before he goes and when he comes out, he tears her to bits.

He won't be back until tomorrow morning; he promised, and I believe
him. In return, I've promised to leave fresh clothes in a marked plastic bag
at the dumpster behind our building, so Evelyn doesn't know.

As for me? I know that in spite of everything that I said to Evelyn about
his kind, Rufus is a lovely, honorable person, except at That Time of the
Month. On those nights I can count on Rufe: he'll find somewhere else to

be. Lovely guy! He won't hurt Evelyn, whom I'm beginning to like better, or Aidan, whom I haven't seen in days—or me—although I don't think he likes Aidan much.

Now, as for Bruce . . . Well. He knows how I feel about Bruce.

As far as Rufus is concerned, the jury's still out.

So that problem is solved.

Now, all I have to solve is Sylvia, who wants to destroy me and take away my beautiful son, the one person I love more than anybody in the world. If what they say about vampires is true, she won't turn me, she'll kill me dead, and if she takes Aidan away from me, I'll want her to. For all I know, she's already a thousand years old, and Rufus isn't old enough or smart enough to deal with that.

It's up to me.

Tonight, I roll with the punches, waiting until morning when Rufus comes back and tells me how it went, although the news may come in as a late-breaking bulletin on CNN.

For now, I have the ancestral crucifix to protect me, but first thing tomorrow, I go out to the religious supply store and buy up every crucifix on the shelves and nail them up in every room in the place.

While my new best friend tells Evelyn some story at four and my daughter kisses her sweet boyfriend goodbye because he won't come back until he's completely recovered from The Change . . . While that's going on, I duck into the living room to give them a little space. I relax a bit, reassured by the ebony and ivory family treasure that stands like a sentinel on the mantel in our living room. You bet I'm exhausted. I don't mean for it to happen, but I fall face down on the sofa—I can't help it! All the anxious breath rushes out of me in my crash dive into the first decent sleep I've had in weeks.

How long have I slept?

Startled, I wake up, knuckling my eyes. Aidan's still out, of course—he's stopped coming home at night, he's in that tight with the slinky, blood-sucking nightmare who's convinced him that she is the love of his life. He thinks they're in love. He cares more about that bitch Sylvia than his very own mother, even though she's older than me by far, and a danger to us all. Evelyn—where's Evelyn? Asleep, I suppose, with a string of dried garlic looped on the bedpost, so she'll be undisturbed until Rufus comes home. And me?

Alone on the living room sofa with deep night showing in every window in the room. And my ancestral crucifix, with all its ebony and ivory and silver nails and halos and fleur-de-lis protective silver elements—*Aidan! My beloved, my betrayer, what have you done to me?*

Along with all my hopes for a happy future, my ancestral crucifix is gone.

THE HOUSE OF THE WITCHES

DARRELL SCHWEITZER

In 'The House of the Witches', the author takes his inspiration, not from Lord Dunsany, but from his *inspiration for the stories in* The Book of Wonder, *i.e. Sidney Sime. 'This is a kind of meta-pastiche, written around an imaginary Sime illustration,' Mr. Schweitzer explains. 'First I have imagined the kind of drawing Sime might have created, then tried to tell the story implied there. Alas that we can't have someone actually draw it, but I can just see that tottering house against a star field with winged things fluttering about the eaves. I did something like this once before, in* Weird Tales, *and we did have George Barr draw it.'*

The author's most recent story collections have been Echoes of the Goddess *(stories in the setting of* The Shattered Goddess*) and* The Emperor of the Ancient Word, *both from Wildside Press. The anthology* That Is Not Dead, *a historical take on the Cthulhu Mythos, appeared recently from PS. Coming up soon is* Speaking of Horror II, *a volume of interviews with horror writers, again from Wildside Press.*

T HE HOUSE OF THE WITCHES PERCHED PRECARIOUSLY ON A basalt spire, far out in the depths of space, an infinite distance from the mundane world, where star-clouds broke against black stone like the froth of an infinite sea. This was not a place that could be reached by any vessel or contrivance of mankind, only by magic, on a broomstick, in an enchanted cauldron, or in the ecstasy of a vision induced by forbidden ointment, though demons fluttered around the high windows like sparrows, and dragons coiled slowly and lazily beneath the eaves.

Still, the house crouched, like a drunken, living thing. It creaked and tottered in extra-cosmic winds, but it somehow never fell: an immense and perhaps always growing pile of wooden gables and balconies, of stone towers and battlements, of brick faces, and even a vast ivory portal carven of a *single piece*. Sometimes the floors swayed and rocked. The windows rarely looked out on the same vista twice, and the house flowed and grew and shifted, like the creation of a mad dream.

You had to be a witch to find the place comfortable. But witches did, either as an occasional resort or a permanent residence. On one high balcony, semi-enclosed behind gingerbread trimmings carved in the delicate likenesses of leaves and flowers and writhing, damned souls, there dwelt three witches of particular note. Jezebel, the oldest, could remember Babylon. That was not actually her name, but she had taken it when wicked names were all the rage. She'd known the original Jezebel and thought well of her: "Great lady," she would reminisce. "Very elegant, with a real queenly presence, even if she did wear too much makeup." The witch Jezebel had grown vast and soft and pasty-faced over the course of centuries, favoring as she did among the Seven Deadly Sins these days Sloth and Gluttony above all others. She could argue with the subtlety of a theologian that those two were just as bad as any of the rest, for all they required less exertion. "If you've got a problem with that," she'd say, "just shut up and think impure thoughts for a while."

She seldom moved now, but lay on her wide couch with her feet up on the balcony's railing. Far below, the fires of Hell burned infinitely hot, but at this distance they warmed her feet comfortably.

On a low table before her, in a space cleared amid the lavish feast that was perpetually spread out before her, she played endlessly at a game like knucklebones. She could have used it for divination, to delving into mighty secrets if she'd wanted, but now it was more of a habit. When not doing that, she often slept, dreaming iniquities and little misfortunes, which she sent wafting out into the universe like a plague of boils. As long as she could trifle with worlds and with fate, lie there and nibble on delicacies, and rattle her knucklebones, she was content.

Salome, who joined her in the game, had taken that name, too, after a series of others. She was considerably younger, little more than a slip of a girl when she and her parents had escaped from the unpleasantness at Salem in 1692. Now she was middle-aged in appearance and had a stern, solemn look about her. But she was Jezebel's boon companion.

The third witch, Annabel, whose name was not particularly wicked, more chosen for the rhyme, was less than a hundred, raised in Brooklyn among gangsters and speakeasies, pale and slinky and still addicted to nearly transparent flapper fashions and sometimes inane phraseology; but to the others she had her uses.

It was Annabel who sat apart from the other two, warming her hands with a cup of hot brimstone-flavored cocoa (something only witches have a taste for) when she noticed the surface of the beverage rippling.

"Ooh," she said.

Jezebel let her knucklebones trickle between her fingers onto the tabletop, heedless of where they fell.

"Someone is coming," she said.

Annabel peered intently into her cup, trying to make some sense out of the little bits of pumice floating there, and merely repeated, "Ooh."

"Someone?" said Salome.

"*He* is coming," said Jezebel. "It can be no other."

"Oh dear," said Salome.

"Ooh, golly," said Annabel.

The other two winced. What kind of a witch says "*Golly*"?

"*Go,* child," said Jezebel. "Go and see."

"Me?" said Annabel.

"Yes, *you.*"

Jezebel picked up a cluster of grapes covered with glazed molasses with small, live insects set artistically onto each one (another witches' acquired taste) and began to devour them rather messily, apparently oblivious of Annabel, but the order had been given, and Annabel rose and went. Barefoot and silent on the stairs, she descended into the depths of the house. She conjured a cigarette in a long-stemmed holder out of the air, and trailed smoke behind her.

Down she went, into the labyrinthine bowels of the house, into the mass of stone and wood and strangely colored, warped glass that shifted as she passed, rooms popping into and out of existence like bubbles, doorways to whole worlds and dimensions opening and closing like mouths. She came to a vast, high hall where hundreds of other witches had gathered alongside the occasional visiting warlock. Wriggling, upright serpents circulated among them with trays of drinks and hors d'oeuvres, but few paid attention to them. There was palpable excitement, tension rising in the whispering susurrus of conversation. The house itself seemed to be come awake, aware, intent on what was about to happen.

Annabel made her way through the crowd, scarcely noticed, muttering no more than the occasional, "Excuse me," until she reached the opening of another stairway, and ascended, or descended, or moved through angles that human (or even witchy) senses could not quite follow, until she emerged onto another balcony, like and yet converse to the one from which she had come, for here she did not gaze down on the distant fires of Hell, but on the starry Abyss, and galaxies splashing and swirling like foam in tidal pools.

She leaned over and studied the stars as she had the floating lumps in her cup. Yes, she saw a comet disturbed from its path. A constellation rippled, then another.

Someone was indeed coming.

But before she could even report back to the others, as she was pitter-pattering softly up a stairway filled with portraits of the famously damned, the whole house shook with a tread louder than thunder. She was thrown against the wall, hard, and one of her flailing hands went right through one of the paintings and the painting yelled, "Hey! Watch it, girl!" But she couldn't help herself. The whole place tilted as if an elephant had just stepped into one end of a rowboat. She found herself trying to crawl up the stairs on hands and knees, which was very undignified, particularly in the filmy, see-through dress she was wearing. The other figures in the portraits seemed clearly agitated as they brushed their shoulders or straightened their ties or polished their medals, making themselves ready to greet some *major* dignitary. A full-length painting of Faust at the top of the stairs said, "Ahem!" in a soft voice as she almost touched it, before she regained her balance and managed to make her way past.

By the time she was able to say, "Yep, somebody's really coming, all right," Jezebel merely replied with a deep and rumbling sigh, "No, *He* is already here."

"Oh my G—!" said Salome.

"Don't say it! Quite the opposite, actually."

"*The* Him himself?" said Annabel.

But Jezebel just waved her right back down again, into the depths of the house. This time, all the figures in the portraits had left their frames. She encountered some of them among the milling multitudes in the great hall, along with quite a bit else: several giants, a Cyclops, a horde shambling and rotting corpses, assorted vampires, and a three-headed dog, not to mention witches of every possible size, shape, and description.

By the time she reported back this time, the dragons that slept beneath the eaves of the towers were uncoiling with fiery yawns, and outside every window she saw flocks of bat-winged demons blotting out the stars. The whole house tilted ever more precariously beneath the weight of their massive, distinguished visitor, who stood so high above the others that when he straightened himself he took out the ceiling and stretched his wings out to brush the clouds of demons aside and touch the stars.

His face was all of fire, his eyes too bright to look upon. Yes, it was definitely him, the Big Mahoff, the Boss, the Chief, the Father of Lies, Lord of the Flies; the one they'd all kissed in a curious place when they'd signed his book, Satan himself, the Fallen Prince of Angels. When he spoke the air seemed to explode. Glass windows blew out into splinters.

Now was the time, he told them. *Now* the season had come at last for vengeance, for storming the very bastions of the enemy, for setting the whole universe to right (or more properly, to wrong), for soaring up out of the abysmal depths and smashing countless worlds, until they, all of them, all the witches and warlocks and dark demons and minions of every sort, the countless, unimaginable dark legions of Sin, burst through the unguarded gates of the Other Place and took the Throne of Creation for themselves—or for him, their leader, to be precise—that He might rule the universe for time without ending. For who said anything about time having an ending? Who said anything *at all* now that the word was out, as even the lowly humans had begun to suspect, that the Other Chap, the Master of Light, the feared and eternal Master had proven less than eternal after all and was in fact *absent*, either absconded or dead, definitely not doing miracles anymore or sending forth sword-wielding, winged hosts, consistently failing to answer prayers, and not even smiting with wrath those skeptical philosophers who doubted his very existence.

"*Now* is the time for the final war and the final triumph!" spoke the Lord of Darkness. "Now let us make all of creation tremble!"

There were considerably more words to that effect. Whatever else Satan's presentation may have been, mind-searing, capable of shaking the stars from their courses, it was definitely not brief.

And though such a discourse would never have descended to such trivialities of phrasing as *when the cat's away, the mice will play*, that was how Annabel summed it up in her own mind as she struggled to make her way back to tell Jezebel and Salome what was happening. She was somewhat the worse for wear, bedraggled, tattered, and buffeted about like a leaf on a roaring wind. By the time she got there, the House was well on its way to transforming itself from a conglomeration of stone and wood and charmingly cut gingerbread trim into a thing of living metal, covered with scales, blazing fire out of thousands of windows like a multitude of eyes, spreading its wings from one end of the cosmos to the other as it made ready to leap from its stony perch and crash over the very battlements of Heaven; by that time Annabel, who was not the most articulate of witches under the best of circumstances, had scarcely managed a "Jeepers," much less any further ineffectual clichés, and no further summation was necessary. It was all too obvious what was going on.

Once more the House shook and heaved, and Jezebel actually slid forward like a fleshy avalanche onto the floor, making inappreciative noises before she finally managed to mutter, "You know, this is going to be a *lot* of bother!"

"Oh dear," said Salome plaintively. "I liked things the way they were."

Annabel managed one last "Gee—"

Jezebel raised herself up with all her strength, caught hold of the couch with one hand, and paused, gasping. Sloth and Gluttony were fine Sins, she knew, but there could be times when they were *damned* inconvenient. Nevertheless, she was the one who was going to have to *do* something. The other two could only flutter and say, "Oh dear! Oh dear!" Annabel's cocoa cup fell from the table onto floor and shattered, making a mess. Knucklebones scattered everywhere. A dish of some kind of sauce splashed onto the floor, making a hideous mess. Salome clung to a drapery hanging for dear life. Annabel managed to flop down on her rump, her legs spread apart, her slinky dress ripping all the way up the side as she did.

"Oops," she said.

It was Jezebel who kept her presence of mind, as she always did. She nodded to Annabel and then jerked her head toward the stairway.

"What you can do, dearie, is ask our guest to come up and have a chat."

"*Him?* Ask *him* to come to you?"

"That's what I said. Go!"

So she went, yet again, but not very far, because soon she found herself face to face with Satan, who came roiling at her up the stairwell like an explosion of fire up a chimney. It was all she could do to scramble back the way she came, and get out of the way before the immense face floated in the air before Jezebel.

The eyes were indeed too bright to look upon. Even Jezebel held up a hand to shield herself.

"You'll pardon me if I don't get up," she said.

"*You* did not attend when I summoned *all* before me!"

Salome whimpered. Annabel cringed. But Jezebel merely said, "I'm not *all*. I'm a special case. A specialist. In my two particular sins, you must admit, I am exemplary. I was *so* hoping you would stop by so we could have this chat, before you did anything rash."

"*What?*"

"Dreadful One, it is only out of the deep devotion I hold for you in the depths of my blackened soul and corrupted heart that I am able to bring myself to tell you that maybe your present enterprise needs a few finishing touches—"

"*What?*"

"It's your image, Sir. A bit old-fashioned. Sure, you *can* rule the universe through sheer monstrosity and terror, but wouldn't it be more elegant to *allure?* Maybe I'd have to ask the young girls, the under-a-hundred set like Annabel over there, but I am pretty certain that we witches don't go in for the winged, clawed horrors anymore. And if you will pardon my saying so, you *reek*, of sulfur and goatiness, and I don't know what all else. Were you not *beautiful* once? How about that again?"

"What do you suggest?" said Satan, his vanity piqued.

Jezebel snapped her fingers. The shattered cup miraculously repaired itself. It sat on the tabletop, steaming, not with hot cocoa, but with something white and bubbly which dribbled smoke over the rim.

"I've prepared a special potion. Drink up," he said. "By my wickedness, it's just the thing."

An immense claw materialized. Satan took up the cup delicately, doubtfully.

Jezebel winked at him.

He drank, throwing back the contents like a shot of whiskey.

The transformation began at once. His whole outline shimmered. Before long he towered only three or four feet above Annabel, and *all* of him fit onto the balcony, no longer goatlike or serpentine or resembling a winged, bipedal dinosaur, lacking scales at all or even horns other than a faint hint of a pair of bumps at his hairline, entirely sans forked tail and without his sulfurous stench. If anything, he seemed to be wearing cologne. He had assumed a far more human aspect, immense but otherwise the extreme archetype and composite of tens of thousands of movie idols and rock stars, the perfect lust object in tight leather pants and a white, silken shirt split open in the middle to reveal a muscular, gleaming chest and a neck draped with jewelry.

And, decidedly, without wings.

Very much to the point, without wings.

Now it was Annabel's job to lean on the balcony in the tattered remains of her slinky dress, a condition of near nudity never being inappropriate for a witch even under ordinary circumstances, much less when she was heaving her assets and murmuring breathlessly, "Hey there, big boy . . . "

Satan turned, leering. He stepped toward the balcony. Below, there glowed no mere stars and galaxies, but the fires of Hell.

And it was Salome's job to give him a firm shove, precisely as Jezebel, shifting her position with more vigor than might have seemed possible, reached out with a cane she had not used in centuries and deliberately *tripped* him.

Then all Annabel had to do was get out of the way, as he let out a yell and was gone, very quick but not quick enough to work out the implications of not having any wings.

Annabel looked down. She thought she saw the Hell fires flicker.

"Oops," she said.

To no one in particular, Jezebel said, "The problem with corrupted souls and blackened hearts is that they tend to think of themselves first. Selfish and lazy, the lot of them."

"Even our vices have vices," said Salome.

"Like fleas having fleas," said Annabel.

"That's right, girls. Now help me up."

They helped her up, and she said, "We three actually do make a pretty good team, you know. Here, have a grape."

Around them, the House of the Witches settled back into its old, ramshackle, infinitely changing, shuddering self, with countless comfortable verandas and porches and balconies decorated with gingerbread trim, perched precariously on its basalt spire amid stars and galaxies, always about to topple off but never quite doing so.

Annabel sipped her brimstone cocoa. Jezebel and Salome played at knucklebones, trifling with the destinies of worlds, but no more than that, and if the gates of Heaven were ajar and the throne of God empty, they must have remained so, because none of the witches ever bothered to check them out.

For the two Sins to which Jezebel was especially devoted are as Deadly as any of the others, but they have the one self-limiting feature that they do not inspire ambition.

Such are the ways of wickedness.

THE ANISEED GUMBALL KID

ANDREW HOOK

A brainstorm with his partner, Sophie, led to the genesis of Mr. Hook's delightfully titled yarn, 'The Aniseed Gumball Kid'. 'I forgot about it,' he says, frowning at the memory. 'But then I found it written on the back of a recipe. A fortuitous find!' The author considers it a nostalgic piece, possibly because he had been reading Ray Bradbury around that time. As indeed should we all!

His most recent publications are the neo-noir crime novel, The Immortalists (Telos), *with its sequel* Church of Wire *to follow in 2015, and a collection of short stories,* Human Maps, *from Eibonvale Press. He has also recently edited an anthology of punk-inspired stories,* punkPunk! *for DogHorn Publishing, and is co-editor of the alt-poetry magazine,* Fur-Lined Ghettos. *You can find him at* www.andrew-hook.com.

W HEN SANDFORD'S WIFE AND CHILD LEFT, HE QUIT HIS JOB and found employment on the opposite side of town. He didn't want to see those familiar places anymore: the street, the shops, and especially the park. He changed his number and scrapped his car. He left his clothes in several black bin liners at a charity shop and restocked his wardrobe from the same store. He styled his hair differently and bought a different brand of toothpaste. Yet there were aspects of his life that bled in from the past that couldn't be avoided; such as the sky.

On sunny days, memories assaulted him through picnic blankets, warm sandwiches, and uncanned laughter. On wet days he was hit by the sloughing of rain from umbrellas and the digital flicker from windows backlit by television sets. On windy days, clinging onto his child's hand couldn't be avoided; that soft grasp. On other days, when the sky wasn't doing anything in particular, just looking *up* acted like a giant mirror into the past, as if above him the world ran along as normal and his life was intact.

Sandford hadn't told his new workmates about his wife and child. He orchestrated conversations so that they never existed. On some levels this was true. For what is existence but memory? Without memory, the past is never present.

Yet he was also careful not to lie; he remained noncommittal. Because lying created false memories which then became true. As true as any memory is truth, and as false as any truth is but a memory. This way, like a rake being drawn across a sandpit, he kept it upon himself to erase his footsteps.

Not to start afresh. Because starting afresh would open old wounds through coincidence. One relationship would remind him of the other. A prepared meal has no allegiance to the cook, but to taste. Sandford saw himself as driftwood on an endless sea. A sea no more than two inches in depth, containing no monsters.

Limiting his world to that of his spatial awareness gave him fresh perspective. People, vehicles, animals: these all seemed to come to life at the peripheries of his vision. As though as he moved forwards he triggered a hidden tripwire that activated a marionetted diorama. These people, vehicles, animals held no life other than that called into presence by his being. Once out of sight they ceased to exist. He became increasingly sure of this during his time at the office.

Sandford had worked in a handful of offices during his life. None of which were remarkable, either through the nature of the work or the workers themselves. In his new office he realised quickly how the staff fell into stereotypes: the dumb blonde, the surprisingly clever blonde, the SF nerd, the fat guy with glasses who blinked too rapidly, the married woman on the verge of having an affair, the token ethnic, the knowledgeable female, the motherly female, the unattractive temp, the chummy boss, the avoidable boss, the workmate who thought you liked him and who considered himself a friend but who you would never see socially. And so it went on.

Over his spiced chicken wrap—he no longer bought fish paste sandwiches—Sandford catalogued his fellow workers and found each correlated with an identikit counterpart in a previous office. Beryl was Carolyn was Cynthia. Wayne was Dwayne was Shawn. Emma was Sharon was Melissa. Raj was Raj was Raj. From this only one deduction could be made: his brain held a finite template of stereotypes from which to draw new people. Similar circumstances created similar people. The more he toyed with the idea, the more he decided to believe that was true. And the more he believed it was true, the more it became true.

After Sandford had been in the office a week he began to stray from his designated desk and spend more and more time at the water cooler.

The cooler faced a ground-floor window onto the street. Inside the office, people were obsessed with figures and targets and productivity and how to do things better. And those who weren't obsessed with those things pretended to be, until distinctions could no longer be made. Outside of the office, on the other side of the glass, life was completely different.

Men walked briskly or leisurely, not subjected to the demands of the workplace. Babies were manoeuvred in prams or pushchairs, unable to engage with the concepts of profit and loss. Cars adhered to speed limits, but their destinations were unknown. When Sandford bent to his knees to generate water from the cooler, he found he could look through the plastic container and view the street anew, distorted. Shapes, rather than figures, flitted back and forth; a cloudscape of colour. Faces, bodies, were blurred. When Sandford stood he experienced a slight dizziness, a rush of blood to the head, which he found it hard to attribute to any one sensation.

From the window, as well as the outside view, and the ghostlike ethereal half-reflections of his nearby colleagues, Sandford could also see marks on the glass itself where it was chipped or dirty or had had a static collision with a bird or a fly. It was this snapshot of reality, like a microscope slide, which began to fascinate him: not just the divide between one world to the next, but the falsely interstitial properties of the divide itself.

When his colleagues saw him staring at the window they couldn't comprehend what he was seeing. In fact, of course, what *they* saw was different.

Different also, was his opinion of those colleagues when they were outside the glass.

Some mornings Sandford would arrive at work early, and then regard his workmates' transformation as they came inside from outside, shedding individuality and creeping into conformity. And occasionally, in the evening, he would stay later and then watch as they became themselves again on the street. They were chameleons, the lot of them. And he was no different.

For some time, this was his existence. In role as observer. A year—maybe two—passed. Those memories which did assail him, assisted by the ever-present sky, became distorted like curled autumn leaves or melted snowflakes or oven burns, until it was impossible to know what had happened and what had actually happened. Most days, Sandford knew that what had happened had never happened. With this in mind, and with the rolling reality both inside and outside the office, he sublimated his life.

Then one morning—crisp, fresh, where the sky was a pale blue, the blue of someone's eyes that he couldn't quite recall—a gumball machine was installed beside the newsagents on the other side of the street. He had a clear view of it through the window, standing by the water cooler. The base was a deep pillar-box red, the middle section clear—filled with gumballs, the top also red. On the side that he couldn't see he imagined a metal dispenser with a money slot and a plate like a cat flap that you lifted to access the sweets. He imagined it thus and therefore it was true. Although his journey to and from work didn't take him past the gumball machine, he knew the flap existed and in some respects hindered access to the sweets as much as it ensured none fell onto the pavement.

Something about the dispenser tugged at something inside him.

When he stood by the water cooler, no matter what time of day, there seemed to be a kid standing by the machine.

At home, Sandford had started hoarding. In direct contrast to the life he left behind, where memory was the enemy, it seemed that behind closed doors he needed to be crushed by every aspect of his new existence.

Free newspapers local to the area were stacked, unread, in date order beside the stairs. Cardboard food packaging insulated the loft, beginning from under the eaves and extending backwards to the trapdoor, gaining height in a roof-ward pyramid. Tin cans, bereft of labels—which were steamed off, flattened, and supplemented the carpet—stood head to toe flanking the hallway like suits of armour in a stately home. Glass jars took up shelving space in the living room: not wasted, their contents contained finger and toenail clippings, the weekly mesh from his hairbrush, spat toothpaste, excrement, and a slowly increasing pile of eyelash, pubic, and eyebrow hair. Each day created less space in the property, reaffirmed his new identity, and shouldered out those old memories like excitable women at a garage sale.

Sandford spent his evenings watching his reflection in the television. A genuine reality show.

Those letters that he received, those that had to remain unopened, were buried deep in the garden.

The kid at the gumball machine would reach into the pocket of his shorts, pull out a coin, insert it into the machine, turn the mechanism, push a stubby finger behind the metal flap and pop the gumball into his mouth.

Sandford would stand by the water cooler, his thumb pressed against the plastic lever, waiting whilst his cup filled to the brim. He didn't have to look at it, familiarity and sound told him when to stop. Instead, his eyes to the gumball machine, he watched the kid chew for a moment, before the boy extended a numb tongue like a black carpet before turning away.

Sandford assumed it was aniseed and so it became aniseed. Not only for himself, but for the kid, too. He assumed the kid liked aniseed, and so he did.

Sometimes, caught up in the moment, Sandford would actually say: "Hey, do you see that kid?" or "See that kid?" or "You see that kid?" But immersed with deadlines and projects and very important matters none of his co-workers paused to answer. Often they didn't look up.

The kid wore grey shorts, knee-length, pockets stuffed with what Sandford could only imagine were sticky handkerchiefs, bits of string, cats-eye marbles, discarded chewing gum, smelly coins, pencils, scraps of paper with ideas for big machines, conkers. And so they were. The kid wore a white school shirt that had seen better days, colour washed into it, the cuffs and collar frayed like a mini-Elizabethan. Sometimes he wore a blazer, other times he didn't. Sometimes he was with friends, sometimes not. Sometimes with a mother, sometimes alone. Yet whenever Sandford went to the dispenser, unfailingly the kid was there.

He experimented. On some days Sandford waited until he was so parched from taking telephone calls relating to product that his tongue flopped in his mouth like a fish thrown onto a beach, until he could no longer function without a drink and he could smell his interior self. On those days, when he approached the water cooler, the kid approached the aniseed gumball dispenser.

On other days, he had barely drunk from his cup before he was back at the cooler, his bladder bursting from the intake, repeatedly filling up and drinking, filling up and drinking, watching the kid feed the aniseed gumball dispenser just as frequently, just as methodically. Yet never looking up, never looking through that glass window at him, at Sandford, just standing there popping gumballs into his mouth and then extending his tongue.

It was on those days—on those frequent water days—that Sandford was more likely to talk or gesticulate to his colleagues. To say, half in jest: "That kid'll rot his teeth, chewing all those gumballs" or "Look at that kid. Do you see that kid?" But his colleagues, few of whom ever seemed to venture near the water cooler—preferring the coffee machine or the kitchen, where they took turns to make herbal cups of tea—might barely look up and nod, before returning to their work. Their very important work which earned them the right and the money to be individuals. Or, so they believed.

One evening, Sandford returned home to find a free newspaper, some leaflets advertising pizza, kebabs, and a nearby Chinese takeaway, a plastic sack within which he might place clothes to donate to charity, and a handful of envelopes—some brown, some white—wedged behind his front door so that he had to put his shoulder to it to open it.

So many memories were trapped in the house that should the bricks and mortar and window frames and tiles be removed there would be a second house held intact within it. A house which Sandford told himself he could quite comfortably live within. And so he did.

Watching his reflection in the television screen, he switched off his mind and drifted into a sleep containing dreams under which he had no control; they were effortless fractal fairytales that swam from past to present and into possible futures. Sandford often couldn't recall his dreams upon waking, but this evening the ferocity of the visions assailed him as though he were standing on a beach battered with twenty-foot waves. Repeatedly images washed over him, drenched him to the bare nerve of consciousness, until he realised he wasn't standing on a beach at all, but before an office window from which fell consecutive panes of glass, as though he were the central figure in a flicker book with each pane a page, altering him as it fell, giving the appearance of movement.

When he awoke, he had a clear memory of his wife and child. The wife and child that had left him some time ago.

Because Sandford had slept fitfully, concentration failed him.

At the water cooler he realised his cup was overflowing onto his fingers at exactly the same time as he realised the kid was not standing by the gumball machine.

"Hey," he said to someone who was passing—Geoff? Jeff? Jess?—"Do you see that kid who isn't there? Do you see that kid who isn't by the water cooler?"

Kev? Keith? Katherine? answered: "Water cooler?"

"Gumball machine. Gumball machine."

"Gumball machine?"

"Kid."

"Kid?"

Sandford returned to his desk, dripping water.

He took a sip. Placed the cup on his desk, where it created a lagoon on the shiny surface. Returned to the water cooler.

There was still no kid by the gumball machine.

After thirty minutes, Sandford had twenty-nine plastic cups taking up space on his desk. Finally, he was getting noticed. But the kid still wasn't by the gumball machine.

Later, after the conclusion of the story, his work colleagues would tell anecdotes about the guy who repeatedly went to the water cooler one winter's morning when the heating had broken and so couldn't possibly have needed one cup of ice-cold water, never mind twenty-nine. Invariably, they wouldn't remember Sandford's name, but they would compare him to other oddballs they had worked with in other offices, those who kept themselves to themselves and who eventually disappeared, often not noticed even in absence until a few days after the event.

"There was that guy," they would say. "Do you remember? That guy with the plastic cups. At the water cooler."

And others would say, even those who worked in different offices, "Yes, that guy." Adding credence to the story from false memories.

But on this day: on the day after the dream of his estranged wife and child, on the day that the kid didn't return to the gumball machine, on *that* day, Sandford had felt compelled to walk out of the office—through the glass that changed everything—towards the newsagents on the other side of the road. As he walked, his memories of other offices, of other street scenes, of who and why he was, were pulled together until all the realities were folded up over his shoulder like a knotted handkerchief held to the end of a stick. Everything contained there.

With each step a new reality closed around him, a pressing reality not dissimilar to the contents of his house, with one significant difference: he was no longer burdened.

Each step was lighter. The sky above threw itself open, freshly painted with soft gleaming clouds.

The gumball machine shone like a beacon, the contents as black as tar.

As Sandford approached, it increased in size; so that when he stood where the kid had stood the top of the machine was head height. He reached into his pocket, a pocket stuffed with bits and pieces, crammed with his memories, and pulled out a coin. It was large and bronze and not of this time. He inserted the coin in the slot and turned the metallic handle. Within the mechanism the coin dropped, and then reality shifted for one of the gumballs and it fell into the dispenser with the sensation of vertigo. Sandford eased it out, sniffed it, then popped it into his mouth.

The taste was strangely familiar.

Sandford looked around for the kid in the shorts, but only noticed a series of faces pressed against the office window across the street, so indistinct as to appear sketches on the glass.

He stuck out his tongue, blackened and numb, and turned away to wait for his wife and his child. Who would be along shortly, sometime in the future.

Easy to Imagine

Ian Whates

Ian Whates currently has two published novel series: the Noise *books (Solaris), and the* City of 100 Rows *trilogy (Angry Robot). 50-odd of his short stories have featured in various venues, with two shortlisted for BSFA Awards, while his work has received honourable mentions in* Years Best *anthologies. His second collection,* Growing Pains *(PS Publishing), appeared in 2013. In his spare time Ian runs award-winning independent publisher NewCon Press, which he founded by accident in 2006. His view of Scarborough as a place of great beauty tinged with sepia—a wistful nostalgia for bygone days—helped inspire 'Easy to Imagine'. Either that or he's just getting old and nostalgic himself.*

H ER NAME IS CHLOE WEBSTER, AND SHE HAS A GOOD imagination.

Chloe always looked forward to visiting her grandpa. He lived in Scarborough, which was by the sea and hilly—as if a giant hand had grabbed hold of the land and crinkled it up—and it was so much more interesting than the flat grey drabness of the North London suburb where she lived with her parents.

This time around they were staying for almost a week—well, five days at any rate. Mum and Dad had gone out for the day, leaving her with Granddad. She didn't mind. She loved Granddad and he was full of stories. He had photographs too, but she wasn't really interested in such flat and lifeless residues. All she needed was a story or a place and she could see the people involved immediately, with far more vividness than any photograph could portray. She watched her grandma now, for instance, bending forward as she . . . *pours tea from a fat-bodied pot through a silver strainer and into the first of three floral patterned cups. A curl of steam rises from the cup as it steadily fills. The cup rests on a matching saucer; both bear a narrow gold rim. The best china; someone important must be visiting. There's movement in the street beyond, as somebody walks past the house, their identity obscured by the intervention of net curtains.*

Chloe had never known her grandma, who died long before she was born, but she felt as though she had, thanks to Grandpa's stories and the images they evoked. He spoke about her often, always with a half-smile or a wistful look. "Your grandma would have loved this," he'd say. Or: "That used to be Annie's favourite." Chloe knew that he missed her dreadfully, but not in a sad or forlorn way. Instead he seemed to bask in the love they so obviously had shared and to take comfort from its memory, while Chloe savoured the warmth of its reflection.

Grandma hadn't died in the sort of way that most people do—from old age or cancer or heart problems. It had been an accident, which happened while Mum was still a girl. Chloe didn't know the full details—she had never seen that particular memory, didn't *want* to see it—but she knew that Grandma had died in an 'incident'. That was how her mother described it, refusing to elaborate. But Chloe had overheard them talking about it and so learnt that Grandma had been run over by a bus. Granddad had never remarried. "There was only ever one woman for him," Mum had told her more than once.

"Well, Princess, what shall we do today, then?" Grandpa asked.

"Go into town," she said at once. "And have an ice cream!"

He chuckled. "At the Harbour Bar, I suppose."

"Yes, *yes!*" She instantly pictured one of their scrummy sundaes . . . *White ice cream laced with dark chocolate sauce piled up in an impossibly tall glass, with a fan wafer standing proud at the top. The woman serving has dark hair, tied back, and wears a bright yellow tunic. When she puts the sundae down she smiles broadly, as if taking pleasure in her customer's delight.*

"All right, if that's what you want . . . "

"And afterwards, chish and flps at Mother Hubbard's!"

"Steady on now, girl, we don't want you being sick, or your mum will never trust me to look after you again."

"Oh please, Grandpa."

"We'll see."

Granddad's home was in a residential street just off the Filey Road, which is a little way outside town. They went in on the bus, arriving at the stop to find no one else there, the little shelter unoccupied, but Granddad assured her they would only have to wait a few minutes. "They run a good service here, I'll give them that."

A bus draws up almost immediately. It is shorter than any she's seen before and the windows are too high up. At the front is a big black radiator grill, which sits directly below the driver's windscreen, and the windscreen looks too small. She wonders how he can possibly see all the things he needs to out of such a tiny window. Above the windscreen is a badge saying 'Wallace Arnold'. She can't help but wonder if this is the same sort of bus that knocked Grandma down.

The bus arrived within a few minutes, just as Granddad had promised. It was blue and long and looked perfectly normal.

They stepped up into the vehicle, confronted by the barrier that separated driver from the paying public, but the man smiled, his face crinkling warmly—everyone seemed friendlier here up north than they ever did back in London—and Grandpa spoke cheerily to him before they shuffled down the aisle to find seats. The bus was little more than half full, and they had no problem sitting together. More people boarded as they came closer to the town centre. A child two rows in front was whining continually and being a real brat. Chloe felt superior and was glad that *she* never behaved like that.

The journey was a mercifully short one—past the college grounds and on—though the last part seemed interminable, as they hit some local traffic. They got off near to Debenhams. Chloe didn't want to visit any of the shops, not today, though Granddad said he needed to go to the bank. She sat down and waited impatiently while he did whatever he had to, and then finally they made their way down the steep road that leads to the seafront.

A man in a navy blue jacket and flat cap holds a car door open for a woman in a pale yellow dress. She has dark brown hair—short but wavy and worn in a bob—and bright red lips. The car, which seems to consist of at least as much canvas topping as it does metal body, is tall and incredibly

*narrow. Chloe feels that it must surely topple over should it ever attempt
to take a corner too quickly. Another vehicle rumbles past, this one open-
topped and squat and nothing like the cars she is used to; instead, it looks
as if somebody began with a horse and cart, took the horse away and
simply stuck an engine on the front.*

Despite her earlier enthusiasm for an ice cream, when they actually
arrived at the Harbour Bar, Chloe settled on a milkshake instead, while
Grandpa opted for a coffee. Her shake was cold and frothy and full of
strawberry sweetness, just how she liked it.

"My Annie used to love the strawberry milkshakes here too," Granddad
said. She'd forgotten for a moment how long the Harbour Bar had stood
here, but then recalled Mum telling her that it had been on this same spot
even when Granddad was a boy.

"You remind me of your grandma in so many ways," he added. Chloe
loved to be told things like that. It made her feel closer to Granddad,
somehow.

They left the Harbour Bar and stepped back into the real world, with
her feeling all full of milkshake. Even Chloe had to admit that it was still
too early for lunch. Besides, she wasn't ready to leave the sea just yet and
Mother Hubbard's wouldn't be open at this hour, so she didn't argue when
Grandpa said, "I fancy going to the spa, are you up for that?"

"Sure, why not?" she replied.

They walked along the front, not hurrying. It was a glorious September
day, with summer evidently determined to make a final stand before
bowing out for the year. For once, the sea breeze, which so often seems to
blow off the water and temper the warmth this late in the season, had
decided to behave itself.

Chloe paid scant attention to the amusement arcades and the shops and
bars they passed on their right and even ignored the cinema, which on
another day she might have dragged Granddad into, pleading until he
gave in, as he always did. Today she only wanted to look out at the sea
and the waves and the sand.

A gull sailed past, soaring effortlessly on outstretched wings, as if to say,
Hey, this is how you really look at the sea.

Two boys, her age or perhaps a little younger, chased each other
across the beach, laughing and shouting, while their parents looked on
indulgently.

A group of children stand just within the lapping edge of the water—a mixture of boys and girls. They all wear vast straw boaters against the sun and high white-collared shirts that look ridiculous to Chloe's eye, and they hitch up the legs of their long trousers as they paddle in the shallows, giggling. Beside them tower a trio of wooden bathing huts supported by huge multi-spoked wagon wheels. These look even more ridiculous than the children's clothes.

"Are you all right?" Granddad asked.

"Yes, just thinking," and she smiled to reassure him.

She stopped walking as the theme to *The X Factor* suddenly sounded, startling her and sending her hand questing for the phone.

Granddad frowned. "Is that the best ring tone you could come up with?"

"There's nothing wrong with *The X Factor*!" She loved the show. Every year she and Mum and Dad would choose their favourites, one from each contestant category, so that they all had four rival acts to root for and follow throughout the rounds—their own private competition. "Hi, Mum!"

"Hi, love, are you having fun?"

"Yes, we're in town. We've just been to the Harbour Bar and I had a strawberry milkshake, and we're going to Mother Hubbard's later."

"Are you now? Well don't go wearing your grandfather out. And tell him I'll settle up when we get back tonight, okay?"

"Will do . . . Are you enjoying yourselves?" She couldn't remember for the moment what her parents were actually doing.

"Yes, everything's good here. Your uncle Tom says hi."

Ah yes, that was it; a sick relative. Boring.

"Listen, love," Mum said, "I have to go . . . See you this evening."

"Okay. Love you."

"Love you too."

She put the phone away and found Granddad smiling at her.

"Checking up to make sure we've been behaving ourselves, is she?" he said.

Chloe nodded. "Something like that."

"Well, we'll just have to make sure we *don't* then, won't we."

They both laughed.

The spa was only a short walk away, and they arrived there shortly after, the number of people thinning out as they moved away from the shops and arcades.

The promenade is packed. Elegant women wearing elaborate bonnets and prim long-sleeved dresses stroll beside men in blazers and white trousers and banded boaters—never touching; there are no held hands or looped arms in evidence here. Chloe notices that all of the men seem to sport moustaches or beards—more facial hair than she has ever seen in one place before—while the women each carry a parasol, some of which are open and held aloft while others are clasped down by their owners' sides in white-gloved hands, ready to be deployed should the sun become too much.

Chloe knew full well that the spa was a special place for Granddad and that he loved to come here, especially with her, perhaps because she reminded him so much of Grandma. She didn't mind—she liked it here too.

The spa stood right up against the edge of the beach, elevated behind a solid brick seawall. It was a grand old building of yellowed stone, with tall windows and domed turrets at the four corners and a low tower at the centre.

"You have to give it to the Victorians," Granddad said. "They certainly knew how to build things. You do know that this place is responsible for much of Scarborough's fame and fortune, don't you?" She did, but only because he had told her as much several times before. "People tend to forget that nowadays."

The setting was as impressive as the spa complex itself. Behind them rose a steep wooded slope, verdant and spectacular in the summer, though a little more muted and shot through with brown at this time of the year. At the top of the slope stood a long line of white buildings—which Chloe knew marked the course of a posh street called the Esplanade—as bright and gleaming as a Hollywood actor's smile.

Her favourite bit of the whole complex was at the far end of the main building: a white bubble that pushed out towards the ocean and was supported by its own little bulge in the seawall. It had various names—her mum always referred to it as the Pavilion, but Granddad said that was confusing because there had once been a Pavilion Hotel in Scarborough. Chloe preferred his name for it in any case. He called it the Sun Room. And that's exactly what it was.

The room was defined by a crescent of white columns which formed the framework for a series of huge glass plate windows—each two or three times the height of Grandpa, and if you squeezed your eyes tight you could pretend there was no glass there at all. The windows gazed out to sea and provided a fabulous panoramic view. The floor was a striking contrast of monochrome crosshatch formed by great black and white squares, like a giant chessboard, and the ceiling . . . *Ah, the ceiling* . . . was provided by the sun and the clouds and the sky. This was an open-air room. Chloe had been here when rain bounced off the chequered tiles and even then it was beautiful, but today, with the sun shining high above them and the sea visible through a host of picture windows with no haze to mask the horizon . . . today was when you saw this place in its full glory.

"Your gran and I had some wonderful evenings here," Grandpa said. "The music, the dancing . . . "

A band occupies the small stage—a raised plinth at the apex of the room's arc, a sort of blister on the bubble. There are a lot of musicians and they look a bit cramped in the small space, but they still smile and the music flows unfaltering. It's night time and the centre of the floor is filled with a swirl of dancing couples, all circling the floor beneath a canopy of stars. Everyone is elegantly dressed and the whole scene has a magical, otherworldly feel.

Chloe suddenly recognises the nearest couple: Grandma and Grandpa! She focuses on Grandma first, fascinated to see her like this, so glamorous, so very different from how Chloe is used to seeing her: pouring the tea or nattering with neighbours or simply pottering around the house. Today she looks radiant, in a navy blue cocktail dress—taffeta, maybe? The pleated skirt falls to just above the ankle, and modesty at the bust line is maintained by a sequin insert, which glitters as brightly as the stars.

Granddad too looks dashing, in a black evening suit—and still a young man, though this doesn't surprise Chloe, who has seen him like this before. The pair glide across the floor, happy and perfectly at home here, though they are soon lost from sight among the other dancing couples.

Chloe is thrilled to catch a glimpse of such a wonderful moment, to share in it, however briefly.

Something catches her eye; a flash of blue, in the shadows beyond the tables on the far side of the dance floor. She recognises the dress immediately as Grandma's and she strains to see more. The woman is with someone, a man, and they're leaning into one another, kissing. Chloe smiles: Granddad and his Annie, together as they were always meant to be.

Then the man turns towards her, and his face catches the light. She sees him properly for the first time and is shocked to realise that this isn't Grandpa at all, that it's no one she knows; a stranger. Beyond him, now that they're no longer kissing, she can see Grandma, who seems anxious not to be seen by anyone.

It reminded her of when she had seen Mum kissing Mr Johnson, who lived next door. Of course, neither of them had really been there. Mum was upstairs at the time, doing the cleaning—Chloe could hear the rhythmic drone of the vacuum—and Mr Johnson hadn't even set foot in the house since the weekend before last, when he and his wife had come round for a barbeque with their daughter, Olivia; 'Orrible Olivia, who was nearly a year older than Chloe and an utterly spiteful cow. Even so, even though they *couldn't* have been there, Chloe had seen the two of them, in the kitchen, as clearly as if they were.

Mr Johnson and Mum, clinging to each other and snogging, just like Grandma and the stranger. What Chloe will recall most vividly afterwards is the way Mr Johnson's hand slides down past her mum's waist to grab hold of her buttock and squeeze . . .

Of course, Mum was initially shocked when she asked her about kissing Mr Johnson, but soon recovered her composure, to laugh and shake her head and say, "Honestly, Chloe, the things you come out with. You're very special, you know that? You've got such a vivid imagination . . . But be careful what you say to others, love, or it could land you in all sorts of trouble one of these days. Other people don't see things the way you do. It's your *private* world, you see, not to be shared with anyone else. I think it's best if you keep it that way, don't you? People might not understand . . . "

Chloe thought long and hard about that. She'd never considered until then that her visions were unusual. She'd always assumed that everyone saw the sort of things she did. In the end, though, she trusted her mum, and from that day forward she kept quiet about them.

She could see Grandma again, but the scene had shifted.

There's daylight now, and two people stand before her. Granddad and Grandma, though no longer dressed in the finery they wore at the dance. They're no longer at the spa but in the street; somewhere in town, she thinks. They're arguing, and she senses instinctively that the row is caused by the other man, the stranger from the dance. Grandma is obviously upset and it looks as if she might have been crying. Grandpa is furious. Chloe has never seen him so angry. He grabs hold of Grandma's shoulders and shakes her. She struggles to break his grip, pushing him away. Chloe is suddenly frightened that he might hit her, and she doesn't want to witness that. But he doesn't; instead he lets go, or perhaps Annie breaks free. It all happens so quickly. Grandma stumbles back, retreating from her husband's fury, and she trips, the heel of her left shoe catching on the pavement. She falls backward, into the road. Only then does Chloe see the bus. She knows that it will never be able to stop in time.

Chloe squeezed her eyes shut, refusing to watch what came next.

"Chloe . . . Princess?"

"I'm . . . I'm all right, Grandpa," she lied, forcing her eyes to open again.

The images had gone. There was only the chequered floor, the white columns, and the sea.

Grandpa looked worried, so she smiled. An automatic gesture and an empty one, but it seemed to reassure him.

"Do you want to head back into town?" he asked. "Mother Hubbard's still won't be open for a while, but . . . "

"No, not just yet," she said quickly. "Maybe in a minute."

She had to calm down, to settle her thoughts back into the here and now. And she wanted to make sense of what she'd just witnessed.

She almost said something then, to Grandpa, but her mother's words came back to her: *People might not understand* . . . Chloe didn't doubt her visions, didn't disbelieve them for a moment, but they were something *other*, to be kept tucked away in their own compartment, separate from the rest of her life. They were there, they were real, but they were different. *Her* imagination. Hers and no one else's.

Nothing she had seen today at the spa, nothing she had thought, changed anything. Mum was still her mum and Grandpa was still her grandpa.

"Are you sure you're all right, Princess?"

"I'm fine, really," she said, and meant it this time. She giggled and cuddled up to him to emphasise the point, his arm automatically going around her. "I was just imagining, that's all."

"Yes, well . . . It's easy enough to do that here," Grandpa agreed.

The two of them stood in silence, cuddling and staring out at the sea.

THE GLASSHOUSE

EMMA COLEMAN

Emma Coleman has lived in Northampton all her life, which perhaps explains why her fiction tends to focus on the quirky and darker aspects of human nature. She has previously been published by Greyhart and NewCon Presses, her first story for the latter, 'Home', gaining honourable mention in Ellen Datlow's Year's Best *as well as being longlisted for the Bram Stoker Award. Among other things, Emma would find it unpleasant to live without darts and David Bowie, but could very happily live without either milky tea or UKIP. 'The Glasshouse' was inspired by the music of Kate Bush.*

MOONLIGHT REFLECTED IN THE GLASSHOUSE, HIGH-lighting implements and surfaces of shiny metal. Some of the cages were as clear as if it was the summer afternoon sun staring down into the see-through house, and I thought, 'Is he out there, just outside and waiting, watching me?'

I was sitting in a high-backed chair and melted into its deep, dark wood. An occasional rustling passed softly through the silence. I saw the full moon; as round and as bright as a military button, way up above me.

"What am I going to say to him?" I asked myself. I had hatred in my mind and nothing but hurt to give him. I didn't know when he would return, but I was determined to stay; all I could feel was his little captives' fear and I didn't want to leave them.

I had seen the old man before, many times, out in the wood. He was tall but stooped, the passing of years weighing him down and his silvery, wispy hair grew long. He seemed to have the weather hanging around him; the wind and the rain but never the sun. He didn't deserve to have that.

As the moon passed over, my fears became more acute. Not for myself but for them.

I shifted in my seat, twitching with empathy; how they must be feeling! The glinting of the moonlight faded and morning was breathing.

"Oh no."

And the first sound of pain pierced my soul.

I'd watch him in the wood. Always alone, he trudged through the trees with a net and brown sack. He'd stop at certain times, listening hard and looking up to the canopy. Sometimes he would shrug his shoulders and continue on his way. Other times he wouldn't.

I wanted to know why he was doing this. So I came to find out. Half of me wished I hadn't come—that I'd just ignored this feeling of anxious curiosity—while the other half was glad to have come, to be there and show love and that not all humans were like him. But still I didn't know what I could do.

The cages were metal and padlocked. I had tried to lift one, intending to carry them out, one by one. But the cage was so heavy, I could barely heave it up an inch before dropping the box back down.

"I'm sorry, I'm sorry!" I whispered urgently, through the bars.

I hoped they knew I was trying to help.

The first time I saw him catch one I was sick with rage and despair.

"What are you doing?!" I screamed, but the old man was deaf to my shouts and he hurried away, the brown sack tied up and safe in his cruel hands.

The next time, I followed him.

He moved quickly and stealthily through the trees and I lost sight of him after twenty minutes.

"What exactly do you expect from doing this?" I asked myself after a sudden feeling of paranoia rose up inside me. "Why can't you just leave him alone?"

"Because he's evil," I said aloud, as the cries became higher and higher and the sun crept up, dousing everywhere with soft, hazy light.

"I wish it was last night again," I whispered through the mesh of one of the cages. "At least I knew you were safe then."

The bird was crying and I was helpless.

I had been determined not to lose him next time he came into view. I wanted to break his soul the way he had broken so many tiny, beating hearts.

I saw him near a gigantic oak tree; he seemed pathetic and insignificant in comparison.

"If only he was," I said, fully knowing how much power he had.

He was leaning against the trunk, no doubt taking a rest after his despicable work, and poking tobacco into the bowl of his pipe. He lit this and drew on it slowly; puffs of blue-tinged smoke hanging in flat webs above his head. Once satisfied, he moved on, the smoke weaving and swirling behind.

I followed the trail with no idea of where I was going to end up. Where did the old man take his little captives? And, above all, what did he do to them?

I stood up straight, fortifying my spirit, and kept on behind him.

I had scarcely believed what I saw: a glasshouse in a small clearing of the deepest and densest part of the wood. A perfect little house made of crystal-like glass. A few net curtains, tatty and full of holes, were drawn over parts of the walls.

"What is this place?"

I'd lost sight of the man moments earlier, but surely this was where he'd disappeared.

Dusk was approaching fast, the canopy making night more threatening.

I crouched down and waited. Minutes passed when I noticed the curtains being tugged back, exposing dim candlelight and the old man pacing about. I saw him fall heavily into a high-backed chair and then pick up something, maybe a sheet of paper or large envelope, but I wasn't sure.

In that moment he appeared to be quite sad; weary, lonely, and guilty. The way he sat hunched and small in that chair, his head barely held up from fatigue and a forefinger rubbing his closed eyes slowly.

Maybe he was tired from his hard day's work. And maybe he was the happiest man alive.

I had waited in that spot; I was frightened by just how dark the night could be. Only the glow from the man's candle provided any light . . . until, as if by magic, the moon had shone bright and strong. I could see trees and logs and the highlighted clouds as clear as day.

The old man stared out from his glasshouse, and I slipped down further behind my cover; there was every chance he could catch sight of me but, instead, he hurriedly blew out the candle and moved away. He had his equipment and was leaving.

I gave him a while to walk on; to be sure he was nowhere near as I moved toward the building.

Peering in, I could make out a table beside the high-backed chair and rows of sideboards, glinting in parts like polished metal, covered with what I assumed were cages.

I found the door secured by two sturdy bolts, and I gently pulled them back.

Deathly silence waited inside.

I moved as quietly and cautiously as the old man himself; I didn't want to disturb anything or cause fright.

There must've been at least thirty cages in that glasshouse, all partially covered with tea towels or old sweaters.

I lifted several covers, trying to make out anything in the dark, but I could only hear rustling and weak chirping. I tried to heave up one of the cages, but it was too heavy. The panicked bird inside screeched and I dropped the box, whispering my pathetic apologies.

"I'm sorry, I'm sorry!"

I felt I was doing more harm than good and so went to sit in his chair; I was going to wait for him. I didn't know what I was going to say; I just wanted to shout and scream, to make him stop.

The cushion had a lingering, cosy heat and I got up, throwing it to the floor. I didn't expect him to have any warmth and found it disturbing to feel his presence. I sat back on the cold, wooden seat and felt better.

Glancing at the table I noticed the paper I'd seen him reading earlier. I picked this up and struggled to read the exquisitely small and old-fashioned handwriting. Bending the manuscript this way and that, I managed to understand what it was that I had found.

A death list.

A neat column of bird names all of which had, neatly written beside them, a price. I slowly read, quietly uttering out what was before me.

"Single wren, five pounds; one jackdaw, three pounds; greenfinch, three pounds; nightingale, fifty pounds; swallow, fifteen pounds; ring-necked dove, five pounds; barn owl, fifty pounds . . . "

The list went on but I could no longer read for I was shaking with rage. I tore the sheet of paper to shreds, the pieces falling around my feet like plucked feathers.

As the night wore on my thoughts grew dark.

"I hate you," I whispered. "I hate you."

Nothing in the world would've induced me to leave and I glanced about the glasshouse, trying to catch a sign of his return and I wondered if he was outside, watching me.

"I'm waiting for you, you bastard."

I was wide awake, the passion burning in my brain, the thumping of my heart keeping me upright and ready to lash out.

The occasional ruffling and fluttering of weak wings passed through the glasshouse.

Hours must've gone by when I noticed the little see-through prison becoming brighter.

"Oh no."

I rubbed my eyes and massaged my stiff neck when, suddenly, the first desperate shriek of birdsong erupted from one of the cages. My heart felt like it was breaking and burning and bursting.

"What can I do? How can I help?!"

The tears flowed freely; I was frantic, my vision blurring as if I were looking into a broken kaleidoscope.

The sun grew in strength until every cage was a musical box playing tunes of despair.

"Please!" I begged them; the noise was too much for me, and I wanted them to stop. I began pacing about, not knowing why, clasping my hands to my ears and whispering, "Please, please don't, please don't."

And then I saw it: a tiny, shining key hanging from a hook by the door. I ran to it, snatching the key and staring in wonder at the power I now had.

"Don't worry, everything's going to be alright!" I laughed out loud. My hand was shaking and I thought, 'I must act quickly, he could return any minute.' I had to release them all.

I began by throwing off all the covers and then, with a prayer, I shakily fed the key into a padlock. A satisfying twist, a click and the lock sprung open, though I didn't open the door; I wanted them all ready to be freed at the same moment.

My hand was trembling even more from the pressure of succeeding but I did it.

I was panting and looking at the unlocked doors, preparing myself to fling them all open and set the captives free, when something caught my eye. There was movement outside and I saw him lumbering slowly through the undergrowth, carrying his brown sack; a tied-up and loaded brown sack and I gritted my teeth.

"You are *not* getting away with this!" I screamed out at the top of my lungs.

I caught a glimpse of his startled, tired face before I lunged across to the nearest cage and wrenched open the door.

As I worked quickly, I heard a faint shout but I continued until only one cage remained.

There was a crash and a small cupboard was sent flying as the old man ran into his glasshouse with a look of utter bewilderment.

"What are you doing?" he cried, his voice wavering.

Standing by the last cage, I replied, "The right thing." And I opened it.

Time seemed to slow down; we stared at each other, his face a waxwork of disbelief. We looked to the cages; I knew he was yelling, "No," but he sounded muffled and far away, and we both heard their wings, their shuffling claws as they got ready to take flight. But then time caught up.

They didn't stand a chance. Eager and desperate, the birds spread their wings and flew fast, fleeing their prisons with such desire.

I was dumbstruck; static as an incredible cold rushed from my head to my feet.

The old man fell to his knees, throwing his hands up to his face and screaming, "No! No! No!" over and over again until he could only moan and sob with grief.

I stared at him, feeling a stranger to myself. Everything was so unreal.

Little, broken bodies scattered the glasshouse. Blood spattered the windows, the see-through ceiling and I wondered dreamily what had happened.

A tiny, white, and beautiful feather drifted down slowly and I watched, stretching out my arm and gently catching it in my open hand.

"What have I done?" I whispered, staring blindly at the brown sack the old man had brought in. It was moving, the bird inside flapping and chirping. He pulled the bag to him and deftly pulled out a blackbird. He cradled her to his chest, whispering and weeping, the tears gathering in his trench-like wrinkles.

"What did I do?" I asked, dumbly.

Without a word, the man carefully got to his feet and walked away, leaving me alone in his glasshouse.

Through brimming eyes I watched as he carried his blackbird. Stumbling among the ferns and bracken, he seemed to me now like an old nature god, serene and timeless and part of the wood.

Crouching down, he stroked the plumage lovingly; a great, hard thumb softly, delicately following the lines of her feathers, all the while speaking to her quietly.

And then the blackbird was released; he opened his large, gnarled hands and she sprang out, stretching her dark, brown wings as wide as she could, flying away into the trees.

The sight broke me. I cried and I screamed.

"God what have I done?!"

My knees gave way and I collapsed, catching my face on the corner of a table, but the pain was blotted out; I felt nothing.

White papers fell gently, mockingly, from the tabletop and I wanted to cause myself so much physical pain.

Screaming again, I grabbed at the sheets of paper, clutching them tightly to myself as if they were alive. When I held one out before me, I could see that same exquisite and old-fashioned handwriting. But this wasn't a death list, it looked like a letter.

'Happy,' stood out and, 'pleased,' and my breathing became slower as I read the words with numb reality.

Dear little Carol,

Thank you for your lovely card and photograph; you looked so very happy to release the pretty blue-tit, and I know how much good it did you. I was sorry to learn of your poorlyness and I hope getting close to your favourite bird helped keep that beautiful smile on your face. I'm sure Mrs Blue-Tit was just as joyful to meet you as you were to meet her. Remember to take care of our feathered friends; they're incredibly precious, just like you.

If you ever have need to call on me and my family again, then please do come. My thoughts are with you and your mother, dear girl.

From your loving old friend,
Samuel Rowntree

I shakily picked up another sheet and read through a similar response; this letter was addressed to a gentleman named Mr Chater, someone who suffered from fear and loneliness. He had requested a swallow; a symbol of his childhood days, 'when the world had been kinder to you than it is now,' Samuel had written, 'and when innocence felt infinite.'

I dropped the letters.

I looked out to catch sight of Mr Rowntree, but he had gone.

Left with the little bodies and the carnage I had caused, I cried my rotten heart out.

ALL THE LAYERS OF THE WORLD

STEVEN UTLEY AND CAMILLE ALEXA

Camille Alexa is very proud of having collaborated on this story with the late Steve Utley. 'In his last correspondence regarding "All the Layers of the World", he spoke in his typically elliptic and bluntly poetic manner of moving "credibly into the incredible—toward something truly inexplicable". I would never have been able to capture the intent of our piece so succinctly, nor am I certain two writers—even two writers writing on the same story, with great affection and respect for one another's work—could ever be said even to have the same intent, much less the same experience, writing being what it is. More pertinent is the last line of that particular email, the spirit of which captures "All the Layers of the World" and the writing of it, at least for me:

... So glad you're having fun with this. Do I know how to show a gal a good time, or what? Yers, Steven

You sure did, Mister Utley.'

Alex C. Renwick has written dozens of short stories and scads of poetry as Camille Alexa. Her solo work appears in Alfred Hitchcock's *and* Ellery Queen's Mystery Magazine, Fantasy Magazine, *and* Imaginarium: The Best Canadian Speculative Writing. *Her award-nominated short fiction collection,* Push of the Sky, *was an official reading selection of Portland's Powell's Books SF Book Club.*

T HIS PLACE WAS SO FAR OFF THE MAIN ROADS, LAUREL'S phone didn't even get decent reception. She coasted along the quiet narrow street, one hand on the wheel and one digging in her purse for the paper scrawled with an address in her loopy narrow handwriting, having a hard time believing she was lost in a town the size of Treasure, Texas, population 894.

But it wasn't as though she'd gotten lost, exactly. More like she'd been hypnotized by the poky streets, by the crooked cottages glowing in sunlight, by the crimson surprise lilies pushing up in neat rows and by the sleepy glances of sleek cats and fat dogs lolling on whitewashed wooden porches with gingerbread trim, relics of another era. The day was one of those perfect first few of spring, temperature just right for a simple cotton sundress, maybe a hat—nothing yet suggesting the blistering glare of the impending Texas summer. It was what Laurel's great aunt would've called *hot-tea weather*, the first two words run together as one. In a few short weeks the temperatures would be topping out over a hundred every day. Then would come month after month of triple digits, nobody willingly going outdoors for longer than it took to get from air-conditioned car to air-conditioned office or classroom or shopping mall. By July, by August, these half-paved streets would be asphalt ovens, melted in the centers and crumbling at the edges. The gingerbread cottages with their swept porches would look dingy and dusty and raw, the paint peeling, white curls and lead-laden flakes littering crisped lawns like party confetti thrown after a wildfire. The cats and dogs and every other living creature would be hiding from the punishing sun, and no one in her right mind would be wandering the streets looking for the Visitors & Historical Center of Treasure, Texas.

And suddenly there it was: a repurposed 1920s Texas shack-style outbuilding with window units choking the small curtained squares, weighing down the sagging wooden sills. The tires of Laurel's sleek silver car kissed the soft rolled edge of the old-fashioned curb. She killed the engine and dropped the keys into her pocket. Though her fingers hovered a moment over her sketchpad and charcoals, she moved instead to press the door handle, open the door, and step out, leaving the flat notebook along with the drawing materials still in their box on the smooth leather seat.

She crunched up the short gravel path, pausing to study the small cannon mounted in front of the squat, sunken building. It seemed all out of scale: the sloping roof, the cannon, the short swath of green lawn studded with wildflowers. All were foreshortened, the colors bright and flat. The cannon looked like a child's toy, stubby, barely three feet long, and painted black over black over black, previous decades' chipped coats visible under the resurfaced gloss like inscrutable bas-relief. A plaque mounted below claimed the gun had been used during the Civil War to fire from the sides of riverboats paddling up and down waterways hundreds of miles away from the wide shallow depression snaking through the middle of Treasure, its patchy silver down the center of the sandy riverbed glinting like liquid tin. The cannon's overall travels were thought to consist of some one hundred thousand miles, ribboning back and forth along the rivers of the South, transported by mule team over land when it had to be. It remained a mystery, whatever force of history or nature had brought it to become abandoned beside a mastodon skull in the sandy bottom of the riverbed stretching away behind the Visitors & Historical Center, winding off past the edge of town. From the small rise where she stood, Laurel could see the river looping past the railroad tracks, past the dinky county highway out toward the countless acres of monotone scrub, a trail of tangled growth sprouting along the water's edge, a shaggy green beard on the otherwise clean-shaven face of the land.

The shuttered dimness of the Historical Center was cool after the street. Laurel ducked slightly to clear the whitewashed lintel over the front door and descended the single step into the low angular building, a muffled shop bell twangling softly above her left ear. She closed the door behind her and stood squinting, feet sinking into antique carpet, eyes adjusting to pale light filtering in slanted rays past shaggy lace curtains and half-drawn blinds.

She studied the shelf by the door, small stacks of brochures neatly arranged. Most were slick advertisements for attractions a hundred miles or more up or down the lone paved road running through town straight as a two-lane ruler. Brochures with titles like *Natural Wonder Caves of the South* or *The Biggest Rollercoaster in Texas* or *The World's Largest Christmas Store: Opened 368 Days Per Year*—one was simply billed as *Mystery Hill*. Sparingly scattered among the rest were simple faded photocopied brochures for more local attractions. Homemade drawings and hand-lettered pages promised such things as the sweetest pies in the county, or river rocks the "exact spitting image of every president to ever hold the office in the United States of America." In these last, the *I* had been left out of *America* in the original photocopy, and someone had written it in on every page in blue ballpoint pen.

"Honey, you here for a tour?"

Laurel looked up, replacing the Presidential Rocks brochure as a small woman approached across the mismatched Victorian carpets. The woman's lurching gait was strangely even, as though she limped equally on both feet.

She returned the woman's smile, a pucker in the small round face. "Hello. Yes, please, if it's not too much trouble."

The woman cocked her head to one side. Her hair, a crisp helmet of white curls, glowed pale lavender in the muted afternoon rays of faded light. "I bet you're that nice magazine girl from the city, come to write about Treasure afore they tear everything down to build that Mall of the Century. From Dallas, was it?"

"Austin, ma'am. But yes, I called last Tuesday."

She gave Laurel another pucker, eyes crinkled by the smile. "Then let me show you around."

There were ancient newspapers and a collection of arrowheads. Swords and firearms dating from the Civil War, a weather-beaten saddle, an operating table that had belonged to the local doctor in the late 1800s. A model of the ferry once used to transport nearby townsfolk across the Colorado River shone soft green and gold.

"And this," the woman said, her graceful-ungainly gait carrying her to a lurching halt beside a lumpy, discolored mound with deep sockets, with pits and scars and uneven patches of varying textures, "is our prize exhibit, our mastodon. Well, just the skull. That's all they ever found in Treasure."

Surrounded by hand-tatted christening gowns and moth-worn needlepoint cushions and gilded chocolate cups brought over from one Old Country or another by grandmothers' grandmothers, the skull perched on a circular Chippendale dining table with no leaves. A large doily rumpled limply beneath the brittle ivory lump, which was big, but smaller than Laurel would've expected.

"It's between nine and twenty million years old," the tiny woman said in her breathy little voice, miniature like her stature, wispy but hard like her lavender hair. "At least, that's what the gal from the University said. And they found it *right* down there"—she pointed vaguely toward a rear wall—"right in the creek, right below the center."

The same skull, then, which had been discovered in such close and unlikely quarters with the painted cannon. Laurel's fingers, tingling, stretched toward the uneven mound. "May I?" she asked.

The woman smiled, conspiratorial, crinkle-eyed. "You're not supposed to, but go ahead."

Laurel pressed her fingers against the ancient bone. It was hard, but surprisingly spongy, hollow-feeling. She wondered if that were an effect of having lain in a sandy creek bed for a nearly unfathomable number of seasons. Water and sand coming and going. Flood and drought and sun and wind.

"Nine million years or twenty," she murmured. "Either way, it's the oldest thing I've ever touched." Then she shook her head. "No, that's not true. I wrote a short piece for the magazine on Enchanted Rock—they say that's a billion years old or more. But this is the oldest thing I've touched that used to be *living*."

"Everything in the center used to belong to the living, one way or another. Our most recent acquisition is that World War Two outfit"—the tiny woman pointed to a particular glass case, one containing a bemedaled Army dress uniform mounted on a leaning, faceless mannequin—"donated by a local veteran just afore he died. Most people nowadays don't appreciate the importance of being connected with the past. Like the people who're going to build that big factory outlet thingie here, or whatever it is. They think the past is something to be bulldozed out of the way to make way for the new." Here she demonstrated, pushing the air with her small wrinkled hands as though shoveling aside invisible history. "But the past is always with us. It moves us along from moment to moment. William Faulkner said—you know who William Faulkner was? They still teach him in schools?"

Laurel blinked. "Yes, of course. The writer."

"Well, Mister Faulkner said the past isn't dead, that it isn't even past."

Laurel found herself wondering what thing of her own, really her own, as each of these relics and artifacts had been somebody's own, might still exist in a hundred years. The list of possibilities was short; her possessions were limited to the anonymous products of industry, her creations to drawings, a painting or two, and the ephemera she wrote for the small arts-and-entertainment print magazine. Their depressingly slim prospects for long-term survival, it struck her, derived from their showing none of the care and craftsmanship that had gone into these cushions and christening clothes before her. The museum was stocked with items from a time when things weren't simply thrown away once they'd fulfilled their original purposes. What would become of the things she had made? What actually became of the mediocre and worse works of art created by people who didn't rank with the great or even the merely truly good? Were they politely consigned to attics to rot away to dust, or circulate through yard sales and flea markets until they just fell apart, or were they rudely cast into the trash with yesterday's coffee grounds? She imagined strata of the detritus of popular culture packed together in the earth, awaiting the attention of some future archeologist, and then for some reason she thought of the barrel of the museum's cannon, with its bas-relief of chipped paint, like a map of the past showing through the most recent surface of gloss.

Her vision dimmed. The room around her became indistinct and unreal for a moment.

The woman touched Laurel's arm, light as the brush of a feather. "Darlin', are you all right?"

"Yes," Laurel said with a start, a shudder running the length of her spine as she brought herself back. "I'm so sorry. But this skull"—she gestured vaguely toward the irregular mass—"it's really very... *captivating*."

The sense of disorientation lingered as she left the museum. She wondered as she got into her car what she was likely to find in the way of a cafe in a town of 894 residents. Though she still felt a little faint, almost dizzy, she decided to wait until she reached Austin to eat. It would mean hours of driving first, but all that stuff in the museum, all that detritus, those abandoned artifacts crowded close in her imagination, making it hard to breathe. Certainly didn't do anything for her appetite.

The road out of Treasure rolled along, remaining seemingly as straight as a yardstick between alternating stretches of farmland and stumpy pine woods, mile after mile. The nausea when it hit her came on suddenly, unexpectedly, setting her stomach roiling. Her hand slipped on the steering wheel. She touched her forehead; it felt cold and clammy, her fingertips coming away slick with perspiration. She pulled the car onto the weedy edge of the road and put it out of gear. The queasiness worsened. She fumbled the seatbelt loose, flung open the car door, and stumbled around to the passenger side. Here, with both hands braced against the side of the car, she lowered her head just in time. The little she had in her came up.

When even the dry heaves had ended she took a wobbly step away from the mess and looked around. No other cars were in sight. What the hell was wrong with her? It couldn't be food poisoning; she'd eaten nothing since that morning. And with the way things had gone this past year or so in the romance department—or lack thereof—no way could she be pregnant. She stood looking down the roadside embankment, which sloped into an evergreen thicket. Nothing moved down there, nothing made a sound above the constant cicadic hum, and yet she had the feeling of being observed by some unseen and unknown entity in the woods. Her heart tightened in her chest. The pulse jumped erratically in her throat and sweat trickled down the back of her neck. *This*, she thought with a strange clarity, *is dread*.

Laurel stumbled back to lean her throbbing head against the side of her car, trying to breathe deeply, evenly, waiting for her stomach to stop its churning, waiting for the sour taste in her throat to dissipate as she repeatedly swallowed. The rounded metallic window trim felt warm under her forehead, the window cool to her touch. On the passenger seat the sketchbook shone, parchment-colored and dry like the pages of the antique bibles back in Treasure's soon-to-be-demolished Visitors & Historical Center. Dry like the brittle edges of starched lace bonnets worn by infants long dead. Dry like the coarse spongy hardness of old bone and tusk.

Draw something: that's what Laurel should do. Sketching always made her feel better, gave her a way to define the chaos of the world, describe it, and organize it. As they had back at the mastodon skull, Laurel's fingers tingled. She ducked in and grabbed her charcoals and sketchbook, ignoring the gentle *bing, bing* of the car's reminder that the door was open and the keys inside. She scrambled over the edge of the embankment down toward the trees, the grade steeper than it had seemed from the road. The chitinous drone of cicadas or some equally persistent insect filled her head more than her ears, making the hard lump of panic rising in her chest feel more present and more distant, simultaneously. Her shoes—suited to the city, to air conditioning and sidewalks, too slick for tromping through Texas countryside—skittered down the slope, sending a shower of gray pebbles and brown winter needles from the evergreen shrubs.

Sketchbook clutched in one hand and charcoals in the other, Laurel flailed for balance, managing to keep upright all the way to the bottom. Underbrush thorns raked bloody furrows in her cheeks and arms during her descent, but she hardly noticed their sting. It had been a long time since she'd lived in the country; Laurel had grown accustomed to steel and glass, to paved jogging paths and indoor concerts and controlled temperatures. She'd forgotten how, out in the Texas countryside, everything bites and stings. Burrs and chiggers, rattlesnakes and nettles. When was the last time she'd even been stung by a mosquito in the city? Not since they started spraying after the West Nile scare. As a kid she'd been taught to always tap her shoes out in the mornings, in case a scorpion had crawled up in there during the night. Did scorpions even exist anymore, in places where humans had taken over? Where they'd laid out their acres of pavement, their tamed xeriscape yards, their outlet malls and their big-box stores?

Her stomach gave another warning heave and she forced herself to calm down. *Breathe*, she reminded herself. *Just breathe* . . . .

Down among the spindly trees, her panic ebbed again. The journalist in her hated such nebulous spasms, such lack of courage in the face of no evident threat. It could strike like that, though, dread. It could creep up, strangle you with its choking fullness.

"See? There's nothing here," she muttered at the scrawny tree trunks, saying it out loud to make it more real. The ratcheting insectoid buzz pressed in from all sides at once, all directions at once, even from above and below . . . .

Below. Especially from below.

She sat with a total lack of grace or forethought, her knees and legs crumpling under her rather than lowering her to the ground. Brown twigs and pointy dead live-oak leaves crackled under her weight. The insect sounds ceased abruptly, leaving the air empty and ringing.

She fumbled a charcoal pencil from the box with trembling fingers. Flipped the sketchpad to an empty page with a rapid shush-shush of rustling paper. No breeze stirred the stiff trees, the clumps of yellow grass. Though spring greenery had been evident back in town, it was still mono-chromatic in the gulley. Brown dirt, brown branches, shed brown needles, brown dropped leaves. Brown against brown against brown.

The charcoal left its first black smudges on the paper the color of sun-bleached hide. Even a few quick heavy strokes calmed Laurel's nerves, made her heart slow its galloping beat. She felt all the layers of the world bearing her up, those countless strata of deposits, of dead things and aban-doned things. Lost things. What was that Faulknerian sentiment the museum lady, an unlikely source for regurgitated English 101 classes, had tossed at her? That the past isn't dead, that it isn't even past.

Black strokes came faster on the paper, harder. Laurel watched her fingers turn white above where they gripped the charcoal, bloodless, almost skeletal instead of merely slender as her grandmother had always praised her for. An artist's hands, her grandmother had said, and Laurel's mother and great aunt had nodded as though a pronouncement had been made, something final decided, a course set.

Laurel sketched faster. The paper blossomed with a mass of dark scribbles and tangled lines, layers on layers, a cutaway view of the earth. Layers of bones, layers of dirt, layers of darkness. Lost objects, ancient swamps, trees, and animals of species that had gone extinct in previous eons. Laurel drew all the layers, all the strata, and all the detritus of everything pressing up from below, drew them one over another, until there was no blank space left on the page, no exposed bits of iron cannon to rust between the topographic coats of thick black paint.

And then she began to sketch the new stuff, the stuff to come, the stuff that would go over the stuff that had gone before. And then she drew more, shooting forward into the future, the stuff that would come after: the malls, the asphalt, the ruined crumbling masses of concrete and stone and glass that hadn't yet been erected over these vast Texas plains. She sketched them as though they had already passed, already sunk to a layer beneath other layers. And then she sketched even beyond that, erecting societies and empires before burying each under the next, her heart crushed against her ribs with the weight of all those future layers bearing down from above, all those strata of buried history, natural and manufactured and imagined and unknown, pushing up from below.

Deputy Garcia wasn't happy to find the abandoned car.

This bit of county highway was a rough-paved stretch of gravelly nothing between one interstate and the next, like so many other farm roads running like capillaries to all the little outlying towns that otherwise would be forgotten ghost blips on the state landscape. Texas had mostly been ocean bed once, flat and enormous. His little girl liked the thumbnail-sized ram's-horn fossils and the tiny limestone clamshells he sometimes picked up for her along the sides of the road or in the scars of dried-up creeks or new building sites.

Garcia radioed in the car's license plate. Someone had left in a hurry; the driver's-side door gaped wide, as if it had been interrupted speaking, mid-sentence. A woman's purse lay on the back seat with a phone peeking out of the top, though you'd have to get a lot closer to the interstate for reliable service. A mess stained the faded white strip at the ragged edge of the road—lost breakfast, it looked like, or maybe dinner from the night before. Car didn't look like it had been sitting long, though; the automatic interior light was dim but still shining. Keys dangled from the ignition. Cute key ring, too, sleek and pretty, something one of those University girls might get at a fancy museum gift shop or as a present from a female relative.

Shading his eyes against the day's glare, Garcia peered up the dotted gray stripe of the road. Nothing so far as he could see, not even a farmhouse. Not even a smattering of mobile homes around a gas station, as was common around these parts. Just miles of scrub, and a small gully with a copse of stunted Texas pine, probably an old creek bed long dried, with just enough seasonal runoff to keep the copse alive, if not green it up every season.

He was still waiting to hear back about the license plate. Maybe the car's owner had simply ducked down into those trees, some city girl after a few lunchtime margaritas needing to make a pit stop, not expecting the long stretch of nothingness along this particular road, not expecting the wallop folks out here expected for their money in the 'rita department.

Garcia was about to turn back when something too regular at the bottom of the slope caught his eye. Something perfectly square where everything else was crooked and twiggy and crumbly.

His boots skidded on small sharp stones as he slid down the rise into the copse. Now he was looking for it, he noticed two furrows raked in the ground mirroring his own, two shallow troughs where two heels had dug in like his dug in, carrying someone to the bottom of the hill.

The rectangular shape Garcia had glimpsed from the road turned out to be a notebook. A sketchbook, in fact, with spiral rings so you could flip it open to a single page at a time—his kid used one for her art classes, though not with paper this fine. The paper was so fine, the top page was gouged and ripped, torn as though someone had pressed a pencil hard enough into the page to make it rip right through. No, not a pencil; here was a box of drawing charcoal, expensive art stuff wrapped in paper and hardened to a point so it looked like a pencil, but wasn't. And near that, a few strands of golden hair, glinting in the sunlight, coming straight up out of the ground.

Lurching to his knees, Garcia scrabbled at the dirt and leaves around the lock of hair. Barehanded digging was hard, small stones and sharp leaves, dirt heavier than one would think. His nails tore, his fingers scraped bloody and raw as they met a layer of solid limestone with barely the soft rounded tip of a human skull and a girl's long wavy locks rising impossibly straight from the hard calcium whiteness.

Garcia rocked back on his heels, realizing there was nothing he could do but radio it in.

Grunting, he stood. He'd seen a lot even in the few years he'd been patrolling, but never someone who looked to have been buried whole and vertical, as though sucked straight down into the earth, even through layers of stone. The limestone itself was layers too, of course: layers of skeletal fragments of ancient marine organisms like the ones his kid collected, all crushed and pressed together by time and force, hardened into solid rock.

Averting his eyes from the shining blonde hair choked with dirt, he stooped to s'tudy the scribbled-on sketchpad, the layers of charcoal forced one over another over another, no picture at all to speak of, at least none he could make out. Leaving it alone—this was a crime scene now, though the copse looked serene and still, offering no sign of struggle, no obvious mark of violence—Garcia wiped his hands on his pants, wiped off the dirt and decayed needles and dead insects and decomposed matter and all the other things that make up living earth. He began retracing his way up the slope to call it in, wondering about the young woman whose picture he'd probably find on her driver's license in her purse in her car with its pretty key ring and its soft leather seats. Wondering what the team would find after they got out here halfway between noplace and nowhere, wondering about the girl buried over her head, like one of so many layers in the earth, like any bit of debris or rotting leaf or fallen log or other ephemeral, passing thing.

CROSSED GATES

ADRIAN TCHAIKOVSKY

Adrian Tchaikovsky is the author of the Shadows of the Apt *fantasy series, the final volume of which came out in July 2014, as well as numerous short stories. When not writing he has a day job for which he commutes through Crossgates station. 'It is real, as inexplicably grandiose as described and is 95% of the inspiration for this story in and of itself, the remaining 5% being inexplicable delays on the Leeds-York line.'*

CROSSGATES STATION HAS AN ABSURD GRANDEUR.

Crossgates itself is a suburb, an appendix to the grand North England metropolis of Leeds. The shopping, I'm told, is good there. I've never had cause to find out. It's just a place the train stops, between the poles of home and work. But the station . . . Crossgates Station is a vast piece of Edwardian redbrick architecture, great expanses of platform spreading out on either side of the twin lines of track, overshadowed by reaching walls where the natural contours of the country have been hacked into, bludgeoned into submission by the will of man. Those walls are louring, buttressed, massive things, fit for a prison and crowned by an overspill of decaying greenery. The overall impression is of something transplanted from another land and time, fit for the arrivals and departures of tsars and emperors.

There was some country house nearby, I had heard, whose family had mandated *There Shall Be A Railway Station*, only, not actually close to the house, not really. Otherwise it might have frightened the horses. So, manorial whim had bequeathed the whole unnecessary glory on unsuspecting

Crossgates, and then been outlived by it, so that commuters on the line from York to Leeds must look and wonder, and be made to feel small and prosaic and faintly awed.

But I always spared a glance for Crossgates Station, when I passed through, just a moment's consideration for the leftover splendour of another age, like a hard node of the past still standing against history's flow.

Which was why I raised an eyebrow when the train pulled up there a second time on the way home.

Any journey taken every working weekday becomes a ritual. Any ritual repeated often enough results in a disconnection of the mind from its surroundings. I wasn't sure, to tell the truth. I glanced up from my book to see those louring red walls on either side of the carriage like genteel clashing rocks, shrouded in the gloom of evening and painted by the flaring white of the station lights. *Did we not . . . ? Have we . . . ?* But I couldn't say for sure if I was remembering a stop of minutes ago or the previous day. Pulling into the same station daily, the memories smudge and blur and are lost even as they are laid down.

Of course we hadn't stopped at Crossgates twice.

I was nervous. Some inner score-keeper was frowning at his notes. The rational forebrain, that thinks itself the lord of all creation and yet is so easily convinced of impossible things, dismissed any potential irregularities. Easier to believe in my own fallibility, that was at least backed by plenty of past evidence.

So I settled back to the book, eyes skipping over the words, reading the same passage over and over as I tried to track down where I'd got to. The train groaned and squealed its complaints as it lurched forwards, and the brooding spectacle that was Crossgates Station at dusk receded into the distance and into memory.

A few minutes later, the train pulled into Crossgates Station and my mind's ability to gloss over the inconsistencies snapped like a rubber band. I was staring out at the tall, brick-lined walls of the cut, the desert expanse of the empty platform, unmistakeably Crossgates because nowhere else on the line is anything like it. The moment of uncertainty ensured that the memory of the last time had not simply been stirred into the general morass of history.

There were plenty of other passengers in the carriage with me, on their homebound commute. Every seat was full. Not one of them seemed concerned: not one of them so much as glanced outside. The haughty presence of Crossgates Station was lost on them. Nobody got up to disembark.

Because, I thought, passengers wishing to alight at Crossgates Station had already done so.

Being English and self-conscious can be a terrible burden, and never more so than then. It was out of the question that I stand up and clear my throat; that I impose myself on the other passengers. What could I say to them? How could I possibly draw their attention to something so unprecedented, yet at the same time so banal? *Look outside! It's Crossgates Station!* I would cry, and they would look at me with judging eyes that said, *Yes we know. You're obviously a dangerous nutter.*

I got as far as opening my dry mouth twice. *I am Lazarus back from the dead, come to tell you all . . . I will tell you all . . .* But it can't be done. You can't tell people impossible things. The fear of being taken for a lunatic was stronger than my fear that we had pulled into Crossgates Station three times without the train needing to do anything so mundane as put itself into reverse.

The train sat there for a while this time, as though sharing my uneasy surprise but equally unwilling to say anything about it. *That*, of course, did register with some of the other passengers, in all the small but unmistakable ways. There were sighs, and then some tutting, and a middle-aged man turned the page of his newspaper slightly fast, the sharp sound indicating with withering panache just what he thought of the state of Britain's railways.

We don't care that we're in the same station for a third time, they seemed to be silently saying, *but at least let us have forwards motion!*

I had put my book away. Alertness seemed mandated, and yet nothing was happening. I was as much a prisoner of the commuter mentality as everyone. Something bizarre and inexplicable was going on with the train, and yet I had no wish to alight at Crossgates because, then, how would I get home? A train that had taken leave of the laws of physics was still a train, even if all rails led to Crossgates now.

There was a brief crackle of static, and the flat, dead voice of the speakers informed us, "We apologise for the delay in continuing your journey, as there is a fault. We are currently looking into remedying the situation and will be underway as soon as possible," and then informing us that the rail company apologized for any inconvenience the delay to our journey might cause us.

There was a stir amongst the other passengers, a sort of jowly, Churchillian *I-should-think-so-too* kind of a mutter. I was unconvinced. I was unsure that a large corporation could be in a position to make any sort of a sincere apology, and in this case I was beginning to think that the situation might be beyond even the most deeply held regrets. However . . .

The harsh double buzz heralding the closing of the doors was heard in the land, and the rumble of the engines built a little, and we were underway. Next stop: Garforth.

Book forgotten, I watched every passing metre of the countryside, hawkish for a glimpse of when *it* would happen. I hung on for the disconnect, that cut-film moment that must surely show where the land east and out of Crossgates turned into the land west and in. It was a doomed venture. I realized I had no idea of what any of it was supposed to look like. How many times had I made this journey? Enough that it had all smeared into a blur in my mind, too much repetition, too many journeys with my nose in a book. There was no tell-tale flicker to show how the trick was done.

And the train pulled into Crossgates station.

This time I stood up. I was going to make my grand announcement: *Crossgates! This is Crossgates!* The words died in my mouth. The bonds of propriety still held me in an iron grip. I just could not impose myself on my fellow passengers: their outraged scorn would be like the fatal gaze of a basilisk. Besides, I had seen enough films where, the moment the hapless protagonist does try to draw the attention of others to the inexplicable, the inexplicable refuses to cooperate. Looking a fool is a social stigma that far outweighs the unravelling of the ways of the world. Or the ways of the rail, at least.

I sat down again, and nobody marked it. I was just one more passenger who thought his stop had come, then realized his error.

I was very possibly the last person on this planet to own a mobile phone and, in protest over having to do so, I almost never had it on me. I resented that people felt they have the right to get hold of me at a moment's notice wherever I am, especially when so many of them are strangers trying to sell me something. I wished I had remembered to bring it then, though. Although . . . even then, what could I say? *I'm going to be late. The train is . . .* What? Delayed? Would that word stretch to cover pulling into the same station for a fourth time?

There was movement at the far end of the carriage, and I froze like a mouse before an owl. For a moment I thought . . . I couldn't say, in the next, just what I'd thought, but it had been apocalyptic.

It was the ticket inspector.

He was a thin, tall man, angular as a mantis, with a large chin and a large nose and a small, neat moustache. In his navy-blazered uniform— some uncomfortable no-man's land between a policeman and a rep for a holiday company—he was stepping down the aisle one seat at a time, a spindly, looming presence at the elbow of each passenger as he asked after their right to be there.

I had a sudden terror that I'd lost my ticket. The thought of *not* being entitled to be on the carriage was an unexpected source of fear: yes, something terribly wrong was happening to the train, but would being *off* the train help? Or would it expose me to worse? The situation was sufficiently unprecedented that I was no longer thinking like a commuter who wants to get home.

French poets aside, you can't *know* existential dread until something happens that makes you doubt the rules by which you exist.

But I had my ticket, always in the last pocket I checked. I was going to just show it meekly and let the man pole his way on down the carriage.

The shadowy, barren presence of Crossgates Station outside intruded onto me, poised around the train like the jaws of a carnivorous plant, as though a single passenger stepping out might be the trigger to snap them shut. As he neared my seat I saw the inspector's eyes flick to the windows, piercing past the distorted reflections to the reality outside.

He knew. In that one glance was a wealth of understanding. Then he locked eyes with me, and knew that I knew too.

"Tickets, please."

Even then, I almost failed to speak. It would have been so easy to just show him my white and orange rectangle of card and let him pass on. To do anything else would be to scale the walls of proper social conduct, which loomed higher around us than those of Crossgates' cut. To start talking lunacy to a ticket inspector was the sort of transgression that might bring the world crashing down.

Except that it had already gone, and so from somewhere I found the courage.

"Excuse me," I started. I was withholding my ticket to keep him there. I was worried that, having seen it, I would cease to exist for him and he would just stilt off and away.

"Ticket, please," he repeated. He knew, and he knew that I knew, but nothing in his manner betrayed it.

"Excuse me," I repeated, "what station is this?"

"Crossgates, sir." His hand was still out for my ticket, wavering a little impatiently.

"Only, we've been to Crossgates before . . . "

"Every day, sir. Ticket?"

"Today," and then, because that, too, left him a get-out, "on this journey. We keep pulling into Crossgates." I couldn't believe how insane the utterance sounded, even though it was true. It was a ridiculous thing to have to put into words. I could imagine any other passengers unfortunate enough to overhear cringing into their seats. I knew the inspector would deny it, and then where would I be? I would have to show him my ticket, and he would go, and then . . .

Crossgates. Crossgates again. And again.

"Yes, I'm sorry, sir. There is a fault."

I stared at him, or tried to. Meeting his gaze was utterly devoid of that connection one feels on receiving the regard of another human being. My eyes slid off his bony face over and over. "A fault," I echoed.

"Yes sir. I understand that all efforts are being made to resolve the issue."

He sounded so very calm about it, so matter-of-fact. I kept trying to start on just how little that reassurance went towards actually addressing the issue; that some fundamental locomotive law seemed to have been repealed. You can buy a return ticket, but every train ride is a one-way trip. In a sense, even if you go back in the same carriage and are hauled by the same engine, it is not the same train, any more than Heraclitus could cross the same river twice. What was the 9.11 to Leeds on the way in, will be the 10.45 to York on its return. They are distinct entities at a level untroubled by the prosaically physical.

Trains are forward progress, the concept made real. Every journey is breaking new ground for them. They do not repeat themselves.

Abruptly, all restraint went out the window. I clutched at the inspector's proffered hand, snagged his sleeve. "We keep pulling into Crossgates!" I said again, with urgency.

I wanted his face to remain calm, but there was something fractured deep inside his eyes. "There is a fault," he whispered, his voice shedding all that professional assurance like a snakeskin.

"A fault on the line?" I was still clutching. "A signal failure."

"A signal failure." On his lips, the words meant something different. "A fault. They're trying to fix it now, sir."

"How?" I was desperately in need of reassurance.

He had none to give. "I don't know, sir."

"And can it be fixed?"

"I don't know, sir." Identical intonation.

I got up, suddenly, and he started back, dragging his cuff from my fingers. For a moment he just stared at me, and his head twitched sideways like a spasmodic tic, a weirdly inhuman motion. He didn't know what I was going to do. I didn't know what I was going to do. The fragile hold of social niceties fumbled and dropped me.

"We keep pulling into Crossgates!" I cried out over the inspector's shoulder, eyes wide as I tried to make contact with someone else in the carriage, anyone else.

"Please sir, it's just a fault," the uniformed man whispered.

"We keep doing it," I cried out to the world. "We've been here four times!"

Perhaps I might have done it, if the train hadn't started up again even then. I had seen my fellow passengers stir a little, as I stuck a finger into their own distant sense of wrongness and waggled it around like Thomas in the wound, but now the train was moving and they were on their way home, and everything was fine.

"No, listen!" but they were not listening. They were hearing, but what they were hearing was a madman jumping up and being unbearably rude and un-English. They all knew the type: the drunkards, the mentally ill, the unavoidably oikish, those who cannot be trusted to behave by the polite rules of public transport. Being of polite society, my fellow passengers just hunkered down, burying their noses in their newspapers and Kindles, and pretended I did not exist.

"Please, sir," the inspector said reproachfully. His face was calm and relaxed, and his glassy eyes stared out from it like prisoners at twin windows.

The train was getting up speed, but there was no hope in me. We would be slowing soon. We would be coming into the station. Coming *back* to the station.

"What's going on?" I demanded.

"There's a—"

"How can it be a fault? How can a fault on the line—"

He was shaking his head.

"A fault on the train, then—"

Still shaking his head, those desperate eyes straying to the dark country-side still passing by outside.

"There's a fault," he said again, sounding sick.

I looked about in the hope that someone might be eavesdropping on the increasingly unhinged conversation, but every commuter was an island, with no intention of receiving ambassadors from any other.

"There must be someone," I decided. By this time it seemed pointless to keep any thought in the privacy of my own head. I turned back down the carriage.

"Please sir, no, sir," came the inspector's hollow voice behind me. I glanced back to see him coming after me, hands on the seat backs, elbows high, picking his way like a spider.

I bolted for the end door, feeling the train start to slow again, feeling the inevitable gravity of Crossgates Station draw us in. And why Crossgates? Did that futile redbrick magnificence hide some genuine significance? Was there some universal anchor buried beneath it that, now activated, could not be escaped?

The automatic door half-opened at my approach, and I shoved it brutally the rest of the way. Behind was the vestibule with the exit doors I had no intention of taking, and thereafter the narrow intersection between carriages, shifting and sliding with the movement of the train, floored by curved plastic plates so that the whole had always seemed to me the kind of articulated throat possessed by some creature that has chitinous teeth all the way down its gut. The impression was never so strong as it was now, and it took all the courage I had to force myself through that grinding throat and into the next car.

Every seat was full, the commuter crowd sitting in sullen obedience as we pulled once more into Crossgates. I opened my mouth and cried my Cassandran warning, hoping someone there would be open-minded enough to take notice.

Some did, but their gazes were incurious, set beneath beetling brows. I didn't exactly travel first class, but the people in this carriage seemed to be a different class altogether. They were squat and solid, heavy-shouldered, heavy jawed. Their suits and coats were stretched uncomfortably taut across barrel chests, and they were all in need of a razor, the women almost as much as the men. I shouted at them again, and one of them leapt up and bellowed back, whacking his umbrella against the baggage rack to make his point. No words came from him, only something that was language's rude, unstructured understudy.

I should have gone back then, but I pressed on down towards the end of the train. Any destination seemed better than my vacated seat, with the shadowy vista of Crossgates gliding into view.

In the next carriage, they were jumping on the seats. They were swinging from the overhead handholds as though it was standing room only. Some still had their shirts or skirts on, draped over shrunken, long-limbed hirsute forms. They paid me no heed, too busy running madly back and forth; feet like hands, prehensile tails and broad, omnivorous teeth.

I picked up speed, pushing on, forcing each door open as I came to it. The next carriage was infested with rats that twined and fought and flurried like grey-furred carpets under my feet, gnawing at the electrics and making nests in the upholstery. In the car after that, the heating was fixed to full on, and the commuters lay torpid under it, sunning the great lengths of their scaly bodies, vaned fins rising high from their spines through rents in skirt-suits and anoraks.

I felt that I was descending an incline, perhaps one not to be measured with a ruler or a spirit level. The far end of the next car was underwater, the slope of the floor making a shore up which the passengers had crawled and lumped, frog-slick sides heaving as they regarded me with eyes that were huge, round, and perpetually appalled.

I approached the water's edge carefully, thinking, *slimy things did crawl with legs* . . . The water was clear, and I could see the lights of further carriages, entirely submerged. Fin-tailed shapes shoaled there, and beyond them things that were not even fish.

I would have stayed there, but there was something wrong with the air conditioning. It made me feel lightheaded and strange.

I backed off, and then I turned and retraced my steps, back up the family tree towards my seat. We were just pulling into Crossgates again.

When I had reached my original carriage again; when I had struggled through those coaches of the somnolent, the cold-blooded, the scurrying, the hooting, the primitive, I found the inspector exactly as he must have been the moment I slipped out of the door, caught in mid-stride. Animation returned to him only as I entered the carriage, so that I recoiled back against the automatic door, which refused to acknowledge my presence and stayed mulishly closed behind me.

He did not touch me, although he had a hand half-reaching, perhaps still mindlessly seeking my ticket. In my absence, something had deteriorated in him, leaving his skin waxy and sallow. His stick-insect movements were jerky and stuttering.

I glanced at my fellow passengers. They were unmoving, each to his or her seat, staring vacantly, some animating spark withdrawn while I had been away.

"What's going on?" I demanded plaintively, though surely matters had gone beyond any convenient answers, and surely this twitching creature was past providing them.

And yet: "Anyone who travels on a train partakes in a potent symbol of order and celestial organization," the inspector said softly, sadly.

No commuter could let that go unchallenged. "What about the delays, the cancellations, the trains that just vanish from the boards, the unexplained stops?"

"The battle with the forces of universal chaos takes its toll," whispered the inspector. "But think: to travel on rails, your course predetermined—what more perfect symbol of universal law can you imagine?"

At last the door behind me gave, and I was in the vestibule, where the doors had opened onto Crossgates Station.

"Sir," said the inspector at my elbow. It was not clear whether he intended encouragement or warning.

The station was shrouded in dusk, and the scattered lampposts seemed fewer, each burning less brightly than before. The nauseous amber glow beyond the briar-crowned walls spoke of a cityscape that I no longer quite believed in. The orange LEDs of the arrivals board flurried and danced, forming no letters I knew, announcing no sane timetable, and yet patently trying with great urgency to communicate some message I was not equipped to understand. It was as though the station was trying to vomit or to scream.

I could have stepped out, but the twilight-grey tarmac had no promise of substance to it. It was like smoke. I felt that, if I left the train, I would fall through this suburban mirage and be lost.

There was that buzz-buzz of the door alarm and the portal slid shut, the train passing on, moving away from that one fixed point and into the gathering dark.

"There must be something we can do," he said.

"Please, sir . . . "

"What? Resume me seat? Become like them?"

"It might be kinder." Eyes like jellyfish swam in the hard plastic of his face.

"And what then?" I hissed. "What happens to the train then . . . ?" but I was recalling my own words, *the trains that just vanish from the boards* . . . Had we vanished? Had the 17.28 just been erased from all records, stripped from the arrivals list of every station between Leeds and York, so that those waiting to embark just tutted and checked their watches and wondered if they could somehow have missed it? Or was it true that the fault lay elsewhere, and that the train was all there was, and the tutting, waiting world had been devoured, ripped apart law by law until nothing but primal entropy remained.

Perhaps the train would become the seed of a new creation.

I could feel us starting to slow again, and a wild feeling gripped me, a reckless unwillingness to just tread the same circle over and over again.

There was one thing I could do.

I reached for the emergency stop handle.

At once the inspector was galvanized into agitated life. "No, sir, no! You mustn't! There is a penalty for improper use! A penalty!"

The train's shuddering progress was definitely assuming the characteristics of re-entry. Any moment now the muted lights of Crossgates would glide into place beyond the doors. I put my hand upon the handle, because a fifty-quid fine was surely nothing weighed against the breakdown of normal services we were experiencing.

The inspector tried to stop me. He grappled with me, but his twig-thin limbs had no leverage to them. The touch of those slick, long-fingered hands was repulsive and clammy, and with a revolted shriek I hurled him away from me, so that he crashed into the wall and slid down it, broken in a dozen places.

Even then, the hungry maw of Crossgates Station was in sight, just opening to receive the first carriages of the train, and I yanked on the handle as hard as I could.

The instant braking motion flung me towards the front of the train, spilling me into that grinding, twisting throat between carriages. Looking forwards, I saw the blank-faced passengers strewn about like shop window mannequins.

I expected us to finish half in and half out of the station. It was not so. As we slowed, so the station began to pull away from *us*, imperceptibly at first, but then receding faster and faster until it was lost in the all-encompassing dark. I realized only then that we had not been drawing up to a stationary station, but had been matching speeds with it as it fled towards some unimaginable event horizon, and now even that was lost to us.

I got to my feet. The ticket inspector was still slumped beside the external door, his rickety limbs in disarray. A thick yellow fluid was seeping from his eyes and staining his uniform in a dozen places.

"There is a penalty for improper use," he murmured. "And we have all paid it now."

"What, then?" I asked him. I could not decide whether I had ruined something, or saved myself from it.

"Now?" One of his eyes closed, a grotesque and unintentional expression of intimacy. "There is no now. Or there is only the now. I cannot remember." Something like breath rattled in his throat.

I stood up. In front of me was the carriage, filled with slack-jawed, deanimate commuters, and with that one empty seat waiting patiently for my eternal patronage. Behind me, towards the rear of the train, lay only devolution, a slow descent back to simpler times, back to the sea, back to the soup.

Outside, there was not even a facsimile of Crossgates Station anymore. I thought I could see stars.

I turned from the wheezing inspector, brushing off his one working hand as he made a last mute request for my ticket. I left the vestibule and reentered the carriage, stopping at that single vacant seat.

Would it be quick, I wondered, if I sat down? Would I know anymore, or would I wink out like a blown bulb, and equally impossible to rekindle? I found that I would do anything rather than find out.

So I walked on. I moved towards the front of the carriage, away from that endless train of temporal regression that my journey towards the rear had showed me.

There was only the driver's compartment there, at the front, but it was forwards, away from the intolerable present and the dragging tail of the past.

When I opened the door, there was only light, as though I had drawn aside a veil into the heart of the sun, or the heart of God. It was the future, in all its golden potential: the future the train itself would never reach.

I made sure I had my ticket ready, and stepped through.

CURSE OF THE MUMMY PAPER

ANNA TAMBOUR

Anna Tambour tells us, 'This story is dedicated to Borderlands Books in San Francisco, which as every cat would know, is a great and good bookstore.'

Anna lives in the Australian bush, where the paperbark and scribblybark trees are inscrutable. Her novels have been shortlisted for the Campbell and World Fantasy Awards. Her short fiction has been published in various venues, including Tor.com. Tambour's latest collection (Ticonderoga Publications, 2015) is The Finest Ass in the Universe.

W E WOULDN'T BE MEETING LIKE THIS—YOU AND I—IF we didn't love books, so before I introduce myself, I'll lay these before you as presents. Truly, you needn't jump on a chair or grab a broom.

A princess, from the late Mr. Pettigrew's collection, was swathed in forty thicknesses, producing 42 yards of the finest texture. The supply of linen rags would not be limited to the mummies of the human species alone; independent of that obtainable from this source, a more than equal amount of cloth could be depended on from the mummies of sacred bulls, crocodiles, ibises, and cats.

—Dr Isaiah Deck, 1855 manuscript proposing the
solution to the great rag (thus, paper) shortage
then plaguing the USA's 800 paper mills

> *An Onondaga county man, worshipful of the golden Eagle and not of the Egyptian Ibis, has put upon the market, 'paper made from the wrappings of mummies.'*
> —[Syracuse, NY] *Standard*, August 19, 1856

Does that reassure?

For though I've been known to utter kitten cries and toy with balls of string, this is no more a 'cat story' than the princess mentioned would have been a cat-story lady, or a cat-story lady brought back to life as some world-conquering villain whose only gentle stroke is to a cat.

Both make you creep away from them, warned perhaps by some instinct against sentiment. We flee from love that smothers, from forgetfulness. Not for us, all that petting, nor dishes set down just for us, always decorated with the glued-on bits and bones of unfinished fish, never quite washed because they're 'for the cat'.

We would rather starve than touch that seaminess.

But seaminess doesn't kill, and no cat ever really died—last-flick-of-the-paw death—from that so-common pain, starvation.

And as anyone who knows cats knows: we love good books—from the light embrace of a papyrus scroll to the luxurious bed of an open vellum tome, to a pile of paperbacks. A good bookshop is, of course, a palace, but a loving home can be a good abode.

At one time I lived in a beautiful place, not here where it snows every winter, floorboards creak and drawers stick, people rush ungracefully about on hard, unmusical footwear, and the air is a nose-offending reek of '99 percent germ killer' and name-brand perfume that no long-time-ago old dung-carrier would have worn. You who know this isn't sentimentalism can call me Keti, for that is what the baker did. *Keti*, by the way, is *fleabane* in your unmellifluous modern tongue.

As to the baker, Niankhum, deserving of a book of psalms to him . . .

Whenever I dropped a rat at his feet, he was properly appreciative. He never asked where the gift came from. And if it needed a bit more chasing, he kept out of my way, even when the rat jumped into the dough trough or fell into the oven's fiery mouth.

He was also quite a reader. There were no booksellers in Niankhum's town but he had a collection that he treasured. It was quite musical when I settled on it, my purrs setting forth a vibration in the scrolls. He'd pull one from under me and read to us, which always turned up my music.

His wife, who liked to think she was my mistress, was the dream of many cats.

A lap that could hold 7 at a time. A face as round and beautiful as the moon.

The baker's wife took care to keep herself beautiful. She rubbed her skin with ground cinnabar, salt, almond oil and honey till it took on the sheen of the baker's finest egg-washed bread. She wore wigs on special occasions but didn't need to, her own hair being so thick that she'd only have to lay on a pallet on the floor and all us cats would comb her thick mane till it stretched out to the door. She made special foods to gain weight, her favourite being milk reduced to cream that she shared thick slices of with 'all my little family'. The other 6 of us grew so fat, they couldn't roam outdoors at night nor leap atop a wall.

Of all women I've ever known—and what cat doesn't know countless hordes—she was the only one who knew how to wear perfume. And *such* perfume. Her secret was to mix balanos oil, myrrh, and resin (what's so secret about that, you say. That's just what the city of Mendes exported for gold and rubies, nothing special to us.) But this baker's wife added an incomparable something extra. This was her secret recipe:

On a hot still summer day, when the sun was looking down upon everything at once, she carried all 6 cats up the ladder to the hot clay of the flat roof where a black-glazed platter lay in waiting. Then she carried up and built a mound of cream slices in the middle of the platter. The 6 didn't wait to be invited. They never noticed her lower a lid upon platter, cream and cats. The dome she had constructed of finest fish bladder looked like a cloudy sky, and the air around them, as the cats ate, grew hotter and hotter till they, if they hadn't been so greedy, would have been panting and scratching frantically to get out and into some cooling shade. But what did those silly sisters and brothers of mine do? They sweated. When finally they had all finished their cream, their coats were matted with sweat. She reached in and took them out one by one, rubbing each down with linen cloths that she packed into a stoppered jar. And in that jar, she macerated her perfume. Like a cat, she knew how to apply it to herself, and as you could expect, knew how to drive her husband wild. Which she did with much more enjoyment, I must say, than any female of my set.

The baker's wife (I don't remember her name, but the other 6 called her with no sense of shameless flattery, Isis) was not only a loving, but a conscientious wife. She would even make up the medicaments for her husband's frequent attacks of constipation: zizyphus bread, honey, sweet beer, etc., mixed to a paste and smeared on linen that she bandaged around his stomach. That doesn't sound bad, does it? But even though I love the baker—(I don't deny that feeling that I first recognised in that melancholy time when the fire roared in the oven and shot sparks into the inky night, in that time before the dung beetle rolled the sun up into the sky, that thoughtful, sentimental, nostalgic time—the baker used to sit on his stool then, humming faintly. Sometimes he would drop his hand and I would rub against it. Otherwise, I curled myself up between his sandaled feet which were always soft and smelt fragrantly of dough from his stamping.)—even though I did love the baker, do!—there are limits to self-sacrifice. And no way would I pick up the etc. in the medicament that his wife made regularly for his constipation. Cat's dung!

Her cries carried to every house in our town and far over the sands to stir the rooftops in the next town, so loud were they that early morning when he choked on a hard crumb in his cup of sweet *bouza*, an unattractive soup of broken hard loaf soaked in water and honey that I used to turn my tail up at, little did he learn.

His death was so unexpected that the next thing the town knew was the smell of his bread burning.

The baker's wife wanted only the best for her beloved husband, and was quite an organiser. Priests were summoned and scurried to the bakery, where they picked him up from where he had fallen, at the foot of his oven.

They took him away to the music of the baker's wife's lamentations. Around her feet milled the 6 accompanists. Their high voices would have been far more plaintive if they had known what was to befall them.

The embalming of the baker took the requisite 70 days, and in all that while, the widow hardly touched a crumb, and lived otherwise, on date vinegar flavoured with water. Mice exported grain both day and night while the 6 lay torpid upon the floor, more useless than ever now that the mice had to climb over them and sometimes had to dig new holes in the walls that were thoughtlessly blocked by a paw or tail or tragic whiskered face.

Indeed, it occurs to me that the 6 reluctantly slimming cats looked like your modern filmmakers documenting a trade route as they lay dilatorily watching fat rats wash their whiskers, themselves watching busy mice lugging the remaining stores of grain, chunks of bread and cakes along the inside walls and out of sight.

Meanwhile, the beautiful widow was in danger of losing her looks, she starved herself so. Still, she cared for nothing other than providing an Afterlife of comfort and joy to her beloved husband. So along with this most unprecedented embalming of the baker and all its costliness (the neighbours did not approve), the widow hired a bevy of builders and painters, and also spent much worry and coin on everything his heart and body would desire in the Afterlife.

Day after day, the widow acted sometimes frantically but oftentimes as if she were sleepwalking. She worked and worried so hard that her smooth brow wrinkled and her hair grew wild as a bush. One morning, she shoved a wig over it and made for the tomb. For today was the 71st Day. The baker's body was ready and the tomb had been built, decorated, muralled, provisioned; and nothing was missing except her presence to farewell her beloved husband on his Journey into the Afterworld. The ritual required her to arrive on foot from their home, the bakery. The priests would arrive from the direction of their temple.

The spectacle of the priests' arrival holding her husband high was part of the scene that she would store in her heart, ready to tell him when they met in the Afterworld, if she had provisioned him well enough that he would meet her.

As she approached the tomb, however, all she could see was a milling of men. Builders, painters, decorators, the owner of the emporium where she bought all the items he would need on his journey, even to the clay donkey.

'Where is our money?' they asked as one.

The widow was shocked. She thought she had paid them, every one, all she owed. They insisted she had not. Her husband had always hated owing anyone money, and would rather go without than buy something on credit. And she had felt the same. I do believe these men were plotting to destroy her, but don't know finance well enough to be sure.

'Come back to the bakery after this and I will find whatever I can to pay you,' she had just said, when four priests approached.

They bore upon their shoulders a board laden with what I had to assume was the baker, now wrapped and smelling so highly of spice and oils that I wanted to run, but I didn't. I stayed in the shadow of the tomb, watching. (And where, you might ask, were the 6 other members of the household whom the baker had provided, through his missus, with such luxurious lives of feast and leisure? Still at home, those layabouts.)

The chief priest stepped forward, leaving the other three to balance what had once been a man plump as a grape.

'Woman,' he said to the widow, 'Your good husband, Niankhum, arrives impatient for his journey.' And the woman the greedy 6 called Isis when they were fat, and Useless in her mourning state of forgetfulness, answered with a stumbling bow and an idiotic 'Is that my beloved?'

From the shadows in her cheeks and the bags under her eyes, I wouldn't have liked to estimate how long it must have been since she last ate or slept, though she must have cried her fill.

'Beloved or not,' said the chief builder, shoving her out of the way, 'I'll not seal this tomb till you seal my hand with coin.'

'What's this?' said the chief priest, striking his staff against the builder's head. 'May Uytsteth give you piles for your attempt to cheat a suffering widow!'

'Where's our offerings?' said one of the priests.

The chief priest turned to the widow

The baker's wife rent her hair. She didn't know how she had forgotten to go to the next town to buy those funerary cakes. Her husband had always made them for the people of his town, but now that he was gone, the ovens were cold. Baking was, of course, not woman's work. 'How could I forget?' she cried.

It was obvious to me. Every thought of food she'd had since her husband's death had been to provide for him in his Afterlife. Like when she prepared his beer, she thought only of him. She lost all interest in her own needs, and the rest of her 'little family' was just an extension of her, in her forgetfulness.

So call me a mouse if I'm wrong. I am sure that she had paid to the smallest coin, everything she owed the tomb-makers and provisioners, and had paid the priests for the embalming.

But whether she had enough coin left to pay for the ceremony that the priests had arrived for with her husband held high between them, is still a mystery to me.

Whatever, as you say now.

The priests dropped the baker in the sand and stomped off, the heels of their sandals spurting up sand.

The builders trashed the tomb, drank all the liquid and took everything they could carry, even to the last unground grain of barley—all the provisions that is, except, probably superstitiously, the pile of inked papyrus, the Book of the Dead.

They left while the baker's wife scrabbled in the sand with a beautiful broken bowl.

She buried him beside the rubble, her tears rolling off the oiled linen before she tipped him into the hole. I wasn't sorry. The likeness was terrible. His eyes had been warm, lively, and crinkled at the corners. And he stank of resins, rather like your germ killers.

I didn't want to leave, yet was too shocked to make plans yet. I followed the widow back to the sad ex-bakery and those 6 useless cats who were so annoyingly self-centred that they didn't do a thing about comforting her, who needed them so much. They complained mightily, however, of the loss of their slices of cream. That night, the wailing was terrible to hear.

The bakery was soon surrounded by old toms, and I don't blame them. She sounded indecent.

Before the pigeons woke the next morning, the front door was shaken by a tremendous banging.

It was old Muhet. I don't know her real name, but everyone called her Muhet behind her back, for she was wrinkled as the plum that loosens your bowels.

'Good morning, Auntie,' said the baker's wife respectfully, though this 'auntie' was but a neighbour, and famous for her nosiness.

'What a sight,' declared Muhet, who rushed past and swept into the bakery, suddenly getting into everything like teeth-grinding grit from a sandstorm.

My siblings scattered. I hid behind a water jar.

'Enough of this mourning,' said Muhet, not even pausing for a polite 'I am unworthy to cross your doorway. A thousand praises on your fragrant . . . ', and she came bearing not a single gift.

She came weighed down, she said, with the demand of the whole town. That the baker's wife marry, and she knew just the man. A baker from _____ (some place I can't remember or she never said, but where misfortune had fallen) was, thank the Gods, free to take over this bakery, and thus, this wife.

And to my surprise, the marriage took place the next day, as if there was no mourning period needed. Where were the gossips, you might ask? Stuffing their faces with bread, now that the oven burst into life again.

This baker wasn't like that last one. His new wife dutifully served him, though her sighs when not in his presence would have made any sensitive cat rub against her leg. Now that she bustled back to work, however, she noticed how thin my 6 siblings had become (they looked now like healthy cats, not filled wine sacks). They took up their places around the room where she gave them milk. When the baker came in for his midday meal and sleep, he saw them eating their cuts of cream and let out a bellow that could be heard on roofs across the town.

He tore open the front door, and raised a foot to kick the nearest cat out, but his new wife rushed between them.

'Remember Efuban?' she said. Seeing his face, she quietly shut the door. Everyone knew of Efuban, who had been stoned by a mob the day he killed a cat, though everyone knew it had been an accident.

'Remember where your food comes from, your dress,' said the new baker. He stormed off and before the door shut behind him, my siblings mobbed the dish again to polish off the cuts of cream. I might have stopped to say, 'Your beloved Isis is crying,' but it wouldn't have done her good. Instead, I followed the monster.

He went to the temple, met the priests, and soon sauntered back, happy as a full belly.

While his new wife was busy with his dinner, plucking pigeons on the roof, he plucked my siblings off the floor till the floor was clean of all 6—all now in a bag, providing a moral about exercise after eating that they have never, unfortunately, lived to enjoy, no matter how many years pass.

Oh, he never noticed me, never knew there was a seventh. Out he went with the bag slung on his back. The noise in the street was too great for anything new to be noticed, though the bag was loud with cries and hisses, 6 cream-filled cats bumping on his back, tumbling against each other, nose to undertail, upside down and everywhichway. He carried the bag to the temple and handed it to the chief priest, who lowered it into what looked like a secret place under the floor. It certainly sealed their cries.

I stayed at the temple and watched. At nightfall, two priests prepared milk together, fussing over the preparation for some reason, but I'd never watched priests before and didn't know their ways. When they were satisfied, they poured it into a pot that one took hold of. The other priest opened the secret place under the floor and pulled up the bag of my siblings. Their cries were so weak and dispirited, they almost caused me a

pang of pity. Like mice they were, lacking all dignity. The two priests
nodded to the chief priest. Then one priest carrying the pot, the other the
bag, and the chief priest carrying nothing but all looking nondescript as
they usually did, they all walked out of town, out to a sandy flat place that
was so featureless that it looked sacred.

And in this place, sure enough, there was a sort of column, with decora-
tions such as I'd never seen, and when I say that, I mean that it was truly
strange, for what *haven't* I seen?

And the priest with the bag of my siblings handed it to the chief priest.
Then the two priests took hold of the pot, raised themselves up as high as
they could and poured the milk into the top of the column. Then the chief
priest opened the bag and tumbled my 6 brothers and sisters, the cream-
lovers, onto the sand.

Instead of running, as any lean cat let out of a bag should, one sniffed,
then another, and in a moment's breath, they had surrounded the base of
the column, which was crying milk. They lapped and lapped and lapped in
a kind of frenzy. This milk was driving them mad with desire. They
couldn't lap fast enough, it seemed. The priests looked on, smiling.

Now I know that I should have pushed them aside to take my place.
After all, I am the oldest and wisest. And I should have known that, cats
being sacred, these priests would be better providers than any ignorant
but well-meaning wife.

I never lived for my stomach, but nothing can slake my curiosity. So I
watched from a low point, and no one noticed me. Indeed, out there lit
only by stars, I wouldn't have been distinguished from a pile of sand.

'These six won't do much to help our count,' said one priest to another.

'But it's something. We need to do more to satisfy them.'

'And if it works—'

'Yes, there's no shortage of scoundrels we can pay to bring us fresh
supplies.'

'But what if we get caught?'

'Who would tell? What's to catch? Look at them. They have chosen to
live again as Bastet's aides.'

I'd been so absorbed listening that I hadn't looked at my siblings, but
now I did. I had to look fast, because in a few moments, one of the priests
had picked up all their still silent bodies and thrown them back in the bag.

The chief priest raised his hands to the heavens, and then rubbed them.

'I do so love,' he chuckled, 'the smell of embalming.'

'I do too,' said one of the milk preparers, seriously enough that he ended up walking a bit alone on the way back.

The next day, in mourning for the missing cats, the baker's wife shaved her eyebrows, earning a beating from her new husband. I know because I dropped in to see how she fared, and could only rub against her legs for a moment once his back was turned. But I had to leave. She had never been anything to me, but I don't like to see a creature that I'm not playing with, suffer.

Back I went to the temple where I almost choked from the fumes while watching the 6 go through the process of permanent preservation. It was hard in a way not to turn madcap somersaults at the ludicrous idea of cats dying and then being preserved permanently by being dunked in goo and wrapped in something that holds them so tight, they cannot even flex their paws to knead.

But the providing of thousands of mummified sacred cats was serious business to this small third-rate temple in a town so lacking in allure that no one had ever tried to raze it.

My siblings were bundled together with a quirth of others into a job-lot, loaded onto a donkey cart and trundled out to some other featureless place in which now sat, supposedly forever, a stone image of Bastet. Quite a beautiful image, I should say. You could almost hear her disdainfully purr. She would never have been able to be caught by a bribe of milk. Not that I didn't think (and still don't) the idea of a cat being a God any less ludicrous than the idea that a dungbeetle moves the sun around. Which dungbeetle? I have eaten many. One crunch and they're gone. They don't strike me as any more capable than a donkey, and actually, they are much less able to do anything. I narrowly missed a donkey's hoof one day, and I can tell you: if that hoof had connected, my history would be different.

So back to the statue of Bastet. The thousands of mummified cats were meant, it must have been, as companions to her. Into a tomb went my siblings at the bakery, the Greedy 6, on top of and surrounded by so many other mummified cats that I could almost hear the cheers of rats across the land. Whatever the priests really thought about cats and Bastet, rats would certainly worship any cat that could be the cause of such a cat-plague of religious contribution.

When night fell, so were the stones lowered upon the tomb. So now I knew, as your mysteries say, where the bodies were buried. The Greedy 6, in that tomb that was buried soon enough, by history and sand. And the baker, Niankhum, in a place unmarked, except by my memory. Do I regret that he was left to starve there in the wilderness of between-lives? To be truthful, I am glad. Once the head priest stuck a skewer up his nose and twiddled it in his brain, he was no more the baker I knew than I am a pickled turnip.

Centuries passed. My curiosity got me in many scrapes and more than a few deaths, but that unwraps another myth you might believe in. Why 9 lives? Why not 5, or a baker's dozen, or 8977? I wouldn't go so far as to say that I'm immortal, but I'm still me.

You've possibly read of me or seen pictures, though I keep out of the limelight, leaving it to those who bask in it. I've sat on poets' papers, posed for painters' portraits, chased balls of scrap-paper tossed by a lonesome limerickist. I've roamed the backrooms of museums where they prepare bodies for a modern Afterlife. I've watched watchmen. I've loved a thousand thousand books, inspired as many tales, but never, if you must know, walked on only two legs (what a waste to use a mere 2 when we have taken or been given 4!). Furthermore, I've never tarried in any place, no matter how young a miewling, if someone called me Fluffy.

As for the Greedy 6? Why shouldn't they be romping free as I am, only caged by the turns of history?

They have one problem that I never knew, that none of them has solved.

Embalming, you see, does change a cat forever.

All that sticky stuff against your fur. It does the same thing as honey to the face. Just try to pull it off, and out comes all your hair. The only way that these cats can come out from their bonds is if they come out—yes, you know already. Hairless. They must wriggle free of their resin-coated winding cloth, and in this act, depilate themselves.

So in addition to greed, they possessed vanity. Such a curse, but they bestowed it upon themselves.

I tried to tell them, but as with their fatal attraction to cream, they would not believe me.

I thought that I'd be telling them for eternity, or as long as we live. Little did I know that there is a way to kill a cat.

Mummy paper. No one makes mummy paper now. Almost no one ever did. But in the 1850s in the busy United States of America, there was a huge hunger for rags to make paper. And likewise, there was at the same

time, a huge digging up of mummies in Egypt. Many of those mummies
were tossed into the hungry maws of steam trains, but others were sent by
the shipload to the New World. And so my 6 siblings became for the last
time, sea cats. They took their first and last steam trip and were then treated
to the incomparable indignities that ended with them becoming—paper.

Not being, like that princess, liable to clog up the machine as a big-
boned body so therefore undressed of what the mill desired—40 yards of
linen—being instead neat little bundles tight as loaves, they were tossed
whole into the jaws of the giant crushing machine. In that shadowy wet
cavernous place, teeth the size of men thundered, smashing, grinding,
ripping the linen to shreds. I saw all 6 of my silly siblings for one fleeting
moment, tumbled from a basket into the maw. The machine crunched
down upon them like jaws upon a rat. I heard not a single miew, though
who could have heard it any more than anyone could have heard their
bones breaking? By nightfall the soup that they were crushed into was:
paper.

All the cats, not just the Greedy 6. All of them who I saw tumbled into
that frightful broth that day—all of them could have done something
through the centuries. Would they have—if they knew their future—torn
themselves loose, freed themselves in the shiphold or on the train, or in the
carts awaiting to be emptied into the terrible maw of that fateful (if you
choose to believe *that*) mill? Freed themselves of their bonds? I ask, but
that is my interfering self. I wouldn't choose as they did, but it can't be
Fate. They were turned into paper and died as cats, became no more themselves than the breadcrumbs in the baker's soup could again be bread.

And though they can never be recycled, there is a scrap of the paper still
extant, I must believe, somewhere. Somewhere?

For as science says: you can't destroy matter.

Such a waste. That a cat can be destroyed is too incredible. I can't believe
it, as you would say when something happens that you know just did.

Such a tragedy. So they were vain. So they were greedy. That's only
human, you might say. And so do *I*!

But:

There's a cat down the street here, living like Bastet herself.

A cat so beloved that I would find life cloying.

She's a bookshop cat. She spends her days catching warm rays in the
window. And her nights? I wouldn't know. But she has rolls of fat, and is
as active as a book.

People point at her, exclaim about her ugliness. But then they enter the shop and try to tempt her to come and let them pet her. They buy books they never thought they'd want, but they do, taking them home, maybe as substitutes for this cat. They become silly in their admiration. They are not themselves.

I would say that she is Bastet herself, if I were a believer. But one thing I do know. She is free.

Her skin is pink as a tongue. She is hairless as a mouse's heart.

THE SEVEN MIRRORS

MARLY YOUMANS

Marly Youmans says, 'After the first portion of "The Seven Mirrors" materialized as a daydream—the fad for seven mirrors, the Charlottesville school, Poe, the central figure and her bike, the cemetery—the rest of the story unreeled so quickly that I doubt being able to catch hold of the original inspiration, any more than one could catch the tail of a fleet ghost in a mirror. In memory, the writing feels like a paean to the energy, imagination, and longings of youth.'

Ms. Youmans is the author of eleven books of fiction and poetry, winner of the Michael Shaara, Ferrol Sams, ForeWord, and other awards. Publisher and editor Sean Wallace says of 'The Seven Mirrors', 'It still remains one of the most stunning novellas I've ever read, in my life.'

T HE SO-CALLED "BLACK WRITINGS" OF HOLBERG HAD circulated for some months at my school in Charlottesville, and many of the girls were wild to try the mystical investigations that had predated Ludwig Holberg's composition of his *Subterranean Voyage*, his account of a journey to the land of the dead. In particular, a mania for the "Experiment of the Seven Mirrors, also called the Pleiades," grew up, and a secret cache of gilt-framed mirrors, pilfered from vanity tables and little-used rooms, was kept hidden on the grounds. My classmates were busy forming collections of necrophiliac objects, letters and curls of hair and scraps of embroidered cloth that had belonged to their great-grandmothers.

I, too, proved not exempt from the general hysteria, though I held myself aloof longer than most. Not until after ninth grade, in the quiet days of summer school, did I join in. The "Seven Mirrors" was my downfall, in part because I already possessed a treasured assortment of objects from an adored dead: a rose taken from his grave in Richmond, a shard of glass worked from between two floorboards in his college room on the Range, and the word *unspeakable*, said to be inscribed in his own hand on an otherwise unremarkable strip of foolscap. I especially treasured the glass, which appeared to be the fragment of a mirror, marked by a trace of dried blood which I hoped might be my idol's own, the very DNA script of him. Once, in a moment of temptation, I had thought of placing the object on my tongue like a holy wafer: had imagined the nick, the coppery taste of blood—the blending of mine with his, the living with the dead. It was a thought that seemed to verge on the foolscap word, *unspeakable*, but it gave me pleasure.

My name was a plain, common *Catherine*, but in the infinite corridors of the internet, I had begun to sign myself as *Ermengarde*. She, I imagined, could succeed where others had failed.

One afternoon I dragged the sack of mirrors out of its hiding place in a hollow tree. I rode to the chosen spot: a mausoleum in a much-frequented cemetery. A year before, I had discovered the hiding place of the key while playing hide-and-seek with friends. My fingers, gripping a projection under the low roof, had accidentally flung the bit of metal onto the pavement. The ringing noise gave me away, but before I scampered toward home base, I tucked the key in my pocket. Afterward I occasionally visited the mausoleum, and I often daydreamed about the musty air, the coffins, the tumble of mouse bones in a corner, the lurid window that shed a stain of crimson and indigo. The intense colors reminded me of "The Masque of the Red Death." The chamber was authentically spooky, far more interesting to me than any horror movie.

Although I sought out the company of the dead, I was careful to avoid the caretaker and passers-by who crossed the soil without much thought for its inhabitants. So many took shortcuts through the cemetery that I didn't worry about being a girl, alone. Or perhaps I was merely careless. On the afternoon of the seven mirrors, my thoughts were not with the living. But since I didn't want to risk being cornered in my private hideaway and maybe having to hand over the key, I leaned my bike against an obelisk some rows from my destination.

The chamber was the same as always, darker and cooler than the outside day, as if it were different from the outer world in climate and in hour.

I propped the seven mirrors on the coffins, measuring with a tape I had brought so that they were in what Holberg regarded as the exact conflguration of the constellation of the Pleiades. Afterward I took out my treasures, and set the rose (red when I snatched it from his grave but now shriveled and black), the word *unspeakable,* and the blood-speckled triangle of glass upon a lid engraved with a girl's name and years. It wasn't quite as late in the day as Holberg recommended, but it was gloomy inside the mausoleum; the noise of my feet on the curled dry leaves gave me a frisson of unease.

All the same, I kept on going. I lit the candle and said the words, conjuring the spirit to speak only truth.

When nothing happened, whim made me snatch the shard of mirror and touch my tongue to its blood, long dried. I don't know what I expected; there was no revelation, no fear of having succumbed to something forbidden, only a sense of solidity and the taste of salt. I measured the mirrors once more before I began again, making an insignificant correction.

A flicker in one of the mirrors: it was caught by another, and, as if a match had been ignited on the other side of the glass, all seven caught fire.

It was not a light at all; or, if it was, it had something about it of the iridescence of decay.

The flash in the depths was a face, pale and dark at once.

"What do you want from me?" The voice was tremulous, broken.

I hadn't thought of a proper question, and I felt a panic of unreadiness, as well as a fright at being in the presence of something unclearly dead.

"Why are you as you are? What are you really?" The question was awkward; I hardly knew what I asked, or what it meant, but the voice seemed to take the words and arrange them to suit itself.

"Why Griswold, you mean? Why let the Reverend Rufus Griswold, small-time literary man, defame my name in my very obituary? Why let him be my executor and give him rein to forge my letters, destroy all memory of friendships, assassinate my very character?"

The image wobbled in the glass like the reflected moon on water, but I felt sure it was really he. The eyes had a lustrous quality that accorded with my own image of the man.

I nodded, and then whispered, "Yes." It wasn't in the least what had been in my mind; in fact, I had never heard of this Griswold. It was a curious name, *gris* with *wold*; I knew enough of languages to think of a drab land in which one could wander forever. *Rufus*: to me that meant nothing but the rufus kingfisher, but wasn't this spirit a kind of king—king of a gray realm? The dying Fisher King flitted through my thoughts; my half-sister, a college junior, had been reading *The Waste Land*, a work she found alternately maddening and confusing. Myself, I prefer somebody like Andrew Marvell when it comes to pondering those little aggravations like the deserts of eternity and the iron gates of life: give me some spine and a good laugh, will you?

"Yes, yes, you might well think it remarkable, more remarkable even than that I should have done what I have done and made what I have made. Did you read my obituary? How much time has passed?" The voice hurried on without waiting for reply, as if he were not concerned with the centuries. "The Right Reverend Griswold. This is what he said: 'Edgar Allan Poe is dead. He died in Baltimore the day before yesterday. This announcement will startle many, but few will be grieved by it. I myself can find nothing in my heart responsive to the news. The poet was well known personally or by reputation, in all this country; he had readers in England, and in several of the states of Continental Europe; but he had few or no friends; and the regrets for his death will be suggested principally by the consideration that in him literary art lost one of its most brilliant, but erratic stars.' That's good, isn't it?"

The voice laughed softly.

"I purposed it; I was the one who chose the man. What is the role of executor if not to execute? Not, as in the common, plebeian sense, to carry out a commission, but in the higher, rarified mode. To *execute*, to decapitate, to annihilate. I cheered, then groaned when I thought of it! My whole life had been on a chasmal pitch, skidding toward that revelation. The birth passage from gloom to pain of light, my father's desertion, my mother's death. Was it not all a fabric of betrayal and unpardonable destruction? A hurtling toward dissolution? Was I not born to suffer, and by adoption to become the accursed child of one who could never comprehend the least motive or spring of my being? Who had no love or sympathy with an excitable, febrile temperament or an artist's soul? Mr. Allan stood as an emblem of this great commercial enterprise, America, which seeks to devour its writers in insatiable bites and gulps! His name at the heart of my own! Was it any wonder that I drank or gambled, trusting in visions and sudden swerves of fortune? Yet freedom from want never came! Not at the University of Virginia, with its serpentine walls that drew my heart to the arabesque, not at West Point—the shame of it, living without means, having not so much as clean linen to my name!

"Years of naked unhappiness . . . I buried myself in my darling child wife. The god Hymen, broken and weeping crimson tears, came to our wedding. I sheathed my very soul in her; the frail scabbard melted away, leaving only splashes of red and memories. Our mirrors were draped in black, so that I grew to fear the nature of the images hidden underneath. My recollections pulsed with blood. They, too, were consumptives and would not stay, growing starved and transparent. None of my literary successes could save me; they brought only jealousy, insult, and feuds. I dived deep, seeking the supernatural at the bottom of a glass. I tried to destroy myself with laudanum, but death howled and spat me out! My ladies, oh, I wanted one of them to save me, to place my fevered head between her cool, naked thighs and let her hold me steady. I didn't care which one. I couldn't care. They were all one woman, one desired constancy, while I was many men. I spun and bobbed like a top until I was forced to drink and drink and drink in Philadelphia, and at last I died, raving as I swept toward the lip of the world and the plummet—"

"Who are you?" But I recognized everything about him.

"I am and am not he, the man Poe. But what is Poe? A veil flung between hope and heaven? An ululation pronounced by a bare-breasted woman on a cliff that looks uncannily like piled bales of cotton? A smear of putrescence that shines like gasoline rainbows? The impulse of an angel, or of a fallen power? Did I say that I myself gave Griswold a copy—borrowed from my employer's bookcase—of Bulwer-Lytton's novel, *The Caxtons*? With my own hand I marked the passage with which he later defamed me, a description of the character of Francis Vivian: 'Passion, in him, comprehended many of the worst emotions that militate against human happiness. His temperament was mercurial, his desires unmet, his history dramatic—yea, unto tragedy and melodrama. You could not contradict him, but you raised quick choler; you could not speak of wealth, but his cheek paled with gnawing envy. The astonishing natural advantages of this poor boy—his beauty, his readiness, the daring spirit that breathed around him like a fiery atmosphere—had raised his constitutional self-confidence into an arrogance that turned his very claims of admiration into prejudices against him. Irascible, envious—bad enough, but not the worst, for those salient angles were all varnished over with a cold repellent cynicism, his passions vented themselves in sneers. There seemed to him no moral susceptibility; and, what was more remarkable in a proud nature, little or nothing of the true point of honor.' You see? That is Poe, a character from a Bulwer-Lytton novel, masquerading under a nom de plume . . . Francis Vivian. My *other* was made not of flesh but of words— and bore a feminine name. I rose again, half woman. Curious, is it not? There's a perversity to the idea of a man becoming a character—blood reduced to a handful of words."

The voice had become excitable and quick; I could hardly keep up with what it was saying. The room seemed filled with a treelike rustling, and an idea that it was *me*—the veins and the nerves of me trembling as if stirred by a gust—flew into my mind. Above this, the syllables continued on, rapid and at times staccato.

"Years before, I had been irresistibly impelled to lie to Griswold when he asked me for an autobiographical sketch. I created another self. *That* Poe was born not in January 1809, but in January 1811. His family tree was old Baltimore stock, its canopy weighty with famous names from the Revolution and British naval history, rooted in English manor soil. Yet this privileged Poe ran wild, was 'dissolute' and 'dissipated'; like Byron, he threw himself into the Greek struggle for independence—but then wandered off to Russia. He was famous in Britain, writing under pseudonyms 'not permitted' to be disclosed. Unspeakable, no doubt!

"Why? Why did I do it? How do I know, when I do not even know what Poe I am any longer? I only know that I wrote out of my own heart's blood, and that neither the states nor their citizens ever gave me ease or paid me a living wage for the red drops of me, and so I died.

"Eternity gnaws at my heel. Who is Poe? What am I? *L'autre?* Progenitor of poets and storytellers to come—or who have come and gone? I swing in time like an orangutan on a child's monkey bars. Such is my fate, to spin and to become—what? The black angel of Baudelaire? The unmanly man of Auden? The blasphemer? The opium-eater, perhaps in yet another Poe's tale? The raven? The defamed star of Griswold? The jingle man of Emerson? The "no milksop or dreamer" of Arthur Conan Doyle? I love that fellow's name; it reminds me of my own labyrinthine journey as Arthur Gordon Pym. Perhaps Edgar Allan Poe is merely a figment of Pym's imagination. So who am I? The double dream of Jorge Borges? Of Georgy Porgy, pudding and pie? Of Joe Poe? Was it I, childless, who in futurity fathered Borges and instructed him in the horror of mirrors and mazes? Who led him by the hand into a labyrinth of words? And who, if not I, taught him that he was Borges and not Borges, as I am and am not Poe and Poe and Poe and Poe and Poe in the infinite reiteration of images in glass? Or am I merely the flight of a bird in and out the windows of a ruined cathedral in a tale by one yet unborn?

"In life, I could have been content with less, with a warm dish of milk by the fire and a wife who cooled and stroked my head, but that was not my fate. The arc of my life was always the same. I kicked at the doors to comfort, but they were sealed against art with the great mercantile seal of America and would not let me in.

"Nevermore, the bird says. Never will and nevermore."

The voice, strangely exalted, echoed from mirror to mirror. It seemed to me that Poe had become a diamond, and that everywhere it turned, I could see new facets of him.

"So I have revenged myself on the states and on the world. I am still read. The literati listened with surprise and alarm as I clawed the sides of my pauper's coffin, wrenched its hinges, and rose with my arms swaddled in poems and stories and with corruption set like a star and a crown on my forehead—"

The face rocked in the mirrors like light on a black stream.

"Hearken," the voice whispered. "What's that?"

I listened, my skin prickling.

"It's just the caretaker, mowing the lawns."

"What is this—where are you?"

"In—In Charlottesville, where you wrote 'Edgar Allan Poe' on a pane of glass in your room. They keep it in a case, you know, like a saint's relic . . . "

There was more shaking, and the light broke into stars and faded away.

I called his name but nothing answered. The candle guttered and went out. I shivered, damp with sweat. The window flung shafts of crimson and indigo onto the floor. As I gathered the mirrors, a line from Poe's "The Power of Words" came into my thoughts: *For wisdom, ask of the angels freely, that it may be given!*

Outside, the breeze felt warm, and the lawn was a deepening green. A boy had his back to me, pushing a mower into the setting sun while a maelstrom of insects burned around him. He looked astonishingly alive, thrusting through that golden furnace of light.

For a moment I was transfixed by the mystery of him; then I darted across the graves in search of my bicycle, the sack of mirrors jangling in my hand. I pedaled along the sidewalk, ducking under branches of crepe myrtles as the mirrors shifted inside my bike bag. Rose, word, and shard were safe in my pack. Exultant, I picked up speed and jumped the curb to the street, zooming to the opposite walk. The mausoleums had gone blue in the shadows when I glanced over my shoulder.

"I wasn't afraid," I said out loud, my voice shaky. "I wasn't."

Bending low over the handlebars, I sped toward school and the hollow tree where I would leave the sack. With luck, I'd be in before dark.

Catherine and Catherine and Catherine, I thought.

"My name is Ermengarde," I shouted to the coming dusk and the trees and the sky's dark sword-cuts, slashed by the birds. Their cries made me feel even more joyful, for they were no Poe's ravens of ceaseless lament but angelic flyers, shrieking *evermore, evermore, evermore.* The colors of houses and shrubs and cars flowered in the twilight as I called out again. Once more I felt the nerves and veins of my body like the silhouette of a red and blue tree. The wind dashed tears from my eyes as I struck hard at the pedals, flying along the path.

I was fifteen, and I had wanted nothing except to be a poet for years and years. Some dreams never happen in the least, but just then I knew my strangeness and strength and the size of my yearning: *My name is Ermengarde, Ligeia, and Madeleine, and I will batter and kick against your doors until they fall.*

Fool!

Oh, sure, I knew my own foolishness. Plenty of times I'd written in my diary in Poe's spooky, crepuscular voice. I loved the paradox of it, the jarring marriage of a twenty-first-century girl with a nineteenth-century man, vain and gothic-hearted. It was a little campy, like putting on an outrageous hat loaded with birds and old-fashioned flowers. Even the fact that I thought of myself as one of Poe's heroines, bound to her lover or brother, was absurd. The vision and the message brought on by Holberg's experiment were genuine, yet, for that day, my dream of being a poet remained undisturbed by words of the visionary man. But hadn't the revelation told me what a terrible fate it is to be embraced by the muse? Had any happiness or contentment come to Poe? Hadn't he wooed and tempted annihilation?

To some degree, I saw what was before me. I remembered the mower, gone golden, the cries of the birds: these were images of life and light, not passages from some underground corridor, strangely lit from a mysterious source. It was these that called to me, not the flare in the seven mirrors. So much intelligence I grant myself, but not more.

I had more freedom than any girl should have. My parents had stowed me in summer school, and the courses were mere play compared to the work of fall and spring term. I knew how to leave the grounds without anyone noticing, and I came and went as I pleased, often without a companion. My close friends were at home, or off traveling with parents who wanted to spend the summer with them. Often I lay on my bed and scribbled in my notebook. I spent hours drawing and erasing and redrawing manga figures. One of them, black-haired and with a small moustache, resembled Poe—a Poe hunched in an oversize jacket with tails, his enormous shoes trailing laces. A big-eyed bird of ill omen perched on his shoulder.

I did not go back to the cemetery. I felt reluctant to return; I had the inkling of a thought that what I had done was wrong or perverse—or something. Sprawled in a litter of pens and drawings and books, I would draw and write by flashlight until exhaustion stilled my hand. The books I chose to read were already familiar to me. I didn't investigate the authors the figure had mentioned, though I had gone so far as to see if Chesterton and Borges were in the school library, a peculiar structure made, like so many of our nineteenth-century buildings, along the lines of a rabbit warren. The secret crannies of the place lured me because they were so opposite to the oversized, light-soaked rooms in my parents' house in Raleigh. I navigated the winding corridors, searching for the books our catalog said would be there. They weren't. I often drifted off with my cheek on a page. My perfunctory prayers were a blur at the edge of sleep. Even there, gripped by the headlong fall toward unconsciousness, the words *lead me not into temptation* disturbed my peace.

One morning a flicker of motion in the large oval mirror that hung on the wall of my dormitory room led me to think with fear of the encounter in the mausoleum. Not anything definite, it was no more than a tug at reality: some stray stirring in one corner. I turned and surveyed the bedchamber, the trailing spread and nightstand, the dresser. The furniture was typical of our dormitory issue, curious pieces with pigeonholes and secret compartments that had the additional charm of being the same ones used by girls who had gone to school on these grounds a hundred years or more past—who might have left behind a message or a forgotten treasure. But they were still, absolutely still, revealing nothing.

At first I thought that the movement must be a mouse. I had been wakened by a scrabbling in the wall the night before. So I lured Princess Delphinium, the enormous blue Persian cat belonging to our housemother, to my room. She sniffed in a half-hearted manner at my sneakers and at a plate that had seen some cheese and crackers in the last week, and then launched herself at the bed, where she promptly washed her paws and fell asleep. I climbed in beside her to read a history of the slave trade for my morning class, but I am afraid that book and cat worked on me like a drug, and I woke only when the housemother banged on our doors, calling "Lights out!" Delphinium lay flopped on my pillow with her copper eyes narrowed, tail switching. She hissed and dived from the bed, materializing on the table below the mirror, where she proceeded to attack, pouncing at the slippery surface and letting out a series of weird, half-smothered howls.

"Catherine!"

It was our housemother.

"Have you got Delphie in there?"

When I opened the door, the cat spat at the mirror and bolted, charging between our feet and streaking down the corridor.

"Whatever was that about?" Mrs. Banister stared at the crooked end of the hall, where a blue cloud of fur arced around a corner.

"I thought that there was a mouse in my room. Something darted . . . " It was impossible to explain that I had seen something on the other side of the mirror. I looked at her, unable to go on.

"Don't get upset!" Mrs. B fumbled at my shoulder blade. I have never been the sort of girl whom one pats, and people who try generally make a bad job of it—not their fault, of course. "You're usually so self-possessed. I'll take a look around."

She came in, glancing from corner to corner, bending to check under my bed.

"You're right up there with the worst of them," she said, observing my nest of clothes and papers. "There's a room check due this week, you know. Why don't you get a box for your drawings and scribbles? That would take care of a lot of this . . . " She made an arabesque motion with her hand.

"Debris," I offered. I relaxed. She didn't see anything because there wasn't anything to see. Perhaps it had been nothing but a mouse.

"Look at that!" Mrs. B leaned over my bed, gathering up wisps of fur. "Would you like to give Delphie a good brushing sometime? I'll pay you in homemade cookies. How would that be? You must be lonesome, with so many of the girls away. The headmistress says that you're not going home between sessions."

Normally I don't take comments about my private life from anybody, and Mrs. B might have been implying something distasteful about my parents. But I was entirely too distracted to care, or to try and reprove her for stepping over a line into territory I normally defended.

"Yes, I'll do that. Maybe tomorrow." As I was glancing at the mirror, checking to make sure that it hadn't changed in any way, Mrs. B passed with the rolled-up fluff in her hand and paused to peep at her reflection and tuck her hair behind her ears. She appeared satisfied with an image notable for its tight curls, fuchsia lipstick, and brows plucked close to the vanishing point.

"Strange how chilly some of these old rooms can be." She stared at herself in the mirror, nodded, and turned away.

Just then, I glimpsed something in the glass.

"What's the matter?" She spoke to me sharply, catching me by the wrist.

"I thought it was the . . . "

Mrs. B wheeled about, looking at the wall opposite. She made a careful examination of the wainscoting and baseboard.

"I don't see anything. But there's a crack in the corner as big as your thumb, and it's amazing the way mice can clamber through the narrowest opening. I'll have maintenance stuff some poison in there. How's that?"

Since my fingers were trembling, I clasped my hands together.

"You're not afraid, are you?"

"Afraid of a mouse? No, of course not." I wanted to say something more to her, but I didn't know what. "Though there are things worth being afraid of," I added.

"Girls and women have to be careful. If you're careful, you never have to be sorry."

That wasn't what I had meant, but I assented. I had eaten that very crumb of wisdom before; it was often hauled out for the inspection of a group of girls heading to town.

When Mrs. B left the room, I scrutinized the glass carefully but saw nothing out of place. I was sorry that Delphinium had bounced away and wished her back again.

Three days later, I saw a decided movement in the glass. Until then, I had felt only a pang of anxiety when passing the mirror, and had avoided looking in that direction. It was difficult, because the big oval was centered on one wall, and reflected a portion of my bed. This time I was propped up on pillows and was in no doubt that I had glimpsed a flash at the left side, near the gilt frame.

I couldn't look away. Clutching a schoolbook to my chest, I stared until I couldn't keep myself from blinking: there was nothing more. The jumping of my pulse died down. Still, I couldn't quit noticing any change, and when I tugged the sheet over my knees, I let out a whoop, startled by my own reflection.

"What's going on?"

Mary Elizabeth leaned in the open door, her blonde hair lashed into a high ponytail that pulled the skin of her face taut. She looked ready to break out in a laugh.

"Just spooked, I guess. Thought I saw something in the mirror."

She came in, peering into the glass.

"Nobody but me. And you. And a whole lot of garbage."

I didn't respond; Mary Elizabeth was no favorite of mine, but I didn't want her to leave. Although I had never thought her very smart, she came up with a good idea.

"Why don't you turn it to the wall? Or cover it with a cloth? Wait a sec—I've got something that will do."

In a minute she came back with a rough-edged length of black cotton in her hand.

"Here—I've been working on sets for the fall play all week. It's just a leftover. I was going to make it into something, but this will be better." She swathed the mirror with the fabric, tucking it underneath at the sides and pinning a bunch of material around the hook at the top.

I was grateful to her for not making fun of me, and said so.

"Oh, I've been scared plenty of times, doing the Ouija board with my brother. We about jumped out of our skins last Christmas."

"Thanks. That looks a lot better."

"Sure. Want to go bother Mrs. B? I was just heading over."

My legs felt quivery, but I got out of bed, letting the papers in my lap tumble to the floor. "All right. I need to comb Delphinium."

"Delphie's such a funny thing. Her face is smushed, like she smacked into a wall and stayed that way." Mary Elizabeth patted her face with the flat of her hand to illustrate.

"That's just the way Persians are." My voice sounded faint. I was glad to leave the room, and I left the door wide open, so that whatever haunted it could have full chance to leave.

When I returned several hours later, the cloth still hung over the mirror. In the evening light, it looked like a dwarf wearing a cloak, his shoulders hunched and head bent. All the same, it was better than a reflection. I went to sleep with the door ajar, in case Delphie wanted to come in.

In the morning she sat humped high on the mat just outside the room. She woke me with a low gargled noise as if a meow had gotten caught in her throat and was strangling her.

I staggered to the door in my nightgown.

"You're not such a Delphic oracle," I told her, loading my voice with scorn. "Anybody could tell something was the matter."

She stalked away on her stubby peg legs with the plume of her tail raised against me. I would have to apologize later if I wanted to stay in the cat's good graces. She was spoilt, I thought; every girl on the hall petted and coaxed her. Though a mere puffball, she ruled the corridors' twists and turns, the crannies and the window seats.

While changing, I felt uneasy and was sorry that I hadn't ingratiated myself with the beast. I had that peculiar sensation when the hair hackles at the nape of your neck because somebody's covertly watching, so I went close to the mirror and fingered the cloth, drawing it up until I could see the reflection of my wrist and the bunched fabric. Then I let it drop. Gathering the rest of my clothes, I carried them to the bathroom and changed hurriedly.

When I returned, the textbook on the slave trade was open on my bed, the pages turned to a section we hadn't been assigned. On the right-hand page was a passage from William Bartram's *Travels*; on the left was a woodcut engraving of a black man in a cage, hanging from a tree. The caption said that birds had pecked his eyes out, and so he asked the passing traveler to put him out of his misery. When I glanced behind me, the cloth over the glass resembled the wings of crows.

Mary Elizabeth breezed in, ponytail skinned back in morning tightness. Her skin had been scrubbed to rose.

"How's it going?" She cocked her head toward the mirror.

"It's not. Or is—going, that is. I want to get rid of it. Gives me the creeps. Listen, did you come in my room a bit ago? Did you open my book?"

"Nah. I don't open books unless I have to!" She grinned at me, her teeth unnaturally white. Her father was a dentist, I remembered, or an oral surgeon. Had he performed his dental magic on Mary Elizabeth, to make her teeth like chalk?

"Must've been the wind." I checked the window—shut. "Or something. I'm off." I threw a notebook and my history book into a pack. "I've got a final this morning."

"Not me. That's why I took set design. No final, no tests, no essays, no nothing. I'll see you," Mary Elizabeth called as I loped down the hall. I was about to be late.

Summer school is simple. I wrote the three essays in less than ninety minutes, afterward going to the library to poke around in the stacks and check my email. I had accumulated a lot of spam, and mingled in with the usual sludge from persons and purveyors unknown were three messages from "Edipo." The name made my arms prickle. Opening them, I found nothing but nonsense, messages in fonts that were triangles and arcane marks; the last, set inside a lozenge, must have been a cartouche, but I deleted before considering that perhaps I could have deciphered the symbols. Afterward I could remember nothing but a jumble of shapes and the little bird hieroglyph that was part of the cartouche.

I had forgotten to put on my deodorant. Fear has its own primal stink, at least if you are barely fifteen.

"How'd it go?" Mary Elizabeth spotted me as I reached the top of the dorm stairs. At the other end of our hall, her blue leather bags stood packed and ready. Her parents were taking her to Florence, she had told me.

"Florence, South Carolina?" It was a joke; people used to go there to get false teeth. The town was the false-tooth capital of the world, once upon a time. That's what my father had told me, and I'd been revolted and fascinated by the idea of people pouring into Florence, South Carolina to render up their teeth in a tooth fairy's nightmare. Or maybe it was more of a dream—a happy tooth-fairy convention. It must've been disgusting, all those tooth tourists with their mouths packed in cotton, bloody heaps of incisors and molars everywhere. My dad, Arvin, had a big set of snappers. He'd had all his teeth pulled at one go. It must have been a right mess of pulp and blood. If he happened to be around a little kid, he'd shoot the falsies out of his mouth like the monsters in *Alien*. It fascinated children, the way a snake fascinates a mouse, or else made them cry. Either way, he had his laugh. For years he could make me roar by sliding them out slowly, slowly, with a great clashing chomp at the end. If my mother caught him, she'd scold him and say that you can take the boy out of Lumberton, but you can't take—you know how the rest goes. Once I heard her tell my half-sister that Lumberton had not *quite* reached the pinnacle of culture. My mother was born in Raleigh, so she considers Lumberton to be a perpetual joke.

"Florence, Italy, you doof!" Mary Elizabeth laughed. She was smart enough to know that I was kidding.

I was going to miss her; we had been the only ones left on our corridor, though there were other girls close by, up and down, separated by stairs that reeled and staggered, often pausing for long, contemplative landings with nooks for reading or gazing out of windows. Not many of us would be lingering for the break, though Mrs. B would be ensconced in her suite, baking cookies and crocheting toilet paper covers in the shape of antebellum dolls—she never left the grounds, so far as we could tell. She had wanted the girls in summer school to move onto her wing, but Mary Elizabeth and I had refused, not wanting the bother. Now I wished that I had agreed.

Mary Elizabeth helped me unhook the mirror and lug it into the hall before she left for the airport. A few hours later I found it back in place; I suppose one of the maintenance crew, vacuuming the hallways before the break, had strung it up again. The cloth was nowhere to be seen. I stared into the depths, which reflected the room but made it appear subtly larger and dimmer. After pawing through my closet and drawers, I draped a sarong square of batik with a design of rose and sky-blue cats over the mirror. My mother had sent it to me from some trip abroad; she was a banker, something I would never be. You couldn't pay me! *The Usurer*, I sometimes called her.

The cats distracted me from what glimmered underneath, though several times I felt sure that I had seen a quick, sharp movement through the veil. When I nerved myself to peep behind the cloth, the reflection was unchanged. At night I had a hard time calming myself to sleep, and I dreamed about a constellation of seven mirrors flashing in a sky of ink. On waking, I felt afraid that the room behind the drape had grown larger and darker while I slept.

Seven of us sat with Mrs. B at the table; there were six more at another table. The numerologist in me couldn't help but note the constancy of seven, the ill luck of thirteen. Two were from Jordan, and a third was from Kenya, so I suppose most of the girls had reasons for staying at school: better, no doubt, than mine. The emptiness of the dining room reminded me of the inside of a mirror. The domed chamber under the rotunda echoed with footsteps, and the two women who had been kept on through the summer break could be heard talking and laughing in the kitchen.

I scraped the sauce from my slice of chicken breast and meticulously cut away the bones and fat. Cutting a thin wedge, I took a bite. The flesh proved sticky and tasted revoltingly of canned fruit. I don't care for cooked peaches, especially when baked onto chicken. I prefer mine straight off the tree, warm and fragrant. When I'm grown, I'll live in Charleston and have fresh peaches all summer long.

Foul nasty fowl. I pushed the chicken perilously close to the brink of my plate and tried some of what I had assumed to be mashed potatoes. It wasn't: pureed cauliflower. Liberally peppering and salting, I stirred the stuff with my spoon.

"Not so bad with butter. They say the head cook's on vacation." My neighbor was a dark-eyed girl I recognized from Algebra. She had been quick to answer, alert to jump at what the teacher wanted, whereas I was sullen—I've always detested math in all its varieties and manifestations. "My name's Sharon."

"I remember you. The math whiz. I'm Catherine."

"I know—I've read your poems in the school mag."

"Maybe I'll have a chocolate bar for supper," I whispered. On impulse, I added, "And I've stopped all that nonsense, as of today. As of right now, this instant, I don't want to be a poet anymore. The money-grubbing citizens of America apparently don't appreciate the art of poetry, so unless I move to Uruguay or Russia or Argentina, I'm going to do manga."

"I liked your poems." She tilted her head and stared at me from under her bangs. "That one about Edgar Allan Poe? With the basilisk and the bird? That was my very favorite." I liked the way she looked, skinny with a big head, tiny nose and chin, and wide, slightly protruding eyes that reminded me of a manga drawing. Her feet were big, too. She reminded me a little of Delphie, who is a real manga beast, with her excessive, sticky-out fur and big copper eyes above a barely visible nose.

"I just don't want to be a poet anymore, that's all. It's like weaving tapestries of unicorn hunts or studying the secrets of alchemy—a dead pursuit. I especially don't want to be a poet like Poe. A damned soul, jumping into hell for the sake of a good line." I rapped on the bowl with my spoon for emphasis, so that the others at the table turned to look at me. And I was a sight worth staring at—I'd worn the slinky black Chinese gown my mother had sent from Hawaii, along with a grand, swoopy hat with a black feather that I called my *Mae West*. Mrs. B had told us to dress for dinner, and I meant to do so with a vengeance.

"Something you want to announce, Catherine?" Mrs. B smiled, though I knew that she was annoyed at me because of the last visit Delphie had paid to my room. The woman adored that cat; a suspicion seized me that there was something unnatural about the relationship. Immediately I dismissed the thought as perverse, a more interesting concept than Mrs. B warranted. The idea came straight from Poe, maligner of the feline. I felt a surge of grief, remembering him. Or perhaps it was denying poetry that made me feel so. Giving up was like being the heroine of a story that starts out one way and ends up entirely another. No wonder I had worn black.

"Sorry," I said, bending over my plate. The hat drooped over my face, as if it sympathized. "A mere disturbance in the dishware."

"We always like to hear from you." Mrs. B had on what I called her God-save-our-good-gracious-queen manner, and she gave me a nod before turning her attention to the glazed chicken. All she lacked was a powder-blue suit, pillbox hat, and a matched set of diamonds. And a couple of billion tucked into her matronly handbag.

Sharon peered under Mae West's ample brim.

"Annie Hudson told me that you had a chunk of bloody glass from Poe's bedroom and a rose from his grave and a love letter—"

"It's just a little shard, and not a letter. Just one word."

"Holberg." She lowered her voice. "Did you?"

I didn't answer.

"Because," she added, "I've got a copy of the *Pleiades*, the whole thing, that my brother sent me. He copied a pamphlet from the rare books library at his college. Have you seen it?"

"No. I'd like to—all I ever got was the mimeographed copy of the instructions that Hager Dinwiddie passed around." I felt sweaty. My shiny

Chinese sheath was wrinkled and creased at the hips. Why didn't they turn on the air conditioning? Perhaps the school meant to save money over break, but it wasn't right. I would have a word with Mrs. B. Her fuchsia lipstick had begun to bleed in the moist air.

"It's even rarer now. My brother told me that the one he had copied was stolen a week later. The librarians questioned him about whether he knew anything, since only three people had asked to see it in the past year—I guess they asked them all."

"Stolen. Wonder whether they wanted to possess or to destroy?" I toyed with a square of pineapple upside-down cake, flipping the thing over to see if it looked any better with the bottom side up. It didn't. "Can I come over after dinner? Why didn't you go home?"

"My stepmother." Sharon gave me a glance, her face without expression.

"Yeah. My parents."

Excusing ourselves, we carried our trays to the kitchen, briefly chatted up the cooks, and whipped out the side door, racing with whoops across the quadrangle, past the library, and into the shadowy back quad. I would've won except that my dress was way too tight. And poor Mae West flapped as though she wanted to sail into the sky. I followed Sharon's habit, avoiding the usual modes of ingress and scurrying up the fire escape. The rickety iron stairs jagged along walls half buried by Virginia creeper. The steps vibrated underfoot, and the bolts in the bricks seemed only tenuously fastened. My slinky black dress popped a thread as I flung myself through the open window, landing on a wide-cushioned bench below. The skreeking of the flimsy stairs and the final shot home had struck me as funny, and now I laughed until tears came to my eyes. Perhaps I was still punchy from stress—too much vigilance with the mirror. When I finally unwound, I sat up and glanced about, wiping my face with a kleenex that Sharon handed me. Her bedroom appeared similar to mine, though the furniture was more ornate. That there was no mirror pleased me; I was weary of duplication.

We talked for a long time. Afterward I lay full-length on the bed, reading the xeroxed pamphlet Sharon had mentioned at dinner. It had been translated into a turgid English that may or may not have been a fair reflection of Holberg's thought.

Meanwhile Sharon was curled on a lambskin rug, flipping through an album of photographs; she had never been away from home before being awarded a full scholarship plus a monthly allowance. Her brothers were as thin and manga-faced as she, I had noted before settling in with the pamphlet. Now and then I read a passage aloud.

"Listen to this: 'The danger inherent in the Pleiades is one of the making of simulacra; that is, a magical objective of the alchemical originators appears to have been either to introduce copies into the world, thereby achieving a kind of faux immortality, or else to erode the boundaries between this life and the next so that vestiges or ghosts might drift across the border. The latter idea of their purposing has been dismissed by commentators in the East, but is still countenanced in certain circles.'"

"Circles of hell, he means," Sharon interrupted, "and certain East Coast boarding schools."

"'However, the creation of simulacra so genuine that a man might take a being for another like himself has not been disproven. It is likely that the idea cannot be wholly dispelled, because if a simulacrum be sufficiently lifelike, the hoax would be impossible to perceive and hence to unmask; in a sense, there would be no mask. Such a creature would be no homunculus or ghost but in all material respects a flesh-and-blood entity capable of bleeding, feeling joy, and dying—yet would not be genuine but a simulacrum! This hard-to-compass description seems to imply that the simulacrum would not possess a soul but be in some sense hollow: man as imagined by the atheists, perhaps. Or man as he might be copied by some fearsome, yet-to-be-invented machine of the next millennium.'"

Yawning, Sharon shut the scrapbook.

"That's a mouthful. Holberg was a dreary old spirit, I guess. Did you try the experiment? You wouldn't say at dinner." She sat up, her eyes on me. "And what's wrong with those poems of yours? I really liked them."

"It's a tragic thing, giving your whole life to make these songs that used to be so important to people, only now they don't even matter." I dropped my grand manner. "Nobody ever reads one. Now and then maybe somebody switches on the radio at breakfast and hears some morose, arrhythmic rubbish about some college teacher who's unfortunate enough to be a poet and how he drinks coffee and reads the paper with his depressed dog. And to the people that hear it, that's all a poem is, some mundane prose thrown through the lawnmower and spewed out like clippings of grass—"

"But yours weren't boring. They weren't, really."

"Keats and Poe and Yeats, they thought it was a marvelous thing to be a poet, but the world changed, didn't it? Who wants to be in the pantheon of poets these days? Who could possibly be on fire to make a poem? Only some nutty weird kid who might actually be stupid enough to go and try and conjure the spirit of Poe. Or the simulacrum of Poe. Probably poets want to design a new video game these days. Why not? Nothing lasts. Or maybe the poets will just sit and watch TV for forty years on their big saddlebag butts. It doesn't matter that 'The Song of Wandering Aengus' burns the mind if nobody ever reads. Because then it doesn't exist. Like one hand clapping—it's just a slap in the face." I pushed my unruly hair into a knot, but it bristled and burst outward. "So there. Nevermore."

Sharon sat up and looked at me, her eyes bright in the lamplight.

"So did you—"

"Yes, I did. I set up the mirrors and called for him, and he came. It took me a while to see what he meant, but I've been thinking, off and on, though I still don't understand everything." I had admitted my success with the Pleiades on impulse, and I now told her about the mirror, though I didn't confess to the mausoleum and the key that was even now weighting a chain around my neck. The idea that I might take her to the cemetery appealed to me—I liked her, better than anyone else I'd met so far at school.

"I don't know anyone else who managed to do it." Sharon stared at me, assessing—what? My weirdness, my fall into temptation, the depths of my madness?

I shrugged. "Maybe we just had an affinity. Me and Poe, pals of the pen." Though I made light of my success, I remembered the salt taste of the blood and wondered if something more than kinship and words had called up the vision.

"Let's go to your room," she proposed. "I want to see that mirror."

I didn't object; the tale I told had been almost wholly occupied with the memory of what had happened in the mausoleum. But I couldn't forget the reflected room and the movements. So it was good to skim downstairs and see manga-eyed Sharon laugh and toss the cloth from the glass. Shadowy with evening, the room's reflection hung motionless on the wall. She sat and watched it for half an hour without blinking, or so she claimed later. I hadn't been sleeping well and dropped into a nap as soon as I slumped onto my bed. She stayed up until one in the morning, drinking caffeinated soda and reading in my notebooks of poems, keeping an eye on the mirror.

I slept heavily, without dreams, and in the morning I found Sharon on the floor, rolled up in a blanket.

"Thanks." I was awake enough to feel grateful to her and half sorry that she hadn't seen anything.

"We could do it again tonight, though I'm positive that nothing strange was in the room. Maybe it just took time to disappear. Or was busy. Who says that ghosts always come when they're expected?"

"You're a mathematician *and* a morning person." I felt groggy: my usual pre-noon condition.

Morning people tend to trample brightly through the moods of those less fortunate, so she ignored me, giving off a big, flashing smile. "Listen, how about we ride out to that cemetery after lunch on Saturday? I've got the whole afternoon free."

Tottering to my dresser, I gulped down a mug of black coffee that had been festering for several days, waiting for a moment of direst need. "Horrible, nauseating stuff," I muttered. I straightened, briefly compared myself to a watered rose—just as quickly ditched the idea—and stretched. While Sharon rattled on about Saturday, I climbed into my closet (I insist on privacy), where I stripped, balling up my black dress and climbing into my ratty old kid's bathrobe with the flying penguins on it. I decided to tell her everything. Saturday sounded like a fine idea. Despite the fact of morning, I felt a rush of euphoria. I wasn't in this peculiar situation alone. When I emerged, Sharon laughed at me; as she was still wearing her clothes from the night before, she went upstairs to change.

Putting my hands on either side of the gilt frame, I stared into an ordinary room. Nothing. Nothing to cause the least alarm, except for a crumpled, slept-in dress. I was glad, and I didn't even jump when Delphie leaped onto the table, nudging my arm with her stunted Persian forehead. I rested my palms against the mirror, feeling the hard, intractable substance against my skin. The world felt safe once more, or as safe as it gets.

"Oh, that's sweet! That's priceless!"

The boy that I'd met only an hour ago—the caretaker's son—swung his scythe and flailed at a stand of chicory. The stems with their blue flowers pitched sideways in the hot sun. Uncertain whether I should bolt, I glanced over my shoulder; Sharon was wandering through the graves in the old section, reading the inscriptions on the tablets. Our bicycles were propped against the stone wall by the street, poised for a quick getaway.

At first it had all gone so well.

I'd been in a buoyant mood at lunch with Sharon and on the ride over, our bikes zooming like dragonflies through traffic. While she poked through the plots, I'd fallen easily into talk with the caretaker's son. We liked the same music—he even had a copy of the Tiger Lilies' rendition of Edward Gorey's macabre tales—and had seen the same obscure Bergman movies and Corman's *The Tomb of Ligeia*. He didn't call them *films,* either; that was good. We hadn't read many of the same books, and his lists of favorites came off as a bit geekish. I didn't mind. As a reader, I'm pretty much omnivorous. By the time we got onto favorite anime, I'd started to have that warm, delicious feeling that you get when talking to somebody you're sure will be a friend, and it didn't begin to ebb until we meandered into Holberg territory. Then everything had gone wrong. As I was telling the story—parts of it—I could see him growing agitated, until I broke off entirely.

"What's the matter?" I followed close behind him, even when he gestured with the blade as though I shouldn't come too close. "You were the one who was interested—you came over to me, and you—you accosted me and asked all about why I came here and seemed fearfully nice—how deluded a woman can be!" My mistake, I knew, I knew, I knew. I'd been carried away by the sudden friendship with Sharon, deluded into the daydream that the world was full of people like me who would, indeed, like me. "It's not my fault you'd heard about the Holberg experiments and were curious—and then you have the nerve to go and get all sulfurous and smoldery and plain old stuffed shirtish—"

"You sneak over here from your refined private girls' school, and you do some hocus pocus thing with mirrors, and poof! Edgar Allan Poe comes to visit and tells you a bunch of stuff about how he damned himself through this Grayworld person—"

"Griswold—his name was—"

"Whatever—Grisfreakingwold! What business did you have messing around here? Who asked you to come and do black magic on our tomb-stones, anyway? If my dad wasn't laid up with shingles, he'd—Didn't anybody ever tell you that it's wrong to do things like that? Don't you have a mother or father or somebody to tell you how to do right?"

He looked as if he might really take the sickle and fling it at me. It's amazing what a good imitation of the Lord of the Dead a teenage boy in a t-shirt and scythe can give, if his heart's fired with an assortment of the seven deadlies. Wrath and pride seemed to be the passions jostling in the forefront. While I wasn't about to cower, I retreated a judicious few steps.

"You assume because you're nice and petted and rich, probably, that you can do whatever you like? That if you want something hard enough, it will happen? Imagine that it'll happen? Is that it? It's supposed to happen for you because you're so damn special—"

Here he hurled the scythe away and looked so thunderously at me that I veered away, letting out a yelp as I caught my ankle on an infant's half-submerged lamb. I tumbled sideways and struck my head on a tombstone: stars exploded and glimmered slowly into the dark, dropping in streamers of gold like the fireworks called *weeping willow*. Then there was nothing but hush and blackness until I heard voices and felt something splashing onto my face.

"What on earth did you think you were doing? Who do you think you are, the Grim Reaper? You might have killed her—I thought she was dead—look at the blood, my Lord, what did—"

"I didn't touch her—she's coming round—she's not dead."

"You're choking her! That's too much!"

Sputtering and coughing, I jerked upward, seizing the arm before my face. I gripped the boy tightly as pain slammed against my head. Exhaling, I cried out, and then held still, trembling. I hate it when people pule and weep. I don't do that.

"Who am I?"

My hand shook as I raised it against the glare. I really didn't know who it was—he hadn't told me his name. My thought was: Damon *the Mower*. (That's because I love Andrew Marvell.) But I didn't say so.

"The Grim Reaper," I whispered.

"Who the hell are you is about right." Sharon blotted water from my forehead with a rag that stank of grease. "Catherine, Catherine, who am I? Do you know who I am?"

"You are manga-Sharon," I said, no doubt a bit dottily. "You are big-eyed anime girl. You are a drawing by Miyazaki."

"She sounds normal, at least for..." Sharon paused. "Maybe we should get her out of the sun, give her a drink of water."

"I'll do it; it's my fault. I've never hurt a girl before in my whole life, and

I'm so sorry." The boy picked me up, kneeling with his back straight and rising quickly, so that I wondered if he were used to lifting heavy objects— tombstones, perhaps.

"Not on a coffin," I said thickly. Just then my tongue seemed an alien instrument.

"No, of course not." He didn't sound annoyed this time, and I wondered whether I had frightened him. "I'll fetch a bandage."

He put me down in the shade of a tree before he took off running. While he was gone, I made Sharon go investigate what he had left at the foot of an angel, near his lawnmower.

"An empty water bottle, a bundle of iron keys, and a calculus book with an exam stuck in the back. Grade of 102. He didn't get the second extra credit problem," she reported.

I moaned.

"Does it hurt?" She peered at me, sympathetic but helpless. "I know— dumb question."

"Another mathematician," I said faintly.

"A violent, girl-hurling mathematician," she pointed out. "But at least he's bright."

"No hurl," I whispered. "Just a stumble." I had torn something—his sense of the spot as inviolable, or maybe his pride. Was that it? I had wads of the prickly stuff myself. Perhaps it was hard to go to school with the sons of C-ville professors and lawyers and doctors, when your father was the local lawn boy to the dead. While your classmate's dad was fighting against tort reform, yours was six feet under, shoveling clay. You might even outdo the others in taste and braininess, but when the big yellow bus stopped, the caretaker's cottage was home.

Soon he pelted back again, carrying a bundled-up blanket. Dumping it onto the grass, he fished through his loot.

"Ice. Put it on the cut," he directed, handing Sharon a plastic bag full of ice. "I've got more in the towel. There's a bandage, but we don't need that yet. I'm so sorry, really I am. It's a fault of mine, getting angry and pushy."

"Yeah, you said it." Sharon rubbed the ice over the swelling around the cut. "And you could've killed her, you know."

He didn't resist the blame, though strict accuracy meant that he'd been guilty of nothing more than startling me. The two slid me onto the blanket, and the boy fixed a cup of cold water.

"Here. Take these. They'll help with the head. It must hurt."

I took the pills without question; it did hurt. I must've drifted off for a few minutes, because when I woke again, the others were mid-conversation.

"Don't think she'll be able to ride the bike to school, not unless she's feeling better," Sharon was saying.

"I can walk you there, or maybe we can call a taxi, and you can leave the bikes in the shed until later . . . "

I watched the boy, letting their words slide away. He had a malnourished, scrawny look to him, though he was muscled. His skin was very pale. That must've been why he had been wearing a hat, I speculated. He wore cheap sneakers with faded black jeans and a white t-shirt.

"What's your name?" I interrupted. "You never told me your name." The words sounded garbled—or gargled, maybe—definitely somehow askew.

"Pendragon." He glanced down at his hands. "Fancy name, isn't it?"

"Just Pendragon?" Sharon looked dubious. One name was for rock stars and certain writers of children's books.

"My dad named me Lee Al, but I don't like it much, even if Lee is a big name around Charlottesville. My friends just call me Pendragon."

"Puh," I said. The syllable didn't want to fall out of my mouth.

Sharon leaned over me, scrutinizing my eyes.

"She's got the same size pupils. I know that's one thing to look for with a blow. If they're not the same, it's a real bad sign."

"It's almost right," I blurted out, my voice too vehement.

"What does she mean?" Pendragon picked up my hand, examined it as though he had never seen such an oddity, and set it down again.

I was counting in my head, though the throb got in the way. There was an N too many. And an A instead of an E, though who didn't misspell Allan? It was an old habit of mine, fooling with names, searching for a message.

"Edgar Allan Poe. Lee Al Pendragon," I said loudly, trying to make them see. My tongue still felt too big for my mouth. "Drink."

"Maybe she ought to go to the hospital," he whispered to Sharon.

"I don't know. There's a nurse at the school infirmary."

"Put on some more ice." Pendragon bent over me, and I stared into his black eyes. *Gravedigger's boy.* The sweaty hair, clumped into pieces, hung down. I could make out a droplet on his eyebrows. I watched, waiting for it to fall.

Even through the ache and pound of my head, I could see that he was a good-looking boy—at least, the kind that *I* thought of as good-looking. *Interesting-looking* might be a better term for it. His nose was straight, and his nostrils flared in a surprisingly aristocratic way for, as he had described himself, the caretaker's son.

"You have a beautiful mouth," I said indistinctly.

"What did she . . . ?" He glanced across to Sharon.

She let out a giggle and held up her hands in surrender. "I couldn't say. But I think she's going to be all right."

How we managed to get home, I hardly remember. The school nurse got fluttery and agitated; she was afraid my neck might be broken. But it wasn't. I do recall that she toted me off to the university hospital, where I slept on a gurney for several hours before returning to the infirmary. Evidently I had an x-ray during that time, and a clan of radiologists had pored over it. No secret messages. I had a concussion and didn't feel quite right for some days. By that time, the second session of summer school had started. I was taking an intensive drawing class, and my teacher encouraged me, though he groaned when he saw the pages of big-eyed creatures and people in my sketchbook.

"It doesn't really matter what you draw," he said in a martyrly sort of tone that reeked of adult resignation. "Just that you draw. I liked your poems in the magazine, by the way. Best ones I've seen in my fifteen years at this school. You've got the gift."

Despite my renunciation of the muse, I felt pleased. I glanced past him at the semi-clad model slumped in a chair. Maybe I had been too hasty. But I wasn't ready to talk poems again.

"Thanks." I picked up a stem of charcoal and rubbed it against the page.

Afterward I met Sharon in the shrubbery walk by the library. She poked experimentally at my bandage and said that it seemed less disgusting than before.

"Want me to go with you to fetch the bike?"

"Got yours already? You didn't tell."

She nodded. "Saw our friend Pendragon edging the lawn. He asked about you, said he'd bring the bike and walk home if you wanted it. He was very polite. Also relieved about your head. I guess he could've gotten into some trouble over that one."

"Me too."

"I gave him the Holberg pamphlet. He asked to see it the day we met, after he clobbered you."

"He didn't *clobber* me."

"Uh." She nodded. "Okay."

"Really. I'm just clumsy. And I'll pick up the bike," I told her. "Maybe I'll do it now and be back for dinner."

"Better hurry," she said.

"If I'm not back, tell Mrs. B that I'm napping in your room, that you didn't want to wake me."

I scrubbed off the charcoal smudges and put on my Chinese gown and the big hat with the dyed ostrich plume. If he could take that, he could handle anything. The dress was narrow, but there was a slit in the back. I could manage coming home on the bike.

The taxi let me off at the corner, and I walked up the block and let myself in at the side gate.

Pendragon was sitting on the edge of a low tomb in the shadow of trees, his head cocked back, throat pumping, a bottle of water in his upraised hand. The scythe was propped against a stone. He wiped his mouth on his arm before he noticed me.

He didn't get up but watched as I picked my way between the graves. For a long time we just stared at each other.

"How old are you?" he asked. He gave a surreptitious glance at my Chinese dress. He was wearing the same clothes as before, or else another pair of faded black jeans and another spotless white t-shirt—that is, bleached but flecked with confetti of grass clippings.

"Fifteen."

"Virginia Clem was thirteen."

"When she married Eddie Poe, you mean. You've been reading."

"Read some Poe," he acknowledged. "Thirteen. That's pretty odd."

"I guess the world's full of strange things," I said.

"Did you really see an apparition of Poe?"

"Well, it sure wasn't the ghost of Jacob Marley," I said. "Not unless he lied through his teeth. A lot of people do fabulate through their teeth, so far as I can tell. Some people even lie through their false teeth. Take Arvin, for instance."

"Arvin?"

"Take him," I said. "Please."

Pendragon raked a hand through his hair, and it stood up in confused black spikes. The effect wasn't half bad.

"It wasn't some kind of female hysteria?" He sounded cautious, as though he knew I would be offended but just had to ask.

"I can show you female hysteria." I adjusted my Mae West hat. "If that's what you want—"

"No!" He glanced at the bandage and hastily changed the subject: "I read the Holberg piece. Did you notice that if somebody really was an 'intrusion into reality,' the way he says, 'a kind of simulacrum,' that you'd never, ever be able to know it? That if reality were to bulge in from another world, or if a copy of someone were to pop up, there would be no way at all to find out? That the simulacrum might not ever find out? Not unless duplicates existed simultaneously in time in the same realm?"

"Sure, I thought about it." I tugged my hat over one ear and scanned him. Pendragon, that is: I looked him over. *He would make a good muse,* a little voice said in my ear. It sounded a lot like Mae West. I could feel the tide coming in over gravel. The grass-growing, boat-floating, kite-lofting mood. So what if I'd landed in the wrong era for the beautiful? It could be a grand night for poems, hiding under the covers with my flashlight, a towel socked against the door.

"I will admit to having a strong imagination. That is, maybe I didn't see so very much in the mirror in my dorm room. Or maybe I did. It's hard to know later on, when memory is ebbing. But I definitely saw a lot in the mausoleum with the indigo and rose window." I fished the chain out of my dress and displayed the key, twiddling it between my fingers.

"You shouldn't have that." The response sounded automatic; you could tell he was pondering something else. "Two years older than Virginia Clem." He paused, tilting his head to look under my hat brim. "Don't you want to know how old I am?"

"Well, if you were an intrusion from another realm, you might be jillions of years old," I said. "How could I possibly tell? And if you came zooming back from the land of the dead, you might be 195 years old, or some such. And if you were a simulacrum, you might actually be a mere babbling infant. So what's the use?"

"I'm almost seventeen."

"Of course you are," I said agreeably.

"You don't really think that I'm 195?"

"No. But I'd like you even if you were a simulacrum. Even if you were fearsomely old. And even if you were Eddie Poe, come back as a mathematician who calls himself *Pendragon*. Which does not seem wholly unlikely."

He seemed to digest this, sitting on the tomb.

"Want to go out?"

"So long as I can climb the fire escape to Sharon's room by nine p.m. That's the witching hour—that's when the Queen comes buzzing by with the Princess Delphinium." I wasn't sure that he'd meant go out *right now*, but I was ready.

Though it wasn't yet five o'clock, the moon was already up, floating like a soap bubble above the treetops. You know they aren't as smooth as they look, soap bubbles; they're all irregularities and stretches and swirls. I sighed with pleasure as Pendragon took my hand. We kicked up the little white moths that look like fairies as we wandered toward the main gates. From now on, I thought, the bit of mirror and the dried rose and the word *unspeakable* would have to take second place to souvenirs of the living. Sun and moon would have to fly to keep up with me and Pendragon. The wind skipped over the wall and ruffled the grass and set the cemetery trees to swaying on their roots.

Why worry that we teetered above the abyss, or that for some all life was angled at Poe's "chasmal pitch?" Nothing would devour me! I wouldn't ask from angels the dark and fearsome wisdom that Poe had desired, or turn peace into strife.

For a fleeting instant, as Pendragon began to swing my hand, I remembered stepping out of the mausoleum and spying a marvel: an unknown figure mowing through a cloud of gold, insects orbiting his head. That was the sunlit mystery that had caught me, in the end. I laced my fingers with Pendragon's, and we ran down the steps and through the iron gates.

The world is magic, magic; I was walking on air.